praise for dave duncan

"Rich, evocative language and superior narrative skills . . . one of the leading masters of epic fantasy." —*Publishers Weekly*

"Dave Duncan writes rollicking adventure novels filled with subtle characterization and made bitter-sweet by an underlying darkness. Without striving for grand effects or momentous meetings between genres, he has produced one excellent book after another." —*Locus*

"An exceedingly finished stylist and a master of world building and characterization." —*Booklist*

"Duncan writes with unusual flair, drawing upon folklore, myth, and his gift for creating ingenious plots." —*Year's Best Fantasy and Horror*

"One of the best writers in the fantasy world today. His writing is clear, vibrant, and full of energy. His action scenes are breathtaking and his skill at characterization is excellent." —*Writers Write*

"Duncan's prose avoids the excessively florid in its description and the archaic in its dialogue, opting instead for simpler narration and contemporary parlance . . . serves as a refreshing reminder that epic fantasy need not always be doorstops filled with manly men speaking in overblown rhetoric and grasping their swords." —*SFF World*

"Duncan produces excellent work in book after book . . . a great world-builder. His fantasy worlds are not mere medieval societies with magic added but make organic sense." —*SFReview*

"Dave Duncan has long been one of the great unsung figures of Canadian fantasy and science fiction, graced with a fertile imagination, a prolific output, and keen writerly skills." —*Quill and Quire*

also by dave duncan

the
Enchanter General

Ironfoot

dave Duncan

Night Shade Books
NEW YORK

Night Shade books may be purchased in bulk at special discounts for sales promotion, corporate gifts, fund-raising, or educational purposes. Special editions can also be created to specifications. For details, contact the Special Sales Department, Night Shade Books, 307 West 36th Street, 11th Floor, New York, NY 10018 or info@skyhorsepublishing.com.

Night Shade Books® is a registered trademark of Skyhorse Publishing, Inc.®, a Delaware corporation.

Visit our website at www.nightshadebooks.com.

10 9 8 7 6 5 4 3 2 1

Library of Congress Cataloging-in-Publication Data

Names: Duncan, Dave, 1933- author.
Title: Ironfoot / by Dave Duncan.
Description: New York : Night Shade Books, [2017] | Series: The enchanter general ; book 1
Identifiers: LCCN 2017006600| ISBN 9781597809177 (softcover : acid-free paper) | ISBN 9781597809306 (hardcover : acid-free paper)
Subjects: LCSH: Great Britain--History--Angevin period, 1154-1216--Fiction. | Great Britain--History--Henry II, 1154-1189--Fiction. | Great Britain--History--12th century--Fiction. | Magicians--Fiction. | Magic--Fiction. | GSAFD: Historical fiction. | Fantasy fiction.
Classification: LCC PR9199.3.D847 I76 2017 | DDC 813/.54--dc23
LC record available at https://lccn.loc.gov/2017006600

Cover illustration by Stephen Youll
Cover design by Shawn King

Printed in the United States of America

Ironfoot

chapter 1

Eighty years before I was born, two of my forebears, house-carls of King Harold, the rightful king of England, died beside him at Hastings, fighting for their liege against Duke William's Norman horde. Ever since then, Saxons have been underdogs in their ancestral land. My father, who should have inherited an earldom, was hostler for the Cistercian abbey at Pipewell, in Northamptonshire—he was a lay brother only and honorably married to my mother. In those days even priests were often married men.

As a hostler's son I grew up with horses. When I was nine years old, I tried to put one over a gate. My experiment ended with the horse on top, me on the ground, and the gate between us. My right leg was badly crushed and healed shorter than the other. Ever since I was able to walk again, I have worn a boot with a metal platform attached to the sole. And so Durwin son of Durwin became known as Ironfoot to everyone except his parents.

So how did a lame Saxon boy make a living in an England ruled by Normans? How did he rise to be a royal confidant and advisor, enchanter general to three successive kings? It seemed a miracle at the time, and still does when I look back at how it happened. No, rather, it was three miracles.

Firstly, the abbot was sympathetic. Every morning during the long months when my leg was in splints, he would send a couple of brawny novices to carry me to the abbey school, so I learned my letters, although I felt no call to take the tonsure. When I could walk properly again, I earned my bread by helping my father, for the abbey was steadily growing and acquiring more livestock. But I had younger brothers following me. As I approached manhood, I knew that I must soon find some way for a cripple to earn his living.

The second miracle occurred when Sage Guy Delany stopped by the abbey. He was gentry and an old friend of the abbot, else the monks might have refused him hospitality, for sages were tainted with suspicions of witchcraft and devil worship.

Guy was on his way to join the faculty at Helmdon, which in those days boasted one of the finest secular academies in England, or even in all Christendom. He was a large man, hefty, rubicund, and well dressed, with a Norman's haughty, well-fed look. He wore a sword and rode a spectacular hunter, the finest horse I had ever seen.

When he prepared to leave the next morning, I humbly pointed out to him that his mount was close to shedding a shoe. My father doubled as the local farrier, but the abbot had sent him off to attend the horse fair at Northampton. Guy was in a hurry. He spoke to his friend the abbot, and soon they worked out a solution. Guy would ride off on one of the abbey's horses, and I would go with him, riding another abbey horse and leading the packhorse that carried his baggage. The plan was that I would learn the road, and then make the journey three times more, at which point Guy would have his horse with him at Helmdon, and I would be back at Pipewell. It made an interesting break in my humdrum existence.

Pipewell and Helmdon lie in the middle of England, but at opposite ends of Northamptonshire, and there is no grand highway between them, just trails winding through fields, meadowland, and forest. Even in summer it would be a very long day's ride, but the weather then was appalling, and we got lost more than once. It took us almost three days.

Guy was intrigued when he learned that I could read and write, for that was very unusual for an untonsured Saxon back then. According to the story he later told, I never stopped asking questions all the way to Helmdon.

When we arrived there, he inspected the academy's stable with disgust, and took me with him when he went to meet Odo le Brys, the dean. To my joy, I was offered the chance to attend classes as a servitor, meaning I would pay no fees, so long as I looked after Guy's horse and the academy's four—which were hacks compared with his. I could hardly believe my good fortune. I hastened back to Pipewell to obtain my father's permission, which he readily granted.

In the abbey most of the monks had been Saxons, but all the senior offices—abbot, prior, bursar, and so on—had been held by Normans. No one ever commented on that; it was just the way of the world. The distinction was much more obvious out in the secular world. In the academy all the sages and most adepts were Norman, as were most of the students, known as squires. Not many Saxon parents could afford to send sons to the academy, or had reason to. The few Saxon students were referred to as varlets, and tolerated as little better than vermin.

At fourteen, I was already one of the older students, so the squires promptly ganged up on me to make sure I knew my place. When I reported to Sage Guy the next morning, he displayed neither surprise nor sympathy. He told me to strip so he could examine my injuries.

"A few loose teeth," he concluded, "and a couple of cracked ribs. I'll cure those for you, but I'll leave the bruises, because otherwise they'll just give you more. You'll have to learn to grovel better."

He then chanted a healing spell over me, which did what he had said it would. I was amazed, because the monks' medical skills had been limited to potions and poultices. If chanting was what this Helmdon place taught, then I vowed to learn it. If I must crawl to learn, crawl I would.

"Can you cure my game leg, master?" I whispered.

"I might have managed that, had I been there when you smashed it, but I can't now. Get dressed and we'll start lessons."

The other sages reluctantly let me sit in on their lectures, but they became more accepting as they discovered I had both talent and ambition. Some conceded that I might make a good folk healer some day, even perhaps be certified as an adept. A sage? A *Saxon* sage? No chance at all.

And even I accepted that—until the date I shall never forget: October 4, 1164. That was the day I stole a bag of tiles and was granted the third miracle.

chapter 2

The academy was a tiny establishment by today's standards, just a circle of thatched cottages connected by a boardwalk. All the buildings had windows with shutters, though, and a few even had fieldstone chimneys, a recent innovation.

In those days serious students who could afford it attended the University of Paris, but King Henry forbade that a few years later, in 1167. Now England has several academies grander than Helmdon ever was, especially the one in Oxford. Still, with a faculty of six qualified sages and five adepts, Helmdon was then one of the largest and most respected schools in the country. Its student enrollment at that time comprised eight Norman "squires" and four Saxons "varlets."

Helmdon claimed to turn out men—never women—familiar with all human knowledge, and it pretty much succeeded. It taught the wisdom of the ancients as it had been handed down to us, including all topics except holy matters, which were reserved for the Church's schools. The curriculum included alchemy, arithmetic, astrology, geometry, grammar, herbalism, history, law, literature, logic, music, numeration, reading, writing, and rhetoric. And also antique song, which was what the common folk called enchantment.

Enchantment was what really mattered, of course.

The Church regarded secular schools with suspicion, some bishops even arguing that any learning other than Bible study was a fast road to Hell, but we could quote Church Fathers like St. Augustine against them. In practice academies were tolerated as long as they did not infringe on religion, which the Church interpreted as broadly as possible. It especially frowned upon the field of study officially called antique song, denouncing it as heresy, superstition, and blasphemy. Confessors could impose fearsome penances on those who used such art, but in practice tended to turn a deaf ear, because the bishops knew that any effort to suppress enchantment would arouse the wrath of the great lords, almost all of whom employed house sages—officially to advise them on law, medicine, correspondence, and so on, for almost no other laymen in England could read, and no one quite trusted even the humblest cleric not to tattle secrets to the nearest bishop.

Enchantment was a large part of a house sage's duties. The king himself employed an enchanter general, and several lesser enchanters under him. The common people put no faith in a medicinal potion that had not been fortified by a chant or two. The monks had never told me that.

The ancient spells were recorded in precious grimoires, some of them centuries old. Helmdon's library of grimoires was one of the finest in England, containing no less than fifty-six books, plus numerous sheets and scrolls tucked away in muniment chests. The spells were mostly written in Latin or French, both of which came in a great variety of dialects. A few texts were in Greek, Hebrew, or even the old tongue, the language of England before the Conquest. Most Normans could understand some of that, or even make themselves understood in it to an extent. I, of course, had learned it at my mother's knee, and I could even read it and write it, which was extremely rare.

Sage Guy, my mentor and tutor, was more open-minded than most of the faculty, and one day it occurred to him to investigate what cabalistic knowledge might be hidden away in these neglected old tongue writings. After six years instructing me, he had come to treat me as if I were an adept, which few others did. I was twenty years old, after all, older than many of the adepts, and no longer a juvenile chatterbox.

So he set me the task of collecting all that material. The other sages willingly parted with what they had, because they regarded us Saxons as ignorant buffoons—which we were by then, of course, after a century of oppression. They forgot the splendid English culture their ancestors had destroyed in the Conquest.

Guy and I were both astounded by the amount of material we accumulated. He had to order the carpenter in Northampton to make a new chest to hold it all.

There were no classes on Sundays, but that particular Sunday an everlasting deluge was keeping everyone indoors. Guy, thoroughly bored, decreed we would not be breaking the Lord's commandments if we looked over the collection. In the course of half an afternoon we set aside any spells that seemed to duplicate others we already knew in modern languages. Then we selected a few short single-voice spells and I chanted them for him. Several of them worked, too—one of them summoned people by name, I remember. Although its range was too limited to be very useful, even men who had little fluency in the old tongue would come running. Another chant would sober up a drunk. I memorized that one and have often found it helpful over the years.

The two-voice spells were trickier, but Guy insisted on trying out a couple of those also. He put his agile mind to it and studied the text with me until he could pronounce it and understand it thoroughly, because merely mouthing the words will not work. Then I chanted the versicles, and he the responses, as cantor. One of the spells worked, the other did not, but that was always a problem. More than half the spells in the grimoires never worked.

We were about to call it a day when we discovered, at the bottom of the chest, a shabby leather bag containing a set of stone tiles about a thumb-joint in size. There were thirty-seven of them; one was blank and each of the others was engraved with a sign of an ancient alphabet.

"Runes," Guy said dismissively.

"Futhorc!" I had met those signs before. Futhorc was the ancient Anglo-Saxon version of runes, the alphabet used by pagans before the blessings of the True Faith were brought to our island five hundred years ago. I had seen a script about them back at Pipewell, in the abbey library, so I was able to tell Guy what each symbol meant, but not why they had been so carefully engraved on tiles.

"Not teaching," he said, frowning. "Divination, maybe? To respond to an incantation without the need for a cantor?"

We both turned to the heap of documents we had discarded. Lame as I was, my youth made me nimble, and he was growing almost portly. So I flopped down on the floor, and he pulled up his chair, and we began hunting for anything that might relate to the tiles. I glanced at each scroll in turn and told him what it was as I handed it to him, for spells are always known by their opening words.

Most of them got tossed back in the chest, but we kept back three single-voiced invocations that sought an answer. All three invoked the Wyrds, the pagan goddesses of destiny, with the enchanter demanding to know what was in store for him. All three were written in the Christian alphabet. Two were almost identical, while the third was a separate creation, completely different.

"Try them," Guy said.

I moved to a chair near the window, for rain was still pounding down, making the cottage dim. I spread the tiles on the table, within reach, then chanted the first of the three spells, which began *Spricest ðu,* "Do you speak?" I felt no sense of acceptance, so I did not bother to reach for any tiles. Then I tried the two versions of *Hwæt segst,* meaning "What do you say?" With the first I again felt no response, but halfway through the second . . . maybe. It was very faint, and it died away before I reached the end of the chant. By then chanters always know if a spell is going to work.

Guy shrugged and moved closer to the fire. "Useless. Put all that stuff back in the chest and someday you can list it all."

But I laid the duplicate scrolls of *Hwæt segst* side by side on the table and compared them. "They're not exactly the same, master. This one uses a dual pronoun to address the three Wyrds in a couple of places. That's wrong! And the other has a dative case noun here instead of—"

"Never mind!" Guy barked. "I've warned you a thousand times that tampering with the ancients' words is not just a waste of time, it can be very dangerous. Oh, God's flesh! Is that the vespers bell already?" He strode across the cabin and lifted his cloak off the hook by the door. I knew the faculty was scheduled to meet at sunset that day.

Guy was normally a logical and patient instructor, but he would take only so much from a brash Saxon varlet.

"And you," he told me as he wrapped himself, "had better get back to the horses, or you'll be trying to rub them down in the dark." He paused with the door half open and regarded me suspiciously. "But put all that old tongue junk away first! You hear me?" Then he was gone.

After six years, he knew me well enough to guess exactly what I wanted to do. As I said, most of the old spells did not work, so the Saxon material was no different from classical in that. The trouble, as I rebelliously saw it, was in the copying. I knew the infinite pains taken by the monks to avoid errors when replicating holy texts. Sages and their scribes had been less careful, and it was common to find divergent versions of the same text. Sages like Guy stubbornly refused to make any effort to correct the texts, not even quite obvious errors. Spells could go bad, they insisted, and men who tampered with them might raise the Devil by mistake.

My mentor and I had gone over this same argument several times, and I had always deferred to his wisdom and authority. But that evening I felt rebellious. To repair an ancient spell would be a triumph, and my Saxon heritage made me especially attracted to these two, whose corruptions were so clear to my eyes.

Hwæt segst was a very brief spell. It would also be a very valuable one if it could be made to work, for prediction is one of the hardest tasks in the enchanter's repertoire. So I took time I could not spare to compare the two versions and memorize what I thought must have been the original text.

Voices going past the door suddenly reminded me that night was falling fast and I had work to do. Most sages used their cottages as both sanctum and living quarters, but Guy had independent income, and soon after arriving at Helmdon, had made an arrangement with Thyra, a widow in the village, penniless mother of two girls. He normally slept there—she had already had a child by him and was working on another—but on a night such as this he might well decide to sleep in his sanctum in the academy.

Hastily I tossed everything into the chest. Except the bag of tiles. I took that with me when I departed.

Helmdon was not much of a village then, and is probably even less now, with the academy gone. The academy was located at the south end and its stable at the north, for no known reason. The entire hamlet could be taken in at a glance, being just a dozen or so cottages with thatch roofs and walls of cob. Understandably, several were then showing damage from the long wet. Windows were narrow slits, smoke escaped through a hole in the roof. Add in a few hedges, vegetable patches, and fruit trees, all strung along a single street that had now become a slow-flowing cesspool, and you have a good picture of Helmdon.

Leaning on my staff, I hobbled along that sodden road as fast as I could go, trying to ignore that pain in my hip that such a gait always caused me. I paused only once, at Edith's cottage. She cooked for the academy, and always prepared a separate evening snack for me in winter, when I could not tarry to eat with the others. That night she knew I was already late, and handed it out to me before I could even knock.

I had to bring the five horses in from the common, wipe them off as well as I could, and feed them. When I had done all that, night had fallen and I couldn't see my hand in front of my face. I was also wet.

My billet was still the hayloft above the stable, heated by the breath of the horses below me and as dark as the inside of a grave. The danger of fire prevented me from having heat or candles, and winter nights were maddeningly long. I climbed up there, stripped off my sodden clothes, and rolled up in my blanket. Then I ate my bread and cheese.

The beat of rain upon the roof barely two feet above my nose was muffled by the thickness of the thatch, but I could hear the steady trickle of water into the barrels under the eaves. This deluge had begun on the eve of St. Matthew the Apostle and hadn't stopped since. Although the lord's crops had been safely gathered in, some of the peasants' lay rotting in the fields, warning of hard times ahead, come spring.

The horses snuffled, farted, and staled as usual, but I was confident that none of them was being dripped on. The mice in the thatch sounded busy, perhaps moving babies to drier nests.

My bed was comfortable enough, and the prospect that what I was planning to do might summon the Devil did not worry me overmuch. My lack of progress at Helmdon frustrated me deeply. I knew everything a varlet could know, and some lore that was normally restricted to adepts. I believed Guy when he said he had asked several times for me to be promoted, but promotion required the faculty's unanimous consent. I had a fair idea which of the other sages had vetoed me, but there was nothing I could do about it. I seemed fated to remain a stable hand forever. I could imagine myself as a competent village healer somewhere, but I was certain to starve to death before I began to earn enough to live on.

The time had come! I would not dare to remove any tiles from the bag, because any I lost in the straw would never be found. Fortunately there was room for my hand inside the bag, and I could read the inscriptions with my fingers.

And so, that horrible wet evening, I began to chant the *Hwæt segst*, begging the Wyrds to reveal my destiny. The old tongue is not a good choice for such an appeal, because its verbs lack the future tense that both Latin and French have. It gets around that by liberal use of flowery language.

"What do you say, oh bird in the tree? Do you croak as the raven or trill as the lark? Gracious ladies, at your loom, what do you spin for me? Is the road rough or smooth? . . ." And so on.

The horses, accustomed to my oddities, paid no attention.

As I told you, an enchanter can almost always tell as he chants whether a spell is going to succeed or not. He—and usually his cantor, too, if he has one helping him—feels a rush of satisfaction that we call the acceptance, a sign that the spirits are hearing his plea.

That evening I felt acceptance. I had met it before, of course, when chanting responses for Guy or another sage, or even performing minor healing spells on my own. But what I was meddling with that evening was a deeper, more potent mystery, and the acceptance was unusually strong, making my hair stir. I was reviving a magic that had not been used in centuries.

Trembling with excitement, I selected the first tile my fingers found. The sign on it was undoubtedly *man*, corresponding to *m* in the Christian alphabet. I let it go, shook the bag, and drew another.

The second was *os*, or *o*, and the third was *rad*, or *r*.

I hesitated. *Mor . . .?* My prophecy would be given in the same language as the chant, of course. *Mor* could be the start of *morgen*, which was "morning," or *morig*, "swampy." Just about everywhere was swampy just then. It could also be the start of more ominous words, but at least I seemed likely to be given a real word.

I drew again, and got *thorn*, or *th*.

Morth was "death" or "destruction."

Starting to wonder just what I was meddling with, I dropped that tile and drew a fifth time. *Os* again. I was not surprised when the sixth tile was *rad* again.

And then I drew the blank tile. Was that to signal a new word coming or the end of the reply? Very old inscriptions usually run the words together, leaving no spaces between them. And I believed that the tiles had spoken, for the acceptance had faded. I drew a few more times but was given no more guidance, only gibberish: *lagu*, *cen*, *wynn*. . . .

So the prophecy was *Morðor*, and *Morðor* meant "murder."

Be careful what you ask for, as the old proverb says.

chapter 3

torn by conflicting emotions, I slept badly that night, as you may guess. Frightening as the prophecy itself was, I was overwhelmed by a sense of triumph. I had revived an ancient incantation that had been lost to the world, perhaps for unknown ages. I had done something that every sage in the academy had insisted was impossible. For the first time I could truly believe in my skill and my destiny as an enchanter—provided, of course, that I did not get murdered first.

Not necessarily literal murder, I reminded myself. *Morðor* could mean mortal sin, or a terrible crime, or even drastic punishment, for the old tongue was often poetic or metaphorical. Whichever way it was intended, *morðor* was definitely not a good prospect.

The drastic punishment possibility was certainly possible, for I had taken the bag of tiles against my tutor's explicit orders. Discipline was very strict in Helmdon—far stricter than today's lax standards. Varlets could be severely beaten. Squires rarely were, with the notable exception of Squire William Legier. I shall come back to him shortly. Sage Guy had never beaten me, but then I had never disobeyed his orders before. A varlet who proved his tutor wrong was practically begging for a beating, or even expulsion. I might find myself limping back to Pipewell before noon, and nothing good awaited me there, for my father had died and my mother remarried.

Literal murder? At first glance, that seemed absurdly unlikely. Who could possibly commit homicide on a penniless servitor like me? But there was one possible candidate—Squire William Legier, who hated me to the point of insanity.

William was a Norman, but otherwise something of a mystery. He was the most recently matriculated student except for Eadig son of Edwin, although at seventeen or so and owner of a creditable mustache, he was certainly older than most of them. The sages would not discuss his background, but his father was rumored to be a wealthy lord.

Then, as now, a knight's son would remain with his mother until he was seven, then serve as a page—for his father or his father's overlord—until he was about fourteen, when he became a squire, entering knights' training, expecting to be belted as a knight at around twenty-one. Then, as now, some squires chose not to work toward knighthood. Some entered the Church, others just enjoyed life as landowners, while a very few studied secular arts and became lawyers or sages.

According to academy gossip, William was a fourth son; the two eldest had been trained for war and the third pushed into the Church, leaving only a secular education for the runt of the litter. Darker whispers suggested that he had been expelled from knights' training after some terrible scandal, like blasphemy or cowardice.

He certainly *looked* as if he had spent some years swinging maces or broadswords, running in chain mail, and all the rest of the sweaty things that squires have to do. Knights are always large, powerful men. He was as tall as me, and until old age gave me my stoop, I was unusually tall for a Saxon.

William had turned up at Helmdon a few months ago, had behaved himself for a week or so, and then started being deliberately obnoxious. Refusing to tolerate such nonsense, Dean Odo had sent him home with—according to rumor—a letter saying that William was totally unsuited to be a scholar, and never would be before the Second Coming of Our Lord. But William's father, whoever he was, had either enormous money or enormous power, because William had returned and remained.

He did not mend his ways, though. He grew worse and worse, skipping most classes, turning those he did attend into riots, and refusing to learn anything at all. Lately he had even taken to wearing a sword, which was totally against academy rules, but more evidence that he had been trained for war, because it takes years of practice to bear a sword without tripping over it or banging into things.

The sages responded with beatings, of course, which William accepted without a murmur. His tolerance of pain was incredible. He seemed unmoved by thrashings that would have any other student sobbing and screaming. I had little doubt that he was in some ways insane, waging a battle of wills against the faculty. So far neither side was willing to concede defeat.

If he despised the sages, many of whom were revered for their wisdom throughout Christendom, his contempt for me was bottomless. In his eyes I was just a crippled Saxon stable hand who should not be allowed anywhere near Norman gentry. For months he had been trying to pick a fight with me. I refused to respond, because I had to, but it was not easy. I would gladly have taken him on with fists. Out of doors, where there was plenty of room, I would have even settled for my quarterstaff against his sword.

He never swung the first punch, though, and I dared not. A Saxon who injured a Norman would almost certainly hang. Back then a Norman who injured or even killed a Saxon would merely have to pay compensation to the man's lord, or owner if he were a serf. If there was any man in England who might murder me that day, it was Squire William Legier. Or would I finally lose my temper and murder him?

Or Guy himself. I had taken the tiles on impulse, meaning to return them before he noticed their absence. That should be easy enough, for he often trusted me to work alone in his sanctum—writing, grinding potions, casting horoscopes. But I had used the tiles to disprove one of the basic tenets of enchantment. How could I not tell him what I had achieved, when the consequences might be so great? Highly respected sages do not enjoy their pupils making them look ignorant.

He did have a temper. I had seen him thrash William several times. Now I had started disobeying, just as William did. It would seem to Guy that the troublemaker's example was starting to spread like rot, so I could expect no mercy. For some unknown reason the academy was powerless to expel William Legier, but I was only a Saxon, and had no wealthy father behind me.

chapter 4

At long, long last the night began to yield. Seeing chinks of gray through the air hole in the gable, I reached for my clothes. I dressed as a peasant in those days, of course, and peasant dress has not changed at all. My basic garment was a knee-length belted smock, which had probably served several generations of plowmen before me. Originally a reddish color, it was now faded almost to gray, and was much patched. The sleeves fell a handbreadth short of my wrists, and I had to take care pulling it over my shoulders or it would have ripped in two. Below it I wore a thin linen shirt, to keep the rough wool off my skin, and leggings that laced to the shirt. They were all still damp from yesterday's drenching.

By the time I was dressed the roosters were crowing. I crawled to the hatch, clambered down the ladder, and prepared to face whatever the day might bring.

My mind was still full of Guy, William, and *morðor* as I went through my morning routine of feeding the horses and shoveling out the barn. Knowing they would not stray far in such weather, I let them loose on the common to graze. They ran at once to shelter under the elms that gave Helmdon its name, huddling close together and looking miserable as the wind whirled yellow leaves down on them.

By then it was daylight, as much as it was going to be. I donned my cloak and hood—the hood was leather and had belonged to my grandfather, the cloak was only waxed linen, and sodden by the weeks of rain. I gathered up my staff and the satchel in which I carried my supply of herbs. That day it also contained the futhorc tiles.

I set off for the academy, hobbling as fast as I could go without pain, swinging my staff, trying to stay out of the deepest mud, but soon feeling trickles of water sneaking in under my hood and down my neck.

No, it wasn't much of a place to live. Looking back now, I am amazed at how accepting we all were of such peasant conditions. Life there was hard and short. Daily I give thanks to God, who has raised me so far.

Even a cripple could make the journey in a very few minutes. I saw no one else out, and heard nothing other than some singing as mothers soothed bored children. The rain was so heavy that even the dogs and geese had taken cover, letting me go by without challenge.

I did have one call to make, though. I turned aside to tap softly on the door of Widow Edith's cottage. Being the academy's cook, Edith raised a brood of four on the leftovers. My mouth began to water as I stood there under the eaves. Even before she opened the door my nose had told me that someone was going to enjoy meat today—possibly only the sages and adepts, of course, but we varlets and squires were allowed some once or twice a week.

Edith was a short, plump woman with more smiles than teeth, ever ready with a quip, but when she peered out and saw me, she slid outside, rather than invite me in, and lowered her voice as we exchanged morning blessings. Behind her, children were arguing over whose turn it was to feed the pig.

"How is he today?" I asked. Her youngest was dying and we both knew it. By long custom the academy provided free medical care for the village, but lately the sages had delegated that unprofitable duty to me. It was an acknowledgment of skill and trust that I really did not want on top of all my other duties.

She shrugged pillowed shoulders. "The rain doesn't help his cough. He's asleep at the moment, Your Wisdom."

I was not then a Wisdom, of course, but I did not bother to correct her. "Then I won't disturb him. Keep him warm and I'll look in on him at noon."

It was Monday. In the morning, I would be tutoring some varlets and junior squires in reading and writing. Monday afternoons might see Dean Odo le Brys lecturing on numerology, Sage Alain on Aristotelean logic, or Sage Rolf on alchemy. None of those prospects pleased, especially the last.

Smoke was rising from Guy's cottage, so I postponed my confession and headed straight to the students' schoolroom, which was just a single-roomed cabin like most of the others, furnished with three benches, a table, one stool, a chest to hold slates and chalks, and pegs for cloaks. At the moment it was cold and dark, but student heat would soon warm it, and I was permitted to light candles on days when the shutters could not be opened. I was anxious to write out a version of *Hwæt segst* incorporating my corrections.

All but two varlets and two squires already knew their letters and would be off elsewhere, studying Latin under Sage Alain. I hoped that Squire William would play truant again. The varlets would cause me no trouble, being Saxons like myself, but squires, not just William, never took kindly to having a Saxon in authority over them.

I had barely lit the last candle when in rushed Varlet Eadig, known as Earwig. He was the newest and youngest varlet, still boyishly shrill and shoulder-high, with hair almost as blond as my own, millions of freckles, and a huge eagerness to learn. He bowed as low to me as he would to one of the sages, and wished me God's favor that day. I responded in kind, thinking that God's favor ought not to include murder, but might.

Eadig draped his cloak on a peg and grabbed a place on the front bench, so that nobody taller could sit in front of him.

"Why are you so old?" he demanded.

"Because it's twenty years since I was born."

He considered that for a moment, nodding to concede that it made sense. "But you know everything, so why aren't you an adept or a sage?"

"I don't know everything and won't if I live to be a hundred."

"But why do you have to chop firewood and look after the horses?"

This was no secret. "Because my father couldn't afford to pay for me to study here. Sage Guy discovered that I had a knack for horses and was eager to learn, so he arranged for me to be a servitor. That means I earn my lessons by looking after the academy's herd." And the people of Helmdon also, I thought with amusement, not to mention teaching trivial classes like that one. "Where are you from?"

"Bicester."

"That's a long way. Your father must have wanted to be well rid of you!"

"Naw. He's a freeholder, and wants me to know how to keep the accounts when I grow up."

"Then why not pay the priest to teach you?"

Eadig grinned. "Because he'd sent my brother to the abbey to learn there, and the monks talked him into staying on and becoming one of them. He didn't want that happening to me."

In my opinion, Eadig's father had been worrying needlessly, but he might have outsmarted himself. While Eadig did not strike me as promising religious material, given time his sharp wits might make him an excellent sage.

Then I heard the bell ring and had to abandon my hopes of writing out the incantation. As voices sounded outside, I handed Eadig a slate and a piece of chalk. No one below the rank of adept ever wrote on expensive parchment. The rest of us used slate or tablets of lime wood that could be sanded clean again.

"Let's get started," I said. "The last letter you learned was *m*. The next one is *n*. Like *m* but with only two legs, not three, remember? So you write as many words as you can think of with that sound in them." He suggested a few, automatically switching to French. Among ourselves, we Saxons naturally spoke in the old tongue, but almost nothing had been written in it for ninety-eight years.

The door flew open with a crash and Squires Lawrence Debrett and William Legier swaggered into the room. Trouble had arrived.

The gap between Saxons and Normans was wider then than it is now. The king and most of the barons spoke only French, and it was rare to meet a Saxon above the level of farmhand. Obviously, therefore, Saxons were incapable of doing anything better, yes? Even sages were not immune to this illogical bias.

Lawrence began to unlace his cloak, saw that William was not going to remove his, and stopped. William stalked over to the front bench and deliberately cuffed Eadig's ear.

"Stand when your betters enter the room, worm."

Eadig jumped up, shooting worried glances at me.

"That's my seat. You sit there, trash!" said William, pointing to the second bench, right behind.

Eadig scrambled out of the way.

I braced for the battle. "Close the door, please, William."

"There's a terrible stink of horse dung in here today, Lawrence."

Lawrence grinned. He was a decent enough boy—not much older than Eadig, smooth-faced, still speaking in a treble register, and very nearly literate enough to move on to Latin and other higher studies. Unfortunately, he was completely bewitched by his hero, William. The door remained open, admitting rain.

"William, I asked you to shut the door."

"I think I hear a dog barking. Can you hear a dog barking, Lawrence?"

Lawrence smirked and said nothing.

I was rescued—that time—by the arrival of my last pupil, varlet Ulf son of Magnus, a slender, quiet lad, who bowed to me and closed the door unasked. Teaching four pupils at four different skill levels simultaneously was never easy; when one of them was intent on making it impossible, the results of the struggle could not be in doubt.

They were all better dressed than I. Not that their basic wardrobe was that different—they did not flaunt their wealth like the peacocks you see around court these days; Helmdon was a rustic backwater, after all. But the quality and condition of their garments put mine to shame. They all owned hooded leather cloaks to keep out the rain; their hems hung lower, and there were no holes in their leggings.

I handed Ulf a slate and chalk and told him to write a letter to someone at home, telling them how to travel to Helmdon. Then the two squires . . .

"William, Lawrence, write out the Lord's Prayer, if you please."

William displayed a goofy expression. "Oh, I can't write, servitor. I get all mixed up with those *b*'s and *d*'s and *p*'s and *q*'s. You have to teach me."

"You wrote a very fair hand when you first came here."

"Must be the bad instruction, servitor. Driven it all out of my head, see? All I can do now is draw pictures."

"Then draw the Paternoster in pictures. But be careful you do not commit blasphemy, or the dean will have to report you to the bishop."

His eyes narrowed at this threat: bishop takes knight. "I won't even try, boy. It must be blasphemy to use the Lord's Prayer as a teaching model. I'll complain to the dean."

I had long ago concluded that William Legier was in some ways utterly crazy. To rouse him to homicidal fury when the runes had warned me of murder and he was wearing a sword could be suicidal folly. That left me only one more die to roll.

"Then go away. I won't attempt to teach you if you refuse to learn."

He showed his teeth in a leer. "Make me."

"I won't even try. Class canceled! Eadig, please extinguish the candles. You may all leave." I limped over to the pegs, donned my cloak, collected my staff, and left. Perhaps my example would rouse the sages to do the same. If teaching ground to a halt, the dean would be forced to expel William, no matter what the cost.

chapter 5

Obviously I must report what I had just done to the faculty, and the way to do that was to tell my tutor. So now I had two confessions to make; my sins were piling up. I plodded along the boardwalk to Guy's cottage. The rain was showing signs of letting up.

Every door of every sanctum in the academy bore a pentacle symbol as a warning that it was warded. In principle these warnings might be backed up by very terrible curses, but in Helmdon they never were, because we all trusted one another, and because someone might trespass by accident—a child, say, or an adult on a dark night. Guy's ward, I knew, merely provoked a violent attack of hiccups. I knocked.

I heard him shout for me to enter. Had I not known the password, I would have knocked again and he would have come to open the door for his visitor. Instead I just recited the necessary four words and lifted the latch. He was combing his hair and he was barefoot.

I blinked as the smoky, steamy air stung my eyes. The hearth in the center of the room both crackled and hissed, as rain came in the smoke hole faster than smoke could escape. The stuffy warmth perversely made me shiver after the damp cold outside.

I knew the cramped little place very well. I had spent hundreds of hours at the table there, toiling over herbals and grimoires under the sage's stern eye, scribbling notes as his lectures droned on, or standing at the bench grinding powders in a mortar. I had filled and labeled most of the jars and vials on the shelves. I had helped him chant healing spells over patients lying on the examination couch, which he had obviously been using as a bed until a few minutes ago.

Guy Delany was an esquire and a keen sportsman, commonly invited to hunt with the local gentry. Although he was of an age with the bookish Sage Rolf, he had kept his youthful energy. That he owned his own horse had been reason enough for the dean to put him in charge of the stables; he was also my tutor, which saved me from receiving conflicting orders from two masters. Guy enjoyed teaching, and two of the squires presently enrolled in the academy were also his pupils. No doubt he earned good money from their families, but he never neglected the Saxon servitor who cared for the horses. After six years the two of us had become close.

Bowing, I said, "God's blessing on you, master." I removed my cloak carefully, trying not to spill too much water on the floor.

"And on you, Durwin." His tone startled me, so I forced my eyes to focus. His complexion was always ruddy, which is a sign of a choleric disposition of course, but I had only rarely seen him lose his temper. Now his face was much redder than usual; his neck seemed shorter, his shoulders bulkier.

I glanced quickly at the old tongue manuscript chest, but the lid was closed, as I had left it. He must have noticed my guilty reaction, but somehow he had already known that I had betrayed his trust. I had no idea how. What a fool I had been, expecting to deceive a sage!

He was frowning. "Aren't you supposed to be teaching the chicks?"

I explained about the intolerable William and my reaction.

Guy's frown became a furious show of teeth. "God's mercy! One day I will smite that lunatic with the curse of Abélard, I swear!"

I had never heard of the curse of Abélard, and had no idea why that learned and saintly theologian should have been dabbling in such evil enchantments. I learned much later that the name was a cruel reference to the operation often inflicted on male calves and colts with a sharp knife. The curse might not have literally sterilized William, but it would have turned him into a gentle, biddable softy. Such maledictions require many voices; they are black magic, which was neither taught nor performed in Helmdon.

"Forget William for now," Guy growled.

Why? Why not just boot his backside out the gate and send him home? That was what was done to any other noncompliant student. I had seen it happen twice in my years there. But I must not pry into what were obviously faculty secrets.

And my mentor was waiting for me to continue. "Let's discuss your failings instead," he said.

I opened my satchel and produced the futhorc tiles.

His bushy eyebrows rose slightly, suggesting that he hadn't known the specifics of my transgression, just that I had done something wrong. He had not, as I had supposed, gone looking for the tiles and discovered their absence. He strode forward, snatched the bag from my hand, tipped the contents out on the table, and began to count them.

"I never took them out of the bag, master," I said, as meekly as I could. "They're all there."

Satisfied that they were, he turned to glare at me again. He held out a hand. "The scrolls!"

"No, just the tiles, master. I didn't take any scrolls. I memorized what I needed."

"Then you weren't using candles in the barn?"

"No, master."

"So you were chanting in the dark?" Apparently that was worse.

"Um, yes, master."

"Idiot! I ought to assay you now for demonic possession. I've told you and told you: never, ever, experiment after dark! A tried-and-true, benevolent healing spell would be safe enough, but anything you are not certain of, or that may be in the least bit ethically questionable, should only be attempted in broad daylight. Never a summoning, of any sort, for instance."

"Master . . . it worked!"

"What worked?"

"The *Hwæt segst*. It prophesied for me!"

"*Don't try to lie your way out of this!*" Guy roared, clenching his fists. "I dragged you out of a ditch, you bumpkinly Saxon ingrate. For six years I have taught you, nurtured you, promoted your cause to the faculty, and you reward me with rank mutiny? Great Heaven, how stupid can a lummox be? Chanting in the dark!"

I was aghast, dismayed. I had nothing to say but I was certain he had never warned me of this before. Looking back, I suspect that he knew he had not given me that warning and was angrier at himself than at me.

He took a couple of very deep breaths, then said, "Get out of here. Now! Before I throw you out, you worthless Saxon cripple. Out!"

I stumbled out into the rain. Only then did I put my cloak on again.

Now what? I must just hope that Guy's rage would fade and he would forgive me. The alternative did not bear thinking about.

Having free time was a heady surprise. I was able to spare some of it to comfort Widow Edith's dying son, dosing him with herbs that would do him no harm and might ease his pain, although nothing could do much good for a four-year-old who looked like a two-year-old and coughed up blood. I had chanted the most powerful single-voice healing spells I knew for him, but I had felt no acceptance and knew that my appeal had been rejected. Even when I had called the academy's best healer, Guy, to help, our joint appeals had been rejected.

Edith knew, of course. As she was bidding me farewell at the door, she whispered, "How long, Adept?"

I faked what I hoped looked like a smile. "If he can make it through until spring, summer sunshine will help."

She was not deceived. Her boy would not see Christmas. "Should I warn the others?"

"I think you must discuss that with Father Osric, mistress, not me." Osric, alas, was a barely literate farmhand, son of the previous priest, who mouthed his Latin by rote and was also a notorious gossip. While not as bad as some rural priests, he was not far below average, either.

The soaked, miserable horses were eager to come to the treats I offered, knowing that rubdowns and oats would follow. I took them back to the barn and gave them the best rubdowns they had enjoyed in days. I found a scrap of writing tablet and wrote notes on the corrections I had made to the futhorc enchantment. Then it was time to go back to the academy for the main meal of the day. No one had tried to murder me yet—although

I suspected Guy had come close. After all he had done for me over the years, I felt sick at having given him cause to berate me.

The rain had faded to a drizzle.

The refectory cottage was divided into two rooms, each with its own entrance. When Widow Edith and a couple of helpers from the village brought in the food, they kept the outer doors bolted until they had laid it out. Starving youngsters clustered outside in the rain like drooling puppies, while their elders had the patience to wait elsewhere.

Even when the doors were opened, the varlets were both expected and wise to let the squires enter the building first. We all ate together, though, packed onto two benches flanking a single table, so that every meal began with a stampede and free-for-all, where the longest, strongest arms grabbed the largest shares. The sages and adepts ate in the other room, and so quietly that we could never make out what was being said, or even hear voices raised in disagreement.

For once I arrived while the hungry horde was still gathered outside. William was holding court, clearly under the impression that he had scored a victory by forcing me to cancel a class. The other seven squires were not disagreeing, but that was probably more out of caution than conviction. The others had all been at the academy longer, and some must have had the wits to question his logic. The Saxon varlets were saying nothing.

"Here it is!" William announced. "Ironfoot itself! The crippled Saxon turd."

Everyone waited to hear my reply. The runes had predicted murder, but that was unlikely to happen in broad daylight and the presence of witnesses. I would have preferred to ignore him as I usually did, but this morning I had responded to his hostility in a very defeatist way. Now I could not see how this stupidity could end without a genuine fight.

"If you would rather fight than learn, Squire Legier, why don't you go off and do so, preferably a long way away from us?"

His eyes gleamed at the challenge. "What are you implying, scum?"

"Nothing that everyone else isn't wondering." Out of the corner of my eye I noticed a couple of sages approaching. They had observed the confrontation. Even so, William might have let the squabble die, for he could gain nothing more by prolonging it and he was not stupid, but his crony Lawrence was. Lawrence laughed, which was intolerable.

William barked, "I will make you eat dung, Saxon! Handfuls of it."

"You and your army? Or just you against me?"

"Just me, and you're going to get the beating of your life, as you well—"

"Sword against quarterstaff, or fists and feet?"

William glanced down at the metal platform attached to the sole of my boot. Sensing his manhood being questioned, he snapped, "You choose!"

"No, you choose. You're the one picking the fight. And you'll have to hit first."

"Tonight, right after—"

The door opened, which was the signal to start the stampede. William, as the largest and strongest squire, led the way, and the conversation was abandoned.

In a company of healthy adolescents who had not been fed since the previous sunset, eating came before conversation, and filling our trenchers took precedence over anything, even sitting down. I did manage to claim a small fragment of meat in my share of the booty, a rabbit's front leg I think it was. That day, though, even after voracious youthful appetites were almost sated, no one seemed keen to start the talk. I suppose we were all wondering what the sages would do about my action in the William problem.

Eventually it was William himself who belched contentedly, wiped his mouth on his sleeve, and said, "Assuming you're still around after classes this afternoon, servitor, and Dandelion Head hasn't dumped you in the cesspool, where would you like to get all the shit beaten out of you?"

A Saxon fighting a Norman had no chance of winning. If he won the actual fight, he would still face a flogging or the hangman's noose.

"I'll wait for you in the middle of the quad," I said. "You have to hit me first or come at me with your sword. And then may God have mercy on you, because I won't."

"Hear the dog yap! I do hate yappy—"

At that moment we heard a loud thump that I, at least, recognized as the sound of a bolt being shot. Then, for the first time in my experience—and I was the most senior student present—the connecting door between the two rooms swung open. Adept Baldwin peered in. Baldwin de la Guiche was the most junior of the adepts, promoted from squire only a couple of weeks previously. His eyes sought me.

"Varlet Durwin, the dean wants you."

"No, no!" William crowed. "Nobody *wants* Ironfoot. You heard wrongly. The dean wants *rid* of Varlet Durwin."

Silence. I took up my staff, rose to my feet, and limped around the table to the door. Baldwin, letting me past, shot me a hint of a wink, then hauled the heavy timbered slab closed and bolted it again.

I had never been in that dining room before. At one side of the long table sat the six sages, all flaunting the short green capes that defined their status, while opposite them, when Baldwin had returned to his seat, sat the five adepts, whose capes were white. These were not normal daily wear, so this was some sort of formal gathering.

Dean Odo le Brys sat roughly in the middle of the sages, and it was to him that I bowed. He was a tall, spare, and stooped man, a tree gnarled by age. His bare scalp was hedged around by wispy white curls that always made me think of a silver coronet, but which explained his nickname of Dandelion Head. One of the most honored sages in the land, he had founded Helmdon Academy back in the reign of the first King Henry and nurtured it into a school with a reputation for great learning. Over the last six years I had watched the old man's powers slowly fading, but he was still the undisputed ruler.

"Ah, Varlet, um, Durwin. You had been ordered to teach a class this morning, but you canceled it. Why?"

"One of the pupils was flouting my authority as the appointed instructor, Your Wisdom. I ordered him to leave and he refused. I concluded that he would prevent me from teaching anyone else, so there was no point trying to do so."

The old man blinked a few times. When he saw I had nothing to add, he said, "Thank you. You and the, um, boy in question, were seen in talk just now, before dinner. Was he threatening you?"

"I think he was trying to get me to threaten him, master."

He smiled at nowhere in particular. "Did you?"

"No, sir."

"Of course not. Anyone else have any questions for the varlet? No? Have you finished your meal, Durwin?"

"Yes, master."

"Then you may leave by this door. Adept, pray tell Squire William to come in."

It seemed as if my rash action was going to produce results.

chapter 6

the entire student body assembled in the varlet classroom for the afternoon lecture, so both William Legier and I were present, to our mutual disgust. He showed me his teeth, but said nothing.

Everyone rose as Sage Rolf de Mandeville shuffled in. Rolf was a brother of Count Richard of Barton, and never let anyone forget it—a fussy, flatfooted little man, with the pale and jowly face of a scholar who lived too much indoors. He shed his dripping hooded cloak, revealing that he still wore his short green cape. Either he had not bothered to return to his cottage to change, or he was hoping to impress us with his importance. I doubted he would impress William Legier if he turned himself into a spotted dragon.

He unwrapped his beloved copy of Robert of Chester's *Liber de Compositione Alchimiae* and laid it carefully on the table. Finally, chafing his hands, he nodded to the assembly and said, "Sit."

Rolf was the least-skilled instructor on the faculty, one who obviously hated teaching and did as little of it as he could get away with. Partly that might be because very few students were interested in his specialty, so the atmosphere in his lectures was one of universal boredom. He was also the least skilled of the sages at conveying authority and maintaining discipline in the classroom. Give him his due, when he did find a student who was genuinely eager to learn—for instance me, who sucked up knowledge like a thirsty horse at a trough—then he would make time to instruct him, and even let him read some of his precious books.

I liked him, though. His saving grace, in my eyes, was that he was a skilled singer and musician. He also taught music and the vocal techniques of chanting, and did so magnificently. If he could only inspire his pupils in academic subjects as he could in those, then his lectures would be treats, instead of ordeals.

"Squire William Legier."

William stood up. "Master?"

"Tell the class what Dean Odo told you a little while ago."

The miscreant insolently folded his arms. "I don't remember."

Rolf attempted a smile, but not very successfully. "Then I shall remind you. He said that any further misbehavior by you will be punished very severely."

"Oh, yes. I remember now. It's exactly what he told me last week and the week before and the week before that and the—"

"Silence! But this time he warned you that the academy has always been careful in the past that discipline shall not be carried to—I did not give you leave to sit down."

"I was tired of standing." William yawned.

He had never been this bad before, but he had picked a good victim in Rolf, who was already flushed with fury and practically gibbering. "That is the last impudence I shall put up with. Your challenge before dinner to fight a man with a crippled leg was shameful. Varlet Durwin, if you have trouble with this boy in future, send someone to summon a sage right away. There will be no fighting, either! Do you both understand?"

We both said, "Yes, master," but William was shaking his head. This squabble would have been childishly petty, had I not had that prediction of murder hanging over me.

"And, Squire, the dean has authorized me to tell you that you are to hand that sword over to him before sundown and you will never bear arms within the academy grounds again. Is that absolutely crystal clear?"

Again William said, "Yes, master," while again shaking his head. Lawrence choked back a snigger.

"And you have been warned that future penalties may be severe enough to injure you!"

William yawned.

"Now," Rolf said, with relief, as if he had solved that problem, "we shall continue our investigation of the role of astrology in alchemy. Who can remind us of the names of the seven planets, in order of increasing distance from the earth?"

Several hands began to rise, but all dropped rapidly when William lifted his as high as it would go.

Rolf scowled, rightly suspecting a trap. "Yes?"

Leaping up, William gabbled at high speed, "Saturn, Jupiter, Mars, the sun, Venus, Mercury, and the moon, master."

Which was the right list, but in reverse order. Rolf hesitated, but he obviously had no choice but to recognize the insolence.

"Now give me the right answer. You obviously know it."

"Well the nearest can't be the sun, because it's been gone for weeks. Saturn, Moon, Mercury, Jup—"

"Stop!" Like a fighting cock, Rolf strutted over to a corner and came back with the thick birch rod that was used to prop the door open on warm days. It was not the normal hazel switch used for punishment, but twice the length, as thick as a man's thumb, and strong enough to lean on. "That was your last chance."

"Last chance for what, master?" William's eyes were wide with innocence, but he had noticed the change of implement. So had everyone. That rod was as good as a club. It could break bones.

"To avoid five strokes of the rod. Come here."

That was a surprise. "You mean right now?" William asked, stepping forward. Punishment was usually administered later, in private.

"You know I do, and any more backtalk and you'll get another five. Bare it!"

"Got nothing to be ashamed of!" Instead of pushing his britches down to uncover his buttocks, William shoved them all the way down to his knees, then brazenly turned to face the class and lift his shirt. Such flagrant indecency was a crime and a serious sin, punishable anywhere. The squires obediently grinned, but no one was brave enough to comment.

"That makes ten!" Sage Rolf was almost squeaking in rage. "Turn around! Lean on . . . And remove that sword!"

Still taking his time, William dropped his shirt, unbuckled his belt, and then balanced both sword and scabbard on Robert of Chester. Rolf squealed with annoyance, and moved his precious manuscript to the top of the chest beside the door.

"Now lean on the table! This needs a stronger arm than mine. Durwin, come here."

Sweet Jesus! Was the man insane? I rose. "Master?"

"Come here!" Rolf handed me the rod. "Use that brawny arm of yours. I've watched you splitting firewood. I am ordering you to give this juvenile idiot something he'll never forget—ten strokes on his buttocks, as hard as you can."

William, who had already spread his torso on the table, straightened up again, glaring furiously. Being thrashed in public was apparently a chance to show off, but to be thrashed by the despised Saxon would be intolerable. And he was rightly alarmed by the much greater brawn I would bring to the task.

I was alarmed also. If I truly followed my instructions, I might cripple him. Had the faculty agreed on this insanity, or was Rolf making it up as he went along? Whatever William's grudge against me had been before, if I did as I was told then a great many men, especially Normans, would agree that he would be justified in taking any revenge he fancied. A nasty situation had just become enormously worse.

"Master," I said, "I do not feel it is appropriate for one student to beat another."

"Do as I say!" Rolf snapped. "Hard as you can!"

Still wondering how to handle this situation, I first took the squire's sword and carried it over to the chest, safely out of reach. Then I returned, testing the weight of the rod. A sage should enforce his own discipline. To order one pupil to beat another was bad enough, but to do so when the victim was of higher social rank than the perpetrator was so outrageous that I could not believe the rest of the faculty had directed it. This must be Rolf's own clumsy improvisation.

William was still standing upright and glaring at me. "You touch me just once with that stick, you Saxon pig, and I'll kill you!"

Kill . . . murder . . . *morðor* . . . *morðor* . . . A prophecy could be taken as a warning, not necessarily a foretelling of inevitable events. But the word *morðor* might also be used for a fearful punishment, which was a tempting interpretation, for I had just been handed one certain way to stop William Legier from attempting anything violent in the immediate future. With ten strokes of that rod I could disable him for at least a month.

"Oh, you refuse the punishment?" Rolf inquired in a tone that could only be described as honeyed.

Suddenly I began to see some sense in this madness. Every sage in the academy had tried beating William Legier and he had always come back for more. Whatever pressure or bribe Legier senior had used to make Dean Odo take back his fractious son, part of the agreement must have been that he would accept punishment if he misbehaved. William had shown he was tough enough to endure whatever the faculty could hand out—or, rather, what it had been willing to hand out so far. So it seemed reasonable that if William ever balked, then he would break the contract. So was I now to be given the job of breaking William? Perhaps Rolf thought he was doing me a favor.

"No! I'll take it." William glared at me. "But I'll give you back double, you Saxon shit!" He spread himself on the table, pulling his shirt up to expose his buttocks.

"Not this week, you won't. As hard as I can, you said, master?"

Still I hesitated, for truly I faced one of the hardest decisions of my life. It ought to feel like triumph—my enemy staked out before me, at my mercy. It didn't. I wanted to fight my own battles, not be handed victory by someone else, but if I refused to obey Rolf now, then I would be knuckling under to William's bullying, practically standing up for him. Life would become intolerable, even if I did not get expelled instead of him.

"Get on with it," Rolf said cheerfully.

With a sense of jumping off a cliff into unknown waters, I wound up and swung the club. William gasped. A line of torn flesh across his buttocks at once began oozing blood. My stomach churned. A faint pink line was the usual mark.

"Excellent!" Rolf said. "That's one. Nine to go. Continue. Harder."

"You really want me to cut him like that, master?"

"When he's had enough he can apologize and promise to behave himself in future."

That was never going to happen. As a Norman himself Rolf must know that men like William would die before they would ever knuckle under to a gaggle of namby-pamby scholars. So far as I could understand the youth's thinking, I thought he must want out of Helmdon because of the suspicion of cowardice that always hung over a knight's son who did not follow in his father's hoofprints. William was going to prove his manhood if it killed him. Or, in this case, if I did.

Slash! Two cuts. This time my victim's gasp was close to a scream. He drummed his fists on the table.

"Squire Legier," I said. "If I do what the sage says, I will cause you serious injury. You may be unable to walk for weeks."

William did not even look around, although his fists on the table were white-knuckled.

"Go ahead, pig, and see what happens to you after."

That might involve Legier family and friends riding to Helmdon to stretch my neck with a hempen noose.

So it was now a contest to see which of us could keep this up longer. Torture was the task of the public hangman, and I had no wish for that job, but the harder I hit, the sooner my victim would cry, "Enough!" Then William would be gone from my life, and Helmdon a better place.

I raised the rod for the third stroke, but it was Rolf who cried out and fell against me, causing me to stagger. Then he crumpled to the floor, thrashing and gurgling. I had never seen convulsions before, but I had been taught about them. Steadying myself with the table, I dropped to my knees, snapped the birch rod in two, and forced the shorter piece between the sage's teeth to keep him from biting his tongue.

"Tancred, Lawrence, help me hold him down!" I shouted. "Eadig, run and bring Guy or the dean. Ulf, get his other arm."

Everyone jumped to obey me, but hardly had the door slammed behind Eadig than the sage began to come out of his fit. His movements slackened and he tried to speak. I removed the bit from his mouth, noting the tooth marks in it.

"Certainly . . . at once . . . evensong tomorrow . . ." Rolf's eyes came into focus and he stared up at all the horrified young faces above him. "What is going on? Help me up!"

I said, "No, hold him down. Master, you should just lie there for a few minutes, until we get a sage here to look at you. You took a bad turn."

What sort of bad turn? Epilepsy? A stroke?

Or a curse? Rolf had in effect been the one to shed William's blood, for I had been only his obedient tool. I had heard of protection spells that would retaliate against an attacker, and if that were the cause of the sage's trouble, then he was lucky to have escaped serious injury.

In burst Sages Guy and Alain, followed a moment later by Dean Odo himself. In moments Rolf was pronounced fit to stand up, and was led off, protesting that he had merely tripped, which was certainly untrue, although he might believe it. William had dressed and returned to his place, but the rear of his smock was bloodstained before he even sat down, which he did very carefully. He glared hatred at me. His lip was also bleeding. I could not help wondering how many strokes he would have endured.

Guy took me aside and demanded the story. I told him in as few words as I could.

He nodded. "Come and see me right after this."

Then he went and whispered to the others. He and Alain departed, taking William's sword with them. The dean remained. Unlike Sage Rolf, he could hold the attention of any audience effortlessly.

"Squire William, are you going to behave yourself now?"

"Yes, Dean. Always."

"I shall suspend your punishment for the duration of this class. If I have to take issue with your behavior, I shall reinstate it and add another ten strokes. We are going to break you, William Legier, break you to the bit, like a horse! Is that quite clear now?"

William nodded grimly. "I hear you, sir." He looked pale, and believingly cowed. Twenty such strokes would cripple him for life, possibly kill him. *Morðor!*

Dean Odo retrieved *Liber de Compositione Alchimiae* from the floor, peered at the title, and laid it on the table. "I won't attempt to instruct you gentlemen in the arcane art of alchemy. I am sure that Master Rolf has already taught you more of it than I can remember. Now if this were Master Robert's other work, *Liber Algebrae et Almucabola*, I might venture to speak on advanced computation, but I think we should stick to the use of the abacus. Varlet Eadig, hand out the abaci. Now, how many of you can manage multiplication and division of large numbers? Oh, come, you are being modest . . ."

The dean quickly performed a simple triage, setting the most proficient students to teaching the basics to the beginners, while he showed those in between, including a strangely subdued William, how to multiply CCIX by XXVII. Even alchemy was better than that.

chapter 7

As the squires were following the dean out, I caught William's arm. "I can heal those cuts for you."

He swung around, balling a fist, and then winced as blood-caked cloth dragged on his wounds. "Keep your shitty hands off me, serf. I'm going to send you to Hell for this. And soon!"

No reply was possible. I did not think I would have any trouble from Squire Legier in the immediate future, but his friends were another matter. Saxons were required to know their place and stay in it.

As senior varlet, I followed the squires out, leaving the juniors to tidy the classroom. The rain still fell, the October evening was drawing in, and I had work to do at the stable while there was still some light. But I had orders to report to my tutor. I just hoped that he was less enraged with me than he had been that morning.

Staff swinging, I trudged along the boardwalk to Guy's cabin, reassured by the smoke trickling through the roof that he was home. I knocked, but then disabled the warning without waiting for his command.

"Durwin! Come in and sit down." He gestured to the chair across the fireplace from his. His tone was encouraging and businesslike.

I was more than happy to sit, because the smoke supposedly overhead was down lower than that, and my eyes were already streaming.

"I apologize for shouting at you this morning. Or at least I apologize for accusing you of lying. I could see you weren't. Now . . ." He peered down at a jug that stood by his chair. "Almost gone. Here, top it up and bring a horn for yourself."

Few Normans would drink with a Saxon. Obviously I was back in the ranks of the righteous. Still coughing, I refilled the jug from the ale keg and returned to the fire. The beer was much better than the beer the students drank.

"I want to know everything that happened," Guy said. "Start with Sage Rolf's fit and what led up to it."

Between gulps of beer, I described the afternoon's events in detail and went on to mention William's farewell threat. He would not seek out any violent exercise tonight, but the younger Normans might plan a rumble to finalize the uppity stable boy who had savaged their hero.

"I don't understand, master," I finished. "William Legier obviously doesn't want to stay here, and I can't believe that the faculty wants him to. If everyone is in agreement, why is there a problem?"

Guy leaned back in his chair with a heavy-lidded sphinx smile to show that sages did not discuss confidential matters with students, which he straightway proceeded to do. "Everyone is in agreement except *Sir* William Legier, his father, who has friends in high places. He is warden of the royal forest of Rockingham, and reputedly a stubborn, opinionated, vindictive old tyrant, exactly the sort of father to inspire rebellion in a spirited Norman youth. It isn't you the kid's fighting, it's his old man."

That made no sense to me at the time. Nowadays, having long been a grandfather, I understand better.

"And how is Sage Rolf?" I ventured.

The smile grew even more sphingine. "Completely recovered, thank you for asking." Obviously that, also, was none of my business, but I detected a hint that the matter might be discussed later. "Why on earth did you savage the lout the way you did? A gentlemanly caning is an invigorating and instructive part of every boy's life. It is not intended to leave lifetime scars."

"Because Rolf told me to. And . . . and because Rolf told me to."

"Sometimes, just between you and me, I think he's an idiot." Guy chuckled and refilled my drinking horn. "We were going to get Fugol to do it, not you. How many strokes did Rolf order?"

"Ten." Fugol was the porter and odd-job man for the academy. He had the brawn of an ox, but much less brain. He could cut two cords of wood to my one without breaking a sweat. The thought of being beaten by him was blood-chilling. Even William would never laugh that off.

Guy winced and shook his head. "How did William take them?"

"William is as tough as an anvil, master, but he wouldn't have lasted the full ten. That was the purpose, I gather?"

"Um . . . well, yes. We decided we've had enough of him. We agreed that instead of just warming his butt, we'd give him the sort of beating a lord orders for a recalcitrant serf, but we didn't mean for you to be the tormenter. That boy is vicious. He'll come after you as soon as he's healed."

"And what happens if we do fight? Is he warded?"

Guy looked startled. "That would be an outrageous. . . . Why do you ask?"

"Because I was just acting as Rolf's tool, and as soon as the first drop of William's blood hit the floor, so did Sage Rolf."

"Ah. No, I don't think that was the cause of his distress." Guy was clearly not ready to offer any other theories yet, but he raised a bushy eyebrow as an invitation for me to do so.

"Then someone cast a curse at Rolf?"

Guy chuckled. "A very strange curse! It reminds me a little of the holy St. Paul, who was struck down on the road to Damascus—struck more drastically, I admit. When he recovered he had changed totally from a persecutor to the most fervent of the Lord's apostles. Our learned, if sedentary, sage has not only made a full recovery, but is ardent in his determination to leave at once for Barton, to visit his brother, Count Richard."

"In this weather?" I said in horror, thinking of the floods and streams between here and there. Every ford would be impassable, every bridge washed out.

"'Come hell or high water' were his very words. He even wanted to ride in the cart! I told him it would sink to the axles before he got out of the village. I flatly refused to authorize use of the academy's horses. No doubt he is even now pouring his pleas into the ears of our esteemed dean."

My mind took flight like an arrow as I tried to recall what words Rolf had mumbled as he was coming round.

"You've thought of something!" my tutor complained. "I swear those innocent blue eyes of yours glow in the dark sometimes. Tell me."

I parried, needing time to think. "What do *you* believe caused Rolf's fit, master?"

Guy said, "Humph!" but did not balk at the impertinence of such a direct question. "I am only guessing, because he refuses to explain, but there's an incantation called *Despero in extremis*, which is basically an alarm bell. It has an evil reputation. I suspect that Rolf used *Despero* to link himself with his brother, Richard, the count. It may have been done years ago, when they were both quite young. Or possibly the count had his house sage link him to Rolf at some time. *Despero* is no party trick, more like a scream for help, because a couple of glosses on the grimoire warn that the effect can be violent when the spell is invoked. 'As of a stroke from Heaven,' one says. The sender expects this; he can go off by himself and lie down before sending the message. But the receiver has no forewarning. He may be in church or riding a horse when Heaven smites him—embarrassing, or even dangerous."

It made sense!

"Out with it!" Guy said. "What have you seen?"

"Not seen, heard. As he was recovering, Rolf seemed to be speaking to someone, talking about tomorrow."

Guy said, "Aha! That fits. Now tell me exactly what happened last night."

He listened intently until I had finished. "Durwin, do you realize what you have achieved?"

"It was an easy one. The errors were very obvious. I had two versions of the same chant, one marred by two grammatical mistakes, and the other by three. Things are rarely that obvious."

"Even so, there must be others like that. We have dozens of spells that don't work—hundreds!"

I thought it safer just to nod agreement than to point out that for years he had been forbidding me to do exactly what he was now hailing as a triumph.

He said, "Damn! You'll have to do it again. I simply cannot believe until I've seen it happen."

"Make it work, you mean, master?"

"I have to see it with my own eyes. Did you notice what's on the table as you came in?"

I glanced around and saw a cloth lying there, nothing else. "No, sir."

"The thirty-seven tiles, in no special order, and each one labeled so I can write down what it means in the Latin alphabet. You can chant it from memory, so finish your drink, and stand up." Guy produced another cloth. He led me over to the table, sat me down on a stool, and proceeded to blindfold me.

This was an ordeal I'd never heard of or imagined. My heart was fluttering like a trapped bird. The Wyrds had given me one prophecy and fallen silent when I asked for another. Would they be responsive again now, on another day? I wished I'd drunk a lot more beer. At the same time I wished I hadn't drunk any.

I heard Guy move a stool on the far side of the table. "Now . . . I've uncovered the tiles. You may begin the invocation whenever you're ready. I anticipate that you will point to each tile, but don't go too fast for me to write down their names."

I said, "Yes, master," cleared my throat, and began. Acceptance came strong and clear, so I could relax and concentrate on the quality of my chanting. I had no idea where the tiles were, but I didn't need to. When I finished chanting, my hand—my *left* hand, although I am right-handed—began to move on its own. I could not have slowed it down had I tried, but I had no need to, for it paused after each move. It seemed that Guy had guessed how the tiles were meant to be used. The blindfold might even have been part of the procedure, so that the chanter need not know what message he was delivering.

I soon realized that this message was longer than the one I had been granted the previous evening. Finally the thrill of acceptance ended and my hand returned to my control.

And Guy said, "Christ's wounds!" I had never heard him blaspheme like that.

I removed the blindfold. He handed me the slate on which he had been writing, and I read what the Wyrds had dictated: *se eorles unlybwrhta sie sweltað.*

He said, "'The earl's wizard is dying,' correct?"

We stared at each other. My tutor looked as amazed as I felt.

"I couldn't see the tiles!" I protested.

"Of course not. Durwin, we have to get you promoted to adept. You're going to be a sage, and a great one. Have you mentioned this *Hwæt segst* prophecy to anyone else?"

"No, master."

"Don't! Not even to Rolf. Because, firstly, most people will not believe you. They'll think you are either boasting or trying to trick them into doing something to your advantage. Secondly, the Church denounces any form of foreseeing most vehemently, as a blasphemous insult to God. Understood?"

"Yes, master." I couldn't help wondering whether, honorable as he was, he hoped to pass off my discovery as his own, and take the credit. I should have had more faith, because I am sure now that the idea never occurred to him.

"Don't your people have a saying, 'Murder wants to be revealed'?"

"Yes, master: *Morðor wile ut.*"

"A murder in Barton would explain the use of *Despero* and validate both your prophecies. Could it be done? Barton, I mean," he said, looking up. "Could you get there in this weather?"

My first instinct was to say I would rather die than try. I remembered Barton, and it must be forty miles away—a tough day's ride for a good horse in good weather, but after weeks of rain? Yet I discovered that I was nodding in spite of myself. A few days away from Helmdon to let tempers cool had obvious advantages. And I was eager to find out if the count's house sage had been murdered.

"You could get old Rolf to Barton even in this pissy weather?"

"Might have to allow two days. Many fords will be impassable, and bridges unsafe."

"If you can't manage it, no one else can. Rolf is no adventurer, so whatever is calling him must be important. You are willing to try?"

"Yes, master."

"Then I'll go and talk with the dean right away!"

"I must see to the horses before it gets dark."

Guy scowled. "Do so, and I'll send word to you later." Then he stood up with an unexpected chuckle. "And we'll see what price we can set on your equine expertise."

chapter 8

i hurried homeward through the deluge, pausing only to collect the snack that Widow Edith always packed and held ready for me. I had left the horses indoors at noon, so my work was easier than usual. I had only to move each one in turn to a clean stall, shovel out the dirty one, and repeat the process. They were restless from lack of exercise, but I assured them that at least two of them would get more than enough on the morrow. They didn't believe me.

By the time I fed and watered them, I was working in almost pitch darkness. Having made sure, for the third time, that the door was securely barred against any possible lynch squad of William supporters, I scrambled up the ladder to my loft, where I proceeded to eat. Normally I ate my supper very slowly, for I had little else to do to kill time until dawn; this time I gobbled, in the hope that Guy's message would come soon.

A trip to Barton would be a welcome break from winter monotony, and a chance to confirm the prophecy even more satisfying. Yet the thought of a two-day trek through deep mud was daunting; horses might be injured or, at worst, swept away with their riders in the swollen rivers. If we had to give up and come home, I would make a real enemy out of Sage Rolf and provide the odious William with an undying source of mirth.

I had just washed down my meal with a draft of rain water when a thunderous banging on the door announced that I had a visitor—either a furious giant or an idiot trying to alarm five horses. I slithered down the ladder as fast as I could and hobbled to the door.

"Who's there?"

"Eadig!"

Right answer, because the most junior varlet always got the nastiest tasks. "Just a moment!" I hoisted the heavy bar from its brackets.

No giant but certainly furious, Eadig clutched a fiery torch that was hissing and spluttering even more than he was. The horses shifted their feet uneasily.

"Can't bring that in here," I said cheerfully. "Frightens the stock."

He responded with some ancient words that should only be used in serious cursing.

"Shame on you, Eadig son of Edwin! Did you come here for a purpose or are you just passing by?"

"Sent to tell you that Dandelion Head wants you." Eadig edged in under the lintel while holding his torch out in the rain and wiping his face with his sleeve. "Coming?"

"Of course. You run ahead. I'll follow."

Needing no second bidding, the lad and his torch vanished back into the deluge. I shivered into my cloak and hood, both still soaked. Then I cheerily bade the horses not to wait up for me, took up my staff, and hobbled off after the messenger.

The dean, not Guy! Did that mean that the journey was certainly on, or just that Guy had been forced to disregard his own warning and mention the runes' augury? If that were the case, I must expect an inquisition before all six sages and even some of the adepts, for mending a broken incantation was unheard of.

I should have made Eadig wait for me. Walking along a flooded lane in absolute darkness with the wind blowing rain in my face was no mean task for any man, and mismatched legs were no help. Fortunately I had made the journey thousands of times before, and I could swing my staff before me like a blind man's cane to locate the hedges, portholes, and raised doorsteps that beset my path. Despite the lack of it to lean on, I managed to stay upright, and came at last to the academy's boardwalk. The only sign of life I had detected in Helmdon was some raucous male singing as I passed the cottage of Mother Gwyn, the ale-wife.

When I reached the dean's house, the beat of my iron-shod boot on the boardwalk was heard before I could knock; the door squeaked open.

"Enter quickly," said Sage Rolf.

I obeyed and ducked under the lintel, blinking in the brightness of the candles.

Rolf, wrapped up to the shape of a dumpling, shuffled back to his stool by the crackling fire. Dean Odo was huddled in a bearskin robe on a chair on the other side of the hearth. Silver wine goblets gleamed in the candlelight. I closed the door, removed my hood, and touched my forehead in salute. I remained where I was, knowing that I would not be invited to sit. My cloak dribbled audibly into the puddle forming around my feet.

"You sent for me, Dean?"

"I did and I am sorry for it, on such a night."

"No trouble, master."

The old man was aging; his hands shook all the time and he forgot things, but it was characteristic of him that he had just come much closer to apologizing to a Saxon than most Normans ever would.

"Sage Guy tells us that you think it would be possible to ride to, um, Barton, despite the, um, inclement conditions?"

I told him I was willing to try if the matter were important. "It will be hard going, and dangerous. Even skilled riders can be washed away by a stream in spate. We may need more than one day."

Shaking his head, Odo turned to his companion. "You heard the lad, Rolf. You still insist on this madness?"

"I feel I must, Dean. I cannot say more."

I thought he was out of his head, and probably Dean Odo did too, but he wasn't. The problem really was more urgent than they could have guessed, more than I even had guessed.

"Very well," the dean said. "I admire your courage if not your wisdom. Bring the three best horses up tomorrow at first light, boy. You will attend our learned sage on his journey to Barton, and a squire will accompany you, just in case you run into, um, human trouble, as well as that visited upon us by the elements."

"Have the cook provide us with two days' fare," Rolf said.

I saluted again. "Begging most humbly, masters . . . I do think it would be wiser to take all four horses. Both for baggage, and because the going will be hard on them." I knew who would have to walk if one of the horses went lame. I might be told to carry the bags, too.

Odo chuckled. "Well, we certainly shan't need them for plowing for a good whiles yet, will we, Rolf?"

"No, Dean. You will check their shoes and legs carefully before we go, boy?"

"Aye, sir." What sort of an idiot did he think I was?

Rolf coughed meaningfully. "The promotion, Dean?"

A snarl of pique escaped from Odo's cocoon of fur. "I hadn't forgotten! I was getting to that. We were most impressed by your reaction to the sage's bad turn today, varlet. It seems you kept your head, took command, and did exactly what was required. Your tutor has recommended that we promote you to adept, and members of the faculty have unanimously agreed."

I had not expected that. It was a staggering surprise, and for a moment I just blinked. I did not believe my rapid first aid in the afternoon had provoked it. This was the price Guy had extracted for releasing his protégé to escort Rolf to Barton.

Emerging from cover, the dean rose stiffly, maneuvered carefully around a heap of scrolls, books, and discarded clothes, and then shuffled across the room to me.

"You are required to kneel," he said mildly, old eyes twinkling. Rolf also came, holding a white cloth that looked like a towel, but I recognized it as an adept's cape.

Clutching my staff with both hands, I sank to my knees, an awkward and uncomfortable position for me. They stood beside me and laid the cloth over my head.

"Durwin of . . .?"

"Pipewell, sir."

Odo sang the versicles and Rolf the responses, an arrangement I regretted, because Rolf was by far the better singer. Nonetheless, the ordination enchantment is a beautiful one, which I had always enjoyed witnessing. Every promotion since I had come to Helmdon had been performed before an assembly of the entire academy, and I could not help wondering whether the reason for mine being hidden away in this private little huddle was truly because of the urgency of Rolf's journey, or because they were ashamed of licensing a Saxon adept. My doubts soon faded as I felt an unexpected rush of acceptance, a sensation normally confined to the chanters. Even the simple words seemed to take on arcane, transcendental glory.

Too soon the ritual was completed. They uncovered my head and laid the cape on my shoulders, pinning it on the left. The old men shuffled back to the fire; Adept Durwin of Pipewell rose shakily to his feet.

"Your certificate will be ready when you return," Rolf said.

"Your Wisdoms, I hardly know what to say. This is a great honor for one of my humble birth." Even in those days there were Saxon lords, Saxon knights, Saxon bishops, Saxon cantors, and even Saxon sages, but in most cases they had benefited by family connections. I was a hostler's son.

"Yes, it is," said Sage Rolf. "Just remember, Adept Durwin, that on our journey tomorrow you will outrank Squire William. I strongly recommend that you guard your tongue around him. I don't want to waste time on the road performing healing incantations for either of you."

"*William?* Master, I cannot believe William will be capable of sitting a horse for several—"

"Sage Guy is performing a healing on him even now. He may not be as comfortable in the saddle as you and I shall be, but he will manage."

"He is the eldest of the squires," the dean mumbled, "and had several years of weapons training before deciding to switch to the academic life."

I had guessed about the training long ago, and could not believe that William's change of career had been voluntary. On the other hand, Barton was halfway to Rockingham, so perhaps the sages, like a skulk of old foxes, were hoping that Sir William's black sheep would bolt for home when he had the chance.

The dean waved a dismissal. "Go and pay your respects to your tutor. A suitable token of appreciation . . ." He took a drink to drown the end of the sentence. I had nothing to offer Guy.

"Take good care of your cape," Sage Rolf said. "Keep it dry. I shall wear mine under my cloak."

"As you wish, master," I said, although it seemed strange that a sage would travel incognito. King Henry had restored order after the Anarchy, so that travel in his domain was usually quite safe now. On the sort of forest trails we must take from Helmdon to Barton, though, almost anyone might seize an opportunity to change roles from groveling peasant to murderous footpad. The threat of magic would be a better defense than an escort of men-at-arms.

"I am in a hurry, and do not wish to be detained on my journey by peasants wanting favors," the old fraud explained.

"Aye, master." That a Norman sage would bother to offer excuses to a Saxon adept was even stranger.

chapter 9

an adept's cape is merely a piece of bleached linen draped over the shoulders, pinned at the throat, and hanging to the wearer's elbows. Yet this rag would make a huge change in my life, marking me as a man of learning. As I hobbled along the boardwalk, I was still trying to come to terms with my new status. I was currently wearing every stitch of clothing I owned, none of it fit for an adept; I would have to find a woman in the village to sew some better garb for me. I could earn a decent living now, if I wished, doctoring the sick in some town or village. I would much prefer to remain at Helmdon until I could graduate as a sage, but that would require money I did not have. My days as a servitor had ended, and I could not imagine the academy allowing one of its qualified adepts to double as stable hand.

Expecting Guy to be alone, I tapped on the door for politeness, but spoke the password—*Vivat Henricus Secundus Rex*—and raised the latch. I found myself looking into the murderous glare of Squire William, who was stretched out on his belly on the examination couch with his chin on his forearms and his torn and bruised rump directed at Heaven. So much for dignity.

"Enter, Adept, enter!" Guy boomed. Seemingly unaware of the swirling cloud of smoke around his head, he was standing beside the patient, dabbing at his injuries with a rag. "Congratulations on your promotion. Long overdue and well deserved, right, Squire?"

"We all get our just desserts in time, master." William continued to eye me, unblinking as a cat.

My efforts to thank my tutor for my promotion collapsed in a violent coughing fit.

"Should have happened years ago," the sage said. "You've got more brains than all the rest of them put together. We shall drink to your new rank and your future employment as sage to some noble lord. First, though, we must cure the squire's scratches. I have applied that excellent unguent you blended last week, so now all it needs is the *Asclepius, Vejovis, Eir* incantation. You know the versicles, I'll take the responses . . ."

"I don't want help from that Saxon scum," William said loudly.

"Well you're going to get it. This is the strongest healing chant we have, and it will work much better with Durwin leading, because he caused the damage. One, two . . ."

I inhaled another breath of smoke and was again convulsed by coughing. Either my greater height explained why I was more afflicted than Guy, or his lungs were inured to it, cured like kippers.

"Oh, pull up a stool," he said crossly. "The spirits won't be offended if you chant it sitting down."

The *Asclepius* was one of Guy's favorites, so I knew it well, although I usually sang the responses. Guy had a fine tenor voice, his gestures were sharp, yet graceful, and the squire's wounds visibly closed as our chanting progressed. At the end, they had healed from gaping cuts to two intersecting lines of pink new skin, and the bruising had faded.

"There! You may be a little tender tomorrow, but I don't suppose you'll be doing any galloping or jumping. Make yourself respectable and be on your way."

Looking uncharacteristically subdued—perhaps he had never experienced a healing enchantment before—William thanked him and dressed.

"My sword, Your Wisdom? I'll need it tomorrow. You took it."

"Mm, so I did." Guy retrieved the blade from under the couch and returned it to its owner.

William belted it on, sending me threatening promises with his eyes. Then he wrapped his fancy hooded cloak around himself, and disappeared out into the night. The smoke billowed again.

Guy returned to his chair, handed me a drinking horn, and proceeded to load both it and his own with wine from a pitcher. He raised his drink in a toast. "To our new adept! One man's lost penny is another's good fortune, as they say."

I had never tasted wine before. I wasn't sure I liked it.

"I am very grateful for all your efforts, master, and especially today. I hope they won't cost you any future ill will."

Guy shook his head. "None at all. When I told Rolf of your offer, he jumped at it right away, and suggested that the time had come to promote you to adept. He's been refusing his consent for years, suddenly he's all for it. Explain that?"

"He expects to have me to assist him with enchantments?" We contemplated that implication thoughtfully until I put it into words: "But surely any earl, such as his brother, must employ both a house sage and a cantor to assist him? Even if the sage is dying, Sage Rolf shouldn't need to bring his own cantor?"

Guy smiled. "One would assume he won't, but he may be playing safe. I did not mention your predictions, of course, but if the message Rolf received confirmed what we suspect, then His Lordship must be deeply concerned. In other words, Rolf may need you to chant the responses in the *Ubi malum*."

"That sounds like powerful lore. 'Where is the evil?'"

"Very effective, and not to be trifled with, as you may guess. I have only seen it used once, and the cantor chanting the responses went into a trance all right. But then he walked out into the town and tried to break into the home of a complete stranger, which was later searched and found to contain a cellar full of stolen property. Unfortunately, that wasn't the evil the enchanter was looking for."

I had been put into trances often enough and had no liking for the experience. To be sent on the track of a murderer in such a state could be injurious to health.

Guy chuckled. "So Rolf will take Squire William's strong sword arm along for protection from mundane dangers on the journey, and your skills to help with the occult when he gets there. A prudent lad, our sage."

I was certain that he just wanted me for my skill with horses. Guy took another swig of wine. "How many horses are you taking?"

"Four, master: three saddled and a sumpter for the baggage."

"I want you to ride Ruffian."

"Master!" The academy's four horses were nags at best, docile and experienced, but long past their best. They pulled carts or plows, and they could be ridden. But Ruffian was Guy's own horse, which he used for hunting, a splendid chestnut, and a holy terror, like all stallions.

"He'll pine if he's left by himself, and he needs the exercise. But I do mean you. I daresay Rolf may be able to sit a privy stool in comfort, but never a wild lad like Ruffian. Perhaps a demonstration of temper when you arrive, so that the learned sage isn't tempted to pull rank on you?"

I suppressed a grin. "Could be arranged, master." Ruffian always enjoyed a chance to show off. And I now outranked Squire William, which was a heady thought—provided William saw it that way, of course.

"Mind, if Ruffian comes to harm, I'll turn you into a toad."

"Aye, master." Toads had it good. Fat flies were plentiful enough.

My mentor shrugged. "Now to more pleasant business! You'll need a grimoire to get you started on your higher studies. Take that one and guard it with your life." He pointed to a thick tome lying on the table. "It is a very old copy, very valuable. I want it back, mind."

All books written on parchment had wooden covers, fastened tightly to keep the parchment from buckling in damp weather, of which we presently had no shortage. Instead of ropes to hold it together, this one had brass clasps. Flattered as I was to be trusted with such a treasure, I would have preferred not to be burdened with baggage of such value, let alone such weight.

"Master, perhaps this could wait until—"

"No, take it. You may have long days to fill while you wait for the roads to dry. Read, memorize if you wish, but speak nothing aloud without expert guidance. You must *not* dabble in any of this by yourself! So far you have studied only field magic: herb lore and prayers to nature spirits and a few of the old gods, long banished from power. This will lead you into more powerful arts, ancient and—in some cases—darker. Sage Rolf has promised to start instructing you in some of the deeper wisdom. Nothing black, you understand, but some routines are suspect in the eyes of the Church."

First a champion hunter and now a priceless book? It almost seemed that Guy was bribing me to abscond with such riches and never come back, but that made no sense; he prized Ruffian and his book collection far too much. Much more likely he was relying on my honesty to make sure that I did come back.

"Can an adept be a hostler, master?"

Guy drained the drinking horn and wiped his mouth on his sleeve. "No. We'll have to find a stable boy for the academy and a sponsor for you. I'll inquire of some of my acquaintances. I'm sure we can find someone who will finance your higher studies in return for a few years' service later."

Someone like Count Richard of Barton or one of his friends? "That's very kind of you, master."

"So who do I get to look after the stables?"

"Rodor the miller's son can do the work, but you'll have to tell him every single thing you need done, and not more than ten words at a time." I thought of Eadig, but neither he nor any of the other varlets was any use with horses. "One of the squires, maybe?" They were manor born, and knew horses, although they would not care much for caring for them. On the other hand, they could always use some pocket money to bribe dairymaids. "If you want a new varlet . . . the farrier has a likely son, a bright lad."

"I'll look him over tomorrow."

"I can train someone for you, when I return." *When.*

Taking that as a promise, Guy nodded. "Come back as soon as the weather improves. The count can see to his brother's return."

"Aye, master." Consent while in Guy's sanctum was easy enough, but I would be under Rolf's orders while I was gone. Besides, I would need help. A lone man traveling with a string of horses would almost certainly end in a ditch with his throat cut. Looking forward to a very hard day on the morrow, I was anxious to be on my way, but Guy clearly wanted my companionship for a while yet.

"If the roads are really bad, you may have to stay over at Northampton. If you do overnight at the academy, pray give my regards to Dean Gilbert. I know he includes Saxon adepts in his faculty, so you can wear your new colors proudly there. Rolf trained there."

I sipped my wine. There was more to that remark than met the ear. Why would Sage Rolf choose not to overnight at the academy? Caring for wayfarers is both a universal duty and a pleasure, especially among the gentry. Aristocrats on the road seek out their peers, offering company and news in return for board and shelter. Commoners apply at monasteries or abbeys, but students of the arcane are less welcome there. Surely Sage Rolf should seek shelter from his old school when he was in the neighborhood? Guy, in other words, was dropping hints that their parting had not been amicable. That might tie in with Rolf's remark that he was not going to show his sage's cloak on the journey. I did not mention that.

Guy raised his horn as if to drink, pondered for a moment, and then lowered it. "I've heard rumors that Count Richard has troubles. He's been fortifying, and that's expensive. He's reputed to be an unpopular lord, greedy and hard on his tenants. He tries to claim more service days and raises his milling fees."

His brother wasn't very likeable, either, but if Guy was hinting at some sort of peasant uprising, then I had a lot more to worry about than rain and mud. Ever since the Conqueror himself, the Norman kings had reacted with extreme violence to any hint of revolt. To be caught up in anything like that would mean quick death for a Saxon.

chapter 10

To feed, water, and saddle the horses, and then bring them to the academy by first light was impossible, but I was nimble and efficient, and I had my caravan on the road very soon after dawn; not that anyone could tell quite when the sun rose that morning, for the rain continued, if not quite as viciously as before. I paused only once on my way through the village, just long enough for Edith to bring out the packed food I had ordered on my way home the night before.

Only Ruffian gave me any trouble, but Ruffian gave everyone trouble, just on principle, and approved of me as much as he approved of any human. He also welcomed a chance to get out of doors, wet or dry, although he definitely disapproved of having to lead a string of his subjects. In his mind, a herd should be led by the senior mare and the stallion should canter along at the rear, nipping laggards' hindquarters at will.

He was still seriously piqued by this when we reached the academy. I tethered the others to a post but remained mounted on Ruffian until Sage Rolf and Squire William emerged from the former's house. They were both wearing chain mail shirts and helmets with nose guards; both bore swords. Rolf's I was certain was only for show.

Having a six-foot quarterstaff slung on my back and a metal platform under my right foot, I was well equipped to annoy any horse, let alone a fireball like Ruffian. The human watchers did not notice the jabs, but he did. Outraged, he launched into a virtuoso demonstration of bucking and kicking all around the yard, generously splattering the witnesses with mud—including the half-dressed varlets and squires who had scrambled out to see what was going on. Ruffian wasn't the only one showing off; I stayed in the saddle and let the stallion continue until everyone was perfectly clear on who was going to be riding whom on the journey.

Then I calmed him down, slipped him an oatcake as a reward, and joined my traveling companions on the boardwalk to apologize for the delay. I was only slightly puffed, and my normal limp hid any effects of the beating my rear had just endured.

"Master," I said, "I respectfully suggest we travel by way of the forest. If we follow the Nene Valley, we'll be up to our stirrups in mud all the way, and then have to risk the bridge at Northampton." In the low-lying farmland, every road would be a stream, every field a swamp, every ditch a trap to cripple a horse.

"Of course," the sage said, as if he'd been planning this all the time. "Provided we don't get lost. There's no sun today."

I chose to treat that as a jest and smiled accordingly. "I have never known the *Mín færeld* to fail, sir."

Rolf shot his eyebrows up into his helmet and looked from me to William and back again. "You don't know the *Quo imus*?"

That incantation required a trio. Before the squire would have to confess that he didn't know a line of it, I said, "I would need to review my part beforehand, master."

"Very well, we'll rely on *Mín færeld*. You chant the versicles and I'll take the responses." That was a reversal of the normal roles for our respective ranks, which might be a compliment on my promotion, but more likely a test of my abilities. If so, it was an easy one, for the *Mín færeld* is a brief and simple incantation invoking the guidance, benevolence, and protection of the woodland spirits; my tutor and I sang it even before an expedition to seek out herbs on the common, and it often seemed to bring us good fortune. Guy justified using a Saxon chant because it was addressed to the native spirits.

So I chanted the first versicle. Sage Rolf responded, singing strongly, although his accent in the old tongue was so bad that I wondered if the spirits would understand a word. Apparently they did, though, for as the spell reached its end, I felt a warm sense of blessing to show that the evocation had been accepted.

Rolf clearly felt it also, for he nodded to me and said, "You have a good voice, Adept."

At which a surprised Saxon could only mutter his thanks for the compliment. William was scowling.

"Squire," Rolf said, "the blessing if you please."

Mollified, William drew his sword, raised it to form the cross, and besought the protection of the Holy Trinity on our journey. I felt no sign that the appeal had been accepted. Prayers must be taken on faith, the priests say.

After that it was a small matter to pack the baggage on Blossom and then hold Sage Rolf's stirrup as he mounted Nithing, the big gelding. The third saddle was on Three Foot and I waited to see if William would make a fuss, for most young men of his rank would take offense at being offered a mare. He didn't, but Three Foot did, rolling her eyes, pulling away, and tugging against my grip on her bridle. I realized then that I had never seen William on a horse, and I detected as much stress in the squire's eyes as there was in the mare's.

Three Foot was scared because William was scared; she could smell the fear on him. Admittedly he was going to feel his bruises, which might excuse some reluctance, but a Norman youth with several years of knight training ought to vault into a saddle like a frog jumping off a lily pad. Certainly William swung up into the saddle skillfully enough, but then sat there with all the lithe suppleness of a tombstone, hands and teeth clenched, eyes staring straight ahead as if the four horsemen of the Apocalypse were heading his way. I carefully did not comment or stare. I tut-tutted at the fidgeting mare and busied myself with adjusting the stirrup straps.

The expedition rode off with Ruffian and me in front, leading the pack horses, Blossom and Dapple. Even yet, there are no real roads in the middle of England, for few of the inhabitants have reason to go anywhere. In summer there are always trails between or across the fields, but that October everywhere was drowned in mud.

I cannot recall a day in my life more miserable than that one. The going was horrible, the rain never stopped, and I could not relax for a moment. My mood was not improved by the fact that my two companions expected me to do all the work. Although we tried to stay on the uplands, even there the watercourses were all brimful. At every stream I had to scout upstream and down until I found a passable crossing. Once I had persuaded Ruffian to try it, the other horses would follow, albeit reluctantly. I wished that he and I were alone, and I could let him have his head on some of the open stretches of grassland.

Not that there was much open grassland, for the higher ground thereabouts is all heavy clay soil, little use for cultivation.

Beech, elm, oak, and ash trees grow there, but not all of it is unbroken woodland. Swineherds ran their pigs in places, deer had left their signs to provoke comments from the Normans, and sometimes the turf had been ripped by wild boar. Here and there were signs of old mines, charcoal burners' hearths, ancient settlements abandoned, and patches of grazing currently in use. It was nevertheless all forest in the sense that the king held the right to hunt and cut timber there, as he does over great swathes of England. Peasants and some lords might have grazing and dead fall privileges in parts, but wood cutting and hunting were strictly reserved, for they represented a large part of the royal income. Salted venison is an important part of a palace diet in winter.

Rolf and William in chain mail would not be mistaken for poachers, and no forester came galloping up to challenge us. Several times we crossed fords where a resident might try to extract a toll from travelers, but either the day was too wet for them to make the effort, or the sight of two swords and a quarterstaff was enough reason to waive the claim.

Shortly before noon the rain slackened to a drizzle, the wind to a breeze, and the sky tried to brighten. Either the blessing or the incantation was working; possibly even both. As long as the spirits kept the outlaws away, no horses went lame, and the weather didn't change back again, I could begin to hope that the rest of the journey could be less stressful.

This would be my first visit to a lord's castle, and with luck I would have some time to myself at Barton, when I could start reading through that tantalizing grimoire Guy had lent me. It would be glorious to parade around in an adept's white cape. I kept wondering how I might send the news of my promotion to my mother and brothers.

I had spoken to no one except my horse for hours when I paused for what felt like at least the hundredth time to study a problem. I was at the edge of a flooded meadow. Somewhere out there in the temporary lake was a stream, but the flow wasn't fast enough to show exactly where. It was a perfect trap to break horses' legs, and it would be up to me to lead the way across—on foot, because my legs were worth much less than Ruffian's. As I reached for my staff to dismount, William reined in alongside. I glanced back and saw no Rolf.

The squire had lost some of his nervous tension in favor of looking thoroughly soaked and miserable, which was at least understandable. He indicated the missing sage's location with a backward nod of his head. "Found a tree that wasn't wet enough."

"I hope the tree appreciates the honor." I did not expect a smile and didn't get one.

"Reach Barton before dark?" he asked.

"Should. I can keep going if he can."

Silence fell. Even the hiss of rain was hushed where we were. I wondered why he had come to speak with me. Then he sneered. "So the serf's been promoted to adept!"

"Better than being a public hangman."

William's eyes narrowed at the jibe. "Congratulations. I hope you don't expect me to call you 'sir' now, boy."

"You can call me anything you want, my lord."

"That's true. 'Impudent Saxon cur,' for instance."

William was a typical Norman, and Normans were perpetual fighters. If they couldn't fight enemies, they fought neighbors; if they couldn't fight neighbors, they fought friends; if they couldn't fight friends, they fought cousins, brothers, or sons. King Henry's family wars were to cause me great troubles in later life.

I said, "Rolf was ad-libbing yesterday when he made me the public hangman. They're planning to give the job to Fugol."

William's eyes narrowed inside his helmet. "Meaning?"

"Meaning that he'll pulp you. They're planning to crush you, Squire! You can't win against that treatment."

"You think so? They'll soon learn otherwise." He spoke with more resignation than defiance. His father had friends in high places. "And you won't be there to see it. Why does Sage Guy favor you?"

"I hadn't noticed that he does, Squire."

"Yes he does! He's always buttering you up in front of the rest of us. Now this! Some of us wonder if you're his bastard."

Saxon Rule One was never to let a Norman bait you.

"I believe he was studying in France about the time I was conceived, Squire. My father was a lay brother in the abbey at Pipewell and a few summers ago the sage stopped there with a lame horse. He borrowed a fresh one from us and I accompanied him to Helmdon so I could take it home. The plan was that I would deliver his own mount to Helmdon later, when it had recovered. He got to know me on the journey and offered to take me on as a servitor."

The way he had put it was that he would shovel knowledge into me if I would shovel dung out of the barn. It had seemed like the opportunity of a lifetime to me, and had indeed proved to be so.

"Why do you want to be a sage?" William demanded.

"I can't be a soldier, when I'm taller on one leg than the other. Even herding and farmwork are very hard for me. I don't have a call to the ministry. That leaves the academy."

William glowered at this logic. "What's wrong with your leg?"

What business was that of his? He had never shown interest in me before. "The right one's a handbreadth shorter than the left one."

"I can see that, idiot. Tell me why."

I told him how I'd fallen when I tried to put a horse over a fence.

The little I could see of William's face went suddenly pale. "How old were you then?"

"Ten."

William wheeled his horse and rode away, either to go back in search of Rolf, or because he needed to puke and wanted to do so in private.

When we came near Northampton, Sage Rolf announced that he would show us a shortcut around it, so we need not go through the town itself. I recalled Guy's hints that Rolf might wish to avoid the academy there, and certainly the shortcut seemed unnecessarily long. Northampton was reputedly the third-largest town in the kingdom, after London and York, and its academy was greatly respected. But all I saw of it was the high wall of the king's great castle there. Rolf insisted on pressing on to Barton, ignoring my urgent pleas that the horses were already weary.

chapter 11

i was heartfelt glad when I saw the top of a church tower above the trees, and then a building almost as high beside it, which Rolf declared to be Barton Castle, his birthplace. Now that we were very near our destination, the rain had almost stopped.

Barton was a small village, although larger than Helmdon, and distinguished by a splendid church, dating from the days before the Norman boot descended on us. Although the church itself was tiny, it had a high and shapely square tower, standing bright against the dark eastern sky as we approached. It was ornamented with what I now know is called strip and pilaster work, and in my innocence I was most impressed. I had not seen a single cathedral yet.

Close by the church was the castle moat, and the trail led straight to a drawbridge and an imposing stone gateway beyond. This looked new, and so must have been some of the new fortifications that Sage Guy had mentioned. The bank on the castle side had been built up higher than the near side, and was surmounted by a wooden palisade that was obviously ancient.

Clearly, Barton Castle had begun life as a typical motte and bailey, a motte being an artificial mound topped by a wooden fort, and the bailey the surrounding area of a few acres, enclosed in a stockade, which was itself usually protected by a moat, whose trench had supplied the dirt for the motte. Such simple strongholds formed a refuge for people and flocks in times of danger. The Conqueror had built hundreds of them all across England, and many more had sprung up during the Anarchy, the twenty-year civil war that had ended when I was a child.

We clattered across the drawbridge, but the gate was already closed. A sentry above issued a challenge, and Rolf shouted his name. The response was quick. A trumpet blew, dogs barked. In minutes a new voice shouted, "Aye, that's him. Open the gate. Welcome home, Sage!"

"Hugh, you old sinner!" Rolf retorted in a tone I had never heard from him before. "Haven't they hanged you yet?"

"I thought the Devil came for you years ago!"

One flap of the gate was opened enough for us to enter, and soon men with lanterns and torches were milling around, alarming the horses.

I have seen many castles since, and with few exceptions they are cramped, overcrowded places. A castle is usually smaller than a village in area and yet contains more inhabitants. It must also provide everything needed to support a garrison in time of siege: stables, armory, smithy, granary, bake house, shambles, brewery, chapel, laundry, baths, privies, and either a well or ample cisterns.

Barton was typical. The bailey was crammed with sheds, cottages, and workshops, seemingly all scattered higgledy-piggledy, not set in rows along streets. Rolf walked ahead within a chattering crowd of welcomers, William trailed behind them, forgotten, and I led Ruffian, who had worked harder than any of us that day and was impatient for the treats he thought he deserved. The rest of the horses were coming behind, more or less following me, but also chevied along by a couple of men-at-arms.

Eventually we came to the keep, a stone building standing on the original motte. Whether it was a recent replacement, like the gate, I could not discern in the twilight, and frankly did not care. Being the last refuge in time of siege, a keep is usually accessed by a long wooden staircase, which can be burned if the enemy breaches the outer walls. Trumpets sounded, and flunkies with flaming torches emerged from the door at the top, followed by a man and woman in fine robes. Rolf plodded wearily up to them, and was duly embraced and escorted inside. William directed servants collecting the Normans' baggage and followed up the stairs.

I managed to rescue my precious satchel before it disappeared with the rest, but clearly I was not to be welcomed into the keep. I was left standing in the mud with five tired, filthy, and hungry horses who were being steadily unnerved by a dozen or so dogs sniffing around their fetlocks. In a few moments, though, a group of stable hands come running and expertly took control of my herd. The man in charge was a burly Saxon, tow-headed like me.

"Alwin, master of horse," he said, taking hold of Ruffian's bridle.

Ruffian tried to bite him and got a punch on the nose for it.

"Durwin, Saxon cur," I said.

Alwin chuckled. "Come with me, Rover, and I'll find you a bone."

I took my staff from its sling and walked alongside. After such a wet day it was a pleasant change just to be on reasonably dry ground. Our way seemed to wind at random through the hodgepodge tangle of cottages and sheds.

"You've come far today." It was statement but also a question.

"From Helmdon." I saw my guide's start of surprise.

"Your master's the count's brother, then?"

"So he claims."

Alwin had not been present at the gate to hear Rolf announce himself, but his name was hardly a secret around the bailey now. Yet Alwin's reaction seemed to suggest that Rolf's arrival was somehow unexpected.

"Saxon curs don't often ride high-quality dog food like this," he said, patting Ruffian's neck and clumsily changing the subject.

"Count's brother borrowed me from my master to get him here. My master doesn't trust anyone else to look after Ruffian, and didn't want to look after him himself while I was gone. Told me to ride him."

"Lucky you."

"You weren't expecting Sage Rolf?"

"There was talk that the count might send for him, but no one expected him so soon, not in this weather. It only happened yesterday around noon, right after dinner."

Aha! I forgot my weariness, but tried not to sound too eager. "What only happened yesterday?"

"You don't know?" Alwin's voice was definitely wary now.

"I don't, but I'm sure the sage does. He suddenly announced yesterday that he had an urgent need to come here and wanted me to guide him. So what happened?"

"The count's sage, Archibald de la Mare. He died. Unexpectedly." Pause. "Some folks ween that he was murdered."

"When did this happen?" I demanded, a little faster than I intended.

Alwin detected my interest and gave me a suspicious glance. "He took sick at dinner, and passed to the Lord just nigh on midnight, they say."

So it was no longer "The count's sage is dying," *Se eorles unlybwrhta sweltað.* It was over; not dying, but dead, *Se eorles unlybwrhta is unlifeas.*

77

The "some folks" that suspected foul play certainly included the count, if he had used the *Despero in extremis* ritual to summon his brother. The house sage himself couldn't have done so, obviously. Now Guy's prediction that I might need to assist with the *Ubi malum* incantation seemed right in the bull's eye. If Count Richard had sent for Sage Rolf because he suspected a murder, then it could only be because he had believed his brother could identify the killer.

The tiles had warned me before it even happened.

At the stables, Ruffian was handed over to a skillful groom who slipped him a treat and told him what a fine lad he was. Leaning on my staff and clutching my satchel, I followed Alwin into the bunkhouse next door. The master of horse kicked away a couple of hounds trying to follow us, and shut the door on them.

The shed was a long space with a dozen or so cots lined up on one side. A big stone fireplace halfway along the opposite wall crackled happily, and the pungent fog of smoke hanging under the thatch was not as thick as I was accustomed to. Candles in sconces along the walls made the room bright. It was clearly a men's place: it stank of men, horses, and oil, while workbenches along the fireplace wall were piled with saddles and other tack, waiting to be cleaned or repaired. Men's clothes lay almost everywhere and were hung to dry on makeshift clotheslines everywhere else. Bundles and baskets had been shoved in under the cots.

Alwin led me along to the middle, to a cot directly across from the fire. "Here," he said. "You sleep here, visitors' place of honor." My designated mattress was piled higher than any with clothes, but he proceeded to tip it up and slide them all off, onto the floor. "Help yourself to anything that the slovenly nithings have left around. Here's a towel. Hungry?"

I was bone weary and relaxed to jelly by the heat and the light and the sense of comradeship. For once I was a Saxon among Saxons, a hostler among hostlers. I could jabber in the old tongue and be understood and accepted. I need not fawn and grovel.

"Could eat a wild boar live." The leftover rations had gone with the Normans' baggage.

"We'll roast it for you. You! Scur!"

He was addressing the only other person present, a shapeless older man heaped like a bundle of old rags on the foot of a cot next to the one the master of horse had just assigned to me. He seemed to be staring into the fire, and had shown no sign that he was aware of us. Nothing of his person was visible except some stringy gray rat-tails dangling from under his hood.

After a moment for reflection this relic swiveled his head just enough to reveal a dirty gray beard and one glittering eye, but the rest of his face remained concealed. He stared fixedly at my boot.

"Aye, boss?" His voice was somewhere between a groan and a croak.

"Aye, you."

"Aye, I. Then we are agreed, and all is well. Unless the horses, your masters, cry, 'Neigh'? And if they cry nay, then surely you must not answer, 'I.'"

"Fool, go fetch some victuals for brother Durwin. Tell the cooks I sent you, mind. Tell them it's for a guest."

With a sigh Scur heaved himself upright and turned toward us. He was surprisingly large in all directions, while still resembling a bag of rags. When he drew close to me, he raised his head so I could see all of his face. It was a wreck, as if it had been stepped on by a roughshod stallion: his nose was a misshapen blob, his left eye had been replaced by a patch of white scar, and his mouth twisted and distorted. He stood there for a moment as if to give me time to inspect this horror, while his remaining eye studied my face to see how I was reacting.

"Food would be welcome," I said.

"Move your fat *ærs*," Alwin said, "before I kick it out of here for good."

I moved aside as Scur lumbered forward, but then the old man stopped and leered a nightmare, toothless smile right in my face. "Will fair to behold fare to be held?" he croaked. Cackling as if this were some rib-splitting humor, he continued on his way. When he opened the door, the fireplace belched smoke.

Alwin tapped his forehead and rolled his eyes to indicate that Scur's injuries were internal as well as external. He certainly had not spoken like an average stableman.

I stripped off my sodden hood and cloak, dried my face on the welcome, if grubby, towel, and then shivered into goose bumps. I was happy that my adept's cape was safely out of sight in my satchel, because to reveal that now would end any chance of informal chatter with the hands. Only in an academy could an adept ever be one of the boys.

As always, I must consider the boot on my leg. I couldn't strip with it on; I could barely walk without it. "Can I borrow some clothes while mine dry?"

Alwin had sat down to watch, perhaps waiting to see how the trick footwear worked. "Said so, didn't I? Here, take the biggest. They should fit you." He rose to collect replacement garments from nearby lines and cots, and dumped them beside me. Then he returned to his perch on the edge of the cot that the man Scur had just vacated.

"Thanks." I turned my back on my host before unlacing my leggings and removing my shirt. After years of living by myself, I was uncomfortable exposing myself in company. I toweled vigorously. I would not have been surprised to see myself steaming. "Tell me how the sage died."

"Archibald? We were all gathered in the hall for dinner, see, just afore noon yesterday. Countess puts on a grand spread at this time of year: fresh fish, onions, beans, apples, bread and butter, and meat three or four times a week! Beer was a bit thin, I thought, and there was some muttering about that. But the fiddler plays for us and sings a song or two whilst we're eating. The sage was up at the count's table, as usual. We'd just gotten started. Chaplain said grace. We'd no sooner seated us down when the sage tried to leave, like as if he wasn't feeling good. Then he sort of stumbled. The count saw, shouted for someone to help him. He was carried out, and Father Randolf went after them. At dawn they tolled the church bell for him."

I donned a fresh shirt, still slightly damp and somewhat tight across the shoulders, then sat down to unstrap my boot. Because one side of my cot was made inaccessible by the clothes Alwin had dumped there, I perforce must sit directly opposite my host, almost knee to knee. I wished he would stop staring at me as if I were some sort of freak show.

The sage's death didn't sound too bizarre; a stroke, or a sudden hemorrhage in the bowels. Why had the count invoked the *Despero in extremis* cry for help?

"An old man, was he?"

"Not near. Doubt if he'd seen thirty winters. Just came here a couple of years ago, after Sage Charles left."

That made more sense of the count's alarm. I laid the boot beside the cot, dropped my leggings, and began toweling my legs. Meanwhile I rearranged my thinking. Death came to all like a thief in the night, as the priests said, but few men in their twenties die quite that fast. Unexpected death must always raise whispers of black magic, and doubly so when the deceased himself had been a sage.

"You mentioned murder. Any reason except that it was so quick?"

The master of horse just shrugged and continued to stare at my knees. A pretty girl's legs I could have understood. I had heard of men who fancied men, but never met any. Alwin's curious taste might explain Scur's parting jest. I felt uneasy until I had pulled on the borrowed leggings—much better quality than those I had just shed—and laced them to my britches as well as I could while sitting. Then I strapped my boot on again, found my staff, and stood up to complete my toilet.

I was still lacing when another gush of smoke proclaimed the return of old Scur, who shuffled along to me and to offer a flask of beer, a slab of bread loaded with a slice of salt fish, and a thick wedge of yellow cheese. It looked good and would have looked better had the old man's hands been cleaner.

Nevertheless I took the offering and said, "Thank you."

Scur rasped a horrible cough. "Half a leg is better than no brains, they do say."

"I know people with all their brains who limp when they think."

The old man greeted my attempt at a jest with a laugh that turned into another cough, and he spat on the floor.

Smoke billowed, a couple of dogs arrived, eager to help me eat my supper, and the hostlers followed, complaining about mud and "that hellish stallion of yours." They were all youngsters. Somewhere in this anthill of a castle there must be married quarters for older men.

As I ate, conversation turned to my journey, the flooding, the harvest, and other less alarming topics than murder, until a distant bell began to sound the curfew. Alwin rose to snuff the candles in the sconces, lighting a torch at the last one, then bade his lads a safe repose and went out into the night.

There was some discussion of whom he had gone to visit, and all the names seemed to be male, but a lot of them were greeted with laughter. We lay down and chatted by firelight for a while, but exhaustion wrapped me up like a shroud. I was asleep before the serious snoring began.

chapter 12

"This one . . . Durwin! Durwin, wake up. *Wake up!*"

Who was waving a lantern in my face and shouting? Squire William, of course; his hair awry, his voice shrill. Two other men stood behind him; hostlers on nearby cots were stirring and growling.

"Wha's matter?" I said.

"Get up! The count wants you."

That worked like a bucket of cold water, no, a lake of it. I sat up. The count wanted me? Me? Wanted *me*? I lay down again to grab for my clothes, which I had placed under the cot on top of my satchel to keep them off the dirty floor—not my own clothes, which would still be wet, the clothes I had borrowed. Voices were warning what unthinkable things were going to happen if certain unmentionable people didn't take those unspeakable lanterns away.

"We'll wait outside," said an older man's voice, and its owner hung his lantern on one of the wall sconces. The intruders departed while I struggled with someone else's leggings . . . my boot . . . someone else's shirt . . . smock . . . my shoe . . . my cloak and hood.

Going to meet a count? I dug the adept's white cape out of my satchel. Then I found my staff, slung the precious satchel on my left shoulder, and was ready to take down the lantern and go to be presented to a count. I hoped I wouldn't make too big a fool of myself. I hadn't shaved for two days. Fortunately my blond stubble was not too conspicuous.

Outside, the sky was brightening in the east. Above the thatch of the cottages, lights showed in narrow windows high in the keep. In the cold stood Squire William, all alone, hugging himself as if to keep warm, although the air wasn't cold. Raising the light, I studied the Norman's face and decided that he was scared. Yes, the boy who would deliberately goad his teachers into giving him vicious beatings was now shivering with fear.

"Come on! Hurry!"

I leaned on my staff and planted one real foot and an iron one. "First you explain to me just what in Satan's shit house is going on."

"Count Richard wants you, Saxon. Now!"

"Tell me why or I won't—"

"Because Rolf is dying. His brother. He's frightened he's been murdered like Sage Archibald."

Appalled but still barely awake, I cried, "And he thinks I did it?"

"No, no, no," William was gabbling. "He wants a sage. Two murders in two days and he asked me if I could explain it and I told him I couldn't but we had an adept with us who was very learned—I stressed that, Adept, I truly did! I told them how highly Sage Guy always praised you, even though you're only a Saxon, and I had to explain why you weren't sleeping in the hall where I was, and the count sent me to find you right away, and see if you can save Rolf, so you must hurry; we have to hurry! The chaplain's giving him the last rites. He's dying."

I was already hobbling along the miry lane. Called to aid a dying man? Who or what did I think I was? I had my bag of herbs in my satchel. I could minister to boils, constipation, or bellyaches, but I had never treated serious diseases, only witnessed them while assisting one of the sages. And the chances that I could unwind a major death curse were less than a moth's odds in Hell.

On the other hand . . . most people don't understand that there are many types of sorcery. Even a sage's brother might not understand the difference between an incantation and a potion. If the killer—and obviously there must be a killer to cause two such sudden deaths in two days—if the killer was using poison, then there might be hope. There are ways of dealing with poisons, even when you aren't certain which poison has been used. Rarely an attempted remedy might make the situation worse, or so Guy had taught me, but those chances were often worth taking, better than doing nothing in cases likely to be fatal.

"William!"

The squire slowed down to let me catch up. He didn't even complain about the lack of a respectful title. "Yes?"

"Dean Odo has taught you—I know he has because I've heard him doing so—that the first half of success is trust. Remember? The sinner must have faith in Lord Jesus, the patient must trust the doctor, and the client must believe in the sage. So the doctor, priest, or enchanter must believe in himself. That is the first step, always the first step."

"I remember, but—"

"No butting! I appreciate that you praised me and that will help, but you must stop looking like a gang-raped milkmaid. You're a Norman and the son of a knight. Straighten your shoulders. Stick out your chin. Be proud of the responsibility we bear. Look eager to see how your hero the adept will solve the problem! I know you're not a coward, because I've oftentimes known you to deliberately bait the sages into welting your ass off. You have a lot more courage than I have, so start using it. While I'm wearing my adept's cloak, you must address me as 'Adept' or even 'master' if you can manage it without choking."

"Tu es un chien merdique des Saxons!"

"And you are a son of Norman warriors being called upon to do your duty as your ancestors did. Can I count on you, William?"

"You expect me to grovel to you, cripple?"

"For now, I just want the respect due my rank, but I demand no less. What happens later doesn't matter."

William uttered a strangled noise that might have been, "Aye, sir." After a moment, he added, "For now."

I lifted the strap from my shoulder and passed him the satchel. "Guard this carefully. It contains a priceless grimoire that Guy loaned me, and my bag of common remedies. Do you recall the favored treatments for poison ingested by mouth?"

"No, Adept."

"Try!"

"Um, vomiting . . . er . . . master?"

"That's one. A feather down the throat, or an emetic of mustard and water. Another antidote is finely ground charcoal. I have all of these in my satchel. If I ask you for anything, it will be in my satchel, clearly labeled." I knew William could read, despite his pretense otherwise, but I did not know how well.

Giving orders to a Norman felt unreal. I would be made to pay for this later. My limp wouldn't save me from the beating of a lifetime if William thought I had earned it.

"Master?" That time it came out more clearly.

"Yes, Squire?"

"A sage and then a sage. The killer is targeting sages. Is it wise for you to wear your cape? He may strike at you next."

Did he honestly think that I hadn't thought of that?

"It is my duty, Squire. If I am to help his brother, I must persuade Count Richard to believe in me and believe what I say, even though I am, as you so perceptively remark, only a shitty Saxon dog."

William muttered, "Yes, Adept."

The door of the keep, at the top of the long staircase, was guarded by four men-at-arms with pikes and lanterns. In one of the greatest surprises of my life, they saluted me. Of course they were only honoring my cape, but no one had ever touched a forehead in my direction before and it felt bizarrely good, at the same time as it increased the nervous turmoil in my belly. It might impress my doubting disciple, but it made me feel even more of a fraud.

The entrance was narrow, so as to be easily defended, and led only to a spiral staircase, which was not the easiest climb for a man wearing an iron sole and leaning on a six-foot staff. At the top, I emerged into what was no doubt called the great hall, although it was no larger than the refectory in Pipewell Abbey. Count Richard's castle was tiny compared to the huge one in Northampton, whose hall must be truly great. It was still dark, unlit except by our lanterns and a fire blazing in the fireplace built into the far wall, possibly heating cauldrons of water for His Lordship's toilet.

I could see that bedding almost completely covered the floor, for the knights, men-at-arms, and male servants would sleep here. A few of them were honored with cots, which probably transformed into benches and tables during the day. The rest slept on fleeces or right on the rushes, like the snoring dogs. Although the bell for matins had not yet been rung, most of the inhabitants seemed to be awake, sitting up or leaning on their arms, quietly chatting, either to their neighbors or in small groups. Word of the count's brother's plight had spread, and the talk must be of curses and black magic.

As I began to walk, silence spread through the hall like ripples on a pond. Thump . . . thump . . . thump . . . staff, iron boot, white cape. A boy dressed like a stable hand wearing an adept's insignia? I kept my chin high and stared straight ahead, studying the tangles on the back of William's head as he led the way between the pallets, heading for the platform at the far end. There were only four beds up there, all vacated. The count would dine on that dais with his family and officers, but it was only one step up, and I managed it without a stumble, aware of a hundred eyes fixed on me.

At that moment, a distant bell tolled. It was too deep and far off to be the castle bell I had heard sounding the curfew the previous evening, and I knew at once that its somber tone proclaimed the sage's death. For a moment the world seemed to freeze. William glanced back at me with the staring eyes of a bird, and his tangled hair emphasized his horror. A second sage dead in two days?

My first thought was relief that I did not have to try to treat a dying man, so could not be accused of killing him when I failed. My second thought was utter shame at the first. I had not liked Rolf, but I had respected his learning and his dedication to both music and arcane studies. No man deserved to die by the treacherous hand of an assassin. I crossed myself, as everyone else was doing, and was murmuring a prayer as the second knell rang out across the night-shrouded countryside.

Could I really help Count Richard identify the killer? The count was certainly the local sheriff, the king's deputy for upholding the law, but I was now the local expert on arcane arts. I gave William a nod and he led the way across to the door at the back of the platform. This he rapped on and then opened, stepping back to bow the adept in. So William was going to play his part, and I must do the same.

chapter 13

nexpectedly, the door led directly into the death chamber; I almost fell over a priest kneeling in prayer at the side of the sage's bed. Rolf had been laid out, with covers drawn up to his chin, so that there was no way of telling whether he had died as peacefully as he now seemed, or wracked with agony. Only the cyanosed condition of his face and the extreme blueness of his lips showed that he was not merely asleep. Although I had attended sickrooms with Sage Guy, I had little experience of corpses. The only one I had seen display that bluish color had been an overlain infant, which implied that Rolf de Mandeville might have been smothered.

Still the church bell tolled his knell.

The room was crowded with furniture and people. Two men stood close to another fireplace, much smaller than the one in the hall. Two women sat on chairs at the far side of the bed, both of them veiled, which was the fashion then, although the veils were sheer enough that their faces were quite visible. One of them was sobbing and almost doubled over, her face in her hands. She peeked up momentarily as we entered, and I judged that she was either faking her grief or at least exaggerating it for the sake of propriety.

A large man stood behind her, hands laid comfortingly on her shoulders. Like her, he wore rich robes trimmed with ermine, so he must be the count and she the countess. He was gray-bearded now, but still impressive, conveying power and physical strength, quite unlike his late brother. He would never be a man to trifle with, and at the moment he had his eyes fixed on the corpse and his teeth bared in a rictus that suggested more fury than grief. Richard de Mandeville might be sincerely mourning his brother, but he was also thirsting for revenge, potentially as dangerous as a wounded lion. A brother murdered in his own house must be intolerable humiliation for him.

The second woman was younger, with wisps of ash-blond hair trailing from under a hastily donned bonnet. She seemed tall and lean, with features carved from ivory, but her eyes were closed and her hands clasped, her lips moving in silent prayer. Normans could be blond, just as Saxons could be as dark as Welshmen. Apart from the tremor of her lips, she might have been a saint immortalized in marble. I found the lack of emotion disturbing: was she bored, or in shock?

The fireplace and chairs with backs showed that in normal times this room must be the family's private parlor, so the door to the left almost certainly led through to the count's bedroom. In a castle this small, two rooms might well be the full extent of his personal quarters.

William quietly closed the door, with himself on the near side, making it eight people, a bed, and a corpse in a small room not intended for such a gathering. The cot that almost filled it had been set up for the family guest, probably fetched hastily after his late arrival. Although the shutters had been opened to the dawn, the room stank of bodily fluids, a common consequence of recent death. A collection of flasks, jugs, and goblets by the hearth told of a late-night party.

The count roared, "By what right do you bring that staff in here?" He had the sort of voice that could be heard across a battlefield.

Startled, I bowed. "I have a game leg, my lord."

"Oh. I see. Battle wound?"

"Riding accident, my lord."

"Ahem. You may keep the staff, then. You are the Saxon adept?" Could he not see my cape? Either Count Richard of Barton was badly rattled by his brother's death, or his brother had inherited all the brains.

"Aye, name of Durwin, my lord. I came as fast as I could."

The priest had risen also, and turned to glare at the intruder. He was a tall, spare man, surprisingly young to be a priest, although his sculptured clerical robes made him seem more slender than he probably was. His features, while handsome, seemed naturally set in a disdainful expression. He was clean-shaven; the coronet of hair around his tonsure was reddish brown. His dislike of me and all I stood for was obvious.

"I thank the Lord who delayed your arrival so that you could not practice any of your foul demonism over a dying man. You can do no good here now, if you ever could, which I doubt. There is no place for heresy in this place of mourning. You may go." His voice, like his sneer, was pure Norman cleric.

The bell boomed again. The two men by the fireplace remained as silent as grave effigies. I peered past the priest at the corpse.

Although Rolf had been no warrior like his brother, he would not readily have submitted to having a pillow held over his face, yet I could see no signs of a struggle. On a chest by the bed stood a wine flask, a rosary, a silver goblet, and a candlestick holding half a candle. The least jostle should have sent them all flying. I lurched a couple of steps around the priest in that direction.

I said, "I have known Sage de Mandeville for many years, Father, and I mourn his passing also. He was a man of learning and skill, who certainly did not deserve this horrible end."

"Nevertheless," the priest snapped, "he has been gathered to the Lord, and the manner of it does not concern you. I said: *You may go!*"

No layman should talk back to a priest, no Saxon to a Norman, so I answered softly, "If my life were in danger, should that not concern me, Father? Yesterday Sage Archibald died suddenly, today Sage Rolf, and I am an adept. I cannot help but feel that this concerns me!"

"If that is how you think, then you should leave this place as soon as you can."

Needless to say, I did not. I knew that my continued presence hung by a thread, but there was a murderer at large, a monster who should be caught and brought to justice. To put that truth in words might enrage the count, who must know it, yet might take the statement as a slur upon his honor and his house. But so far he had not backed up the priest, which was promising.

I said, "I would not presume to call Sage Rolf a friend, Father, but I feel an obligation to bring his murderer to justice."

"Murderer? Guard your tongue, my son! And even if there were such a crime, how do you imagine you could find the culprit? Will you draw up a horoscope? Or cast bones? Do you expect blood to flow from his mouth if the murderer approaches his bier?"

Still the count stayed silent. Surely he must want to know the truth about his brother's death?

I stuck my neck out another furlong or so. "I may be able to name the killer when I have learned more." I looked to the count. "May I examine your late brother's hands, my lord?"

The priest said, "Certainly not."

"*Why?*" Even in the hallowed presence of death, Count Richard was a loud man.

Still the bell tolled.

"Because the color of your late brother's complexion suggests that he was suffocated, my lord. If so, he may have fought his murderer, and his fingernails may show signs of a struggle."

I knew at once that I had erred. The priest did not shrug his shoulders, but his contempt somehow seemed to blaze more strongly. The count lost interest in me.

"There was no such struggle. My brother was taken sick in the night. I was here when he ceased to breathe and I assure you that no one suffocated him."

"There are other ways to identify a malefactor, my lord," I said hastily. "There are ways to kill at a distance." Such as poison. I laid a hand over the goblet on the chest, but did not lift it.

"You can summon demons, for instance," the priest said.

"I cannot do so, Father, although I do not doubt that others can." I removed my hand. "I rode with the deceased all day yesterday, and I can testify that he was strong and in excellent health then." I had so many questions to ask, but I was a Saxon interloper whose credentials and even religious orthodoxy were both in doubt. I folded my arms as if pondering while I considered the corpse. "Did he, for example, say anything in his travail?"

The countess surged to her feet and spoke for the first time, in a strangely harsh voice. "He babbled, and mostly in the Saxon tongue." She turned to bury her face in her husband's ermine collar. "My lord, this is intolerable! This insolent *serf* comes here and accuses you of letting your brother be murdered in your own house? Have him whipped and thrown in the moat."

In the second brief glimpse I had caught of her face, I had again seen no signs of weeping. Women were expected to display grief extravagantly, but it appeared that none of the countess's sobs for her brother-in-law had been genuine.

Her husband wrapped an arm around her. "I won't go that far, my dear, but he won't bother us more. Come, let us go and be alone with our sorrow. Matilda, you too."

The younger woman opened gray eyes whose pale lashes did not do them justice. She rose also, without sparing a glance for me or her dead uncle—assuming that she was the count's daughter. Her lids were no redder than her mother's and her face seemed cold and quite indifferent to the gruesome surroundings. In more normal circumstances I would have trouble keeping my own eyes off her. She reminded me of someone, and I could not imagine who.

Fortunately, Count Richard had not noticed my impudent inspection of his daughter. "Bertrand, see that my brother's remains are appropriately tended and cered. Issue instructions for the mourning. Father Randolf, you will arrange for his internment? Hugh, show the adept and his boy out. See them on their way as soon as their mounts are fit to travel."

Everyone bowed as the baronial family departed into their chamber. The two men who had remained silent by the fireplace throughout all this now stepped forward. The younger had a soft, bookish look to him, already showing a stoop and the screwed-up eyes of someone who has to hold things close to his nose to see them properly. From the instructions the count had given him, I deduced that he was Bertrand, and probably held some such title as castle steward.

The taller and older of the two must have been the one addressed as Hugh, for he had his eyes fixed on me. He made no comment as I lifted the flask from the chest, judged its weight to make sure it still contained some wine, and handed it to the surprised William.

I turned to bow to Hugh. "May God preserve your lordship."

Two very shrewd gray eyes were still watching me. "Let us go out to the hall and have a friendly gossip, Adept Durwin."

chapter 14

the hall had been transformed. Bedding had vanished, tables and benches had appeared, and the shutters stood wide, letting the slit windows admit as much light as they ever would. People, mostly young servants, were coming and going by three doors, all of which seemed to open to spiral staircases. At least one of those led upward, doubtless to an attic where the women and girls slept, behind a stoutly barred door. The cots had gone from the dais, being replaced by a single long table, the high table where the count would preside over meals, and where murder had struck down Archibald, the house sage.

I confirmed then that the keep was not a recent construction like the gateway arch. The ceiling beams were smoke-stained, the plaster was flaked by water damage in some places. If Count Richard was strengthening his defenses by crenelating, he had not progressed to upgrading his living quarters.

The man called Hugh led the way to one end of the high table and gestured for William and me to sit, while he scooped up a stool and took it around to the other side. There he sat, leaned brawny arms on the planks, and smiled grimly across at William. The squire had been smirking at me, probably amused that I had been thrown out on my ear. Under the older man's regard, he colored.

"Squire, I don't think that's a very safe place to keep the flask of wine your master pilfered so slickly."

William brought the flask up into view and set it on the table, while shooting me a furious you-will-pay-for-this look.

"Have a drink if you're so thirsty, Adept," the big man said.

I smiled with relief. Count Richard had not impressed me as a deep thinker, but that did not mean that there were no intelligent people in Barton Castle, and now I had found one. Or he had found me. "It would be more than my life is worth, my lord."

That won a nod of approval. "No lord. I am Sir Hugh Fiennes, the count's marshal. I've known the de Mandeville brothers since we were all boys together and I know Rolf would never have attempted to ride that stallion you brought. Alwin told me last night that the monster was like to wreck my stables. Rolf's skills were in his head, not his thighs. So which of you two shavers is the virtuoso horseman?"

William turned even redder and closed his eyes as if praying for the floor to open beneath him.

I said, "I rode Ruffian, Marshal."

Hugh nodded again. "And you think Rolf was murdered." The marshal spoke as if horsemanship made a man's opinions more valuable, and he might even believe that. He was around fifty, at a guess, of an age to have fought through much, if not all, of the Anarchy, and he had the look of tough-as-leather warrior accustomed to battle and command and appraising men. Although a marshal had originally been the man in charge of his lord's horses, the office had grown over the years; Hugh probably outranked everyone in the castle except the count himself. He very likely ran the place on his lord's behalf. French would be his mother tongue, but after a lifetime of dealing with grooms, farriers, saddlers, sutlers, and loriners, he likely spoke and understood the old tongue much better than the count did. The countess had referred to Rolf's lapse into it as if she did not know it at all.

"I do not *think* he was murdered, sir. I *know* it."

"Indeed?" Hugh looked more amused than doubting. "You laid a hand over the goblet, but you tucked your little finger inside it. Then you folded your arms and put your fingers in front of your mouth as some folk will do when they are trying to solve a problem. You put the wine on your tongue and tasted poison?"

William had missed that small trickery; he was wide-eyed.

"Not my tongue," I said, "and not taste. Just my lip was enough. It is now tingling and will likely soon go numb."

The marshal reached for the flask, shook it, then removed the stopper and raised it to his mouth.

"One drop, no more!" I warned, and watched the test repeated. "It takes a small while to work, and that is the danger. I postulate that the sage wakened in the night and felt thirsty. He had likely been drinking with his brother for some hours before retiring?"

Hugh nodded. "Of course."

"So he poured himself a drink, but he was two-thirds asleep and still drunk. By the time he realized what he had swallowed, it was too late. He probably tried to make himself vomit. I thought I could smell vomit . . ." I scored another nod for that. "Then he must have gone for help, but he might have been losing control of his legs already, and certainly would be having great difficulty speaking."

"Yet you dared to taste it?"

"Only the merest trace, Sir Hugh. In very small doses it has medicinal uses. That's why I know about it. Sage Rolf must have swallowed a very large amount."

"And why did you think he had been smothered?"

"Because that potion causes the victim to stop breathing. He suffocates."

"What's it called?"

I decided to gamble on Sir Hugh's continuing approval. "I may be right about poison, sir, and still be mistaken about which poison was used. It would be helpful if I could speak with someone who heard what the dying man was trying to say."

I braced myself for a roar that I must answer the question, which was surely how the count would have reacted. Hugh, though, just smiled.

"What do you think he was trying to say?"

"I expect he tried to call for me, because otherwise none of you would have known to send for me."

A nod said I was right again. "It was the countess who worked out that he was calling for an adept. That was when we sent for the squire, here, and he told us about you."

"Her Ladyship said that he spoke in the old tongue. With respect, sir, he rarely did that, and didn't speak it clearly. I think he was thinking of me and trying to quote the herbals. In his confusion, he may have forgotten to give the French name, which is *aconit*. He may have tried to mention a slowing heartbeat, burning pains in his stomach, and so on, but mostly he would have tried to tell them the name of the poison. It comes from a flower we Saxons call monkshood."

Now Sir Hugh did look impressed. "Exactly right. You see, the three of us sat up late, after the rest of the family left: Richard, Rolf, and me. We talked and drank until long past midnight. That sounds callous when the reason for our reunion was the sage's mysterious death, but we had not had such an occasion in several years. Rolf was born and raised here, and this was the first time he'd been back in a long time. I told the servants to set up a cot for me out here, just about where we're sitting, so I would not fall over a dozen men on my way home in the dark. When Rolf fell into Richard's chamber babbling, retching, in terrible distress, Richard fetched me first of all. I heard much of what he was trying to say, and monks were mentioned several times, in both tongues and even Latin. I did not know of this monkshood plant."

I pushed ahead. "So who could have left that poisoned flask there for him to find?"

"Me," the marshal said, and stopped to glare at William, who had moaned in horror. "I said I could have done, boy, not that I did! Or the count could. But there had been other people in and out, earlier."

"After the bed was set up?"

"Yes." He smiled. "It had to be after that, didn't it? You talk sense, Adept; you'll make a fine sage some day. Several people came and went. Many folk wanted to greet him. Let's see . . . Wacian the bottler supervised the servants setting up the cot. He chased them away as soon as they were done and was the last of them to leave. If it was not his hand that put that flask there, he should know whose did. Bertrand du Blois, the steward, was next to leave, I think. Later the countess, Lady Matilda, and Father Randolf made their excuses. That left the three of us, drinking and reminiscing. My lip is burning, as you predicted. So where did the killer find this monstrous potion?"

Careful! Sir Hugh might already know that. He had admitted to being a suspect, and he was being oddly cooperative, ignoring his lord's orders to evict the meddlesome adept from the keep or even from the castle. It was a reasonable hypothesis that Rolf had been summoned by his brother to discover how Sage Archibald had died, and the same killer had struck again to prevent him from doing so. If Hugh himself was the culprit, then he was now trying to find out how much I knew or could guess, prior to silencing me by locking me in the castle dungeon until I grew old and mad.

"It is prepared," I said, still frantically wondering how far to trust this shrewd and unlikely ally, "from the roots or leaves of the monkshood plant, usually as a tincture, meaning that the deadly matter is extracted by steeping the ground-up roots in strong wine. It has several uses in medicine, despite its toxicity; most often it is applied to the skin to ease pain, and it will stimulate urination. It is also known as wolfsbane, because foresters use it to keep down wolves. I would expect that Sage Archibald kept some in his sanctum. . . . If I might be allowed to look there?"

For a moment the old campaigner studied me in silence, as if trying to decide whether to encourage my insolence or just hang me out of hand. I bore his inspection while trying to seem like a learned, honest, and trustworthy sage, but aware that in the other man's eyes I was more likely just a brash, callow, meddling peasant, an increasingly sweaty one as the ordeal continued.

Then Hugh nodded. "You truly believe that your arts will lead you to the killer?"

"Unless you or His Lordship have reason to accuse someone, then I truly believe I am more likely to unmask him than anyone else is, Sir Hugh. He is a cunning fiend, but I have been trained in the logic used by the ancients." The learned Aristotle might not be much help here. More likely, there would be something in the grimoire Guy had given me, perhaps the incantation he had mentioned, *Ubi malum*.

"He has killed twice already. It seems he either hates or fears sages."

"I am prepared to take that risk, sir."

"How long?"

"At least a week."

Hugh glanced at William. "Well, lad? Should I trust this Saxon adept, or is he all mouth?"

William looked at me.

"He is very largely mouth, Sir Hugh, but if he says he can do it, then I believe he should be allowed to try."

"Angels preserve us! Very well, Saxon. You can have three days, counting this one. Talk with anyone. Wear your cape; if anyone questions your authority, refer them to me. You have the run of the castle. On Saturday we'll talk again."

Blessed saints! This was more than I could have dreamed of. "The count, sir—"

"Lord Richard was humoring his lady, who is understandably distraught. Do not pester him or his family, of course. But if you can prove to him who killed his brother he will cut out the scoundrel's liver with a rusty knife and reward you famously. What are you going to do with that flask?"

"Empty it into the pits, perhaps. It is too dangerous to leave around."

Hugh hesitated, then nodded. He turned to scan the hall and waved. The page who came sprinting to learn his bidding looked as if he'd been stamped with the same die as Varlet Eadig—freckles, peach face, and all, although his dress was fine enough to mark him as a Norman.

"John, this is Adept Durwin. He and Squire William have the freedom of the castle. Show them the sage's sanctum, so they can move in there. Then find the fool and tell him this, also tell him he's to make himself useful by helping the adept with his work."

"You mean *Scur*, Sir Hugh?" the boy asked incredulously.

"Unless you'd rather do the job yourself?" Chuckling, the marshal rose to his full height and nodded to me as I levered myself up also. "There you are, Saxon—a place to sleep and a guide who knows everyone and everywhere. Anything else?"

If there was to be incantation, then I would need the help of someone who could read and write in both French and Latin: Father Randolf could, of course, but he would never cooperate. The count himself must have some education, since he had invoked *Despero*. And he would have a secretary, likely a cleric in minor orders.

"That should be plenty for now, Sir Hugh. I am most grateful for your trust and—"

"Get to work, then."

He gave me no chance to thank him for a half-witted guide and booby-trapped accommodation.

chapter 15

i managed to descend from the platform without falling flat on my face. As I headed for the exit stair, I was much aware of young John at my side, wide eyes scanning me from cape to boot.

"I have met Scur," I said. "I didn't know he was the count's fool. Tell me about him."

John hesitated, unsure how to address a Saxon adept attended by a Norman squire; our names gave away our respective races before we even opened our mouths.

"I have been told, Adept, that he was a childhood friend of the count's, and a doughty man-at-arms in his day. They say the count knighted him for his valor in the attack on the Isle of Ely, but the very next year, at the Battle of Lincoln, his face was smashed in with a mace. He hasn't been right in the head since."

"I don't think I would be, either, if anyone smashed my face in."

John flashed a cheeky grin, reassured that I would not eat him. "Nor me, Adept. Scur's crazy. He talks sewage that nobody understands."

William, on my other side, would not be happy to hear that, but I, from our one brief conversation, suspected that Scur's sewage might contain lumps of truth. A fool must learn to guard his tongue.

Then came the very tricky process of descending a narrow spiral staircase. I managed it without disaster, and was relieved to find myself outside in a bright, breezy day at the top of the wooden steps leading down to the bailey. Sunshine, even!

"That there's the sanctum, Adept," the page said, pointing over the roofs of the cottages. "The tall one."

Other than the keep we had just left, there seemed to be only two buildings of more than one story in the bailey, so I could see the one he meant, but between it and us was the maze.

"You'd better lead us there. It wouldn't look good for an adept to get lost."

John laughed and proceeded to skip all the way down the long stairway much faster than I could follow, but he stopped to wait for me at the bottom.

"You should clip his ear, Saxon," William grumbled as we descended. "Impudent brat."

"He's young," I said. "In a few years he'll learn quality manners, like yours." My assistant did not answer that.

Down on the flat the boy set a brisk pace, leading us through the tangle of buildings. Other pedestrians stepped aside for the man in the white cape, men touching forelocks, women bobbing curtseys. I acknowledged each with a nod and a smile, wondering how many hundred people lived within the bailey.

"Count Richard fought for King Stephen in the troubles?"

The page's young face froze. "At the beginning . . . so I have heard, master. But he is a loyal subject of King Henry now."

"As are we all, of course." The Anarchy had been twenty years of insanity. Much of it is long forgotten, except by sages, monkish chroniclers, or other learned persons, but it is burned into the memories of those who experienced it, few as we are now. I was only a child when it ended.

After the first King Henry's son drowned, the king made all the barons swear loyalty to his daughter, Maud, widow of the previous German Emperor, although neither England nor Normandy had ever been ruled by a queen. When he died, they were told that he had released them from their vows on his deathbed, so they switched their allegiance to a man, her cousin Stephen. That testimony was not exposed as perjury until after Stephen had been crowned, and an anointed king could not be un-anointed. Maud tried to take the throne by force, but neither she nor Stephen was an inspiring leader, and in the end it had been Maud's twenty-year-old son, another Henry, who succeeded. In the last ten years he had done much better than either his uncle or his mother, establishing peace and order, ruling with a hand of steel.

"Lady Matilda is the count's daughter?" Matilda and Maud are the same name.

"Aye, sir," John said. "Was married to Baron Darcy, but after his passing she came back here, sir, with her brat."

William caught my eye then. If Richard had no son of his own, who had been heir to the earldom? Matilda's son or his great-uncle Rolf? The rules would have leaned toward the child, likely, but they were not written in stone, as the Anarchy had shown. In this case the decision would likely have been made by King Henry himself, their overlord. Now Rolf was dead, and Baroness Matilda had been one of the possible poisoners.

Or did Richard also have sons, perhaps grown up and living elsewhere? While I was trying to frame a way to put that question to John without revealing the way my mind was working, the page halted and pointed along an alley even narrower and more noisome than most, a favorite garbage tip from the look of it.

"The sanctum's along there, Adept, sir."

"My thanks to you, page. Now, when you have found Scur and given him the marshal's orders, pray ask him to come here to me."

The lad hesitated. "If he refuses?"

"Then tell the marshal. But Hugh might assign you to be my guide instead, so you'd better sound as fierce as you can."

For a moment it seemed as if John would reply with some shrill Norman obscenity, but then he grinned. He ran off and I was left with my squire, who was looking very wary indeed.

Together we plodded down the alley, which was in truth only a miry and narrow gap between two buildings, tapering toward the end. Indeed it might even be a dead end, for all we could see ahead was a blank wall. When we reached that, though, there was an even narrower way leading off to the right, although it was so restricted that I had trouble not scuffing the knuckles holding my staff.

The wall on my left was a blank, the back of one of the wattle-and-cob cottages, but to my right two shuttered windows flanked a door marked with a sage's pentacle. The building itself was of stone and two stories high as expected. Likely it was old, and the lesser structures had crowded in around it over time.

By accident or design, the entrance was now very private, which is a common feature of sages' sanctums, since both they and their clients often prefer to keep their dealings secret. The windows were guarded by stout iron bars and oak shutters. I went on past the first window and the door to examine the sill of the second window. The alley ended there, at a wicker screen which more or less concealed a privy.

I glanced up to the window above the one that had caught my attention.

"William?"

"Saxon?" We were alone, so I was back among the swine-herds and latrine cleaners.

"There's mud here. Could you scramble up and see what was going on upstairs, if there was anything going on upstairs?"

"Why should I want to?"

"Because I can't. Show me what a runt I am."

William handed over the satchel and the wine flask, gripped the window bars, and walked up the wall until he could put his feet on the ground floor window sill. By clutching the top of one bar, and stretching his other arm as high as he could, he just managed to get a grip on an upper window bar. Then he could straighten up.

"All I can see is another shutter. If you'll go in and open it, I'll tell you what's in there."

"The shutters are closed because it was raining on Monday. You can come down now."

William pushed himself off backwards. His boots hit the mire—*splat*! He flailed his arms wildly and might have sat down in the muck had he not backed into the wall opposite. "So what does that prove?"

I eyed him; we were much the same height. "It proves that only someone as tall as us could climb up to spy through that upstairs window."

"Seeing in isn't the problem," he said, "as long as the shutters are open. Getting up there is. But he could have used a hook. Even a kid could get a grip on the upstairs bars then, and pull himself to take a peek. The sill was lower than my collar bones, so a kid would be able to see over it."

"True. And spying must have been his purpose. I can't think how or why else anyone would leave mud on the window sill. Even all the recent rain didn't wash it off. It's interesting."

"Why?"

"Sage's hunch. Upper rooms contain beds and intriguing things can happen in beds." Not many people had William's strength, but there were plenty of nimble youngsters around. With some forethought and preparation they could have spied on the sage's upstairs activities. I handed back the flask and satchel, then returned to the door.

The door was a serious challenge, and I suspected I had been secretly delaying this confrontation. There was no key-hole. Seemingly, all I need do was press down on the latch and push the door open, but the pentacle was a warning that a sage had laid a hex upon it. This castle was not tolerant and trusting Helmdon, so the consequences for entering without an invitation could be dire. The pentacle was old and faded, but that did not mean the warding had not been renewed often. I spread my hand over the sign, not quite touching it, and yes, I could feel the spell, a faint chill.

William was standing back expectantly, waiting to see the fun.

Who, other than the murdered Sage Archibald, knew the antiphon? Probably no one. Hugh was testing to see if I was all thunder and no lightning. I beckoned William closer.

"This door is definitely hexed. Feel it."

"No."

"It's a trick you'll have to learn."

"I'll wait for a qualified teacher."

Ever since I was a child, my parents had taught me that I must never lose my temper with a Norman. "If I tell you how I think it can be opened safely, will you try it for me?"

"Eat shit, Saxon." He set his big jaw defiantly.

"Your lack of trust is disappointing, William."

"Yes, but that spell was set by a sage, and you're only an adept."

"Well, will you promise to do something for me if I die trying?"

Aware now that he was being baited, the squire said, "What?"

"Go back to Helmdon, clench one of those big fists of yours, and punch Sage Guy on the nose as hard as you can?"

"I think that might be even more dangerous than what you are about to do."

"So do I. That's why I asked. Will you?"

William scowled and repeated, "Eat shit, Saxon."

When he would have backed away again, out of earshot, I said, "Stay and listen." Then I drew a deep breath and began in a low voice, *"Pater noster, qui es in caelis . . ."* After the amen, I made the sign of the cross, opened the door, and went in. I closed it in the squire's face when he would have followed.

Fortunately enough light came through a ceiling hatch to show me where the furniture was, because my first task must be to open the shutters. The ground floor was a single room, larger than Guy's sanctum at Helmdon, and boasting an imposing fieldstone fireplace and chimney. Otherwise it was quite similar, with a workbench, a table, stools, a couch under a window for examining patients, a couple of chests . . . but what caught my eye right away was a wall of shelves, laden with jars, bottles, and boxes. Now if the bottles were all clearly labeled and stacked neatly in alphabetical order, with a gap in the *m*'s, or even the *a*'s, I would have identified the source of the poison that had killed Rolf. They were a wild mixture of sizes, arrayed higgledy-piggledy, and none seemed to be labeled.

The room was dusty, but remarkably tidy, much tidier than any sage's cabin at Helmdon. A stuffed crocodile hung from the ceiling while one wall was decorated with a boar's head and a wolf's head with silver eyes, and another was painted with ornate planet and constellation symbols to increase the mystique. Sage Guy's sarcastic tongue would scourge such hocus-pocus, but he earned most of his income by teaching. Sage Archibald had been required to provide cures, charms, or horoscopes to layman clients from Count Richard on down. Probably he had not charged the servants anything, or very little, but part of his job had been to keep the castle staff happy, and first impressions are important. To be fair, the decorations were faded and shabby; they might date from long before his time.

The table was bare except for two silver goblets, standing side by side. I sniffed at each of them and decided that they had held wine. There was no sign of a wine flask though. Nor were there any books in sight, which was impossible. Any sage needed at least one grimoire.

The door squealed open again and a taut voice said, "May I enter, Adept?"

"Certainly. You spoke the password, so you can enter. That was lesson one."

William entered, slamming the door. "Listen, you yellow-haired dog, I'll play your flunky in public, but I'm keeping score. So far you've just earned a moderate pounding, but push your luck any further and that crappy leg of yours will be the least of your numerous deformities, understand?"

"No!" I snapped. "What I do understand is that you're an ignorant young thug, which is not your fault, and determined to remain ignorant, which is. I was trying to teach you something. The Helmdon sages beat you and that just makes you worse. I was hoping you were smart enough to learn by example, and maybe even ask an intelligent question once in a while."

William gritted his teeth and said, "Then how did you know that the Lord's prayer would deactivate that hex?"

"I didn't. But what I learned at Helmdon was that a ward on a door is a form of curse, and there is nothing in the lore to prevent an enchanter from making it a very terrible curse, invoking major powers. But to put such a ward on a door that might be opened by mistake—in the dark, say, or by a child, or even by the sage himself in a fit of distraction—would be a major sin, even a crime. So most sages are content to use minor spells for wards. They may make you itch, or stagger, or at worst go blind for a while. Such minor enchantment cannot stand against the Lord's Prayer. Do you understand?"

William nodded angrily.

"So now you know how to open that warded door and most others like it, but do not let anyone hear or see how you do so. It's a secret of the craft. Have you learned something?"

"Yes. Thank you, most gracious master. I will remember it with gratitude while I kick your guts out."

I ignored that. "But here's something you can do that I can't. Pull over a stool, climb up, and take a very careful look at those shelves. Do not touch anything. They're dusty, as you can see. The rest of this place seems sparkling clean, so I expect Sage Archibald had a maid dust everywhere once a week or so, but wouldn't let her touch his potions. I want to know if the poison in the wine came from here. Check if there's marks in the dust where something's missing, or has recently been moved."

Without a word, my reluctant assistant thumped the satchel and poisoned wine flask down on the table and did as he had been told—for once. I set my staff aside and clambered up the ladder to the loft. Air slots in the upper portions of the shutters admitted enough light to show a chamber both larger and more grandly furnished than the count's withdrawing room. Besides the spacious bed stood a stool, a clothes chest, and a four-branched candelabra. A thickly woven rug covered much of the floor; the walls were hung with tapestries, and the bed itself was draped with brocade curtains, presently drawn back to reveal an untidy heap of pillows, bedclothes, and a thick fleece mattress. The bed's rumpled state was in marked contrast to the persnickety tidiness of the rest of the cottage. Sage Archibald de la Mare had died at the noontime dinner; had he been a late riser, or had he been using the bed for morning entertainment with the person who had drunk from the second goblet? Or had he been sick that day and died of natural causes?

The chamber pot had been emptied, which might be significant.

Moving awkwardly around the room, I opened the shutters for better light and peered in the closet, where I learned that the sage had owned no less than three fine robes and a spare sage's green cape—assuming he had been wearing another when he died. Most curious of all were some flimsy garments, loosely woven of so fine a thread that I thought it must be silk, which I had heard of but never seen. Below those lay a pair of man's shoes and several pairs of fur-lined slippers, some man size, some dainty. I tucked all these back in the closet and went back down.

Still no books!

William was still standing on a stool beside the shelves, hunched over under the low beams.

I said, "You're in luck, Squire. The bed's wide enough for both of us."

There was nothing improper about men sharing beds when necessary in those days, any more than there is now, but I doubted that Sage Rolf would have made the same offer. William said nothing, but his skeptical glance was meant to inform me that I was the lucky one.

I chuckled. "Where did you sleep last night?"

"With the knights."

"Amid the rushes, spittle, and gravy in the hall?"

"No worse than that kennel you were in."

"But you were lucky," I said. "If the sage had let you board with him, you might have drunk of the poison before he did."

William conceded the point with a grimace. "I thought of that. I don't know where my baggage went, or his. I didn't bring much, but the hauberk and sword are mine." Legacies of his knighthood training days? Chain mail was enormously expensive, so who had outfitted the bedeviled squire? I still did not know why William had switched from knights' training to apprentice sage. In his eyes that would have been a huge demotion.

"We'll ask when we go to the keep for dinner, and if dinner doesn't happen soon there will be a third sudden death."

My attempt at humor was ignored. "I found something up here, Saxon. There's a gap and the dust shows that a jar or bottle has been there until recently. If you would . . ."

I was already handing the poison flask up to him.

"Yes, it fits. Exactly. You said the tincture was made with wine? So the murderer just took the whole bottle of tincture and left it by the sage's bedside!"

Why did that feel more horrible than adding poison to a genuine flask of wine? No wonder Rolf had swallowed a lethal dose before he realized, for the tincture would be highly concentrated. And who else knew how to open the sanctum door? As William was handing down the flask, I saw the underside.

"Wait! Hold it higher, don't tip it. See what's written on the bottom?"

"You read it. The light's bad up here."

If William's reading ability was so poor that he couldn't sound out a simple word like that, then he would be no help with the serious incantations I hoped to use to find the killer. True, the light was bad up there and the writing a mere squiggle, probably made with a piece of lead. I took it to the window.

The word was *Aconit*, but the gap it had come from was nowhere near the left end of the top row, where the alphabet should start.

"Put it back where it should be, now we can identify it. How are the ones next to it labeled?"

William took the jar from one side and held it so I could read the name on the base: *Misteltan*. Then the other side: *Mustum*.

"The sage was inconsistent. He labeled the monkshood *Aconit* in French, but filed it between mistletoe named in the old tongue, and mustard named in Latin. But now we know where the poison came from to kill Rolf."

I was getting somewhere. Rolf had been poisoned in the count's solar with monkshood. A sage did not jump to conclusions. Sage Archibald might or might not have been poisoned, but not necessarily with the same toxin. "What about the other gaps?"

To extend his search, William had to descend, move the stool, and then climb up again; he checked all the other spaces and reported that none showed incriminating clean areas. By then I had located a tinder box and lit a candle. He repeated his search with that and met with no more success.

"None of the others look as if they have been moved, Saxon!"

Someone thundered on the door, hard enough to make it rattle on its hinges.

"Time to play squire again," I said.

William glowered, but jumped down.

"Wait!" I said. "I expect you are about to meet the most dis-figured man you have ever set eyes on, Sir Scur. Be gracious, because we need his help."

William opened the door. Without a blink, he bowed.

"Sir Scur? Pray enter, sir. The adept is expecting you."

"And so were you." In came the ragged ogre—gray-bearded, one-eyed, and hideous as a nightmare. There was nothing wrong with his voice though; it boomed. "Half a man told me half a leg wants half a head." Scur is a Saxon name, and he spoke in the old tongue.

"That is no less than the whole truth," I said.

"What more can you ask for?"

"What more can you offer?"

"If you ask but half a question, you may lack all of an answer." The jester stumped over to the nearest stool and balanced his bulk on it, overlapping all around. "Ask the wrong questions and you'll get the right answers but fail to profit by them."

A jester could probably keep this up all day.

"Then answer me this: who else, other than Sage Archibald, came into this sanctum?"

The old man leered toothlessly. "Why, half the world, Adept."

"A ladies' man, was he?"

"As most men are, given the chance."

"But not all?" I said, thinking of Master of Horse Alwin.

"Some hunt in other forests. Those rarely have a game bag as fat as Archibald's."

That was a clue to something. "What was the secret of his success, do you know?"

"Aye. Any man can make mistakes, but he could unmake them too."

William was standing behind Scur, owl-eyed as he tried to follow the patter.

I took pity on him and switched to French for a moment. "Squire, why don't you go and locate your sword and baggage and Sage Rolf's, may he rest in peace? Ask for servants to bring it here. Also find the bottler, Wacian. Tell him I want to speak with him, and we need a fire here and a couple of days' fuel. They'll pay more heed to you than they will to me." That unsubtle flattery might not be true while I wore my adept cape, but William brightened and departed.

As soon as the door closed, I got back to foolery. "I know Rolf was given poison, so I suspect Archibald was too. Did you see him take sick in the hall?"

"My good eye did not, for it sees only the good in the world. My bad eye sees nothing."

"I was told some pages carried him out. Do you know where they took him?"

"Far away, and now he is much farther away."

"Where did he die?"

"Why, on his deathbed, young sir."

Curiously, I felt that the fool did want to help, he just couldn't make a direct statement. It was no surprise that a bang with a mace would scramble a man's brains forevermore, and after half a lifetime as a fool, he had become addicted to speaking in circles.

A house sage would normally treat the sick, so who had tended the dying Archibald? "Did they bring him back here?"

"And who would have let them in?"

An evasive answer, but a hint that the password was not generally known. Whoever had stolen the monkshood tincture that killed Rolf must have known it.

I reached across the table and pulled the goblets closer. "Will you take a draft of wine with me, sir?"

Scur stared at me, his solitary eye seeming to wobble, as if looking for a way to escape. Finally he said, "Half-head will drink the second half if half-leg drinks the first half." He was saying that he would trust no wine bottle in this place. Nor would I, but I knew that the Rolf poison had come from here. What was his reason to be cautious?

"I think your half-head works better than my whole one, because I haven't found any wine here; not yet, anyway. Do you know where Archibald kept it?"

"For safekeeping, he stored it by choice in his belly."

"Aye," I said patiently. "Before that?"

"Before Archibald, Sage Charles kept it in yon chest." But Scur also shrugged as he spoke, making the simplest answer he had given yet.

"You have not been in here since then?

"Would a seeker of beauty ask me in?"

"What happened to Charles?"

"He went the way we all go, so 'tis said."

"Aye, but what was his reason?"

"He had no reason, for that he lost his reason." The jester evidently liked that jest, for his eye glinted and his distorted mouth twisted in what might have been a smile.

"A reasonable reason. Who is Count Richard's heir?"

"Why, his son, who else?"

"His son's name?"

"Sir Stephen."

Short questions seemed to be the answer. . . .

Perdition! Re-thinking that thought, I decided this smart-aleck way of speaking must be catching. But the son was either a grown man or at least adolescent, for his name certainly dated his birth to before the day his father changed sides in the Anarchy.

"And where is he?"

"After the king."

"Aye, but *where* is he?"

"After the king."

I laughed. "How many horses back?"

"More than he would like but fewer than you'd expect."

"Sir Scur, I was told you'd lost your wits, but your wit greatly exceeds mine. So tell me true: if someone murdered Archibald, then that same person must have murdered Rolf the next day in the fear of being unmasked by his arts. Do you know anyone who might have wanted Archibald dead?"

Unexpectedly, the old warrior heaved himself to his feet. "Aye," he said. "Too many for half a head to hold." He tramped over to the door and was gone.

Still, he had been surprisingly helpful until then—more helpful than Sir Hugh had expected, perhaps? I had learned that Archibald had been a ladies' man, which did not surprise me after I had seen his bedroom. Lechery and adultery might stir up much trouble in the tightly closed society of a small castle. The count had a son at court, who would obviously be his heir, so inheritance had not been the motive for killing his brother. The potion had come from the sanctum, to which few people had access. I was making progress.

But logic alone could never solve a crime. Not all the sages from Abélard, Anselm, and Aristotle to Zeno could help me with this problem. If the killer was a sage himself, then it would be only fitting to catch him by enchantment. I reached for my satchel and took out Guy's spell book.

chapter 16

i saw at once that reading the grimoire would be more like boar hunting than berry picking. It was a scrapbook, pages of varying ages and sizes collected—purloined, possibly— and stitched together. The pages were all of calf parchment, densely covered with minute text, edge to edge, top to bottom, and many were palimpsests, sheets scrubbed clean and reused. Most incantations were in Latin, a few in Greek or tongues I did not know yet, possibly Arabic or Hebrew. Except when the writing changed from one scribe's hand to another's, or even from one century's style to another, it was hard to tell where one spell ended and another began. Most required the standard two voices, but I found some singles and a few triples. They were in no predictable order and the pages were unnumbered, so there was no helpful index.

I hesitated for a moment over *Super inimicos meos*, which was a solo, a defense against enemies. The thought of William throwing a punch at me and hitting invisible magical armor was tempting, but if sages could render themselves invulnerable to attack, then why had two of them succumbed to poison in the past two days? I carried on, thumbing page after page, lips moving in silence.

When I came to something called *Malefice venite*, "Come, villain," I thought this should be exactly what I needed, but it was complex and required three voices. Eventually I found the one that Sage Guy had suggested, *Ubi malum*. Although it was long, most of the chanting was done by First Voice. The responses were short and cued by the preceding versicle, on the lines of:

Versicle: "Come and aid me with your eyes, all-seeing Argus of the thousand eyes, I task you to seek out the evil that beset me."

Response: "I am Argus of the thousand eyes and I see what you need to see."

Versicle: "Come, hunt by my side, great Nimrod of Shinar . . ."

And so on: Orion, Saint Eustachius, Aello, Celaeno, Ocypete, Sir Galahad, Saint Hubertus, Michael the Archangel, and a dozen other hunters and seekers, each being summoned in turn and announcing his or her presence. This was powerful magic indeed, and just reading it made my hair stir like hay in a breeze.

The room brightened as the door swung open. William entered, bowed ironically to his superior, and then said, "Enter . . . Enter . . ." until the sanctum was filled with servants: six men, one housemaid. They brought bags, bundles, firewood, the missing swords and armor. They all glanced nervously at me, so I made myself inscrutable, although not invisible, keeping my finger on my place in the book.

"You wish the woman to put fresh clothes on the bed, master?"

I nodded, and the housemaid scrambled up the ladder, brightening my day with glimpses of shapely ankles. A man went up after her and other men began tossing bundles up to him, some of which I recognized as baggage from the previous day's journey. One of the boys hastened to the hearth and knelt to set a fire.

William came over to the table. "Sagacious Adept, Wacian the bottler and other senior servants have accompanied the gentry to the village church for the funeral mass. The rites for Sage Archibald de la Mare, that is. The mass for Sage Rolf will be held tomorrow."

"So dinner may be a little late?"

"More than a little, I fear."

"Well, we have much work to do, and too much food spoils the concentration."

"Yes, master. I thank you for this wisdom." William's expression was mocking, not grateful, but at least he was playing to the audience behind him.

"Watch that none of them tries to make off with anything," I whispered. I was thinking of poisons, mostly, for there was little else to steal. It was highly unlikely that any servant could read the names on the bottoms of the jars or bottles, or would know what the names implied, but the castle swarmed with so many servants that they tended to be effectively invisible, like fleas.

It had not occurred to me until then that some anonymous menial could have stolen the monkshood. Without effort, I could think up several motives for a servant wanting to murder a sage. The sanctum was well kept, with no cobwebs or mouse droppings in sight, unlike several cottages in Helmdon I could think of. A sage would certainly not do his own sweeping and dusting, but no one had mentioned Archibald's employing an adept or other cantor to assist him.

The invasion did not last long. William shut the door on the last of them and promptly dropped his lackey mask. He headed for the ladder.

"I found the chain mail and swords, but I'm going to go through the bags and see what's missing."

"That can wait. If anything is missing, you'll never get it back anyway. There must be writing materials around somewhere—*Stop!*"

On the point of opening one of the chests, William froze.

"I haven't checked that one for warding yet." I rose and lurched across the room. I felt for that eerie sense of cold, but failed to find any. Then I opened it myself, to keep William from telling me to. "Clear," I said. "I tested the other one earlier."

I was not surprised to find that an unwarded chest contained little of interest, although there were pens, smoothed wooden panels, and ink; also slates for quick notes or teaching. A couple of those bore Latin lessons in a shaky, immature hand, but might have been there for years. A thick roll of astrological charts might be worth examining some time.

The first chest, the one I had looked in earlier, held philosophical paraphernalia: mortars and pestles, crucibles, chopping boards, silver knives for cutting mistletoe, a small crystal ball, many varied dishes.

No wine, no more silver goblets—*and no books!*

"Bring something to write on."

William hesitated, but then decided not to balk this time. He returned with four sheets, tablets, an ink bottle, pen box, and a sand bottle. "Is there aught else that my lord requires?"

"Yes. Are you going to continue posing as a cretinous shithead, or could you possibly manage to be helpful for a little while?"

William swelled as if about to charge, fists clenching. "Depends what you want, peasant."

"What I *need*. Put your ass on that stool. I need someone to chant the responses to the incantation *Ubi malum*. If you are going to keep pretending that you can't read and write, then I'll have to ask the marshal if the count has a secretary or someone else who can help me."

William's face had gone back to its idiot mode. "You're the adept, Saxon. I'm just a squire."

"One of those spoiled brats who is too stupid to learn to be a priest or a sage, but is scared to follow in his father's footsteps?"

The color drained out of his face and for a frightening moment I thought I had gone too far.

"Take that back or I will make you eat your teeth."

"I'll take it back when you admit that you're a fraud. You pretend to be stupid to provoke the sages at Helmdon, but you're not, and they know it. If you were as obtuse as you act they wouldn't bother with you. That's a stupid game, but this isn't a game, Squire. We have a killer to catch and hang before he kills anyone else. Can you read this?"

William took one look at the page and said, "No." But there was a hint of disappointment in his tone.

"It's not easy, I admit. So I will have to read out the responses and you will have to write them. You can read your own writing, I hope?"

"In French, yes."

"And you have no idea what *Ubi malum* means?"

"'Where is the evil?'"

Astonished, I said, "Right! Bad *thing*. Not bad person, unfortunately, but if we can perform it correctly, this chant should smoke out our villain, or at least put us on his tracks. We'll practice it over and over until we know we can sing it perfectly, then you will buckle on your sword, I'll bring my staff, and we'll go and denounce him."

After a fateful moment when success hung in the balance, something overcame the boy's obstinate contempt for learning—the attraction of participating in meaningful magic, or a vision of him actually getting to use his sword, or just shame at being inferior to a Saxon. He nodded. "I'll try a line or two, but one day you'll kneel at my feet and eat dirt until I tell you to stop." He sat down and opened the ink bottle.

Feeling as if I'd just broken a horse, I turned to the beginning of the spell. "It begins with a long preamble by First Voice, that's me, asking where the evil lurks, the darkness, deadly sin, and so on. I call on all spirits and powers of light to aid me. Then you answer for the spirits."

William looked skeptical, but he listened to the first few words of the response, screwed up his face in concentration, and laboriously spelled them out, letter by letter. Even seeing upside down across the table, I could tell that his penmanship was superb, every letter laboriously crafted in Carolingian miniscule. His spelling wouldn't matter, because only he had to be able to read it.

After a painful few minutes, we reached the end of the first response. Now to the next step, which I fully expected to be much harder.

"Tell me what it means, because you can't just make noises like a trained jackdaw. You must understand, too."

"It's a recipe for beef soup."

I said nothing.

William closed the ink bottle, wiped his pen, and shouted, "*I don't know!*" He folded his arms and glared murder.

"Then I'll have to teach you, won't I? And you will have to learn. This is going to take all day, Squire, and perhaps all day tomorrow. We'll get tired and our butts will grow sore with sitting; our eyes will ache, and we'll growl and snap at each other, but it must be done. Will you go back to Helmdon and say that Rolf was murdered, isn't that a shame, but you didn't even try to catch his killer? This is worth the effort! I know I'm tough enough to do it. Are you?"

There was only one way an adolescent Norman could answer a challenge from a Saxon cripple. "I'm tough enough to tear your slimy tongue out."

"I'd turn you into a toad if someone hadn't beaten me to it. You won't help—is that what you mean?"

"No. I mean I'll do what you want and then I will kick you into a jelly and break every bone in your filthy body. Do you agree to *that*, you insolent peasant pig?"

"I'll agree to let you try, any time after I've exposed the black-guard who killed Sage Rolf. Now deliver. This incantation is mainly Church Latin with a couple of lapses into French Latin. First response . . . the verb comes at the end, of course . . . *Omnes spiritus et potentiae summonitionem meum audire . . .*"

My reluctant apprentice scowled mightily. "'All spirits and powers hear my summons.'"

I gaped at him for a moment and then laughed aloud with equal parts astonishment and relief. "Where in Hell did you—"

"In Hell!" he snapped."What's next?"

We went on to the second response. Again he wrote it out in a hand no monkish scrivener could have bettered and this time he rattled off the translation without hesitation.

"That's better than I could do," I admitted, hoping that honey might work better than vinegar.

"I can do anything in the world better than you can, you glorified serf."

"You promised to prove it."

"Including fighting. Next?"

At that point we were interrupted by a tentative tap on the door. William jumped up and strode over to it.

"Enter. No, it's quite safe if I say so. Come in, John."

The page entered, eyes flickering around like moths as he assessed this dangerous, secret place.

"I was sent to tell the adept that dinner will be ready when the noon bell sounds and he may eat at the knights' table, and, um, you at the squires' table, and I am to show you where to wash your hands."

William said, "Food at last."

I reached down for my staff. "Thanks, John. Welcome news. The knights' table is the first one below the high table, I assume?"

chapter 17

acian the bottler was an imposing man of ample girth, with a spare chin, a ring of keys on his belt, and a Medusa stare that could have frozen the French king's army. He deeply regretted that he was unable to assist the learned adept at the moment, as he had a dinner to supervise. He would certainly wait upon the adept at the earliest possible moment thereafter. His manner suggested that around Easter next might be convenient.

With that, I had to be content. I had come to the hall as fast as I could, so I could choose a place at the extreme end of the table. There, I could lay my staff along the base of the wall, where it would be within my reach but not trip anyone. The high table grandees sat on stools, lesser folk on benches—which probably became beds by night.

William had stopped on the way to watch some squires at weapons training, pointing out that he could take his cue from them, because they would not likely be the last to arrive at the trough. I suspected that he was worried about meeting a peer group doing a real man's job. If he were mocked, he would surely feel he had to prove himself in a fight. Then I might have to find another assistant.

Order of arrival in the hall had nothing to do with the order of being served, of course, for that would be determined by rank. Everyone had to sit at their assigned table, and the hall began to fill up in groups and patches. I expected to be given a wide berth by the knights themselves, but there I was mistaken. The first to arrive plumped himself down on the bench beside me. He was not much older than me, but very much larger and also sweatier, as if he, too, had just come from weapons training, possibly wrestling stallions.

"Kendryck of Stane, Adept," he announced. He had a friendly, weather-beaten face and flaxen Saxon hair.

"Honored, Sir Kendryck. Durwin of Pipewell."

"Lucien of Leicester," announced a second knight, settling opposite. He was older, swarthy, and certainly Norman. His expression was less friendly, but perhaps more genuine.

"So!" Kendryck boomed. "Was Sage Archibald murdered?"

"I do not know yet whether he was or not. But I am certain that Sage Rolf was."

The knights exchanged glances.

"Your art tells you this?" Lucien asked.

"It does."

Questions began flying, too fast to finish answering before more arrived:

"One sudden death is murder but the other is not?"

"I don't know, but I intend—"

"How can you be so sure of one and not the other?"

"I've just started my—"

"How did Rolf get here so fast after the first death?"

"That's a secret of—"

Other knights were arriving, being brought up to date, and joining in the interrogation.

"How did you bypass the curse on the sanctum door?"

"Another secret—"

"When are you going to accuse the killer?"

"When I have—"

"Aren't you frightened he will strike at you next?"

"Sirs! Sirs!" I held up both hands. "Your Honors . . . first, yes, I am aware that the villain may seek to treat me as he did the two sages, but I am intent on doing my duty, just as you always are. When I know who committed these crimes, I will report to Sir Hugh first, or to the count himself. And I would be most grateful if you noble knights could help me in a small way."

"How is that?" asked Sir Lucien, and the rest fell silent to listen.

"I am attended by an apprentice, William Legier. I need his help if I am to unmask the murderer. He is a proud lad with many fine qualities, but you have many squires of about his age here, and I worry that some of them may question his manhood because he is not in knight's training. That is not by his own wish, I know. He desperately wants to be, and I fear that his father, an honored knight, has forbidden it, for reasons that the boy will not discuss. I also know that his nature is to accept any challenge, any challenge at all from anybody. He will not be able to aid me if they damage him."

"Damage him?" Kendryck said. "Those young devils will grind him to meal. We'll pass the word, right, hearties?"

"Tell them the adept will turn them into sheep."

"Be an improvement. They're all horny as goats already."

Other voices agreed.

"But the kid will be fair game afterward?" asked another knight. "We'll have to promise them that. I'll tell them." He rose and went to the next table, where William was already pinned within a crowd of his peers. Beyond them, the third table was filling up with stablemen and a man wearing a farrier's leather apron, showing how much the count valued his cavalry. All other servants were ranked lower and farther from the seat of power.

The hall was almost full. At the high table, I recognized Hugh the marshal, Father Randolf, and Bertrand the steward, but there were also three men I had not seen before. Two of them were tonsured, and I guessed that they were the count's clerical staff.

I turned to Sir Kendryck. "Where did Sage Archibald sit?"

"Mm?" The knight looked blank. "Anywhere he wanted. High table, of course. Count and countess always sit on the chairs in the middle, but unless there's guests or a feast, Count likes folks to move around, change neighbors."

That made sense. Life would become very dull if you had to converse with the same people every mealtime. I posed one of the questions I had been intending to ask Wacian.

"And where was the sage sitting two days ago, when he was smitten?"

"Don't know," Kendryck said cheerfully. "I'd just gotten back and I was helping with the horses, so I missed the meal. Had to eat in the kitchen with the scullions."

"I had my back to them," said Sir Lucien. "By the time I looked around, he was on the floor and everyone jumping like hares."

"Me too," said a third. "Looking the wrong way, I mean."

This seemed like a conspiracy of silence, but apparently their ignorance was genuine, because the query was passed along until an older knight two places away leaned around his neighbor to answer it.

"At that end, next to the priest."

I thanked him and considered what that might mean. Diners at the high table sat along one side only, so that everyone there faced the hall. I must conclude that only one of the other diners, the priest, had been close enough to Archibald to slip poison into his food or drink, and Archibald would have had no neighbor on the other side to distract him while it was being done. It's a poor answer that doesn't raise a new question, as Guy liked to say.

The conversation was ended by Wacian ringing a hand bell at the far side of the dais. Everyone rose, the hall fell silent, and the count entered from the personal quarters, with the countess on his arm and two women following behind. All four wore black. The woman directly behind the countess was the widowed daughter, Baroness Matilda, in a gown of fine material and cut. The fourth, likely her lady companion, was some years older, and more humbly dressed, although still in black.

The count and countess went to the chairs in the center, the women moved along to empty spaces at the far end from me. The count surveyed the hall, then glanced along the table to locate the priest, and nodded a signal.

Father Randolf said grace, mainly in Latin, which not a dozen people present would understand, but switched to Norman French to lead a brief prayer for the soul of the count's brother, so recently deceased. Then he took a moment to mention the funeral of Sage Archibald, although he somehow conveyed the idea—without actually saying so—that prayer wasn't very important in his case because any sage was doomed to burn in Hell for trafficking with the Devil. After the amens, everyone sat down and the noise started up again. Footmen marched in from the staircase, holding loaded platters overhead. Being a fire hazard, the kitchens would be out in the bailey somewhere.

"What happened to your leg?" Kendryck asked, as a convenient conversation starter. I told the story. The knights made sympathetic noises and began to relate narrow escapes of their own.

The high table was served first, then a drinking horn and a trencher of stale bread were dropped before each of us; large jugs of ale followed, and after them came the food dishes. Hands grabbed, knives and spoons wielded, trenchers piled high. Up at the high table it was the same picture, with the food communal, everyone dipping into everything within reach. No one received individual dishes. Even the beer was laid out in jugs for diners to refill their horns—or beakers, in the case of the notables at high table. Furthermore, at the high table the food was all served from the front of the table, meaning no footman had to go around the end of the table, where Archibald had been seated. The sage had not had any reason to turn his head away from his neighbor. How could anyone have poisoned him under these conditions?

But just because Rolf had been poisoned did not mean that Archibald had been. Guy's grimoire had contained a few very nasty curses. I had skipped past them as soon as I realized what they were, but now I wondered if I ought to take a better look at them, or find the dead Archibald's library to see what might have been available there.

Worse yet: if a potion could be stolen from the sanctum, so could a grimoire, or several grimoires, for some enchanters own more than one. Fortunately a death curse must be a very dark and evil incantation, which would likely need more than one voice. I must keep in mind that there might be more than one person behind the murders.

The food was closer to cold than warm, but there was plenty of it, and fair variety: fish, ample bread, ample goose grease to spread on it, mountains of beans and peas. There was even enough pork for everyone to get some. I feasted, although I could not match the efforts of Sir Kendryck, who was eating like a whole herd of starving horses, feeding food into his mouth with one enormous hand while the other grabbed more off the trencher.

Many of his fellows were as busy, although Lucien, being older, was less voracious.

The count was deep in conversation with the marshal, Sir Hugh Fiennes; I detected a glance or two in my direction.

The buzz of conversation gradually withdrew to the far end of the hall, where the minor servants sat, and then died away as all mouths were put to more urgent uses. A young fiddler began playing, strolling around between the tables. He soon added a sad lament, singing in langue d'oc, the French of the south. Troubadours were fashionable now, because Queen Eleanor was known to be a connoisseur of their art.

After a few songs, the fiddler withdrew to the far wall to take a break; conversations sprang up like January snowdrops.

"Courtly love!" Sir Kendryck snorted—apparently he was capable of breathing while engulfing food. "I prefer the real thing."

"Sure you're old enough to manage the real thing now?" retorted his other neighbor, thus starting a bout of vicious elbowing.

"Is there much of it goes on here?" I inquired blandly. The dead sage's rumpled bed intrigued me.

Kendryck's blue eyes bored into mine. "Fornicating or fantasizing about virtue?"

"Shock me."

"You expect me to gossip like an old woman?"

"Oh, no. I'm sure His Lordship keeps his household firmly on the path of righteousness." In fact I was sure that—in private—the unsubtle young Kendryck would dish the dirt with all the tact and boisterous enthusiasm of a dog sidling up to a bitch in heat, and probably provide much grist to others' mills on his own account.

"Tell you later," he mumbled.

The count was eating while listening to Hugh. His wife had not let grief dull her appetite, nor had their daughter's companion, but Matilda herself was merely picking at what she had on her trencher. She seemed wan and depressed. Was she mourning her Uncle Rolf or Sage Archibald? Why *did* her face seem so familiar?

A sudden loud jeering whipped my head around. It came from near the entrance and grew louder and closer, accompanied by a tinkle of bells. A large, shabbily dressed man was approaching the head table in a very clumsy, flat-footed dance. This could only be Sir Scur, the count's fool, although his head was hidden inside a keg-sized mask of blue fur—probably dyed with woad—shaped as a giant rabbit's head with grotesquely huge ears. No finicky diner need see his mutilated face.

He stopped before the high table, not far from me, jangling his bell-strung baton at the count, who did not seem much pleased.

Then Scur swung around and waved his bells at the hall in a bid for attention. The audience had already hushed, eager to hear the entertainment.

"Today we are not in a mood for frivolity!" the count announced in tones even louder than his usual officers' bellow. His sour-faced wife looked furious. Perhaps she always looked furious.

"Aye, my lord?" Scur was quite audible, too, even inside his mask. "Is it not when you are most downcast that you are most in need of levity? Furthermore," he declaimed, with a wild swing back to face the hall again, "we bring you glad tidings! Know that your house today is most extraordinarily blessed, by a great miracle."

"And how is that?" Sir Hugh asked loudly. The count's deputy's duties might well include playing straight man for the fool.

"Is it not so, good sir, that mortals walk upon the earth?"

"It is certainly true that mortals walk upon the earth."

"And do not angels soar like birds in the heavens?"

"Verily, angels do soar like birds in the heavens."

"Then, behold!" Scur stomped over to me and gripped my upper arm to raise me. It might be many years since the old warrior had wielded a broadsword, but he had not lost a swordsman's ferocious grip.

Resigned to being today's goat, I stood up.

"Why here, good sir," the fool continued, "is your miracle! For he stands on the earth with one foot and soars above it with the other. Surely he is half an angel?"

The standard of humor in Barton Castle was not high: the audience rated that as very funny. Although few of them could have seen my platform boot, no doubt I had supplied much gossip already. They laughed and cheered and banged things on the tables. Even the count laughed, and I would not expect him to display much wit. I bowed to him, and then to the cheers.

"But wait!" the jester cried, waving both hands. "If he is half an angel, he must surely be only half a sage. So, in faith can he be a whole man? Can he be a good Christian?" Nobody answered, of course, waiting for the punch line. "Well, let us make sure of that, and baptize him!"

Having failed to recognize impending danger when the fool had tucked his baton in his belt, out of the way, I was taken by surprise when he tipped a beer flagon over my head. The audience considered that the funniest event of the millennium. The giant rabbit capered around, jingling his bells again, enjoying the applause. Fortunately the flagon had been close to empty.

I stayed on my feet, wiping beer off my face and licking my fingers. In a moment I was noticed and the laughter stilled.

"Sir Hugh," I cried. "Is it not a brave rabbit that mocks a silver fox? I will turn him into a frog!" I bellowed some meaningless Latin at him, waving my hands wildly.

Sir Scur made his exit, pretending to flee in terror. End of show. That was perhaps the feeblest joke I had ever made, but it was good enough for that company. I was applauded for taking the ribbing in good heart. I sat down.

Sir Hugh said something, the count nodded. The marshal stood up, large and imposing, and the hall hushed.

"We all mourn with His Lordship and his family on the tragic and unexpected death this morning of his brother, Sage Rolf de Mandeville, may Our Redeemer cherish his soul. Adept Durwin came to Barton in his train, and will be staying here for a few days. He is young, but has studied for many years under Rolf and other learned sages at the famous academy of Helmdon. We apologize to him for the fool's pranks and thank him for taking them in good part. The adept will serve here as best he can until a new house sage can be found. He has the count's full confidence. Pray make him welcome."

Applause.

The adept in question was astonished. My demonstration of the poisoned wine must have been reported by Hugh to the count and must have impressed him just as much. Could I possibly live up to the expectations I had raised?

And—I wondered, admitting a shamefully selfish idea I had been suppressing—if I could expose the murderer, would the grateful count be willing to sponsor my continued studies at the academy?

A footman handed me a cloth to clean off as much of the beer as I could. Sir Kendryck rammed a killer elbow in my ribs and leaned close. "What do you want to know?" he whispered.

Where to start? "Was Sage Archibald popular?"

"Not with the men."

"Who was he humping?"

"Well I'm too busy at the moment to go into that. Come with me after the meal, and I'll try to tell you who he wasn't."

Two silver goblets smelling of wine, an unmade bed in the home of an obsessively tidy man, and now a second witness testifying that Archibald had been a lecher. Father Randolf's disapproval of him was understandable.

chapter 18

By the time another grace concluded the meal, the dogs were already feasting on the discarded trenchers. High table diners trooped out, as did the servants, except the few who began collecting horns and platters. Shouted at to go back to work, the squires reluctantly obeyed. Soon only the knights lingered—squabbling, mocking, quaffing beer, and arguing about the chances of the truce breaking down so the king could resume the war in France. There was no fighting going on anywhere, except for some minor troubles in Wales, and there would be no honor or profit in lancing a pack of hairy barbarians there. Knights are always bored in peacetime, and nothing could possibly happen until spring at the earliest, they agreed. The king was rumored to be coming to hunt in Rockingham Forest, which was not far away. I knew that this was William's father's province, but I didn't say so.

Then Kendryck, having eaten enough for three men, heaved himself to his feet.

"Come along, then, silver fox," he said. "Your pelt looks a bit mangy. Let's get it properly groomed."

Of course he descended the spiral staircase much faster than I could, but mended his manners to stay at my pace on the

stairway down the side of the mound. He talked of the tourneys he had entered in the summer, and bragged of ladies whose
token he had worn, hinting at the rewards they had provided
when he won.

I could not resist asking, "Only when you won?"

"Or wasn't too badly concussed in losing."

He led me to the castle laundry, a large building near the gate,
where women boiled clothes and hung them up, both indoors and
outdoors. The interior was a steamy labyrinth of corridors between
wet sheets and baskets of dry garments. Many women were busy
in there. Kendryck seemed to know them all and tried to envelope
each of them in an enormous bear hug before introducing her to
me. The young ones were willing to flirt, the old ones scolded, but
all of them seemed well-disposed to the jovial giant, just as all of
them regarded the new acting sage with wary respect. Kendryck's
special favorite seemed to be one called Megan, who was built on
the same monumental scale as he was. He hoisted her clean off
her feet, and then she did the same to him, in what seemed to be
a standing comedy act in that company, likely because her name
means *strong* in the old tongue.

Once all the byplay was finished, Kendryck uttered an audible aside about, "A wild ride, that one!" and began selecting garments at random, picking up, comparing, discarding until he was
satisfied. Then he found a private corner and told me to strip.

"You'll impress in this," he said, admiring the gentleman's
blue robe that had been his final selection.

"I can't wear that!"

"Of course you can. You must. At the moment you look more
like a stableman than an adept."

And probably still smelled like one, too, since I was one most
of the time. I undressed as fast as I could, much aware of women's voices and footsteps just behind the draperies.

"All right, girls, he's naked now. You can come and look!"

"Stop that!" I protested, grabbing for the robe, which of course he whisked away from me, but I was much less troubled by Kendryck's wicked grin than I had been by Alwin's creepy stare the previous day. Which reminded me, once I got hold of the robe . . . "I got those clothes from Alwin last night. I haven't gone back to find my own."

"Don't bother. They all get mixed up, and we wear whatever fits both us and our rank. What did you want to ask me?"

"I'd like to know about the time Archibald was smitten, and how—and when—he died. He couldn't tend himself, so where was he taken and who looked after him?"

"Father Randolf would know."

"Father Randolf doesn't approve of adepts. He won't help me."

Kendryck snorted. "Try him. Even a priest must see how the battle is going after what Hugh said. That's quite a boot you have there. Do you get shod by cobblers or farriers?"

"One leg each. What happened to Sage Charles?" Rolf's murder could be explained as an effort by a worried killer to escape detection, but there was still no obvious motive for Archibald's death.

"He died, so I heard."

"Where and how?"

"Old age. He got so bewildered he didn't know a potion from a poultice. The count found a monastery to care for him."

"Northampton?"

"No, somewhere far away, near some family he had."

So Archibald had not been murdered by a dispossessed Charles wanting his old job back. Discard that hypothesis.

"What academy did Archibald come from—Northampton?"

"Dunno. He spoke like a Londoner, all sick-cat meowing."

Almost any sage would grab at a chance to be a count's enchanter, so now the hints of bad blood between the academy at Northampton and Sage Rolf might extend to include his brother, Count Richard. Without that antagonism, Northampton could probably supply the count with a replacement sage before nightfall, even if only a temporary one. If the count must send farther afield, my tenure might last for a week or two.

Sage Guy would be wanting Ruffian back, now the rain had stopped and the hunting could resume.

I slung my white cape on my shoulders and wished I had a mirror.

"Come on, then," Kendryck said. "You look imposing now, very *potent*. You do still smell a bit beery, but that's better than stinking of horse like me, because you have a good excuse. I've got to go, or the marshal will have my hide for saddle leather. Can you find your way back to your lair?"

Without waiting for an answer, he led the way back out to the fresh air, managing to pat a few behinds on the way, including Megan's, but she was not the only one who responded with encouraging sniggers of delight.

When they were safely out of earshot, I said, "Now tell me about Archibald's lady friends."

The knight chuckled. "Well, you just met at least six of them. Married, unmarried. I'm guessing, but there were few skirts he didn't lift. He had an unfair advantage."

"Scur told me. If he hit the bull's eye, he could provide an abortion?"

"Didn't matter who'd scored, he could."

"You mean that was his price?" I asked, disgusted.

"I mean that there was a potion to be swallowed and a spell to be chanted, during certain actions that only he must perform, although I have it on good authority that he wasn't as well qualified as some of the rest of us." Kendryck twisted his big mouth into a lecherous smirk.

Even an adept knew of herbs reputed to abort unwanted fetuses, and a qualified sage probably had other techniques also. I did not believe that unwelcome coupling would be part of any of them. What Kendryck was describing sounded like outright extortion, a sage requiring women to provide sex as payment for an abortion. If that was Archibald's procedure, it could easily explain his murder—either by one of his victims or by an outraged husband wanting revenge for being cuckolded. Or for the loss of a future child.

Mercy! Just about anyone in the castle might have had a motive to kill the scoundrel. But some of those fancy garments in the sage's bedroom had not belonged to laundry maids.

"Saxons, Normans, low, or high?" High like barons' widows? Was that what Scur had refused to discuss?

Even the ebullient Kendryck knew where this talk could lead. He shot me a warning frown as he said, "Anything's possible. You go that way."

I thanked him and lurched off along the alley indicated. When I spoke the paternoster and entered the sanctum, I found William seated at the table, hard at work, writing—truly a miracle!

He regarded the newly glorified adept with unconcealed scorn. "Must I kneel to you now, my lord sage?"

"Not unless you want to. I just thought I'd show you how hard work and dedication can raise you in the sages' calling. How many responses have you left to go?"

"Three."

Only three? Something very strange had happened to Squire William Legier. His writing was clear, his spelling as reasonable as anyone's, and it soon became evident that he had worked out the meaning of most of the text without any help from me. The kid was the absolute model of perversity! Give him something to do that you both knew he could do, and he would die in torment rather than do it; give him something far beyond his skills, and he would die proving he could.

And while I was marveling over that, he said, "There's a stupid error in the third versicle."

A moment later he asked, "Why are you sitting there with your mouth open, Saxon?"

Because I was remembering all the hundreds of ancient spells that didn't work in modern times and my triumph at repairing the *Hwæt segst*. If William, whose training in enchantment was basically zero, could see an obvious error, then why hadn't some sage noticed it a century ago and corrected it? *Because it was deliberate!*

Some ideas are so obvious when you think of them that you cannot imagine why they aren't general knowledge. Magic must never be allowed to fall into the wrong hands, because it is the enchanters' livelihood, yes, but also because it is dangerous. So it must have been the custom in ancient times to write the spells with mistakes in them, like trip wires to catch the uninitiated. And somehow the secret had been lost.

"Show me," I said. Yes, it was obvious. I dipped my pen and corrected it.

"I've heard Sage Guy warn us that we must never change the wording," William said suspiciously.

"That's what we tell the beginners." And what I was going to correct Guy on when I got back to Helmdon! "Glad you caught that, Squire. You amaze me. You've had knight's training and you've also been taught by priests."

"Mind your own business, Saxon."

"I am both jealous and impressed." I sat down and took up the book. "Read me what you've done, one response at a time, working backward."

"Why backward?"

"We always rehearse incantations backward, because if you don't, and make a mistake, it may work in ways you do not want. And you'd better tell me the meaning of each one also."

"In what language?"

"Either, but not Latin."

About halfway through, William looked up with a worried frown. "You are going to have me pretending to be the voice of the Archangel Michael? Isn't that blasphemous?"

"No more than people playing the holy family in a mystery play. You're only claiming to pass on his words, not be him." A well-split hair, that.

Still uneasy, William continued reading.

When we ended with the first response, I laid the book down and grinned at him.

"What's so shitty funny, Saxon?"

"I'm trying to imagine Guy's face when we get back to Helmdon and you turn in an assignment like this for him. He will positively pee in his shoes!"

"What makes you think I ever would?"

"Wouldn't you like to see his reaction?" Getting no reply, I said, "Squire William Legier, I always knew you were smarter than you pretended, but I am truly impressed with what you're doing here! This is great work, as good as anything I've ever done or can do. Your Latin is better than most priests', and your penmanship as fine as any I have seen. Who trained you?"

William scowled fiercely. "You called off those castle dogs. You're *mothering* me!"

"I just said I needed your help, which I do. The challenges were only put off, weren't they? You can mash them all later. How many have you got lined up?"

"Seven."

Oh, Blessed Mary! They would kill him. I said, "You're lucky. I've only got one."

"You're going to be first. I wasn't even counting you. You make eight."

"No, we Saxons stand aside and let our betters precede us; I'll go last. Now let's keep on and see if we can get this *Ubi malum* finished before . . ."

Someone knocked at the door.

chapter 19

Wacian the bottler graciously accepted William's invitation to step inside; he had promised to spare the adept a few minutes, so here he was. He did not deign to peer around at the crocodile and other curiosities, but I could not tell whether that indifference was feigned to preserve his dignity or genuine because he was already familiar with the sanctum. He must have noticed my new garb, but his pudgy face expressed no reaction. Likely he approved of that transformation; since the count had accepted this whippersnapper as acting sage, he should dress the part. His bow to me was calculated to the inch.

"You had something you wished to ask me, Adept?"

I was assessing our respective stations. Wacian was head of the domestic servants, likely reporting directly to the steward or even the countess, but he was still a servant. I was a scholar, so the servant must remain upright and the adept stay on his stool. William, having closed the door, was standing by the shelves with his hands behind his back, playing respectful retainer.

"I do have, and I thank you for coming. I am anxious to know what happened on Monday, when Sage Archibald, may he rest in peace, was stricken in the great hall. You witnessed this?"

"No, Adept. It happened very suddenly. I did not see him rise from the table, but he fell almost at once. Some persons cried out, and then I observed Father Randolf going to his aid."

"They were sitting together at the end of the table?"

"The left-hand end, yes."

"Whose left hand?"

"His Lordship's."

Of course. That was the side of the hall with the entrance. At dinner, I had put myself at the other side, out of the traffic.

"And who sat next the priest?" I asked, mostly to gain time to think of my next question.

"Elmer, the clerk."

"I don't think I know. . . . Can you tell me the order of seating I saw today?"

Even that surprising request failed to move Wacian's static features. "Certainly. From right to left or left to right?"

"From the left, if you please, with their titles or offices."

Barely drawing breath, the bottler rattled off the list of today's diners: Lady Aveline; Baroness Matilda; Toland the treasurer; Galan the count's secretary; Sir Hugh the marshal; His Lordship; Her Ladyship; Father Randolf; Sir Bertrand the steward; Elmer the clerk; Hervé the wardrobe keeper. Upon request, he repeated it more slowly, and certainly the persons I knew fitted where he said they would.

"I took the liberty," Wacian continued, "of asking Sir Hugh whether you should sit at high table in future, after what he said about you today as being the sage's temporary replacement. He said he thought that would be premature."

"I'd much rather sit with the knights and watch. The fiddler—"

"Arth the troubadour."

149

"Thank you. Did Arth go anywhere close to Sage Archibald during that dinner on Monday?"

"Arth had not even begun to play, Adept. The sage was overcome before the squires' table had been served."

"So the fool had not performed yet, either?"

"No, Adept."

Archibald, Randolf, Elmer . . . trying to visualize that scene, I sensed the maddening itch of an idea that is forming but has not yet hatched. Who had sat next to Elmer on Monday? That couldn't matter. It seemed impossible that even the sage's immediate neighbor, Father Randolf, could have slipped poison onto his dinner unseen. And everyone ate from the same serving dishes.

The clerk, Elmer, I recalled as a pale, somewhat vacant youth, lacking the weather-beaten complexion of the knights and others who spent most of their days outdoors. It was very likely one of Elmer's robes that I was wearing at the moment. But why, on Monday, would the haughty Father Randolf have chosen to sit beside him? Were his confessions so meaty that even his casual conversation was worth hearing? Sage Archibald's might have been.

"Am I correct in thinking that the first persons to arrive choose stools close to the center and latecomers have to sit at the ends?"

"It is rare for anyone to leave a gap, Adept. That could be taken as a slight."

Something didn't fit. I looked at the two goblets on the table. "Then on Monday, Sage Archibald must have been the last, or one of the last, to arrive?"

"That is so. He entered barely ahead of the count. Had he been a few moments later, he would not have been admitted."

"And did anyone come with him?"

I had to wait a moment for the answer, but there could be only one answer, and Wacian had to give it. "His Reverence."

Thunderbolt! Something had been bothering me all along about the death of Sage Archibald and now I saw that it was the timing. A tiny voice at the back of my mind had been asking me what poison could have worked so fast that it would have felled its victim before the end of the meal. Some might, but only in such enormous doses that they would be detectable by a trained sage. Wacian had testified that the victim had collapsed only minutes after the meal had begun. For a moment I stared at the two goblets right in front of me. They were the only goblets I had seen in the castle, almost certainly the sage's personal property. They were also the murder weapon, and I should have seen that much sooner.

It suggested a way of identifying the killer: *Morðor wile ut!*

"When it became clear that the sage was seriously distressed, who organized the stretcher party to carry him out?"

"I did." Wacian's tone implied that nobody else gave orders to servants when he was around. "But we had no stretcher handy, and stretchers are not practical for taking an invalid down such stairs."

"So what did you do?"

"I had one of the porters carry the learned sage down on his back, with two others going ahead to steady him if he stumbled."

"Was the sage conscious or unconscious? In pain? Convulsing or unresponsive?"

Wacian actually frowned. "I cannot testify to his condition, Adept. He was talking, but his words were hard to make out, and what I heard made no sense. He kept covering his face with his hands. I don't think he understood what was happening."

"Where did they take him?"

"To the infirmary." Where else?

"Who went with them?" The bottler himself would have remained at his post in the hall.

"Father Randolf and Her Ladyship."

He could hardly have named two people less likely to cooperate with an upstart Saxon busybody like me. Hugh had forbidden any questioning of the count or countess.

Curiously, I cannot recall anyone mentioning that lady's name to me during the days I spent in Barton Castle. She was always just "the countess" or "Her Ladyship."

"Where could I find the priest?"

"Usually in the chapel at this time of day." The bottler implied that any idiot ought to know that. "In the morning he is more often at All Saints' in the village."

It would seem, then, that Rudolf was both parish priest and castle chaplain, but that made sense when that grand old Saxon church stood right outside the gate.

"Another topic on which you can advise me, Wacian . . . the last thing the sage did before going to his final meal was to drink some wine—here, in his sanctum."

The bottler allowed an eyebrow to rise in doubt.

"The goblets were still here, on the table," I said, "and everything else was perfectly in order. Perhaps he felt sick already and did not feel moved to tidy them away. But I am puzzled by the absence of a wine flask. As bottler, you are in charge of the count's wine?"

Of course, and I was a fool to ask. "I am, Adept. The wine arrives in barrels, and I oversee its transfer to jugs as it is needed. Only Her Ladyship and I hold keys to that cellar. Her Ladyship prefers imported wines to the homegrown, and the new season's vintage has just begun arriving from Bordeaux. Not a good year, I am afraid."

"And if someone other than the count himself wishes a jug of wine?" I saw that I was starting to pry into matters that did not concern me.

"Certain persons are entitled to request wine from the count's cellar. I keep a record, of course, which I supply to the steward at the end of each month."

That might limit the list of suspects, if the poison had been administered in the sage's sanctum. "Sage Archibald would have been one such person?"

For a moment it seemed that Wacian would balk at revealing the secrets of his craft, but either Sir Hugh's commendation overcame his scruples, or he wanted to defend his own efficiency. "As it happens, owing to the unusual demand in Northampton just now, our vintner failed to deliver on Saturday, and we ran out of wine. I was able to supply some high-quality mead to make up the shortfall, but I regret to say that Her Ladyship was somewhat displeased. Early on Monday the vintner delivered four casks, and I was able to resume the normal distribution. I assure you that a flask was delivered here, to Sage Archibald, and I saw him accept it."

I managed to avoid sending a meaningful glance to William: there was a mystery here. "Explain your 'normal distribution.'"

Wacian's momentary hesitation was as good as a deep sigh from anyone else. "Senior retainers—those with private quarters—are allowed wine from His Lordship's store, for their own use or for entertaining friends. I decant the wine and take it around . . . I mean, I accompany the porter who takes it around, and I make sure that it is safely delivered to the right persons and no one else."

"I am sure that your job requires unusual vigilance, and you appear to be commendably diligent."

"Thank you, Adept. I do try to be. On Monday, as the previous supplies had mostly been exhausted, almost everyone returned an empty, or almost empty, flask and received a full one. Sage Archibald definitely accepted a full flask that morning, and returned an empty. I gave him number seven, as I recall, although I should have to inspect my notes to be certain. The flasks are numbered on the underside."

I puzzled for a moment, then asked, "Who did not receive a new flask?" I wasn't sure why that mattered, but it felt like the next question.

Wacian frowned, uncomfortable at discussing community affairs with an outsider. "Well, Father Randolf wasn't there, but he has given me authority to enter his vestry in his absence, and I did so. Very little had been removed from his flask but I replaced it anyway, because he uses it for the sacrament, and it should always be fresh. Number four, I believe. Master of Horse Alwin was away; Treasurer Toland was at work in the counting room."

"What would happen to the wine you recovered from Father Randolf?"

"Unless it smelled sour, it would be returned to the supply."

Did that explain why the murderer had removed the rest of the draft that had killed Archibald—in case it was returned to the general store? But why take the flask as well, instead of just tipping the balance outside, on the ground or in the privy?

"One last matter, if you will bear with me. Last night, you supervised the setting up of a bed for Sage Rolf. And you would have been the last servant to leave?"

"I did and I was."

"There was a chest alongside his cot. Did you or anyone else leave a flask of wine there for him?"

"Anticipating that he might feel thirsty when he awoke, I saw that a jug of water and a beaker were left there. Indeed, put them there myself."

"Squire, show him, please."

William lifted the monkshood tincture down from the shelf and offered it to the bottler.

"Not like that, no. What I placed there was a single-handled jug of Dudley pottery painted with blue and green chevrons and two-thirds filled with fresh rainwater. The beaker was decorated to match."

I thought back to early morning. There had been at least two jugs among the empties I had seen in the death chamber, so the killer had likely brought the flask and made the switch unnoticed. I gathered up my staff and rose. "I thank you for coming, Master Bottler. You have been most helpful. You will perhaps direct me to the chapel. . . ."

Another knock at the door. William dutifully crossed the room and opened it.

"Sir Scur, master."

"Bid him enter."

"Ha!" the fool said, doing so. He had shed his rabbit mask and wore his shapeless old rags. "I see you have caught other prey, fox, and one already stuffed."

The bottler did not even look at him.

"But when the rabbit enters his earth, the fox flees," I countered. "Thank you again, Bottler. The fool can take me to the chapel."

"What? Marriage so soon? Being of one flesh, then, shall we make a three-eyed, three-legged monster?"

Behind Scur's back the bottler rolled his eyes in the first human gesture I had seen from him, then promptly departed, as if ashamed of this outburst of emotion.

"Fool, I wish to speak with Father Randolf, so you can guide me to him."

"Aye, but not lead you to righteousness."

What did that mean? Scur kept dropping tantalizing hints that he knew things he could not or would not spell out.

"William," I said, "you will finish the responses and then you had better copy out the rest of the incantation, because your hand is much more legible than the original. Some parts are quite obscure, so leave those until I can guide you."

William said, "Yes, master," with a look that suggested I had just added two more kicks in the crotch to our future settlement.

chapter 20

despite the lateness of the season, soupy mud was steaming in the afternoon sunshine. Trudging along at Scur's side in the general direction of the keep, I said, "You wanted to see me?"

"No more than anyone would ever want to see me."

"Then why did you come to the sanctum?"

"To lead you to the chapel."

"How did you know I wanted to go to the chapel?"

"You said so."

"Wherever you're taking me, our conversation is going nowhere." Sir Hugh had instructed him to help me and probably he had come to see what I needed, if anything. "Can you think of anyone who had reason to want to murder the sage?"

"Ah, half a head can only think of half the people."

"You used that joke before. How about men? Do you know any men who might have wanted him dead?"

"Might might be right or might might be wrong."

Now I had made him mad. "True. On Monday, when the sage was stricken in the hall, where were you?"

"Far enough away that no one can accuse a poor fool of sending him to Hell."

"Are you sure he went to Hell?" That was a harsh judgment on a man, even from a jester who made his living by insulting people. Hugh had said that Scur knew everyone and everywhere.

"I hope not to have to go there to seek him."

"But that would be the first place you would look?"

"Yesterday you would have found him in here," Scur said, halting at a doorway. "And today you will find another of his kind."

We had arrived at the castle chapel, a small stone shed, starkly plain. It seemed that successive counts of Barton had relied on the village church and made do with a mere token place of worship inside the bailey. The door stood open. Peering in, I saw Rolf de Mandeville's coffin on trestles taking up most of the tiny nave, with the count himself kneeling in prayer beside it.

Not wishing to disturb, I backed away and turned to Scur. "Where can I find the priest?"

"Why, where he is and nowhere else!" The ogre leered in triumph. "But had I any similar ambition, which God forbid, I would start looking around the other side of this workshop of his."

"Thanks." I walked away. Even if the old man's gimcrack ranting was not his fault, it did become wearing. Why could he not just come out and tell me what he knew or suspected?

Around the corner I discovered an even smaller building attached to the church. Smoke was drifting up through the hole in the thatch, and the door was ajar. My shadow alerted the occupant.

"Enter!" the priest intoned.

I entered.

"Oh, it's you." For comfort, Father Randolf had furnished his cell with a chair, a small table, a plank bed with a blanket folded on it, and a stool. He had a book in his hand. Vestments hung on a hook behind the door. This nook must serve as vestry and perhaps confessional, but he took his vocation very seriously if he slept there also. He might have a rectory in the village as well. "Did you come to make confession?"

"I came to ask you a few questions about the death of Sage Archibald, Father."

The priest sighed angrily, closed the book on a finger to mark his place, and clasped it in both hands on his lap. "Sir Hugh can issue orders to everyone else except His Lordship, but he cannot instruct me. I fail to see why I need pander to your nosiness, Durwin."

He had not told me to sit.

"Father, the reason the count allowed the marshal to make that announcement today, was that I had proved to Sir Hugh earlier—proved beyond doubt—that the count's brother was murdered. The flask of water that had been placed beside his bed had been replaced with a flask of deadly poison, which I identified by name for Sir Hugh. I also know where it came from."

Randolf's face darkened in anger. He closed his eyes in prayer for a moment, crossed himself, and then said, "Very well. Or very evil, rather. Sit down, my son! What do you want to know?"

For starters, I want to know if you did it.

I perched on the stool. "On Monday, you and Sage Archibald arrived late at the hall for dinner. That was why you were sitting together?"

"Beware of jumping to incorrect conclusions, Boy Logician. I disapproved of the heretical, even pagan, leanings in much of Archibald's philosophy, but that did not mean I spurned him as a dining companion. He could discourse on subjects that few others hereabouts could. We enjoyed verbal sparring quite often. Are you suggesting that I poisoned his food? He had hardly begun to eat. Indeed, I am not sure he ate anything. He drank two beakers of wine, though."

"I am quite certain that he was not poisoned at the table, Father. Do you know why he was late?" Had the two of them been sharing a flask of wine in the sanctum, perhaps?

"No. I met him on my way there. He seemed unsteady and confused. I thought at first he had been drinking, early as the hour was. But he complained of his eyes. I saw him safely to the hall. He had some trouble on the stairs."

"Did he say where he had been?"

"No."

"Did he say anything, then or later, about poison?"

"Not a thing. He mumbled a lot."

"And when the porters carried him out, was he responsive? Was he in pain?"

"He cried out as we left the hall. I remember naught else."

"You stayed with him at the infirmary until he died?"

"I did. He was the sage, and who will heal the healer? We soon realized that there was no time to send for another. The roads were almost impassable—two hours to come from Northampton! I administered extreme unction just before he went into coma."

"Did you by any chance," I asked, "notice his heartbeat?"

I knew from the priest's surprise that my diagnosis was correct.

"I did. It seemed extremely strong and rapid, indeed racing."

"Unsteady on his feet, dry mouth, confusion, fast heartbeat. These are all marks of a poison known as dwale, Father. It dilates the pupils, which is why his eyes were blinded by the light."

"Rain was falling in barrelfuls!"

"I expect that was why you did not realize it was the light that distressed him. I thank you. He was poisoned before he even reached the hall. You have confirmed what I suspected."

"And you have confirmed my secret fears. I apologize for misjudging you, my son. You are wise beyond your years."

"That is gracious of you, Father." And it was. How often did this stone-faced, stiff-necked pastor ever apologize to anyone other than God? He was handsome, nobly born, ordained young, and undoubtedly destined to be a bishop before he was thirty.

I slid awkwardly down off the stool and knelt to receive a blessing. Even if a priest is a sinner, his blessing is still valid. The Church says so.

Outside in the afternoon sunshine, I went back to the tiny chapel. The count had gone and two women kept vigil there in his stead, both so heavily veiled that I could only guess who they were. I went to the far side of the coffin and knelt to offer prayers for the soul of the man I had brought to Barton just the day before.

I also prayed for wisdom and guidance so that I might bring Rolf's killer to justice.

chapter 21

Back at the sanctum, I told William what I had learned from the priest.

"You think that the sage was poisoned here, in his own sanctum?" He stared in horror at the two goblets still standing on the table like monuments to murder.

"I do. He could have been drinking with a visitor and turned his back on him for a moment too long. Or Archibald himself was trying to poison a visitor and took the wrong draft, but that would not explain who killed Rolf the next day."

"'Dwale,' you said, master?" We both turned to look at the shelves.

"The Norman name for it is *belladonne*, because ladies sometimes put drops of it in their eyes to make them beautiful. In the old tongue it is called *dwale*, because it is used as a sleeping draft. Even a slight overdose is extremely deadly."

"So what happened to the wine flask, master?"

"You tell me," I sighed. "If the poison was in the flask, how did the poisoner escape its effects? And why not just tip the rest of the wine out in the alley or the privy and leave the flask itself here? If the dwale was in one of the goblets, why bother removing the flask? Unless . . . perhaps Archibald put it up on the shelf with the other bottles?"

William rose and went over to the shelves to inspect the undersides of the various flasks that resembled the one that had killed Sage Rolf. He found none of them unlabeled, as the wine flask should be, but he did find a jar labeled *Belladonne* and brought it over to me. It was half full of black dwale berries, likely gathered not long ago. I told him to put it back where it belonged. As few as ten berries can kill a man and no doubt the raw taste of the fall's new wine might mask the flavor. On the other hand, anyone expecting wine in their mouth would notice an invasion of berries, so the raw material had been processed somehow. I would have to examine every jar and bottle to discover if there were any potions or ointments that might contain dwale extract.

William had completed a fair transcript of the responses. Doing the same thing for the sage's versicles was going to be harder, because they were longer. Some words were almost illegible and there were a few whose meaning had to be guessed at. An incantation improperly performed or understood would either fail to work at all or produce unexpected results. Sage Guy had warned me not to try any of the grimoire spells on my own.

Sage Guy had not foreseen two murders.

This time I wrote while William read out the Latin text, translating as he went. He was fluent in Church Latin but had to be helped when the text shifted into the French version, because it was Parisian French, not the Norman dialect he would have grown up with. The important thing was that now he was willing to try, enjoying the challenge and the importance of what he was doing. Several times we had a studied argument about the meaning of a word or phrase, disputing like sages. For the time being we had become a team. When we reached the end, I felt stiff, and flexed my shoulders; he glanced at the windows and the warm light of sunset.

"Food is provided in the hall around dusk," I said.

"Can't we try this now?" William asked, looking suddenly about five years younger than he was.

I shook my head. *Ubi malum* was definitely the sort of summoning spell that Guy had warned me not to chant after sundown. "We'll have to go through it several times from back to front. And after that we may need to try it several times in earnest before it works, if it ever does. I'm not a sage, only an adept—as I believe you know."

William ignored the sarcasm and just shrugged, disappointed. We looked at each other. Then we both grinned like kids, although it wasn't clear whose idea that was. The sun had not quite set yet.

"Very well," I said. "Just once tonight. It won't work and we may be dragged down to Hell by an army of sharp-toothed demons, but let's try it."

The squire leaped up. "And I have to wear my sword?"

"If you wish." A sword would be little help against the aforementioned demons, but in the unlikely event that the incantation did happen to work, we might stumble upon a dangerous killer.

William fetched his sword and two candles. I played along, laying one end of my staff on my thigh, ready to hand in case danger materialized. Then we gathered the tablets together and exchanged nods, and I began the chant: *"Ubi malum est . . ."* After the prologue came the evocations, starting with Argus. William responded. He had a good singing voice.

Back and forth we chanted, I appealing for help, William replying for each entity summoned. As the incantation progressed, his voice began to change timbre from response to response. I assumed that he was poking fun at the magic, which was a stupid and dangerous thing to do. It wouldn't make any difference in this run-through, but he must be warned not to indulge in any such nonsense tomorrow, when we were really trying. Then I sensed what he must have felt sooner: acceptance! The spirits were responding.

I had the last word, calling on the entities assembled to expose the evil. Then I dropped the tablet, which clattered onto the table. My whole body seemed to come out in goose bumps as I felt the rush of joy and power. Never had I sensed numinous presences so strongly—but then I had never participated in such a major incantation before.

"Praise be!" I croaked, dry-mouthed. My first effort as not just an adept but as a sage, and it had worked at the first attempt! Well, it was doing *something* at the first attempt.

And William . . . William was staring straight through me, his face as wooden as Bottler Wacian's.

"William? Squire Legier?"

Very slowly, William rose from his stool and drew his sword. His eyes did not lose their mindless stare into the far distance.

Oh, mercy! I scrambled to my feet also. What had I done? What had I summoned? I was an arrogant idiot to tamper with powers I did not understand or control! I might be going to die for my presumption. Quarterstaff against sword was a fair match outdoors, where there was room to wield the longer weapon, but indoors a man with a crippled leg would never withstand the likes of William, especially a William possessed.

"William, what's wrong? Put up that sword!"

Showing no sign of hearing, William slowly turned until he faced the door, then began moving toward it, carefully placing each foot as if just learning to walk. God in Heaven . . . Guy had told me of his own experience with this incantation: *the adept went into trance . . .*

I followed, slamming the sanctum door behind me. I had been put into trances often enough. Going in is easy but coming out can be a painful and dangerous shock. Sword in hand, William paced along the grubby little alley to its opening, paused there like a dog sniffing the wind, then chose a direction and began to walk faster. I limped after him, staying close. The bell in the keep was summoning the residents to supper, and they were responding, men and women both. They stared in alarm at the sword-bearing youth advancing like a walking corpse, looking neither right nor left. And he was speeding up, outpacing the cripple who so frantically lurched after him.

A band of knights came around a corner, chattering loudly and generally ignoring everyone else, as was their way. They could not ignore this, though. Fortunately none of them was armed with more than a dagger.

"And just where . . ." one of them began, then stepped back hastily as the sword continued to head straight for him.

I recognized a flaxen mop higher than the other heads. "Sir Kendryck! Let him pass!"

The knights turned to see who dared give them orders, then stepped back.

"Sir Kendryck, I need you!" I panted as I hobbled by. "William is sleep walking. Someone go and tell Sir Hugh I need him, quickly."

The other knights guffawed at the idea of a mere adept summoning the marshal, but by then I was past them and I had my oversized Saxon friend striding along at my side.

"Is this sorcery, Adept? You enchanted him?"

"Yes."

"*Scitte!*"

"Don't let anyone stop him until you know where he's going. But don't let him hurt himself—or anyone else."

"Me especially," Kendryck said in his usual breezy fashion, but nothing would ever ruffle him. He lengthened his stride until he was close behind the madman.

Rounding one more corner, William headed straight for the main gate, which the guards were just swinging shut. I foresaw disaster, but sent Heaven a quick prayer of thanks for Kendryck, who bellowed at them to wait a moment, to let the squire through, and also the adept just coming . . . and to send word to Sir Hugh that all three would need to be allowed back in again.

Gasping, perspiring with both exertion and terror of what might still happen, I ran the gauntlet of the guards' suspicious stares and left the stockade. The gate thundered shut behind me. I might have to spend the night out here, but I had much worse trouble on my hands than that. Whatever had drawn William out here could not be the murderer, who had proved himself to be a trusted resident of the castle. We might be hot on the trail of a poacher or a heavy-thumbed, price-gouging butcher. Guy had warned me the effects of the spell were unpredictable: *he walked out into the town and tried to break into the home of a complete stranger . . .*

But William had not gone into the village. Still clutching his sword, he was stumbling along the edge of the moat that encircled the stockade. He was finding the bank hard going in the dusk, for it was overgrown with thistles and brambles, sloping down into rushes at the water's edge; and it was much harder going for me. My clerical gown had not been designed for rough terrain or my lopsided hobble. Soon I lost sight of my quarry, but I could see some of the guards from the gate parading along the top of the stockade, watching the chase. Other people had begun to join them. Whatever was going to happen was not going to lack witnesses.

Then shouts broke out ahead—Kendryck's roars of anger combined with shrill, almost animal, screams that could only be coming from the entranced William. There was a fight going on. While the kid was a brawler and tough as chain mail, he was no match for a hulking, seasoned warrior like Kendryck. He would be slaughtered. Again cursing my own folly and presumption, I tried to go even faster, but my good foot slid in the mud and I promptly fell flat on my face. The spectators on the battlements were laughing at something, although apparently not me, so nobody was dying yet.

By the time my staggering gait had brought me to the battlefield, the fight was over. William was sitting in the brambles, sobbing like a whipped child. Kendryck was standing over him, drenched in the blood that still ran from his damaged nose. He was also supporting his right arm with his left hand in the way people do when they have broken a collarbone.

"What in the name of Hell have you done to him, Adept?" he roared. "I'd rather fight a she-bear any day."

"He's pugnacious," I conceded, going down carefully on one knee to examine the squire. "William?"

"He stopped us," William sobbed in a twisted, warbling voice quite unlike his own. "We were going to get it and he stopped us! It's over *there*." He pointed an arm at the moat.

There was no sign of his sword anywhere, and that would have to be found. The crowd of spectators along the top of the stockade had grown. Many held torches as the October dark closed in.

"William, say a prayer. Say a Paternoster."

"We couldn't get at it from the other side, so we came around, and then he *stopped* us. We were going to kill him, Sage, but he was too strong for us."

"You did a job on him." There would be the devil to pay over this, I was certain. "Now say a prayer."

"We'll get it for you now." William tried to rise and I pushed him down.

"Say *Pater*, William. Say it! Now say *Noster*."

The boy repeated the words as if they were just noises at first, and then faster, and gradually more in his own voice. When he had finished and crossed himself he peered up at me and said, uncertainly "Adept?"

"Yes. Say another Paternoster, just to be sure."

"Sir Kendryck!" bellowed a voice from the other side of the moat. "What is going on over there?" It was the marshal himself.

"What's going on here, Sir Hugh," Kendryck roared back in a very nasal distortion of his own voice, "is that I have just had the *scitte* beaten out of me by a runt half my size. The adept cast a spell on him. I got his sword off of him, but had to throw it in the moat to keep him from taking it back. He's stronger than a stud bull! He's broken my arm, loosened half my teeth, and mashed my face to jelly."

"Saints preserve us. What was he doing, anyway?"

"He was trying to walk across the moat, Marshal." Kendryck was having trouble holding his nose to stop the bleeding while his only good hand was holding up the opposite elbow. Even in his pain and humiliation, he still gave the impression that he was enjoying himself, with laughter lurking just below the surface.

"Adept, you'd better explain all this."

"I think . . . can you see anything below you, Sir Hugh? The squire thought there was something . . . down in the rushes, I expect. In the water."

Torches were held out, arms pointed, voices mumbled.

William began to rise, spurning the hand I offered.

"Better now?"

"The voices have all gone. You enchanted me!"

"Entranced you. It was part of what we were doing. What were you looking for, do you remember?"

William shook his head, frowning, still somewhat dazed.

"Hope you know how to shtop my node beeding, Adep'." Kendryck was taking his humiliating injuries amazingly well, but there was no disgrace in a swordsman being overcome by enchantment.

Men cried out in alarm on the castle side of the moat—they had found something. The marshal's bellow drowned out the rest, shouting across, "Sir Kendryck, come back to the gate and bring those two lunatics with you."

chapter 22

The gate was opened just enough to admit the three curfew-breakers, bringing them face to face with a torch-bearing crowd. The man in front and indisputably in charge was Sir Hugh Fiennes, but Master of Horse Alwin stood right behind him, together with several of the knights whom I had met at midday dinner, which felt so long ago now. And at least half the population of the castle, it seemed, had gathered in the background to watch.

"Sweet Jezebel!" the marshal roared at the sight of Kendryck. Then he looked at the scratched and waterlogged, but otherwise unharmed, William. "This *brat* did that to *you*?"

If he expected Kendryck to apologize or whine, he should have known better. The big Saxon was determined to find it funny—which was the best defense when all his peers certainly would. "Well, Marshal," he said in his stuffed, nasal voice, "he did start with a sword. I got hold of it, but I needed both of my hands to overpower one of his, so he still had a fist free to punch with. I think he broke a few of my ribs. And after I got the sword away from him and threw it in the moat, he went after it and I had to go after him and haul him out. . . ."

The marshal rounded on me. "Adept, you enchanted this squire of yours?"

"Um, yes, sir. Well, entranced, but not . . . not like that, sir."

"Not like what? Explain!"

Almost without realizing it, I saw a chance to wrest some advantage from this setback. "I tasked him with finding the evildoer, sir. I did not grant him magical fighting powers. He is by nature an extremely powerful fighter. I shall reprimand him for losing his temper with Sir Kendryck."

Sir Hugh turned to stare at William. "Are you, indeed?" he demanded of William. "I was told you accepted several challenges at dinner today."

"Yes, sir." William had recovered most of his wits and was having trouble keeping a straight face—small wonder when he had roughed up a man so much bigger than himself.

Hugh could still glare, but his voice gave him away. "What's going to happen when you have to make good on those contests?"

If any of them would dare face him after this.

"I'm not planning to inflict any serious damage on them, sir, just adjust some of their manners."

Someone at the back started to laugh. Sir Hugh swung around in anger. "What are you all doing, standing around there gawking? Go and eat if you want any supper. Alwin, find dry clothes for the squire and clean ones for Kendryck. Adept, you'd better treat this victim of yours. As soon as you've done that, report to me. I'll likely be with His Lordship."

"Yes, Marshal." But I could not restrain a question. "May I ask what it was that William had located in the moat at the base of the stockade?"

"It's too dark to tell. We'll look again in the morning, but I think it's only a dead sheep."

The total silence that followed suggested that he was the only one who did.

The castle infirmary was one of the larger sheds, having room enough for four beds, three chests, and a table. As soon as candles had been set in the sconces and I had located the rags that served for bandages, I began by plugging Kendryck's nose to stop the bleeding, and then fashioned a sling to support his useless arm—nothing difficult so far.

"I'll give you a potion to deaden the pain," I said. Dwale, maybe.

"Oh, no you won't. It'll put me to sleep and I've got plans for tonight."

Alwin arrived with clean clothes for the casualty, accompanied by a dry William. Alwin insisted on helping the patient strip off his tunic and shirt. Broken ribs were not an injury I had ever treated before, but I knew the principle and the problem was easily located at a swelling welt on the right side of the knight's chest. When William saw that, he ostentatiously inspected the knuckles of his left hand for damage. There did not seem to be any.

I bound up the ribs as tightly as I could. "I think they're just badly bruised, but I suggest you refrain from strenuous exercise for the next week."

Kendryck tried to shrug and winced. "I'll make her do all the work, then." Alwin helped him dress.

I was left with no further excuse for delay. Telling my helper to tidy up after me, I set off to report to the marshal.

Doctoring Kendryck had taken longer than I realized. Servants were converting the great hall from dining room to dormitory, so it seemed that I would miss supper. I was told that Sir Hugh was with the count, but no one offered to knock on the door for me, so I did it myself and was told to enter.

The parlor was much changed from when I had seen it that morning. Now it was back to its usual purpose. Rolf's deathbed had been removed, the other furniture rearranged, fresh rushes spread on the floor, and the air smelled pleasantly of lavender and wood smoke. Count Richard and the marshal sat at a small table, dawdling over a generous spread, but a third stool stood empty beside them, which was encouraging.

I touched a knee to the floor.

"Welcome," the count said. "Come and sup with us."

Saints! Last night I had bunked with the stable hands. Since then I had identified two deaths as murder, pulled off a major incantation, treated the victim of that enchantment, and now I was breaking bread with nobility. "I am honored, my lord."

Lord Richard grunted to imply that I should be.

Sir Hugh said, "Wine . . . no, wait." He filled his own goblet from the wine jug, drained it, and then filled mine.

"Sir, that wasn't necessary!"

The count said, "I am ashamed to admit that I agree with Hugh that you deserve that reassurance. Too many of your calling have died within my doors. Tell him, Hugh."

The marshal was holding the remains of a goose leg. He finished chewing and swallowed. "If that's a sheep down among the rushes, it's the biggest sheep since Jason and the golden fleece. It may not be a human body, but I think it is, and I am willing to bet that it's the remains of a boy called Colby."

"Sage Archibald's varlet," the count added. "He disappeared about a week ago. He had only been here a month or so and was reported to be extremely homesick. We assumed he'd run away."

No trenchers here! I had been provided with a shiny metal plate, which at the time I thought must be silver. Looking back,

I am sure now that it was only pewter, but it impressed me. I began loading it with cheese, bread, cold roast goose, onions, and pickles. "Homesick enough to take his own life, my lord?"

"Granted that self-murder is a very great sin and we wish him no ill in the next world, we must hope so. But a sage's lad followed so closely by two sages . . . now I fear he may have been the first victim of the same killer."

"I fear so also, my lord. The incantation I performed was designed to seek out evil, and although the wording did not allow me to name the evil, surely murder must be the worst. I had hoped the spell would lead me to the killer of your brother and your sage. But instead it led me to another body. So I believe that the third death must be connected."

My listeners exchanged glum glances at having their fears confirmed.

"Have you established how Sage Archibald died?"

"Aye, my lord. He was poisoned, but not with the same poison as Rolf. He was sitting at the end of the high table, so my first thought was that his neighbor, Father Randolf, must have done it, but I soon decided that this was impossible."

"I could have told you that!" Count Richard roared. "To suspect a man of God of such crimes is unthinkable. You will not get far if you waste time on fantasies such as that."

"No, my lord. Of course you are right. I soon realized that no poison known to my craft causes death so quickly, and he must have ingested the toxin before he even reached the hall. Father Randolf met him on the way here, when he was already confused by the venom. Without the priest's help he might not have arrived at all."

"Randolf setting a fine Christian example," the count murmured. "But I keep you from your repast. Eat up. Wine, Hugh?"

For a few moments he and the marshal discussed the damage caused by the deluge, now apparently ended, while allowing their guest to eat in peace. Inevitably, they came back at length to the problem of the thing in the moat.

"We'll start at first light," the marshal said, "and keep the rabble away until we know what we've found. I sent word to Randy, because he'll want to be there. It will have to be done before the funeral mass, I'm afraid, but I'll warn the gatekeepers to let him in."

"A body that has been in the moat for over a week may be unidentifiable. Pike and eels, not to mention maggots."

His Lordship did *not* have to mention that while I was eating.

"That is so, but he was only a boy. There can hardly be two of his age missing. I hope the priest will not quibble about giving him Christian burial."

"I shall have a word with him if he does," the count said darkly. "Three funerals in three days! Word will get out."

"That . . ." The marshal hesitated, glancing momentarily in my direction. "That might not be altogether a bad thing, my lord."

"What'ja mean by that, eh?"

"Mean it can't be kept secret any longer, Dick."

The count grunted, but he nodded, admitted to understanding the hint this time.

Whatever they were discussing was clearly not intended for the Saxon lad, who was content to continue sampling the finer fruits of the rich. The wine was sweeter by far than the sample Guy had given me to celebrate my promotion, even if the bottler had reviled it. The cheese and white bread were superb, too. I had noted the marshal taking another goose leg from the heap, so I took a second for myself, and more onions too. Never in my life had I had eaten meat twice in one day.

There were two questions I greatly wanted to put to the count. Either might give serious offense, but the first could probably be answered by no one else, so eventually I would have to risk it. Not yet, though. Finish the meal first!

Seen at close quarters, the count's axe-blade nose had probably been broken and expertly reset at some time in the past. I would certainly try healing spells on Sir Kendryck's, but doubted I could ever do so fine a job.

"'Harassed,' I think you said," the count mused. "Did you mean just boyish bullying? Or worse?"

"Worse, I fear, my lord," Hugh said. "They don't talk to me, of course, but my squires keep me informed of trouble. They told me after he disappeared that the other youths seemed to have accepted Colby quite well. There was some hazing, naturally, there always is. But nothing unusual. But . . ." Hugh grimaced. "He was a pretty kid."

"Who, then? Archibald himself?"

The marshal chuckled. "Archibald's tastes were quite orthodox, to an extreme degree. Let me ask around, Dick. I don't want to go accusing anyone without cause."

"Of course." Richard de Mandeville turned his piercing eyes back on me. "I would have you sing for my brother tomorrow."

"I should be honored to do so, my lord. I will try to be worthy of his instruction."

The old man nodded, staring into the past. "Rolf always loved music. Even as a child, he was always going around singing: lays, psalms, anything he had heard. Remember, Hugh? I will tell Father Randolf to call you forward, lad."

Hugh had spoken that morning as if he and the de Mandeville brothers were all about the same age, but graybeard Richard looked a generation older than Rolf had. Now he carried a burden he might never lose: his brother had come hastening to his rescue and been poisoned in his house. He roused himself.

"Have you other incantations in your armory, Adept? Can you identify this monster for us?"

"I hope so, my lord. I will need time . . . I feel like a squire called upon to lead an army."

Hugh chuckled. "Rank matters a lot less than fortitude, lad. I remember a stable boy, probably younger than you are now, who charged into the Battle of Winchester on foot armed with only a battle-axe, and brought down three mounted knights. I think he singlehandedly held up King Stephen's forces long enough for the rest of us to get Empress Maud away to safety."

"I'll do my best, sir, but don't expect me to match that." I hadn't charged anywhere since I was nine.

"You've met him—Alwin. He fights like a madman, as if he were immortal, and there isn't a horse in Christendom he can't handle. That's why the lads put up with his odd ways. And if you are wondering whether Alwin abused Colby, I assure you that he has no interest whatsoever in children. Hairy chests are what speed his heartbeat."

"Let us know if there is anything you need," the count said, as if he was about to depart. "This matter is most urgent."

Why? "I'd like to be there when you raise the corpse in the rushes, if I may. And attend Sage Rolf's funeral. And . . ." *Go for it!* "There are a couple of things that still puzzle me, my lord. . . . They may be irrelevant, but may I ask two possibly impertinent questions?"

Sir Hugh raised his eyebrows and drained his goblet.

The count frowned and growled, "Ask them and I'll tell you how impertinent they are."

The more I saw of these two, the more certain I became that Sir Hugh was not only the count's right hand but most of his brain, too.

"On Monday your house sage collapsed at dinner and died a few hours later. I suspect that you summoned your unfortunate brother by the use of the incantation *Despero in extremis?*"

The little room seemed to go very still.

"Why do you think that?"

"Because I was present when he heard you. He—"

"Had a sort of fit. He told me when he got here. What of it?"

"*Why?* I am aware, my lord, that a sage is a valuable retainer, but a man of your station could easily find a replacement in Northampton or London or many places. Why was Archibald de la Mare's attack so important, so urgent, that you used a major incantation, which I assume you and your brother had been holding in reserve for years?"

"Told you he was good." The marshal reached for the wine jug.

"Yes, it is impertinent. Is your second one any more respectful?"

"It may be completely irrelevant. Your lamented and honored brother, my lord, forbade me to wear my adept's cape on our journey, and kept his green one under his cloak. He insisted on detouring around Northampton. If he had enemies there . . ."

Count Richard was shaking his head. "That is not irrelevant, but not what you think either. I see I must take you into my confidence and should have done so sooner. But no one, absolutely no one, must hear of this!"

Worried now, I pledged my word.

"Are you as skilled in astrology as you are in the other arts you have demonstrated?"

"I have been taught the principles, my lord, but the answer is no, I have had no experience outside the classroom. Just as each knight may excel with a particular weapon, some sages favor some of the many arts available." I, for example, dearly wished I had a set of futhorc tiles with me, but Guy had refused to lend me his. I suspected he had wanted to try my mended version of *Hwæt segst* for himself.

The count shrugged. "Archibald was. Incredibly so! He foretold my son-in-law's death before it happened, and my daughter and grandson's return before she even made that decision. A month ago he warned me that I was in very serious danger. Not necessarily death, he said, but devastating."

The sage had not foreseen his own murder, but even skilled astrologers are often blind to their personal futures.

The count folded his big fists together on the table and stared at them. "The day before he died, he told me that the trouble would come from the king."

The king? I had certainly not expected that. Sir Hugh was watching me closely.

"King Henry is currently in this area," the count continued. "He often comes here for the hunting, but he is currently holding a council in Northampton Castle. My son is one of his gentlemen of the chamber. His Grace disapproves of private castles, and it was only through Stephen's good standing with His Grace that I dared request permission to repair some of my fortifications. He will likely want to see for himself what I have done and plan to do. I expect him here any day."

Saints preserve! My hand shook as I reached for my goblet. *The king?* Why hadn't they told me sooner? This changed everything.

"So when Sage Archibald was so mysteriously stricken," the count continued, "my first thought was of King Henry, may God preserve him. He is notorious for his mobility. He rarely spends more than three or four days in one place, and his moves are totally unpredictable. He announces plans and changes them without warning . . . you are nodding?"

"Um, I wasn't aware of doing so, my lord. But I do see the danger. You were worried that Sage Archibald suspected a treasonous conspiracy and was silenced so that he could not sniff out the traitor."

"Exactly. Anyone planning to assassinate the king, God forbid, will have difficulty just knowing where to find him. The present council was announced well in advance, but striking at him in his own fortress of Northampton Castle would be close to impossible. Here in Barton he would be much more vulnerable. Remember that his great-uncle, the second King William, was struck down by an assassin's arrow. If the traitor or traitors know that he is likely to come here, then their task would become much easier.

"That was why I called for my brother. He agreed he would come at once. He came and met the same terrible fate as Archibald."

And now the burden fell on my shoulders.

Implications buzzed like flies in a slaughterhouse. Even if no attempt was made, a nobleman honored by the arrival of his sovereign but then having to explain on his knees that he couldn't guarantee his liege's safety in his own house would face absolute ruin and possibly a few years in the Tower of London.

Sir Hugh broke the silence. "It's easy to see why Archibald and then Rolf might have been seen as threats to the traitors, but the boy Colby disappeared a week ago. He was a newcomer to the castle. I can't see him being part of such a plot, or a threat to the plotters."

"I can," I said. "Someone left muddy footprints on a downstairs window ledge of the sanctum. If Colby was spying on Sage Archibald, he may have overheard dangerous secrets."

Sir Hugh thumped a fist on the table. "By George, you're fast, lad! And now everyone knows it. You'd better keep close watch on your own back from now on."

"We have a fine king," I protested. "But who would want to harm him?" Must we return to the Anarchy? Chaos and civil war again?

Sir Hugh snorted like a horse. "Louis of France, for one. Even the pope! Lad, the man is the most powerful monarch in Christendom. He rules all of England and half of France—Normandy, Anjou, Aquitaine. Anyone with that much power has enemies."

"Or Bloody Becket," the count growled. "That upstart treacherous clerk! That's what the council is all about, they say—to bring Becket to heel."

The Archbishop of Canterbury? If any of this scandal had reached as far as Helmdon, it had not seeped down to the innocent boy who tended the academy's horses. News of Crown and Church at loggerheads appalled me.

"So I have answered your second question also, have I not?" asked the count.

I pulled my scattered wits together. "Um, yes, my lord." Rolf had not wanted to advertise that a sage was riding to Barton on a mission of such urgency that it justified traveling in weather any sane man would shun. And if he had passed through Northampton itself, he might have run into old friends, or his nephew, Sir Stephen de Mandeville.

The count smiled bitterly and drained his goblet. "Then summon up all your arts, Adept, and track down this monster who has made my house an abattoir. Remember that this game is being played for very high stakes, possibly even your king's life and the fate of half of Europe. Succeed, and I will be very generous. I bid you both good evening—and sound sleep."

We bowed as he rose and crossed the room to disappear into his bedchamber.

Hugh sat down again and gestured for me to do the same.

"I wish you had asked me those questions," the marshal said. "He is more worried than I have ever known him, and that is all my life, nearly, for I was fostered here. It is the only home I can remember."

And now it was in danger.

"Then tell me, Sir Hugh, who has recently come to Barton Castle? We are hunting a trained sage. He knows poisons. He is cunning, for he has overcome two of his own kind, and he must have entered the warded sanctum to obtain the poison that killed Rolf. He could be disguised as a knight, or a stable boy, or almost anyone."

"You think I haven't wondered that? No one since the Colby boy, I am certain. Everyone else has been with us for many, many years, or at least many months—long before the council was called. Except you and your squire, and you were not here to poison Sage Archibald. I am certain of this: I know everything that goes on in this castle." He poured out the last of the wine for me.

"Besides," he went on, "the poisoner must have been present in this room after the servants left. We agreed on that, did we not?"

I nodded. "Wacian told me he left a jug of water there. The poisoner switched it for the flask of poison. Unless Wacian is lying . . ."

"It is easier to imagine a rock flying. After he left there was nobody here except me and family, and I count as family."

"And Father Randolf, I think you said?"

"He's family, too—Richard's nephew, his sister's son."

That explained some of the arrogance, and also the count's anger when I had suggested the priest as a killer.

"A future bishop perhaps?"

"No perhaps about it—one of his father's brothers is a bishop. He has state on one side of his family and Church on the other.

But the boy's clever and straight as an arrow. He'll be a lot better bishop than some of those greedy, power-hungry preachers around Becket."

The count, the countess, the baroness . . . "Lady Aveline?"

Hugh shook his head. "She wasn't present that night. Usually she is, sitting in the corner like a mouse. She's just a servant, really, widow of a knight, which is why she is referred to as Lady Aveline. Childless, she gets to live in a castle and keep Matilda company until she can find a husband. Aveline can, I mean. I thought she had her eye on your patient, Sir Kendryck, but he's chasing other game at the moment."

Megan? I couldn't resist it: "Big game?"

Hugh smiled and nodded. "A worthy wench."

Two wine goblets on a table . . . Had Lady Aveline had occasion to consult Sage Archibald professionally that fateful morning? But if the motive behind these killings was to kill the king, everything else faded into unimportance.

Count, countess, sage, baroness, priest, marshal . . . just family and trusted retainers. Possibly the bottler. One of them had to be a murderer.

"How deep is this rift between the king and the archbishop?"

"You mean could it be deep enough to cause a man of God to commit murder?" Hugh shook his head. "I can't believe matters would ever come to that. The countess could tell you. She's more interested in such matters than I am, or even Richard. Randy would know, but he would give you all of the archbishop's side of the matter and not a word of the king's. Or ask Kendryck. He went to Northampton at the weekend, and there is a brain inside all that brawn. Adept," he said with sudden anger in his tone, "is it possible to enchant a person into committing a crime and then forgetting about it?"

"I don't know, sir. I am only an adept, and do not know the limits of enchanters' powers, especially dark powers like that. I did not order my squire to attack Kendryck. He did so because the knight tried to stop him from doing what the incantation required him to do. And he can't remember what happened while he was in that trance."

For a moment we brooded in silence. Then the marshal smiled. "You're out on your feet, lad. Go and get some sleep. Things are usually easier to see in daylight."

chapter 23

ugh insisted on sending two men-at-arms with lanterns to see me safely back to the sanctum. It was a flattering gesture, but a worrisome one, a reminder that my public display of magic earlier in the evening must have attracted the enmity of the unknown killer. William was already flat out and snoring; his presence warmed the bed, but not as well as five horses had warmed the academy stable. Aware that the killer knew how to bypass the wards on the door, I closed the hatch and placed a stool on it.

Without doubt it was the most comfortable bed I had ever lain in, but despite that, for almost the first time in my life, I did not sleep well. Long before dawn I started fully awake, recalling that the count had provided me with another motive for the murder of Sage Archibald. If his theory was right, then a common thread tying Rolf's death to Archibald's—and possibly even to Colby's—was a fear of being unmasked by magic. The killer himself was either an actual sage, or at least wise enough in the arcane arts to open a warded door and identify poisons. My task, therefore, must be to discover the incantation he feared. If necessary, I could add a third voice—the clerk Elmer probably had a smattering of dog Latin—and try the *Malefice venite* in Guy's grimoire. But I had not yet discovered Archibald's library. The killer might have removed it.

Or not. I slid out of bed into the cold night air.

When the roosters began to call and the windows showed gray, William came scrambling down the ladder, half dressed, unshaven, and tousled. I was at the table, surrounded by books and lime wood tablets.

"You never sleep?"

"It's a waste of time. I found Sage Archibald's grimoires, see?"

"You are too farting good to be true, Ironfoot! Where?"

I discovered that I very much enjoyed baiting my reluctant assistant. "There had to be a hiding hole. It wouldn't be under the floor, because you don't store books in damp places. So I looked around, and wondered why the fireplace was so big." The hearth itself was barely two feet wide, but the masonry extended at least six feet farther on one side than the other. "So I scanned for a warding, as I showed you. Try it—but don't touch!"

Growling obscenities under his breath, William passed an open hand over the face of the stonework in ever-widening circles. "No!"

"Try that big square slab. Strewth, man, it even looks like a cupboard door!"

This time the squire nodded. "It feels cool, maybe."

Progress at last! "It was easier for me," I admitted. "The curse was very strong—far too strong, I'd say, when anyone might brush against it by accident. It was vicious! I'm not sure, but I think it would have burned its victims, or given them an agony in the bowels."

"So what did you do?"

"I exorcised it."

"A demon?" William demanded, alarmed.

"No. 'Exorcism' comes from a Greek word meaning to call out an oath. I removed the spell, in other words. Then I replaced it with one of my own." I was bragging, wallowing in my own cleverness in performing a difficult incantation, but I could justify some of my vaunting if it would just inspire William with an interest in enchantment. "Go ahead and try it. The password is *William Legier.*"

He shot me a hard look. "Keeping it simple so the thick oaf won't forget it?"

"No, keeping it relevant so you won't think I'm lying to you."

William spoke his name. Nothing happened.

"You have to say that and then push."

That done, the slab yielded slightly, then swung forward to reveal the cavity behind.

Pause, then: "Thank you for this lesson, master."

However the words were meant, and they sounded sincere, they made me feel like a loudmouth, arrogant braggart.

"The lesson being," I said, "that anything one sage can do, another can undo. And in one of these grimoires I've located an incantation I think can help us: *Morðor wile ut.*"

"*Morðor?*"

"Murder. *Murder wants out.*"

William shrugged, and then smiled, running a hand through his tousled hair. "Will I get to thrash any more knights?"

"You can thrash anyone you want as soon as we've caught the killer, if that's the reward you want."

"One adept and seven squires will do nicely." But he was still smiling. For the first time ever, we were sharing humor. The partnership was prospering.

I sighed. "Meanwhile we have to go and watch a child's body being fished out of the moat. Not something to look forward to. You'd better get dressed."

The prospect would have been even less inviting had we been required to help. As it was, adept and squire shivered on the cat-walk, peering over the parapet in the cold, hard light of sunrise. The stockade was rotting in places, patched in others, and in still others both patched and rotting, which was not surprising if it was almost a hundred years old. It was built of hardwood of some sort, but not oak, the most durable of timbers. I kept wondering if the catwalk itself was sound enough to support so many people.

Father Randolf was present, too. Arrogant he might be, but he took his calling seriously, for he need not be involved until the thing in the rushes was confirmed as a human corpse.

The marshal was in charge, and his knights were keeping other people away, although some villagers had gathered on the far bank to watch. Hugh could have had porters do the work, but he laid the disgusting job on a couple of nimble young squires. They were lowered on ropes by some of the larger knights, with Kendryck excused because of his injuries. The youths wailed dramatically as they sank to their waists in the icy, stinking water, staggering as they tried to find footing in the mud and reeds.

"What is it?" the marshal shouted.

"It's sheepskin, sir," one called.

They must have been tempted to let it go at that and get pulled out sooner, but they didn't.

"There's a bit of a leg sticking out at this end," said the other. He turned his head away and retched.

Their next problem was to fasten ropes to the slimy package without totally submerging themselves. Fortunately the bundle itself was bound up with ropes, so they could attach the hoists to those. Even when they had done that, their ordeal wasn't over, for the gruesome load rained water down on them as it was being raised. By the time it reached the top of the stockade, a stretcher was waiting for it. The priest tried to say a prayer right then, but Hugh made him wait until the shivering squires had been hauled up, thanked, and sent off to clean up. Only then did everyone bare their heads in reverence.

As the shrouded stretcher was being lowered down to the bailey, still dribbling water and worms, William said, "Now what happens, master?"

"They'll take it to the infirmary, I expect. Then we'll see who it is."

He shuddered. "You don't need me there, do you?"

"Not in there," I said, "but I want you outside it with a wheelbarrow. You can bring a porter to push that if you want. A pitchfork might be a good idea, too." Leaving my appalled assistant to work it out for himself, I followed the cortège.

The stretcher was laid on the infirmary floor. Hugh dismissed everyone except the priest and me, but I had already guessed that I would be given the horrible job of opening the parcel. The stench of moat and decay was overpowering. Refusing to use my belt knife, the one I used at table, I hunted through the stores until I found another.

"Tanned sheepskin with the hair outside," I said, "bound with ordinary hemp cord." Which I then cut. "Any chance of identifying where either of those came from, sir?"

"None," Hugh said. "We have a thousand fleeces in the castle and a hundred miles of rope." Both he and Randolf were standing several paces back, near the open door where the air was fresher.

I knelt, awkward as always. "This is a rug of six or eight fleeces sewn together; it's far too big for one." I cut the ropes and pushed the wrapping open with the knife. "You do have pike in the moat."

It was obvious that something had been scavenging the corpse, for there was little flesh left on the head and legs. The arms and much of the thorax were better preserved, having been harder to reach. Bloated by gases, the torso had swelled inside its wrapping, keeping out the larger flesh eaters, yet it was still infested with some sort of worm or maggot. I struggled to focus on each separate detail, because to look at the overall object and see a body was unbearable.

"The gristle on this leg bone isn't set yet, so just a youth. Even a couple of twelve-year-old molars are not fully through yet. Fairly tall for his age, I would think. Traces of hair, light brown. Did Colby . . ." A spasm of nausea made me turn away.

"I think it's Colby," Hugh said. "You agree, Father?"

"I didn't know the boy well enough to be sure. He obviously didn't bundle himself up like that, so we can rule out self-slaughter. Can you tell us how he died, Durwin?"

"No, Father. He could have been strangled or poisoned or stabbed and there wouldn't be any evidence left."

"I will arrange for Christian burial. Did he have any family in the area, Hugh?"

"I have no idea. We can ask Wacian to make inquiries."

The priest said, "Cover him with the shroud, Adept, and I will send the gravediggers to collect him."

Priest and marshal made a fast exit.

Still on my knees, I peered more closely at the corpse, but I could find no puncture wounds, no marks on the neck tissue. There was just too little evidence and there were too many ways for a strong adult to kill a child. Wiping my hands as best I could on bandage rags, I rose and went to investigate raised voices outside. I found the marshal, the priest, William, and a porter, with both a wheelbarrow and a pitchfork. William had mysteriously recovered the sword that Sir Kendryck had thrown into the moat. Randolf was making the noise.

He spun around to accost me. "Explain this sacrilege! The boy says you told him to fetch this obscene object." He meant either the fork or the barrow. Didn't matter which.

"I did, Father. I mean no disrespect to the departed. The fork is to grip the fleece, not to move the body. I want the fleece pulled out from under him and taken back to the sanctum. He would be left on the stretcher."

"What sort of morbid purpose can possibly justify such a gruesome interest?" The priest was scarlet with rage.

I kept my voice as respectful as I could. This was my business, not Randolf's. "It is a long shot, but I believe the fleece might lead us to the murderer."

"After you have practiced some black art on it, I suppose?"

"I have an incantation that might provide some information."

"Satanism! This is too close to necromancy. I forbid you to do any such thing."

"With respect, Father, the body is your concern. The wrapping is a secular matter and I am charged by His Lordship to track down this monster who has murdered three people." I looked to Sir Hugh, hoping for support.

Hugh was stone-faced, not taking sides. The listening porter was goggle-eyed with horror, either because of this talk of murder or at my defiance of the priest. William was enjoying the spectacle, eager to see how I would fare.

Randolf made an obvious effort to control his temper. "And I say you are committing mortal sin. You will report this insubordination at your next confession. Hugh, my son, you will forbid such desecration?"

The marshal had not reached his present eminence by avoiding issues. He sighed. "Adept, there must be no desecration. You will not disturb the body of this unfortunate youth in any way. Father, the fleece is a valuable property in its own right; it should be salvaged and returned to its rightful owner, but the common folk fear to touch anything so closely associated with death. You are protected by your calling, and I consider it both brave and public-spirited of the adept to offer to exorcise it, once the grave-diggers have removed the corpse."

"Thank you, sir," I said humbly.

Randolf spun on his heel and stalked away.

The marshal looked at me, I looked at the marshal. Neither of us put the thought into words, but we were both wondering: why so much anger?

"Sir Hugh, I am commanded to sing at Sage Rolf's funeral. Can you spare a reliable person to see that the barrow and its contents are taken to the sanctum and remain otherwise untouched?"

The big man nodded, understanding exactly what had not been said. "I'll send Sir Kendryck. You've damaged him so much that he's no good for anything else. You'd better wait here to instruct Kendryck in what is needed."

"You are kind, sir. William will be coming to the funeral also, of course."

The moment the marshal was out of earshot, William said, "Enlighten me, master, as to why a priest should be so frothed up over a sheepskin rug."

"I don't know, Squire. I was hoping you could tell me. I wonder if he's aware of the incantation *Morðor wile ut*? Meanwhile, I need you to hightail back to the sanctum. I left the grimoires in full view on the table, and I don't want them to disappear during our absence."

chapter 24

The village church was a tiny building attached to the east side of its great tower, somewhat like a foot on a leg. It had been built to hold the population of a village, not a village plus the garrison of a castle as well. Although few would have remembered Rolf, for he had been gone from Barton for many years, everyone who could walk turned out to pay respects to their lord's brother. Those who could not pack inside just crowded around outside. Father Randolf had the door and shutters left open so they might hear.

Even so, he kept the proceedings short, for he was a man more of righteousness than comfort, and the cold gloom of the Saxon church set a matching mood. Yet its ancient stones were kind to music. Forewarned by the mass and a hymn from the congregation, I limped forward when summoned, eager to hear my own voice resonate in such a space.

The priest gave me a note on a pitch pipe, although I did not ask for one. Hoping to be worthy of the man who had taught me, I sang a troubadour ballad of farewell, "Sparrow Passing By." It had been one of the dead man's favorites and I tried to render it with all the craft that Rolf himself had put into it when he sang it. The church cooperated fully, and I finished with tears in my eyes. As I returned to my seat I noticed quite a few sleeves being used for wiping.

"Master," William said on the way out, "that was very fine. I am sure that Sage Rolf himself would have applauded."

That was the first compliment I had ever received from him. I said, "Thank you, William, I appreciate that."

At the church door, Rolf's brother the count said the same with much blinking. I reluctantly decided that this was not an appropriate moment to raise the matter of sponsorship for my continued education, and made a note to confess the sin of pride at my next confession.

When William and I returned to the sanctum, we found the wheelbarrow parked outside, and a lanky youth pacing up and down, trying to keep warm. Even without the fact that he was dressed as a squire, one glance at him would have been enough to tell me whose brother he was.

"This is Squire Kenric, Adept," William said.

Kenric hesitated, then touched his forehead in salute to me. "My knight said you wanted this guarded, Adept."

"I don't want it, but unfortunately I need it. Thank you. . . . Before you go, did you know the sage's boy, Colby?"

"No, Adept." Kenric's expression stated emphatically that a knight's squire did not associate with riffraff like that.

"Pity. Then you may go with my thanks."

Kenric stiffened, turned pink, and said, "Squire William . . ."

The other fighting cock bristled to match. "Squire Kenric?"

"My knight has ordered . . . He says that you are so dangerous that I must withdraw my challenge to you."

William took a moment to consider this request and ooze a few bucketfuls of contempt. Then he looked to me. "What do you think, master? Should I permit this? This muttonhead said he would make me eat my balls."

"Squire, I have warned you and warned you," I said sternly. "Sooner or later you are going to kill someone with those fists of yours. That man you battered yesterday was very lucky that I was available to stop you and save him from permanent deformity."

Kenric gulped appropriately.

William sighed. "Oh, very well. You can stop worrying, boy. I'll let you off this time—provided you make a full apology at the dining table, with a frank admission that I am a better man than you are."

Kenric shuddered. "He just said I must ask. I'd never apologize to trash like you."

William beamed. "Then I will make you polish your horse's shoes with your tongue as I promised."

Normans! They conquered France, they conquered England, Sicily, Russia, Jerusalem . . . anywhere they went. Living was what they did to fill up the time between fights, and in their eyes it wasn't nearly so much fun. Now they were teaching honest Saxons to think the same way.

"Good. I'll be there, snot." Kenric strode off with a spring in his step.

William gave me a triumphant smile. "See? Now will you stop trying to mother me, Saxon? Do you want me to bring this, *yuck*, load inside?"

"Not yet. We still have to rehearse the incantation. No one can get at it without our seeing them through the window."

The grimoires were safe in the secret locker where William had put them, but we were almost out of tablets to write on. I set my helper to sanding the used ones clean again with the sandstone block and began transcribing the versicles for *Morðor wile ut* onto one of the blank ones. Sanding was a standard chore for a sage's varlet, but a hated one. A couple of days ago William would probably have rammed the stone down my throat, but he accepted the assignment without a word of protest.

While he was doing it, I made his life more interesting, and also instructive, by reading the text aloud and having him guess the meaning of each phrase. In those days adolescent Normans usually denied any knowledge of the old tongue at all, but many had picked up a smattering from their nursemaids when they were little. I had been told that this long-forgotten skill often emerged when one of them found himself alone with a pretty girl.

I was halfway through *Morðor wile ut* when someone tapped softly on the door.

Scuffing his hands together to clean the dust off, William jumped up to answer the summons, then announced, "A woman wishes to see you, master. Says she is Udela the seamstress, relict of Udell."

I sighed. *That new sage the count has appointed—a Saxon, can you believe it? So young! And a cripple!* Now that my reputation had spread, every sore finger and constipated bowel would be trooping in to get a good look at me.

"Bid Widow Udela enter, then." I rose.

She had dressed in her best, although a seamstress would always display her own handiwork. Her gown, bonnet, and shawl were finely made and of passable material. She was likely in her late thirties, but still attractive enough that she should not remain a widow long. Clusters of lines around her eyes suggested that too much close work was taking a toll on her sight—I hoped she did not expect me to treat that. She wore a purse at her waist.

Udela curtseyed. I acknowledged with a respectful nod, not quite a bow, but she seemed flattered.

"I am Adept Durwin, mistress. Pray be seated there and tell me how I may serve." I sat down as she settled on the stool I indicated.

"It is a medical problem, Adept." She glanced at William.

"A good physician keeps his patients' secrets like a good priest keeps his flock's. My assistant would not talk either, but he will leave if that is your wish."

To my surprise she nodded. If mere nosiness was her motive and all she wanted was to be the first to consult the new sage, then she should have just invented a headache and asked for a powder. If she were about to plead some woman's complaint, why had she not brought a female companion along for decency's sake? Or was indecency what she wanted? Had Archibald's womanizing tarred all sages with the reputation of stud rams?

Or she might have come to kill me.

"William," I said. "That person that Squire Kenric did not know . . . I would dearly like to speak with any close friends he had." I spoke in French, but yet still guarded my words because in those days many Saxons understood more French than they usually admitted.

Yesterday my squire would likely have responded with an obscenity. Today he said, "Of course, master," and went out.

Relict Udela studied her hands. "It is three years since Udell died, Adept. There is a man . . ."

I said, "Ah! If it is the state of your soul that concerns you, mistress, then go seek out Father Randolf. I am concerned with bodily things, and I am old enough to know what happens when a man and a woman are inflamed by passion." And not just in theory, although my experience was more limited than I wished.

She did not smile, nor look at me. "In truth, Adept, now there is another man."

This time I waited.

"And I will not tempt him into sin so I can pass off my previous transgression as his. He is honorable."

And she was not a skilled liar. My staff lay on the floor, I had nothing within reach that would serve as a weapon. I was undoubtedly stronger than she, but if she came at me with a knife to expand her collection of sages, then I might not be nimble enough to survive her attack. But William had seen her, and William would flatten her if she lay in wait for his return.

"You come seeking a miscarriage, mistress."

She nodded.

"That is simple, a draft that I can mix at once, a short spell I will chant, and two days' extreme discomfort. And a confession to the priest. Promoting miscarriage is not a crime, but it is a sin."

She sighed, perhaps with relief, but still did not look up. "In payment—perhaps a pair of gloves for the winter? My stitching is much praised, and I have some offcuts of kidskin that will serve."

"Count Richard will pay me," I said, although he had never said so, only that he would reward me if I could unmask the killer. "And a simple procedure like this would barely be worth three fingers, let alone all ten. But I must be quite certain that your problems are caused by what you believe, and also that matters have not progressed too far. If you will lie down for a moment on that . . ."

I stared at the bench under the window, with its hard leather surface. A thought stirred; I put it away for later.

"Adept, despite what I have told you, I am not a loose woman."

"And I am not a loose man. All I need do is lay a hand on your belly and palpate . . . and feel the size of the lump. You need not undress and it will take but a moment. Go and fetch a witness if you will."

Then as now, women's garments were voluminous, because the Church insists that they must mask the shape of the female body, lest it lure men into lechery.

Silence.

"Or just tell me the real story."

"I was sent by another," she whispered.

"To find out if this sage demanded the same price as the last one?"

She looked up, startled. And nodded.

"I have not lied to you about that. Were I that sort of lecher, you would have no need of gloves to make payment. But you are wasting my time. Go and fetch the other woman."

Udela shook her head. "She must not be seen . . ."

What lady could be so noticeable? And if she were who I at once suspected, what was her real motive in wanting to lure me to some unknown destination? I could not believe Baroness Matilda could want dalliance with Saxon trash like me, and she was one of the suspects in Rolf's murder. Was this a trap?

"I fear my present duties are too pressing for me to go calling on her today."

Udela nodded doubtfully. "If she comes here . . . you will be discreet?"

"Mistress, I have said so. If she needs my skills, they are available for the asking. There will be no price to pay, and I will not tell, or threaten to tell, her husband, lover, brothers, or father. But I have other, much more urgent, matters to deal with, so please decide."

"Then I shall go and ask her. It is not far."

I saw Widow Udela out and went back to work.

A sharper knock on the door came a few minutes later. Taking up my staff, I went to open it and invite the caller to enter.

She was tall, slender, and draped in black, including a heavier veil than I had seen her wearing in church that morning. She passed me without a word and marched over to the table, where she turned around before sitting on a stool, so she was facing me as I followed her from the door. Nothing of herself was exposed except pale hands clasped on her lap. No more than four women at the funeral had been garbed like that. I went down on one knee, steadying myself with my staff.

She drew breath. "Do you kneel to all your patients, Saxon? Rise!"

I stayed where I was. "I saw that turquoise ring as you went by me in the church, my lady." And now I recognized the whiff of rose water.

"Stand up, I said!"

"As my lady commands."

I rose. Baroness Matilda lifted back her veil and looked up at me angrily. For a few moments I just returned her inspection.

The angle was awkward for her, but gave me a perfect view of her glorious face. Seeing it fully for the first time, I realized why she had seemed so familiar: she was Edla. When I had first arrived at Helmdon, a gawky, lamed, and hopelessly homesick stable boy of fourteen, I had fallen head over heels in love with a girl in the village. Edla had been the same age as me, but taller, long-legged, and incredibly gorgeous—the same flaxen hair and gray eyes as Matilda, a complexion fresh as a summer dawn, lips to set men on fire. I had never dared speak to her, and within weeks she had been swept away into marriage by a boy from the next village. I still saw her sometimes, on market days, wizened like a dried apple, fat and toothless from childbearing, bent from field labor, her face weathered and blotched. Four children in six years—Matilda must be almost exactly Edla's age, but Matilda had borne a single child, which she would have fobbed off on a wet nurse at birth. She seemed as eternally young as a pagan goddess.

I was the first to look away. Matilda had not blushed, but I feared that I was about to. And I was not so spellbound that I had failed to notice her complete lack of interest in her surroundings. Not even the stuffed crocodile had deserved a second glance as she entered. She had been here before.

"Udela explained my problem to you?"

"We discussed ways to promote a miscarriage. I explained that it could be done with a potion and a simple incantation, and I would charge no fee."

The critical question, of course, was what Sage Archibald had charged for the same treatment, and whether the lady had submitted to his sexual blackmail without success. Red-hot meat hooks would not drag such questions out of me.

I had wondered why Udela the seamstress wanted to terminate an early-term pregnancy if she were about to remarry. Seven-month babies were a dozen a penny in Norman England. Tongues might wag, but most peasant fathers would swallow their doubts, especially if they were offered a healthy son. Gentry were less flexible, obsessed by the inheritance of wealth and the purity of bloodlines.

Matilda's family had the resources to let her bear a child in secret and foster it out. Was the father of such low status— stable boy, cowherd—that she dared not confess even to her mother? Udela's story of an impending betrothal would make much more sense if it applied to Matilda. Although common folk's weddings were often no more than an exchange of promises before two witnesses, landowners like the de Mandeville family made great festivals of them. Manors and forests might change hands.

"And tell no tales?"

"My lady, I will swear that on a bible if you so wish. You can trust Udela?"

"She has been with me for years. She makes all my clothes, and now my mother's also. She came back with me from Kilpeck."

For the count's daughter to pursue a secret love affair in an overcrowded cage like Barton Castle could not have been easy. Had Udela's cottage been the trysting place? And what of Lady Aveline, Matilda's companion, whose purpose was to provide respectability to a single lady. What had her silence cost?

"Proceed, then," the baroness commanded.

"I must ask some unpleasant questions, my lady. How long since your courses ceased?"

"The third was due a week ago."

Not a chance. Even at four months, her figure would not give her away in the draperies worn by high-rank ladies, but my trained eye ought to be detecting hints in her face already.

"I shall need to examine you. Please rise."

She did not. "What sort of examine?

"Just feel the swelling of your belly."

"For what purpose?"

"To confirm that you are as far advanced as you think."

"I have walked this road before, Adept. I know of what I speak."

"So do I. If you do not trust me, please find another healer."

"You are insolent. Proceed with the treatment." Her cheeks reddened. She was not accustomed to backtalk from servants.

"My lady, I must rely on my training and experience," I said stubbornly. "Enchantments can cause serious trouble if wrongly applied. I must consider my reputation."

"*Your* reputation? Who cares about a boy mountebank's reputation?"

"I do. I do not wish to be spoken of as Sage Archibald was."

She bit her lip, which was probably an admission that I was in the right. "You are very young," she declared disapprovingly, although she must be younger. "You have performed this service for other women?"

"I have watched my tutor do so many times and done it twice under his supervision."

"Very well." She stood up and turned her back on me.

I pressed a hand to her belly and concluded that she might not be with child at all. If she were, it was a very recent conception. I retreated a couple of paces; she sat down again, folding her hands carefully once more. She was accustomed to deference and groveling obedience. If I inadvertently murdered a baroness I would hang.

"You are not so far along, my lady. Indeed, I cannot be certain that you are with child at all. The treatment I can offer might be dangerous if you are not. Even if you are, it may make you very sick for some days, so you would be wiser to wait a couple of weeks to make sure that it is needed at all."

"You will not be here in two weeks."

"Possibly not," I admitted. I must return the horses to Helmdon. "The academy at Northampton would—"

"Out of the question! Give me the potion now and instruct me in its use. I will take it if I find it necessary."

"Alas, I cannot. The incantation is part of the treatment and must be chanted at the same time as you drink the infusion."

"Did you not hear my orders, Saxon?" She sounded like her father.

"And if you die, what happens to me?" I decided I must risk treading near the forbidden topic. "Did Sage Archibald ever treat you for anything—chant over you, for instance?" I had never heard of a spell that would induce a false pregnancy, but it would not be an impossibility. Matilda was a strikingly beautiful woman. I already judged that Archibald had been a very evil man, and my opinion of him would be even worse if he had used his skills to cozen his victims into believing that they were with child when they weren't, so that they would keep coming back to him for more fake treatments.

Matilda flamed like tinder. "That lecher? No respectable woman in the castle would go near that slimy, odious rogue!"

Yet she had not peered around at the cabalistic decor when she entered. She had been here before. But that proved nothing, for the castle had been her childhood home.

She was not done. "I do not know why my father put up with him for so long. I would never have consulted him were I dying in agony. Give me the potion!"

She wanted confidentiality, that was all, treatment from a transient healer who would vanish within days and take her dark secret with him.

I shook my head. "I promise you, my lady, that I will treat you as required before I leave Barton. Your problem may solve itself before then."

"I have silver!" she said furiously.

Enough silver, perhaps, to pay for two more years' instruction at Helmdon? To my own astonishment, I managed to resist the temptation. "That will not be necessary. I rely on your father's generosity."

"Men have starved doing that," she said. "Do not smile at me, Saxon. I am not jesting."

chapter 25

So I lost a patient and made an enemy. Matilda departed in a fury, slamming the door. Cursing myself for a stubborn fool, I went back to my favorite stool to continue my work.

I had hardly dipped my pen in the ink before William entered, escorting a boy dressed in rags, well patched but very greasy.

"This is Bearn, master. Best I could find."

"Nothing wrong with him as far as I can see. Sit down, both of you."

Bearn flopped down on the floor, crossing his spindly legs.

"I meant on a stool."

The brat looked alarmed. "Not s'posed to sit on furniture, master."

"Bearn's a blackguard, Adept."

I could see that. The lad's face needed a good scrub, his hands might never be clean again, and his arms and legs were patterned with old burn marks. Kitchen drudges like him were cleaners of pans and turners of spits. The only good thing about a blackguard's job was that he would eat well, even if only on scraps and leftovers.

"Stay down there if you like. You heard about Colby?"

"He's dead."

"Were you surprised?"

Bearn shook his head, showing no emotion. Was he stupid or just ignorant? He was close to being a slave and might never be much more than that.

"You were friends with Colby?"

Shrug. "We played ball when he had nothin' to do and I had nothin' to do."

"Did Colby often have nothing to do?"

"When his master sent him out to play."

"Have you ever been inside this room before, Bearn?"

Nod. "Poultry man brought me when cook spilled hot fat on me." He raised an arm to show a scar that made me cringe; even William winced. Bearn himself did not seem to think it was anything special.

"What did the sage do about it? Did he give you something to drink to ease the pain?"

Bearn worried over the question for a moment, scratching his scalp vigorously. "He said to spread white of an egg on it," he concluded doubtfully. "But cook said 'twould be a waste of an egg and used goose grease, same as usual."

"Did the sage tell you to lie down there?" I indicated the bench under the window.

The boy shook his head, obviously wondering why this odd man kept wanting him on *furniture*. What I was hoping to learn was whether there had been a sheepskin rug on that bench to make it more comfortable for patients being examined, although I doubted that Bearn's testimony would be reliable. If pressed at all, he would start giving whatever answers he thought were wanted.

"Did Colby sleep in here?"

"Nay. Slept in the hall. Shared his blanket with me, 'times."

So Archibald had sent his helper away at nights and some-times even during the day. His disrepute was confirmed again.

"Did you ever see upstairs?"

The boy glanced up at the loft and shook his head. "Ain't tall enough."

"You mean when you stood on the window ledge?" I pointed.

Nod.

"But Colby could see in, couldn't he?"

Bearn grinned. "Watched humpy-bumpy!"

Clearly he didn't realize that voyeurism was wrong and could be dangerous—it might have been fatal for Colby. Meanwhile I had the problem of how to reward a boy who wore rags, lived on floors, and had probably never seen money in his life. Give him a good blanket of his own and it would be stolen from him before nightfall. Treat his head lice and he would just collect a new infestation.

I reached in my pouch and found a farthing. "Thank you, Bearn. You can go now. Give this to the cook and tell her that the adept said you have been very helpful and are a good boy, and she is to give you lots of sweetmeats."

Bearn's eyes lit up with wonder. He grabbed the coin. The door slammed, leaving a thoughtful silence.

"You think Archibald killed Colby, master?"

"It's certainly possible. We saw mud on the windowsill." So the boy had been a nosey-parker, but what had he learned that justified his death? That the sage played humpy-bumpy with the baroness? My eyes turned to that hard examination bench and I remembered that half-hatched idea that had troubled me earlier. It ought to have at least a rug on it, if not a fleece. But the fleece now reposing in the barrow outside my door was too big for it, so that idea didn't work.

Archibald had been Colby's master and could have shot him off home in seconds, but that might not have seemed a safe enough solution if the boy had overheard a plot to kill the king.

"Let's get back to work on the *Morðor wile ut*," I said.

Life was not so simple, because the keep bell began summoning the castle residents to dinner.

Emerging from the sanctum, William and I were confronted by the smelly, weed-festooned, and utterly repulsive heap in the wheelbarrow. William cast a nervous glance at the man he had now taken to calling "master" even in private.

"You really think this fleece will tell us who murdered the boy?"

"No harm in asking it," I said, while it occurred to me that it might also provide some mundane evidence that would be admissible in a trial.

"You want me to stay and guard it in case someone tries to steal it?"

"That's a noble offer just before dinner, but I'd rather you went around by the gate. No one but the killer will want to go near the horrible thing, so warn the guards to arrest anyone trying to take a fleece out of the castle during dinner." I knew it could never be that easy.

William took off at a run. Of course he didn't want to be late at the trough, but he was also becoming willing, even eager, to please. I decided it must be a pack hunting instinct surfacing, and went in search of dinner.

Sun and wind were fast drying the ground. The way back to Helmdon ought to be in much better shape now, and I had five horses I had sworn to return there. Where did my loyalty lie? Tracking down a killer was the count's job, not mine, but the chance that the killings might be related to a plot against the king made it everyman's. And Rolf had been one of my tutors, making his death an obligation that wouldn't go away.

Hearing hooves and laughing voices, I turned a corner and tracked the sound to a line of horses being led in from the gate. All of them, men and beasts, had clearly been exercising hard, and the quadrupeds were now being taken for a rubdown. The one in front was Ruffian, and the man holding his reins was Alwin. Seeing me, Alwin changed direction to come over. He was grinning and so, I suspected, was Ruffian.

"Greetings, Master," I said. "And shame on you, you faithless brute!"

Ruffian twitched an ear and curled a lip.

"Oh, he's a big softie," Alwin said, patting the stallion's neck. "But give him his head and he'll outrun the Devil! We love each other dearly." He was clearly enjoying his conquest.

"Sir Hugh told me there wasn't a horse in Christendom you couldn't ride."

"Nay, I've met several. Must go before this fine fellow takes a chill. . . . Care to share some wine this evening and talk horses, Adept?"

"Sorry. Too much work to do." I hoped the way I shook my head conveyed more than my words.

"Pity." The master of horse understood the message. He smiled sadly and led Ruffian away to his rubdown and warm mash.

"Adept Durwin, sir," Wacian declared magisterially, "Her Ladyship instructed me to present her compliments and invite your presence in the parlor before the meal."

Was this good news or bad? Unable to decide, I thanked the bottler graciously, and stumped off to the dais to knock on the private door. The count's voice bade me enter.

Count Richard, Baroness Matilda, and . . . and her mother the countess, whom no one ever seemed to name, were seated around the fireplace, sipping wine. All three wore black. The only other person present was Lady Aveline, who stood demurely in a corner, clasping a book. There were no empty seats.

I bowed to the nobility. "You sent for me, my lord?"

"We did," the count said. "You are full of wonders, Adept! Sir Hugh had to leave on an important mission, so could only briefly tell us how you recovered the body of that unfortunate child. We should like to hear more."

"I have almost nothing more to report, my lord. As I explained earlier, I am only an adept, and my assistant, while eager to learn, is a rank beginner. Your honored brother, were he—"

"Quite. Do we know how the child died?"

"Impossible to be sure, my lord. As Father Randolf said, it could not have been by his own hand, unless some evil person cruelly hid his body later to deprive it of proper burial. But the condition of the body was such that it was impossible to tell what was done to him."

The three women all crossed themselves, even Aveline, who should have been pretending not to be listening. The count frowned darkly. "These deaths are a blot upon my house and the murderer must be caught as soon as humanly possible. Is there anything I can do to speed your inquiries? Anything you need?"

"Just some more time, my lord."

His Lordship's frown became a grimace. "Which may be something I cannot grant. That magic you used to find the corpse—you said you hoped that it would lead you to the killer. Cannot you use it a second time?"

"We can try," I said. "Sometimes . . . more often than not, incantations, especially the long, complicated ones, fail to repeat, as if the spirits invoked feel they had answered one appeal and do not want to be bothered with more. But we can try. And there are others that might help."

Lord Richard lowered his voice, although everyone in the room would still hear him. "Do you suspect anyone in particular?"

Eek! The only indisputable fact was that the poison that killed Sage Rolf must have been put beside his bed in this very room by one of a tiny group of people, most of them his family. The only safe answer was, "Not yet, my lord. I hope to learn more this afternoon."

The count grunted angrily, and stood up, causing his companions to rise also. "Let us go and make an appearance." He offered his arm to his wife. Baroness Matilda rose, turned toward the door, and waited expectantly.

God's eyeballs! I was expected to squire a baroness into dinner? I moved to her side and offered my arm. Instead of laying fingers on it, she ignored it and followed her parents, without a glance at me. So I was allowed to escort her, but touching was forbidden. It was a deliberate snub, although probably the audience in the hall would not notice.

What could I say? That she reminded me of Edla, my puppy love, a villein's daughter, now baby-maker for a plowman? The same perfectly chiseled bone structure, a complexion as smooth and pale as ivory. . . . Something about the baroness's face had changed, though, and it took me a moment to realize that she had darkened her eyelashes. Like my own, her lashes were normally so pale as to be invisible. The change had turned the extreme pallor of her pearly irises from an oddness to something rare and precious.

To my alarm, she went to the stool next-but-one to her mother, leaving a gap. Remembering what Wacian had said about the implications of leaving a gap, I accepted that I must sit between the baroness and her mother. My appetite promptly died of fright.

We all sat down, the priest said grace, and the food began arriving, almost hot.

The adept's promotion had been noticed by the common folk. William's eyes were bulging. Kendryck's grin would have swallowed Jonah, whale and all.

What did the ruling class discuss at dinner? One certainly did not ask one's patient how her false pregnancy was progressing. Judging by the way she was heaping her plate with boiled mutton and slices of venison, she was not yet troubled by nausea.

Her mother must take precedence, of course, and it would be up to her to choose the topics.

The countess was being more fastidious in her choice of food, picking out easily chewed items. Her teeth must bother her, because a sunken cheek showed she had lost many of them on the side I could see. I moved a basket of pickled eggs closer to her.

She nodded her thanks and, as if she were reading my thoughts, murmured, "Do you have a remedy for toothache, Adept?"

"Not with me, of course, my lady. But I have some meadowsweet, which many people find reduces the discomfort until the tooth puller can be summoned. Do you wish me to send my helper for it?"

"That is most kind of you. Not now, but I will send a boy after dinner. There is a barber in Northampton who is very skilled at extractions."

Relieved that I would not be ordered to perform that service, and before I could think of a suitable follow-up, I was addressed by my other neighbor.

"I have never met an adept before."

"And I have never sat next to a baroness, my lady. That is a much greater honor."

She glanced at me coquettishly. "You sang most wonderfully in the church this morning. You have one of the finest male voices I have ever heard."

"Your ladyship is most kind, but such a talent is a gift from God, nothing I can take pride in. Indeed, such a gift can be a burden, for it imposes the duty to develop it, which can require much work."

She sighed. "Like beauty?"

What was the correct response to that? Who was she calling beautiful? I was hopeless at such courtly banter.

"Beauty that is fated to bring joy to one man and great pain to all the rest? But no one could know more about that than yourself, my lady."

She approved my mot with a nod, and promptly slashed her verbal blade at me again. "Beauty can attract a lot of unwelcome attention, can't it?"

She was trying to make me blush and likely succeeding. I wished she would turn to her other neighbor, Aveline, and leave me alone.

"You must know infinitely more about that than I do," I said.

"Modesty carried to such extremes is rank falsehood. Are you going to catch the killer, Durwin?"

"I hope so, my lady, given time."

"But you may not have time. We are expecting a very important visitor, have you not heard?"

"You think that he is the intended victim?"

"Of course! We do not normally go around slaughtering people in Barton Castle. Sage Archibald was predicting disaster for my father's house. Slug that he was, he was also a fine prognosticator, and would surely have unraveled the entire plot before the king arrived, so he had to be slain. Then my uncle, an even cleverer sage, arrives in his place!"

On that reading, a mere unripe adept would be no threat, so I was safe.

"And the boy, Colby?"

Matilda hesitated, a slice of venison poised just before her lips. Her eyes narrowed. "If he was the boy I think he was, then he was a notorious little busybody, prying into everything." She put the meat in her mouth and licked her fingers. "But he was probably irrelevant. I expect he caught his master with one too many married women and Archibald himself got rid of him. Wouldn't put it past him."

I would. Why would Archibald murder his apprentice when he could just kick his butt out the castle gate?

"Then whom do you suspect of causing his death, Baroness?"

She leaned closer, so I had to bend my head for her whisper. William and half the squires were watching all this with open glee.

"That creepy Saxon stable hand, Alwin. I do not know what it is about him, but he sets my teeth on edge!"

What bothered her, no doubt—and she might not even be aware of it—would be that the master of horse was immune to her smiles and glances. I decided the stakes were too high to worry about politeness.

"But he did not have the opportunity to plant the poison beside your uncle's bed."

Matilda smirked around a mouthful of pheasant. "Is that what you were told?"

I, who was enjoying the pheasant, a treat I had never tasted before, very nearly choked on it. Alwin had left the bunkhouse at lights out, when all humble folk were supposed to be in bed.

And the next morning, before Rolf was even cold, Sir Hugh had known enough about Ruffian to ask who had ridden him on the trip from Helmdon. Alwin had gone to the party? Hugh had been lying.

"If what I heard was in error, my lady, pray enlighten me with the truth."

She gestured vaguely with a pheasant leg. "He came in to report to Sir Hugh and stayed a little while to chat with my uncle. They knew each other well, of course, from the old days."

"Adept Durwin!" said a chilly voice.

My head whipped around like a weathercock. "My lady?"

The countess's smile could have skinned a wild boar. Aging women did not appreciate being neglected in favor of their ravishingly lovely daughters.

"My husband has explained to you the need for an urgent solution to our mystery?"

"Indeed he has, my lady. He fears that these terrible crimes may be only the prelude to an unthinkable atrocity."

"Then you appreciate the burden you bear."

"I wish I felt worthy of it. But I cannot understand why anyone would want to do such a thing. Has everyone forgotten the Anarchy, the time of troubles?"

"Are you not aware of what is happening in Northampton even now?"

"I have heard that the king is in conference there with his nobles."

"And with his bishops. You do know about the new Archbishop of Canterbury? Thomas Becket, barely two years in the see of Canterbury, and he spits in his king's face!"

Sir Hugh had told me that the countess could explain the political situation to me. It seemed she would now do so whether I wanted to hear it or not.

"Helmdon is a very isolated place, my lady. I should be most grateful if you could repair my ignorance about the dispute between His Grace and the archbishop."

"Oh, it is quite simple. His Grace should never have appointed such a man. Becket was just a clerk, and then a diplomat—an able diplomat, which means he was good at lying—but never a priest. For five hundred years the monks of Canterbury have elected the archbishop, but this time they bowed to the king's bullying and accepted the layman he foisted on them. Becket was no more a priest than Elmer or Galan along there, but they ordained him faster than a deathbed confession. Was he grateful? Not at all. He took the bit between his teeth and defied his sovereign."

Perhaps he was trying to prove to the Church that he was not just a royal lackey, but worthy to be their leader in England? New brooms notoriously sweep clean.

"Defied how, my lady?"

The countess issued a snort that Ruffian might have admired. "He refuses to allow the king's courts to try clerics. Only the Church can judge them, he says. And it is true that those in holy orders have always been tried by church courts first, and then handed over to the civil law for punishment. In serious cases, that is. But Becket does not allow even that. Church trial is all he will admit, and the worst penalty an ecclesiastical court can impose is degrading to the laity. What is that to a priest who has committed murder?"

"My lady!"

"Oh, it has happened! Priests can be as wicked as other men, even wickeder when you consider the vows they have taken. But Becket just defrocks them and lets them walk free. Hang them, I say!"

"Aye to that," I muttered, staring along the table to where Elmer the clerk and Galan the secretary were seated together.

Both were tonsured, so they had been admitted to minor orders, but they probably had no intention of advancing to the priesthood. The test for a cleric is always that he can read a text handed to him, and there were thousands of such men in England. Even I, if I ever found myself on trial, might claim *privilegium clericale*. But neither Galan nor Elmer had entered the room where Rolf had died.

The countess was aiming the sword of justice at someone else entirely.

"My lady!" I whispered. "Are you suggesting that a *priest* might want to murder the king?"

"Why not? A priest fanatically loyal to the Church might want to support Becket that far, for the king is certainly running out of patience with the archbishop. I have it on very good authority that he is now in danger of the royal displeasure."

"Morðor wile ut!"

"What?"

I had forgotten that Her Ladyship did not understand the old tongue. "Beg pardon . . . an incantation I am planning to try, which may lead me to the killer."

Her Ladyship smiled in grim approval. "Try hard, young man. Try very hard. Expose the killer priest and I will see that you are well rewarded."

chapter 26

i had expected that the death of the Colby boy would be announced at dinner, either by the count himself or by someone else, but there were no announcements. Either Colby had not been important enough or the daily obituary had become too macabre. Neither the troubadour nor the fool performed. Dinner in the castle that day was a somber affair, and even the servants' buzz of conversation seemed quieter than before.

William was waiting outside when I emerged from the stairwell. He looked me over mockingly, then bowed low.

"Much better," I said. "You're learning!" I strode by.

He fell into step beside me. "What did you learn, master?"

That the countess suspected the priest and her daughter the master of horse? But those accusations had sounded more based on spite than evidence. That the king's arrival now seemed much more likely than I had been told before? But William knew nothing of that.

"Oysters. If you're ever offered one, don't accept. I thought I would puke all over the table. What did you learn?"

"That the baroness has taken a real fancy to you. I thought she might drag you off to her bedchamber before the end of the meal."

"She's just a tease. She was flirting to make me blush."

"She succeeded."

"Shut up or I'll turn you into a woman."

"You bloomed like a rose!" William chuckled, then dropped the subject. "We going to chant the *Morðor* now, master?"

"Soon. The count wants us to try the *Ubi malum* again, but I'd rather see first what we can learn from the goblets and the fleece."

My assistant nodded happily. "*Ubi malum* only if I get to beat up some more knights."

The wheelbarrow and its disgusting load were still where they had been outside the sanctum. Enchanter and cantor settled at the table to finish writing out the *Morðor wile ut* incantation. Then I had to make sure that William understood the unfamiliar words. We rehearsed it twice backward.

"If this works," I said, "don't expect to raze any more knights. But you should reenact the murder for me."

"One goblet or both?" William asked, eyeing them tensely. Despite his bravado about battering knights, he was showing rare courage in accepting another trance without protest. I had not forgotten how Sage Guy had introduced me to a dozen varied different trance states in a single week—to give me confidence, he had said, but the experience had left me close to gibbering. One thing Squire William Legier never lacked was confidence.

"Both, I think. Often the spirits refuse to answer any incantation a second time, and we don't know which goblet was Archibald's and which the killer's. They're quite dry, so if you mime drinking from one of them in your trance, you won't get poisoned."

"What if both people answer?"

"They won't, only the victim's spirit will cry out. The murderer is still alive and doesn't want anything let out. Ready?"

William nodded grimly. He clasped a goblet in either hand, one on each side of the tablets on which he had written out the responses.

"A murder wants out," I chanted, "so spirits of the dead attend. Let the veil be raised . . ." This incantation, I realized, was very close to necromancy, and should perhaps be performed in darkness, even at midnight itself, although the grimoire had not mentioned that. The text was much shorter than the *Ubi malum*'s, invoking no entity by name except the victim, Sage Archibald.

William had the last line. He sang the final response: "Justice! Give me justice, that I may find peace."

I felt a midwinter chill settle over me. My flesh rose in goose bumps, my scalp prickled. I stared apprehensively at my assistant, who was frowning at the goblet in his left hand as if it felt cold, or hot, or had moved on its own.

William said, "Ugh! Where do you think old Wacian finds this swill?"

But he was not speaking with his own voice. He did not even look like himself. He was still recognizable, but he had aged ten years. His face had lost its youthful freshness, his hair was lanker, his pose on the stool more of a slouch.

Then he smiled, slack-lipped, at the empty space beside my right shoulder. "But I need it after all that. You do inspire a man to keep trying, my dear. Bottoms up, as they say. Ah, I forgot that you prefer bottom down." He laughed, then raised the goblet to his mouth and swallowed several times, as if draining it.

He was speaking like a Londoner, an accent familiar to me from hearing Friar Pious in the Pipewell Abbey. Kendryck had said that Archibald spoke that way, so I had no doubt who was speaking through William.

"Well, let's hope so, this time. But your efforts to fake ecstasy weren't very convincing, my dear. You made the problem with pleasure and only with pleasure can you be rid of it. Until you can achieve that, the spell likely won't work. If you haven't dropped your burden by tomorrow, we'll have to try again." He scowled for a moment, as if disliking what he was hearing. "Then keep your little secret. You must say this for bastards, they come out in their own good time. You sure you don't want that wine? Mustn't let it go to waste . . ." William raised the right hand goblet and quaffed the imaginary wine in that.

For a moment he fell silent, his face twitching through a series of expressions. Then he screamed. Goblets and stool went flying as he surged to his feet, screaming again and again. I leaped up and lurched around the table to him, leaning on it for balance. I wanted to grab William in a hug, treat him as one would a ter-rified child, but I was too conscious of what had happened to Sir Kendryck. Instead I swung a hand and smacked him across the face as hard as I could.

I had half expected my next experience to be coming around on the floor, flat on my back. But that didn't happen. Instead William, suddenly silent, staggered backward, eyes coming into focus. He regained his balance and buried his face in his hands. "Oh, Jesus!"

Now I did hug him. "It's all right. You're back. You're alive."

"Where was I?"

Probably in Hell. "It doesn't matter. You're here now, in Bar-ton. Sit down." I lifted the stool upright and pushed William down on it.

"What happened?"

"You—Archibald—drained the second goblet, and that must have been enough to make a fatal dose. He didn't die here, but that second draft doomed him." So the unknown companion had made some excuse to avoid drinking the wine? Dwale berries had a sweetish taste. "You—he—were talking to a woman, but her name wasn't mentioned."

I knew of one woman in the castle anxious to miscarry, but that didn't mean there couldn't be two. And if the whole bottle had been poisoned—as now seemed possible—that might have been done by an earlier visitor, not necessarily a woman.

William sat for a while with his eyes closed, hunched over and hugging himself, shivering as if cold. Then he looked up ruefully. "So you didn't learn anything?"

"I learned that my hypothesis was correct: he was poisoned here, in the sanctum, by drinking from those goblets, both of them. He was entertaining a woman who was consulting him to procure a miscarriage. He had blackmailed her into having sex with him and probably not for the first time. If his soul is in Hell, that doesn't seem too unjust."

William squared his shoulders. "Then we'd better try the fleece next."

"All right, but this time you take the versicles and I'll do the responses."

"No!" my assistant barked. "I'm the cantor. I'll do it." He headed for the door. William was truly a glutton for duty.

I found my staff, gathered up our notes, and followed. William had already lifted the handles and was trying to turn the wheelbarrow toward the door. The alley wasn't wide enough.

Despite its size, the fleece might well have come from the sanctum, for the bare wooden bench there cried out for a covering. Archibald couldn't have treated all his patients in bed.

"Leave it there," I said. "We don't want the stinking thing inside. We can chant here. No one will interrupt us, I'm sure." The pitchfork was still leaning against the wall; I moved it some distance along the alley, just to be on the safe side. People in trances were unpredictable.

"You sure you don't want to exchange song sheets?"

"I am not scared!" Glowering, William took hold of one edge of the fleece. He held out his other hand for the tablets. "Begin . . . *master!*"

I began. I almost hoped that the incantation would not work this time. Indeed I thought it probably couldn't work, unless Colby had been murdered right on the fleece. If he had been killed elsewhere and then wrapped up in it later, then it was merely a shroud, not part of the murder.

But it did work, and the reenactment began just as fast as it had the last time. Releasing both fleece and tablet, William staggered back against the wall of the house opposite me and then slid to the ground, where he could struggle with both hands and feet against an unseen oppressor on top of him. He made choking sounds, twisted his head free for a moment to utter a few muffled sounds in a shrill boyish treble, and then fell silent while his face began to turn purple. His struggles slackened.

"William!" I roared. I dropped to my knees and slapped the squire's face again, although not as hard as I had last time. "William, William! Come back! You're all right. You're—"

He sucked in a huge gasp of air and blew it out in a wail. Then he went limp, but his eyes opened. He lay there, panting and staring up at me.

"I was choking."

I nodded. "He forced you down on the bed and smothered you, using an edge of the fleece itself, I expect. You put up quite a struggle, I think."

William pulled a face. "You didn't learn anything?" *After all that?*

I let him puff for a few moments more before helping him up. He was in disgusting shape, and I not much better.

"I learned that we're both going to need clean clothes."

"So he didn't name the man who was killing him?"

"Not by name, no. But there's something else this fleece can tell us. Fetch the pitchfork."

William frowned and went to obey, displaying his mud-soaked back. "Now what?" he said as he returned, fork in hand.

"Sir Hugh said there were a thousand fleeces in the castle. That's clearly an exaggeration, but I saw at least a dozen in the hall alone, and they all must be cleaned sometimes, or they'd all be stiff with vermin."

"So?"

"And they can't all be the same size or quality, right? So they must be marked somehow, to make sure that they go back to their rightful owners. How would you mark a fleece?"

"On the back!" William said, lighting up. "With a branding iron."

He grabbed the pitchfork with both hands, dug the prongs into the fleece, and dragged it out of the barrow, spreading it on the ground, wool side down. It filled the width of the alley, which was narrower than almost any bed, and its smooth side was almost more revolting than the weed-and-mud covered side we had seen so far. William scraped the dead worms and other muck away with the side of the prongs, and in one corner he exposed a clear mark, a cross.

He looked around at me in horror. "The priest's?"

And I had to nod. "The little vestry beside the church has a plank bed in it, which suggests he must overnight there sometimes. I saw a bed, but no mattress, no pallet, no fleece. Does he strike you as the sort of ascetic who would sleep on planks as a matter of course?"

William just shook his head.

"And I said that Colby's spirit spoke no name through your mouth. But I did make out a title. He said *Na, Fæder, na!* at least twice. And also *Miltsung!* which means 'Mercy!' He was begging the *priest* to have *mercy*."

"But, master, you said that Sage Archibald was talking with a woman!"

"I did," I said, "although she never spoke, so I could be wrong about that. I don't think I am, though. Either we have two murderers, or the whole bottle had been poisoned beforehand by an earlier visitor—who needn't have been a woman, just a social friend. Killing anyone is a vicious act, but leaving whole flasks of poison around where anyone may drink from them is as ruthless as you can get. That was what happened in Rolf's case, too."

Only one person I had spoken with had admitted to finding Archibald an amusing companion.

chapter 27

"Now what? *Ubi malum* again?"

I shook my head. "You've been entranced more than enough for today. Besides, I don't want you beating up on Father Randolf. First, you and I both need to visit the laundry and the bathhouse. Can you lift that horrible thing back into the barrow?"

William pitted all his strength against the weight of the fleece, now soaked with even more mud and mire, but he had barely raised half of it when the pitchfork tines began to bend under the load. They had been designed to lift hay, after all. So enchanter and cantor had to join forces and haul it up by hand, thus coating us both in even more filth than before.

"To the laundry!" I commanded. "And bring the barrow."

My assistant looked at me in disbelief. "Why?"

"Because the exercise will do you good, sonny. And also," I added in case he took my humor at face value and proceeded to devalue my face, "because I need the laundresses to confirm that the horrible thing belongs to the person we think it does." I set off along the alley, and soon heard the wheelbarrow squeaking along behind me, being dragged backward by William, until he found a place wide enough to turn it.

Clean body, clean clothes, but what was I going to do next?

No sheriff was ever going to put much weight on what I claimed that my cantor had said while supposedly in a trance. It was doubly hearsay. A more experienced—and qualified—enchanter would no doubt have arranged for other witnesses to be present. I had not done so because I had not trusted my own abilities. That had been a beginner's mistake, but it might have cost me my only chance of bringing the killer to justice.

Father Randolf's anger outside the infirmary when I literally claimed the fleece off the corpse's back now seemed deeply suspicious, so either Sir Hugh or the count must be warned that the priest was at least implicated in Colby's death. Randolf had also been one of those present when the poison was placed at Rolf's bedside. There seemed to be no way to tie him to Archibald's death except the common use of poison and the fact that they had arrived at the great hall together, both of which facts were merely suggestive and far from proof of guilt.

A priest might know, or just assume on faith, that the Lord's Prayer would de-fang the sanctum door. Every priest was educated to some extent, as most laymen were not, so he could read the names on bottles and vials, and might know which were notorious poisons. Whoever had stolen the aconite to kill Rolf could have stolen dwale to doctor the wine that had killed Archibald. I might not have enough evidence to hang a man, but in my eyes it was quite enough suspicion to justify keeping Father Randolf well away from the king.

The goblets' evidence was not admissible, and that particular trance was not repeatable: according to a marginal note, the murder reenactment would only work once. It seemed impossible that the scraps of conversation I had heard had been Archibald talking to another man. If Randolf had poisoned the sage's wine bottle earlier, before the woman arrived, then why had the priest and sage arrived at dinner together? The evidence did not add up, and the venerable Aristotle himself would have been hard-pressed to apply logic to it.

It was twenty years since the First Lateran Council had forbidden priests to marry, and the Second had reaffirmed that ban only five years ago. Yet the Church might as well forbid the rain to fall as forbid men, whether ordained or not, to father children. A desire to conceal a forbidden conception seemed an absurdly inadequate motive for three murders, even for an ambitious priest. Many bishops had "nieces" and "nephews" they were especially fond of. But a plot to kill the king would be high treason, and must be kept secret at any cost. That was still a more believable motive.

By the time I had worked that out, my laboring squire and I had arrived at the laundry. In both Helmdon and Pipewell good housewives spread their sheets on the grass to bleach in the sunshine, but lack of space within the bailey required the castle's linen to be hung on lines, and who should be doing just that than the mighty Megan, happily singing a song about her gallant lover—without, of course, identifying him by name. She stopped and stared in horror at the grisly load approaching.

"You want *us* to wash *that*?" she demanded of me, her tone lacking the respect due an adept. "That be the one the murdered boy was wrapped in, God save his soul?"

"Amen to that, good woman. No, I don't want it washed, at least not yet. But you do wash the castle's fleeces?"

"There's not many as can lift a wet fleece, Adept." Grinning, she flexed her massive arms, clenching great hands that were red and rough from her labors. If that didn't bother Sir Kendryck, it was none of my business.

"I don't doubt it. I want you to explain to me how, when you have washed a fleece, you know whose it is?"

She hadn't thought of that, and the jollity drained from her face. "Each one bears a mark, Sir Adept," she said reluctantly.

"Such as?"

Megan was certainly uneducated but she was not stupid. "A crown for His Lordship's, and he has four that belong to him, not that he sleeps under them all himself, understand. The sage's has a star with five points."

On the point of saying that the bench in the sanctum had no such covering, I remembered that the bed in the loft did. I nodded for her to continue.

"Sir Hugh's mark's a castle; Master Alwin's a horse; Sir Bertrand's has squares." That probably implied an exchequer cloth for counting money. "There's others with other marks, Adept."

"Keep listing them, all you can remember."

She certainly knew why I wanted to know, and I was sure now that she was deliberately not mentioning the priest's mark, as a possibility too awful to contemplate. But when she ran out of suggestions, I said, "You haven't mentioned the one on this fleece. Do you want to take a look?"

She shuddered as she shook her head. She seemed to have shrunk, drawing herself in, and she was fixedly not looking at the load in the barrow.

"Then the person who murdered the child must have brought the fleece into the castle with him? Or might he have stolen it from someone who does live here?"

Megan brightened at this wonderful escape from the unthinkable. "He never locks the vestry, sir!"

"Father Randolf? And his fleece is marked with . . .?"

"A cross, of course."

"This cross?" I lifted back a corner of the fleece to show her. She nodded.

"Thank you, Megan. We'll leave this barrow and its load here for the time being. Over there, please, William."

After we had cleaned up at the bathhouse and appropriated clean clothes—a red robe for the learned adept this time—we headed for the stable. William was clearly interested to know what was coming next. I knew, and didn't want to think about it. My only hope was that I would be able to report to Sir Hugh and thus postpone the inevitable confrontation when the count heard the news.

At the stable Sir Scur was resting on a hay bale, head back, apparently enjoying the sunshine. I halted in front of him.

The old man opened his eye. "You were told to shed light, not block it."

"I will shed some if you do. Do you know where Sir Hugh is?"

"Aye, that I do."

"Where?"

"Why, I know it right here." He tapped his temple.

William found that funny, which didn't help.

"Tell me where Sir Hugh is."

"He is on his horse."

"And where is his horse?"

"Underneath him, good sir, where else should it be?"

"He's not back yet," said a new voice. Master of Horse Alwin was leaning against the doorpost, blond hair shining in the sunlight, wistfully lecherous smile in place.

"Thank you," I said. "And the count?"

"He has ridden out with Sir Bertrand to inspect flood damage."

"I would be grateful if you would tell whichever of them first returns that I have news to report." Oh, pray that it be the marshal!

"Bad news?" No doubt Alwin was reading my expression.

"No more murders, anyway."

"The best of tidings these days," said Sir Scur.

chapter 28

i headed glumly back to the sanctum. Despite the evidence and the countess's accusations against the clergy, I still found it impossible to believe that a man of God would callously murder a child and two men to conceal plans to assassinate the king. Worse, I was out of ideas. It would be unfair to subject William to more incantations that day, and the only one we had practiced was the *Ubi malum*, which had led us to the murdered Colby.

There must be a better incantation to use than that one, for *malum* meant "thing"—neuter gender. So what would it lead us to this time: the flask of poisoned wine that was so worryingly missing from the sanctum? No doubt that had been emptied, rinsed, and returned harmless to the bottler's store. Even enchantment might not be able to identify it now, and what good would it do us anyway?

"Now what?" my cantor demanded, and I realized that we were passing a practice ground where squires were hammering up a thunderstorm with wooden swords and shields. William looked like a starving dog eyeing a heap of juicy steaks.

"Go and join in if you want to. I have to chew through another two or three grimoires."

William was gone like an arrow.

To each his own! I went back to the sanctum, making a mental note as I entered that I should exorcise the door and install a ward of my own choosing. Everything seemed to be as I had left it, but I climbed halfway up the ladder to check that no one was lurking in ambush up there. My timidity showed me how much I had come to rely on my stalwart squire to defend me from violence.

Having retrieved all the grimoires—six of them, counting Guy's—I settled down to serious work, starting with the two volumes I had not yet had a chance to study. Many of the spells appeared in more than one volume, and sometimes with curious variations, some of which were so blatant that even the most hidebound Helmdon sage would be hard put to dismiss them as copying errors.

Early on, I found the *Ubi malum* with two summonings omitted. Later came the *Malefice venite*—"Come, villain"— which I had already rejected as too complex . . . except that I was looking at a shorter version requiring only two voices. I read it through with rising excitement, for it was far more specific than the *Ubi malum*, which only sought after some evil thing. This text allowed the enchanter to name the crime whose perpetrator he was summoning. I already knew, or thought I knew, who had smothered the boy Colby, but with this I could summon the person who had poisoned Archibald and Rolf. I limped across to the supply chest for clean tablets and ink, then went back to the table to copy out the parts.

Soon I ran out of clean tablets and had to set to work with the sandstone, erasing our copy of *Ubi malum*. I should not have let William go out to play.

A thunderous pounding on the door startled me. For a moment my hair stirred, as I wondered whether just concentrating too hard on an incantation, thinking about it too deeply, could activate it. Had I unwittingly summoned the killer already? Impossible! I heaved myself upright, realizing that I must have been sitting there for an hour or even two. Before I could reach the door, the banging was repeated.

I opened it and found myself face to face with a ferocious baronial scowl. For a moment I just gaped. Nobility never went calling on commoners!

"Well, do we have your *permission* to enter, Saxon, or will you leave us standing out here in this quagmire?"

"Enter, of course, my lord! You honor my—" I backed up a pace to avoid being bowled over as the big man stormed in. I was about to kneel, when another voice spoke.

"And me too?" The speaker was a younger man, finely garbed and wearing a sword. Unlike his father, he was smiling, but it was the fond, tolerant smile of a superior—the sort of smile that could turn instantly to anger.

"Oh, enter, Sir Stephen, and welcome."

The knight did so, raising an eyebrow to acknowledge the identification. "Thaumaturgy or the nose?"

The nose, yes, but more the jaw. He was a younger, slimmer version of the count—younger, slimmer, and brighter of eye.

"No great art, sir. You have inherited your father's noble features. Pray be seated, my lord, sir knight. I have no hospitality to—"

"We'll stand," the count snarled. "I was told you had news for me."

His tone did not sound promising. "Unhappy news, I fear, my lord. The fleece in which the boy's body was found belonged to, um, Father Randolf."

235

"I know that," the count barked. "It was stolen more than a week ago."

"He did not say so this morning when we—"

"He does not need to explain himself to you, boy!" Count Richard moved threateningly close, as if about to bite me. "He came and told me this morning."

"But he had not reported its loss until now? Why? A valuable—"

"Because he is the priest! Hanging thieves is not his business; saving souls is. He knew he would hear sooner or later who had taken it, so he could claim it back and impose a penance."

About to continue objecting, I bit my tongue. Father Randolf's rage when his valuable fleece was dragged out of the muddy moat was understandable, whether he had dropped it in there himself with a body in it or not, but the fact that he had not reported it stolen sooner seemed deeply suspicious.

"Well?" the count roared. "Is that all you have to tell me—something I already knew? You would have me accuse my own flesh and blood, a man of God, of murdering three people in my own house, just on the basis of that?"

That and Colby's dying words addressed to a priest, although those were, in a sense, contradicted by Archibald's speech to a woman.

"So far I have no other evidence that would be accepted by a sheriff, my lord." In those days each sheriff was responsible for maintaining the law in his shire. It was a few years after this that King Henry began the system of sending his own judges out on assizes.

"Well, 'so far' is too far. You're a fraud and a mountebank, and I am of a mind to have you soundly whipped for it. I need this place to billet a score of men tomorrow, so you and your thuggish young helper can get those horses out of my stable by dawn and move them and yourselves off my land as fast as you can move, understand?"

"Aye, my lord."

"And defang that door, so it won't maim them."

"Aye, my lord."

"Tonight you eat in the kitchen, you hear?"

"Aye, my lord."

His Lordship wheeled around and headed for the door. "Come, Son. Your mother will geld me if I don't deliver you into her loving embrace most suddenly."

"Tell her I'm enjoying a leisurely piss, Father. I'll be along in a minute."

Stephen saw his father out, closed the offending door, and then looked around. "This grotto's a lot tidier than it was in Charles's time. Sit!" He waved me to a stool. As he walked under the stuffed crocodile, he reached up to tap it on the nose. "Charles used to call this lizard Maud. When he was talking to King Stephen's supporters, it was the Empress Maud; to her supporters, it was Queen Maud, Stephen's wife. We had a plague of Mauds in those days. If we billet twenty liverymen in here, the first thing they'll do is drain all those bottles. What happens then?"

I said, "It'll leave more room for the living."

My humor was rewarded with an engaging grin. The young knight moved around the table to sit opposite; he leaned forward on his forearms. "So, tell me how you found the boy's body."

He listened intently, nodding impatiently when I began speaking of things he already knew. "And what was the other evidence, which my father did not want to hear?" He frowned at the report of Archibald's words to an unknown companion, and even more so at Colby's dying pleas.

"I do agree with your noble father that it is hard to imagine a priest committing such crimes," I concluded tactfully, not mentioning that the countess was of the opposite opinion.

"I don't," Stephen said darkly. "The king has just been hearing of more than a hundred cases of clerics escaping virtually scot-free after deeds as bad—rape, murder, manslaughter! That Randy is my cousin hurts, of course, but if he is indeed guilty he has forfeited any claim on our loyalty. If we can't have witnesses, he must be judged on facts, and so far those are worrisome. What do you plan next, Sage?"

"I am but an adept, sir."

"But you have almost completed your apprenticeship, surely? I am not wholly ignorant of your craft—Sage Charles taught me some rudiments, and I know that the most renowned enchanters of Europe would be proud to match what you have achieved in the last two days."

Oh, flattery, flattery! I explained my situation at Helmdon, and why I had remained a varlet so long. I did not mention my former hopes that Count Richard might sponsor the remainder of my training, for I thought Sir Stephen was quite quick enough to see the problem. Moreover, Stephen had the king's ear, and that raised prospects too heady even to think about.

How could father and son be so alike in looks and so unalike in manner? Richard was a rough warrior, who had fought for the greater part of his life and might well have taken a few taps from the same mace that had ruined Sir Scur. The suave Stephen was a courtier, too young to have seen much warfare at all. I reminded myself that manners could be deceptive; courtiers carried their knives under their cloaks.

Stephen glanced at the window. Daylight was already starting to fade. "I must go. Forget what my father said. You stay on here at Barton and track down the monster. What do you plan next?"

I explained about *Malefice venite* and the knight's eyes widened. "You mean the culprit will just walk in here and confess?"

"Not necessarily confess, sir, although he might. The author—whoever he was—claims the villain will feel a call, but will come for what he believes is some purpose of his own. We may get other visitors also, of course, quite innocent. The glosses—I mean, marginal comments added by later users—suggest that the power of the incantation seems to be limited to about a mile, which I would take to be a Roman mile, and the delay may amount to a day or even slightly more. In other words, the quarry may not arrive right away."

Stephen nodded. "The Council of Northampton," he said, "has ended. Becket was found guilty of contempt for failing to answer the king's summons in person last month, and His Grace leveled many new charges, mostly of embezzlement committed while the knave was chancellor. He escaped under cover of darkness and has probably fled the realm. I doubt if he will stop running until he can fall on his face before the pope. He is finished!" No question where Stephen's loyalty lay.

"The king has announced that he will leave for Rockingham Forest at dawn tomorrow, stopping by here on the way." His frown softened into a smile. "But that doesn't mean much. He is notoriously unpredictable. He can say that and then leave us standing around all day with our horses saddled. I have known him swear that he will stay where he is for a week and then decide to move out an hour later. How soon can you chant this miracle summons?"

"When I have prepared fair copies, sir. The hand in the grimoire is antique, crabbed, and hard to read. Then my cantor and I must rehearse it until we can perform it without errors or hesitation . . ." Clearly Stephen de Mandeville wanted a straighter answer than that. "By dawn, no sooner, sir. It is unwise to chant any summoning during the hours of darkness."

"Work as fast as you can!"

"I will, as God gives me strength, sir."

The knight sprang up. "Eat in the hall tonight, anywhere you fancy. My father has—with Father Randolf's blessing," he added sardonically, "declared a suspension of mourning for my uncle. It will be a free-for-all, but don't let the partying distract you. When you are ready, send word to me in the hall, no matter what the hour. I will take a bed on the dais, and see that mine is closest to the parlor door. I intend to witness this enchantment of yours, and I will tell my father that he must not evict you to billet the king's men. I don't expect His Grace to linger at Barton anyway. He yearns to cut to the hunt."

I was still bowing when Stephen reached the door. He turned to say something; there was a loud knocking. He opened it.

"Lord's mercy! What happened?" Then he looked to me. "Must you bid them enter, or can I?"

"You can, sir. Anyone within."

"Come in, then, all of you," Stephen said, and stepped aside as two hefty squires obeyed, supporting between them a very limp William, bleeding and barely conscious.

chapter 29

Stephen slammed the door shut, eyes blazing.

"Lay him here," I said, indicating the bench.

William gurgled and tried to pull loose from his holders. His face was a mass of bruises, his fists cut and swollen; blood trickled from his mouth and nose. Through bubbles of blood he insisted, "Amallrigh'! Amallrigh'!"

Grinning, they let go of him. His knees buckled like string, and the smaller of the two—who was still enormous—caught him up like a baby and spread him on the bench.

I exploded, cutting off Sir Stephen.

"You were forbidden to fight him, you great thugs!" I roared. "Goons! Apes! Your knights forbade challenges! Who was in charge of that lesson?"

"Sir Lucien of Leicester, Adept," said the smaller with a smirk. "But the lesson was over. He'd gone. It was your ferret here who started it. He tried to pick a fight with Squire Colbert, and when Colbert refused to cooperate, your man kicked his kneecap and called him a—"

"Is Colbert the one they call Goliath?" Stephen said, and his air of authority instantly quelled everyone else.

"No, sir, that's Squire Delaney. But after Colbert called it quits, sir, this lunatic did go for Delaney. Lordamercy, sir, *nobody* takes *him* on! Delaney knocked him down six or seven times and, when he wouldn't stay down, got mad and began to kick him. The rest of us decided we'd better stop it."

"This's the boy who trashed Sir Kendryck?" Stephen asked, and everyone agreed. "Was he enchanted this time?" he asked me.

"No, sir. But he is obsessed with a need to get back into knights' training. I don't know why he ever left it."

"Maybe he damaged too many others?" suggested the larger squire, and quailed under the look he got from Stephen. His companion grinned, though, and I was hard put not to.

"How are his victims?" I asked, wondering how I was going to complete my task without my cantor. I had known that my own agenda at Barton included finding a noble sponsor for my future education. I hadn't seen that William might have secret plans of his own along the same lines.

"They'll live, Adept. Delaney will, anyway." The squires obviously found the situation funny. "Nobody cares much about Colbert."

"Then, if you will be so kind, carry this wretch to the infirmary so I can treat him, and inform the other two that I will do the same for them." I looked ruefully at Stephen. "I will need someone else to help me with the incantation, sir."

"No . . . won't! Yo' won't!" William struggled painfully to sit up. "Whach you need? I'm yo' helper." He had lost two teeth and no doubt several more were loose.

"He needs someone with some brains!" Stephen snapped. "When you've patched him up, Adept, come to the hall and eat. I'll tell Elmer to help you, and he can find you there. Now I must go." And go he did, banging the door.

William struggled to his feet. He swayed a few times as the rest of us watched in fascination, but he did not fall. He blinked at the table. "Whach you nee'done, master?"

"What I don't need is blood all over the books. So we start at the infirmary with lots of bandages."

"Ri'. . . ." Step by unsteady step, William headed for the door. The squires exchanged admiring glances.

"See he arrives safely, please," I said. "I have to collect a few things here, and I'll join you there."

I began the treatment by chanting a healing in the hope of saving his loose teeth; it also stopped most of the bleeding. The sun having set, I had to work by the dim light of a single lantern. The two bearers had gone, and neither Colbert nor Delaney had come by for treatment. Healer and patient were alone.

"Why?" I asked as I bandaged William's battered ribs. The damage was mostly on his right side, suggesting that either his shield-work had been better than his fencing, or Goliath had done his kicking there. "I can tell by these muscles of yours that you've had years of training with sword and longbow. You write a flawless hand and your Latin is far better than most run-of-the-mill priests', yet you try to keep anyone from finding out. Now you're a trainee sage and hating every minute of it. Tell me why."

"Min' you' own business." William was sitting on a stool, half naked. He was clearly in pain, but to clench his fists or bite his lip would just make things worse. Sweat trickled down his face, but so far he hadn't uttered a single groan.

"But you owe it to me. I found an incantation that should bring the killer right to my doorstep, and I needed your help with it. You have let me down badly."

"I should ram that staff of yours down your throat for that, you prattling, gutless, Saxon cripple."

"It's true."

"Doesn't matter. I probably will, yet."

"Your promises don't seem to mean much."

"Just wait and see. The Legier motto is *I do my best*."

"But you didn't! You failed."

For a moment it seemed that even this argument would be refused. Then William said, "Suppose so. All right, story now, payment later. My father's a knight, two of my three brothers are knights. I was the baby, but at fourteen I could take the next two without working up a sweat and at fifteen even Arnolph, the eldest. At sixteen I was a squire and my horse fell. Was out cold for three days."

There but for the grace of God went Durwin of Pipewell.

"After that, I . . . After that, every time I went to get on a horse I . . . I peed in my britches. *I couldn't help it!* They all laughed at me, of course."

Of course.

"My father said if I couldn't be One Who Fights I would have to be either One Who Prays or . . . or worse."

Worse was One Who Labors, a peasant, the third estate.

"So you chose the monastery?"

William nodded. "I gave my oath I would stick it for a year."

"And there you did do your best? You slaved at Latin and writing and the rest. You learned all that in one year? And?"

"And I prayed up a shit storm. But then he wouldn't let me leave. I showed him I could mount again, even gallop or jump hedges, but he said the family would be better off with me as a bishop or an abbot than another fighter."

The brothers would have found that even funnier, as it meant one son less to divide up the old man's leavings when he took his place in the heavenly choir.

"So then you made yourself so intolerable that the monastery had to throw you out?"

"Wasn't hard."

"I suppose not." Easier than Helmdon, no doubt. "I think I know the rest. You saw the man who was with me in the sanctum."

"Not seeing very well," William admitted, peering around with eyes puffed down to slits.

"He was Sir Stephen de Mandeville, the count's son and one of the king's gentlemen attendants. He was furious at what you had done, but he was impressed."

"He was?" William brightened.

"Impressed by your courage, not your brains. He has influence. He could probably override your duty to obey your father, and he might be able to sponsor me to study at Helmdon without being a servitor. So let's both do our best, Squire Legier. Agreed?"

William did not return my smile. "Always."

I brought the lantern close to inspect my handiwork. "I think that's as much as I can do tonight. Anything I missed?"

"My crotch. Goliath wears very heavy boots."

That problem took two more incantations all to itself. I could not imagine how he had managed to walk at all.

"Now," I said, when I had done what I could. "I have to go to the hall. For some reason there's a party on. I will give you a sleeping potion and then—"

"No you won't."

"It will deaden the pain."

"Satan take the pain! I have work to do and the pain will keep me awake. Help me on with that shirt."

As a man sows, so shall he reap.

William insisted he was not hungry, which likely meant that he did not want to show his sausage-meat face in the hall. I took him back to the sanctum and showed him the text that needed to be transcribed when he had finished the sandstone work. The kid could barely see and had trouble holding the stone, but he set to at once as if nothing had happened.

I paused at the door as I was leaving. "William?"

"Ironfoot?"

So I wasn't "master" anymore. "I just wanted to say that you're the toughest man I ever met. You may be crazy, but by God, you're a warrior!"

"Sod off," he said. "I don't need your approval."

Even before I reached the keep, I could tell that official mourning had been suspended. All the shutters on the great hall's windows stood wide, letting out light, music, and a roar of conversation. A party to honor Sir Stephen's visit, perhaps? It couldn't be the king, because the guards on the door had obviously been drinking. Seeing me, they cried out fake warnings about Merlin arriving.

At the top of the stairs, the noise was louder than anything I had ever heard except thunder. Off to my left a group of men were playing trumpets, fiddles, and recorders, accompanied by women jangling bells and tambourines, plus Sir Scur in his rabbit mask playing bagpipes. In the center of the hall, very cramped, a circle of younger folk were dancing, their hands joined in a great circle.

To my left was a group of knights, Sir Kendryck and his cronies, all of them flushed, leaning on one another, and doing more than their share of noise-making.

"He's here!" Kendryck bellowed. "Look out, everybody, the dragon's keeper has arrived. How is the little shit?"

"Hard at work," I shouted back. "No partying for him."

"Tyrant! We're going to match him up with a bear."

"Won't be fair on the bear," Sir Lucien contributed, "unless we chain his ankle, not its." That was greeted as the joke of the century.

Peering over heads to locate the cause of this celebration, I found it on the dais. The de Mandeville family was there: Stephen and Matilda, with their parents and the usual attendants, Father Randolf, Lady Aveline, Sir Hugh, and Sir Bertrand. But the count and countess were not occupying the chairs of honor. There sat their daughter and a well-worn, weather-beaten man whose graying beard failed to hide the sunken cheeks of someone who has lost most of his teeth. He was undoubtedly old enough to be her father, probably even her grandfather, yet such matches were not uncommon. Everyone was smiling and laughing, dressed in their best. If any of them was faking, it was being done well.

I staggered as a massive arm landed across my shoulders to support a portion—about two hundred pounds—of Sir Kendryck.

"Baron Weldon!" a blast of wine fumes proclaimed in my ear. "King's new chief forester! Huge promotion. Needs new wife to take to court. Very fast betrothal and even faster wedding!"

Fast or not, no doubt this had been in the wind and explained the urgent need for an abortion. Or had I solved that problem by insisting that the blushing bride was not as far along as she had feared? A *really* fast wedding might come soon enough to legitimize her little mishap in the eyes of the world.

"She seems happy enough."

"Going to court!" Kendryck roared confidentially. "Even if the old prune can't give her much of what a woman needs, there'll be lots of pretty lads there who can."

Norman lads, not Saxon, if her attitude toward me was normal. "Good for her. Where's the food?"

"Over there." Kendryck reeled more or less upright. "Cummon, I'll harbinger you." He stormed into the human forest, ruthlessly plowing a furrow for me that I could never have created alone.

The food was being laid out on tables and snatched away by hungry diners just as fast. No one was sitting down. I rinsed my hands in the bowl provided and set to work with the rest, although making no effort to keep up with Kendryck.

"Adept, sir?" The speaker was the clerk, Elmer—lank, pallid, tonsured, and worried. "Sir Stephen said that you might have need of my services tonight."

I nodded while hastily swallowing a mouthful of bream. "I did think that, but Squire William is the most stubborn man the good Lord ever invented, and insists that he can do what I need."

Elmer's eyes opened wide. "But the story is . . . I mean the squires were laughing that he won't see straight for a month."

"He never admits to human frailty. If I do need you later, where could I find you?"

Elmer went into a long and complicated travelogue, describing how to find his cottage, ". . . near the farrier's, not the blacksmith's forge near the gate, but the one near the stablemen's barracks."

"I know the barracks. Start me from there."

ironfoot

The second directions were easier. "But please knock softly, Adept, so you don't wake the babies."

I promised not to waken the babies and of course had to inquire and so learn that there were three of them, the oldest not yet four. Waken a brood like that and you would rouse the whole castle.

"It's not likely I'll need you, though," I said, realizing that I was learning to expect miracles from Squire William Legier.

Once I had eaten, I had no more reason to remain there, so I piled a platter with the softest foods I could see and conscripted John the page to carry that and a flagon of wine back to the sanctum. William, with his contempt for pain, was still hard at work. I insisted that he take a break and some refreshment, while I took over the copying.

Mouth full of food and loose teeth, William uttered a long mumble that was probably, "So what's the party for?"

"Baroness Matilda has found herself another baron, Baron Weldon. High in the king's favor, it seems."

"Grew up near Weldon—never heard of any baron."

"Then you'd better run and warn the count that he's marrying his daughter to a fraud." End of discussion.

Next we had to proofread the copies and correct the mistakes, of which there were remarkably few, considering how poor the light was. Even then I wasn't satisfied.

"Verse eleven doesn't make sense," I said. "*Ineptio?* Why a verb? Why would a criminal play the fool? I think it should be *inepte*—badly."

My squire's attempt at a smirk twisted into a grimace of pain. "I've heard," he mumbled, "old Guy ripping you to shreds for wanting to change even one letter in a script."

249

"But I've known where a change made an incantation work, when it wouldn't before. Let's see . . ." I needed time to find the three-voice version of *Malefice venite* in Guy's grimoire, but when I did, I could confirm that it included that same versicle. My hunch had been right, the word should be *inepte*. In this case I suspected that the corruption had been a genuine scrivener's error, not a deliberate trip wire. Even so, over the centuries such tiny copyists' errors could mount up and any one of them might render an incantation useless.

In the next hour we corrected three more such mistakes by comparison with the other version, and one that I had to make on my own authority, because the versicle and response in question were not present in Guy's copy. I struck them out.

William howled at seeing his work defaced. "How can you do that?"

"Because," I said, "it's unicorn fewmets! It's another deliberate trap to keep the uninitiated from dabbling in matters beyond their ken. Why would this versicle appeal to a Germanic pagan god in the middle of a Latin prayer? Just so the spell won't work if it falls into the wrong hands, that's why. The original sage who transcribed it put that in to deceive the ignorant. He knew it was there and could ignore it."

I was suspicious of another couple of wordings, but did not dare tamper any further with the text. By the time we had read the whole incantation through twice, from back to front, William was spitting blood from his loose teeth and I could barely keep my eyes open. Midnight was long gone.

"Bedtime!" I said. "We both need sleep. We'll summon the killer in the morning. You're out on your feet."

In fact William was seated, but even he didn't argue that time.

chapter 30

By dawn, a few hours later, we were dressed and ready, if not well rested. I wanted to go and fetch Sir Stephen, but William insisted that this was his duty, and limped off to fulfill it. Unhappy at the prospect of trying an unfamiliar incantation before a witness, I read through it a few more times, becoming more and more certain of discrepancies in at least two places.

William returned. "Says he'll be here in a moment." He sat down at the table—gingerly.

"Why did you pick a fight with Goliath? He's the giant, the biggest of the squires, yes?"

"'Cos I knew I could beat the small ones."

"He slaughtered you."

He showed bloody teeth in a grin. "No shame in losing to him, and I got in a few good ones before he got me on the ground and started the execution."

Then I understood. "So no one else is going to challenge you after that, and some knight may want to enlist you?"

William managed something close to a smile. "Oh, you do understand? I was starting to wonder."

Soon afterward, he opened the door for Stephen, bright-eyed, resplendent in an embroidered robe of purple linen, and apparently freshly shaven. He was wearing a sword, which was a troubling sign of the faith he put in my ability to summon the killer.

His smile at William seemed genuine enough, free of mockery. "How are you this morning, Squire?"

"I have felt livelier, Sir Stephen."

"I heard other accounts of the fights. They suggest you should be in need of a month's bed rest."

"They stopped short of driving a stake through my heart, sir."

Stephen laughed and turned to me. "Where do you want me, and which murder will you start with?"

"I do not need to name names, only the crime committed, sir. If there is more than one murderer within range, they should both respond. I shall be happiest if just one person arrives and confesses to all three crimes."

Stephen nodded grimly. "Three people making separate confessions would be the ruin of our house."

Enchanter and cantor sat at the table, but I put Stephen on a stool at the other end of the room, on the pretext that he would be hidden by the door when anyone entered. My real reason was that I found the prospect of a witness unnerving and wanted him as far away as possible, as if that made any difference.

After that, there was nothing to do but begin.

"Set the pitch," I told William, who was having trouble speaking, let alone singing.

William chanted a few words; I nodded. "Fine! Here we go."

First versicle; first response. Second versicle . . .

And finally . . . nothing.

"Didn't work!" I said.

"You can tell?" Stephen asked, surprised.

"Yes, sir. Let's try it again, Squire."

Again nothing happened.

"Then I'm going to try a couple of—I hope—corrections."

Ignoring William's impertinent sigh, I opened the ink bottle and made the additional changes that instinct told me were needed to make sense of the text.

And on the third attempt, it worked. I felt a huge surge of power, a sudden extreme sense of urgency that rapidly faded away. Again William bared his bloodstained teeth, this time in a leer of triumph.

"Success?" Stephen asked.

"Yes, sir. Something should happen. If he's within the castle, he should be here soon. If he's out in the village, he'll need a little longer—although it depends on how long he can resist the call. Some people are more resistant than others. I know because there is a less potent summoning that my tutor uses on me when he and I are searching for herbs in the forest. When he's ready to leave, he can call me back to him. If I am gathering something valuable, I can resist the urge for about ten minutes, but then I start to itch and twitch and sweat and the compulsion becomes unbearable."

Stephen leaned back against a complicated astrological horoscope and folded his arms. "If you can pull this off, Adept, I think the king will offer you employment. In fact, I am sure he will."

My heart leaped like a horse going over a hedge. I must not flub this! "Sir, I honestly believe I have been very lucky so far. My tutor warned me not to try enchantments on my own yet, and I disobeyed him only because the need was so great. I cannot guarantee to meet with such success in future. I cannot call myself a sage without at least two more years at Helmdon. Two years of full-time study, that is."

The knight's smile said he understood the problem. "That might be arranged. You would have to be on call, of course, in case of emergency, and His Grace would expect you to pay off your debt with service after your training is completed."

"You are making my dreams come true, sir."

Stephen smiled and shrugged at the same time. Generosity was easy when you had the royal purse beyond you. "And Squire William? You have—"

Someone knocked on the door, and all three of us jumped. William rose and limped across to open it.

"This seems too soon," I said. "It may just be happenstance."

William said, "Enter, Father."

Stephen and I exchanged horrified glances.

"Whatever have you done to your face, my son?" the priest asked as he stepped inside, raising a hand in blessing. William shut the door, and stayed close to it.

"I was exercising with some of the squires, Father."

"And how are they this morning?"

"I hope they will live, Father."

The priest's gaze switched to me—rather too quickly, I thought, but then I was looking for signs of guilt. He seemed to be breathing harder than usual, as if he had been running.

"Durwin, my son," Father Randolf said, "I just stopped in to apologize for my unseemly display of temper yesterday morning. Such rage is a sin in any man, and especially in one of my calling."

"You always had a vicious streak, Randolf."

The priest wheeled around in a swirl of robes. "Stephen?" Then he took in the grouping—the squire leaning against the door, the knight wearing a sword, and I at a table covered with texts. He had been addressed by name, not by his title.

He strode over to me, snatched up a couple of tablets, and scanned the Latin text. Then he angrily threw them down.

"So you think your deviltry has summoned me here to confess to murder?"

"That is the presumption," Stephen said, rising. "They summoned a murderer and you responded."

"That is an outrageous suggestion! All clergymen have renounced violence. How can you accuse me of such a monstrous crime?"

"Easily, Cousin. I remember lying on the ground with you on top of me, trying to throttle me while you banged my head up and down. Father had a devil of a job hauling you off me. I had thrown your favorite ball into a holly hedge, as I recall. And now you honestly claim that you came running here to apologize for some cross words to an insignificant menial you despise as a mountebank?"

There was a painful pause. Then the priest bowed his head and clasped his hands. After a moment he crossed himself and looked up. "No. I didn't know why I had to come here, but I did. Clearly I underestimated the powers of darkness." He pulled up a stool and sat down, beside the table but not facing it. Stephen did the same. William remained by the door.

"You expect a court to accept witchcraft as evidence?" the priest asked the knight. Adept and squire did not matter now.

"No, but my father will believe me, and probably His Grace the king will also. You will not be allowed within a mile of him."

Randolf shook his head with contempt. "Faugh! You think I have designs on him next? No, this is no great assassination conspiracy you have exposed. I killed the boy Colby in a fit of ungovernable fury. He was an odious, prying little cockroach! He came by the vestry one morning. I thought he wanted to make confession or discuss confirmation, but it turned out that he had been spying, mostly on what his master was up to with female patients, but on some other matters also. He did not want to confess to me, he wanted to blackmail me. I lost my temper—and this time Uncle Richard was not around to control me."

"What, exactly, did you do?" Stephen asked.

"I threw him down on the fleece and smothered him with it. Once I began, I had to finish, and I did. When I was certain he was dead, I wrapped his corpse in the fleece and hid it under the bench. I barely left the vestry for the rest of the day, you may be sure. I could think of nowhere to hide the body permanently within the castle, nor could I smuggle it out by the gate, and it would start to stink fairly soon. So that night I tied the bundle up with rope, carried it to the wall, and dropped it into the moat."

Thus might a man admit to swatting a mosquito. I was appalled to see no sign of regret, no repentance or human sympathy. Poor little Colby had not been a person at all. *He was a nuisance, so I killed him.*

Stephen's face was white, and I suspected that my own was, too. That a man of God would confess such a crime with such indifference!

"And is that all?" Stephen demanded. "There have been two other unnatural deaths."

"I admit to both. Archibald was a skilled sage, especially masterful in astrology. He began to drop hints. I realized that he suspected me of being responsible for his varlet's disappearance, and once he knew where to direct his arts, he might very well uncover evidence that would incriminate me." He glanced at me. "As this callow boy has now managed to do, so I'm sure it would have been easy for a qualified and experienced sage. I slipped in here one morning and poisoned his wine supply. When I saw him stumbling around on his way to dinner, I knew my scheme had worked."

"It did not worry you that he might share that poisoned wine with a visitor?"

"Archibald was not one for sharing, and he drank more than most. I expected him to finish the wine by nightfall."

"And how did you pass by the pentagram to get in here?"

"I once asked him . . . We were sitting here one long winter night, arguing about the dark arts. I asked him what would happen to a child who tried to open the door. He laughed and said not much. 'It will feel like a blow on his funny bone, that's all.' And it was exactly like that."

Sensing that there was to be no attempt to escape, William had taken the stool by the door that Stephen had vacated. If there was to be any violence, it would most likely be started by Stephen, who seemed tempted to tear his cousin apart. I suspected that neither William nor I would try to stop him.

"And our Uncle Rolf?"

"The same reason. He was at least as skilled as Archibald, probably far more so, and he knew that he had a murderer to find, which Archibald had not known for certain." He gestured at the shelves. "It was easy. I took the poisoned wine flagon to the castle and switched it for the water bottle by his bed. When this Saxon boy turned up in his stead, I thought I was safe, but he straightaway found Colby's corpse wrapped in a fleece that could be traced back to me, and I realized that I was in great peril. That was why I lost my temper."

"Lucky that I had witnesses there to defend me," I muttered, but no one paid heed.

"And you relied on Archbishop Becket to defend you? You believe that the Church will defrock you, but that will be your only punishment?"

Randolf shook his head. "That is not true. I will undoubtedly be confined in a monastery for the rest of my days."

"A layman would be hanged."

"But I am a priest. Not a righteous priest, a disgrace to my calling, I admit, but still a priest, and a secular monarch may not touch me." He smiled and I longed to punch his arrogant face in.

Stephen grimaced, as at a bad taste, and looked to me. "I repeat what I said earlier. His Grace has great need of men with such ability, Adept. If he sends for you when he is here you may use a cane, but a quarter staff is too easily turned into a weapon to be admitted to his presence."

"I understand, sir. I can walk with a cane. May I just ask the witness how he knew which bottles up there contained poison?"

Randolf curled his lip at me. "You suspect me of lying—me, a priest? On another of those nights Archibald and I were whiling away in idle gossip, I reached for what I thought was the wine bottle on the table and he laughed that I had better not drink from that one. He had been working with it, mixing a sleeping potion for a patient in pain. He mentioned the name, dwale, and then listed some others that were as deadly. I had to gamble that he would not recognize the taste. Evidently he did not, any more than Rolf did, the following day."

"You will come with me now to repeat your confession to my father," Stephen said.

Randolf rose obediently. "And then you will send me with an escort to the bishop in Northampton? But please not Sir Kendryck! Whatever my sins, they do not deserve another four hours' torment in the company of Sir Kendryck."

"In my opinion," Stephen said as he opened the door, "your sins deserve an eternity in Hell."

The door closed. Enchanter and cantor sat in horrified silence for a while. We had triumphed, but the victory tasted like ashes to me, and apparently to William also. Two men and a boy had been ruthlessly destroyed by an arrogant popinjay who lacked the decency even to pretend remorse.

At last William said, "How could a man like that become a priest?"

"He isn't a priest. He never was and never intended to be. He's a politician. He has a count for an uncle on one side and a bishop for an uncle on the other. He had his eyes on the king's council or even the Roman curia. He probably keeps a cardinal's hat among his spare underwear. Makes me ill. Don't know about you, Squire, but I'm going back to bed."

"Sounds like a good idea, master, but before you do, I'd be really grateful if you would sing another lullaby to my nuts."

chapter 31

Distant cheers and the strident cry of trumpets awoke me like a peal of thunder in my ear. *The king!* Suppose he sent for the Saxon miracle worker and men-at-arms came to drag me naked from my bed at this time of day? I threw off the covers and massively collided with my squire, who had been similarly inspired.

Very few minutes later we were both dressed, groomed, and downstairs. Waiting. And waiting. And still waiting.

Impetuous but relentless, tyrannical but famous for his justice, dreaded by his enemies and adored by his followers, irascible, exuberant, terrifying, inexhaustible, and overwhelming, Henry the Second by the Grace of God, King of England and Wales, Duke of Normandy and Aquitaine, Count of Anjou, etc., etc., lord of a third of Europe, was a fanatical follower of the chase. He swept into Barton like a whirlwind at the head of a company of about sixty. That was a tiny fraction of the hundreds who would accompany so great a monarch on state occasions. Even a bishop or the abbot of a great abbey might lead a larger train, but the fact that more were not needed was a glowing tribute to the strength of the king's peace, which he had restored after the chaos of his predecessor's rule.

He was at that time thirty-one years old and just completing the tenth year of his reign.

Would a monarch eager to be about his pleasure waste time on trivia like some crippled Saxon youth who had lucked into the answer to Count Richard's domestic problems—admittedly unusual domestic problems? He had come to inspect the crenellation, perhaps to collect his new chief forester, Baron Weldon, and then be on his way. Conceivably he might nod agreement if Sir Stephen—a great power in Barton Castle but a very minor attendant in the king's household—managed to catch the royal ear long enough to mention a promising adept who could be engaged at a very minor cost. Of course he would not waste royal hunting time in receiving the lad. Why did I think I mattered?

Then a fist thundered on the door and the way Squire William hurtled across the room to open it testified that my latest incantation had worked well that morning.

I was close on his heels, of course. Outside loomed a giant, seeming to fill the narrow alley from side to side. I had seen this colossus eating at the squires' table and I marveled anew that William had survived their encounter. What was new was the magnificent shiner he now sported.

"Squire Delaney of Carlton!" William said. "Feeling better now?"

"Deal with you later," the titan growled. "The adept is wanted. I was told to give him this, or I'd break it over your head." He offered a stout oak walking stick. That someone—almost certainly Stephen—had made the notorious Goliath play page was a wicked jest.

I set off as fast as I could, leaning on the unfamiliar cane, flanked by an urgent Squire Delaney and followed by William. He still had a limp, but it was no worse than Delaney's. William had not been invited but was undoubtedly coming in the hope of being admitted into the royal presence. A man might live a long lifetime and never see more of his monarch than his image on coins.

Came a taunt from behind: "Say, Goliath? The adept has an enchantment that cools hot balls nicely. Worked on me, might work on apes. You should ask him to try."

"Next time I'll kick harder, then."

"You'll be able to sing soprano in church. . . ."

The insults did not sound serious, more like banter between two men who had tested each other and were satisfied by the results. I could have cured his black eye also, had he accepted my offer the previous evening, but a man whose friends called him Goliath was probably the sort of he-man who never accepted help from anyone.

But then we arrived at the stairway up to the keep, where a squad of royal archers stood guard. Master of Horse Alwin was there to identify people. Goliath and I were allowed to proceed, but William was turned back and joined the crowd of spectators.

The great hall had changed yet again. Three clerks were bent over a small table by the door, scribbling furiously. The only other furniture in sight was the count's grand chair, up on the dais, presently unoccupied. Men were standing around everywhere, speaking softly, and almost all wearing green hunting garb, including the count. The absence of women showed that this was a business meeting, and only a very privileged few stood on the dais: the count, Sir Stephen, Baron Weldon, Sir Hugh, four men I did not know—and the king.

Although not especially tall, Henry Plantagenet was burly, and already starting to put on weight. He was still more beefy than plump, yes, but most of the men present were knights, and beefy by definition. His hair was reddish, as was his thin mustache, and his face was heavily freckled. He had a large head, which he bore thrust forward aggressively, his blue eyes never still. He rarely sat down, even to eat, and even those engaged in private conversations never took their gaze away from him for more than a second or two. The most powerful man in Christendom after the pope, he was restless, fidgety, yet fully intent on whatever he was considering at the moment.

I stood by myself and studied the protocol: when to bow, when to kneel. A few men were left on their knees to state their business. In general, the king seemed displeased. The news that a priest, a Norman aristocrat, had confessed to three murders would not have improved his mood, whatever it had been before he heard that. He must gain some satisfaction from the news, though, for it fully supported his contention that the clergy should be subject to the full weight of the law.

Then he dismissed a man impatiently and strode across to the group containing Stephen, who had noted my arrival and nodded to me. Now he beckoned, and it seemed that the hall hushed for a moment at the sight of a tall youth hobbling forward on a cane. Who was this in a cleric's robe, untonsured, and most likely a mere Saxon from the look of his flaxen mop?

Feeling my hand shaking on my cane, I mounted the dais, bowed, and went to be presented.

"Adept Durwin of Helmdon, Lord King," Stephen said.

I would have knelt, but the king said, "No. Come over here." He turned and strode across to a window—he never just walked anywhere.

No one followed us. *Not just an audience, but a private audience!*

Henry turned his back on the rest of the company and assessed me with the bluest eyes I had ever seen. "What happened to your leg?"

I told him.

He dismissed the matter with a nod, but then came a hint of smile and a twinkle. "I have heard a very improbable account of your actions here during the last few days, Durwin. I want to hear it from your own lips." He spoke the French of Anjou, softer than the Normans'.

I told him, stressing that I had disobeyed my tutor's orders only because the need seemed to justify it. I tried not to brag, but I didn't deny my success either, and I gave full credit to William's astonishing assistance. I was taller than he, but not by much, and I felt much smaller under his intimidating gaze. It hardly flickered until I had finished.

Henry was a marvelous listener, guiding the speaker with nods that were almost imperceptible and yet signaled, either that he already knew that so move on, or that he hadn't known that but he took the point. He interrupted with questions only twice.

At the end he asked, "How old are you?"

"Twenty, Lord King."

"Old to be merely an adept."

I explained again, as briefly as I could, but I felt bound to mention that it was my skill with horses that had made me indispensable to Sage Rolf's travel plans. That, and not my philosophical skills, had finally freed me from servitude in the stable and promoted me to adept.

"What do you plan to do next?" the king demanded.

"I hope to continue my studies at Helmdon, Lord King, although—"

"And become a sage?" The king did not smile, but the sense of menace faded slightly. "Let us hear what sort of advice you will give, Sage-to-be. Count Richard petitioned for leave to repair his stockade, which was in danger of collapsing, and which permission we granted. But he has gone beyond that, replacing the entrance with a stone barbican, and starting to replace the stockade with an ashlar curtain wall. Now he wants to crenellate and greatly extend the keep. How would you counsel us to answer his plea?"

I ought to have fainted dead away on the spot, but didn't. Obviously the king was not asking me for military advice, for I knew nothing of warfare. Nor could I imagine how a knack for enchantment could be relevant. What then?

"Sire, I knew Count Richard's brother for six years. I have known the count himself for only four days, admittedly at a time of great stress for him, when men tend to reveal their inner selves. Even knowing that he originally fought for your uncle against your royal mother, and later switched sides, I can say only that I have not seen or heard any reason to believe that he is not totally loyal to Your Grace. If a secure castle here would be of advantage to Your Grace, then I believe the de Mandeville family could be trusted with it."

My answer won a twinkle in the royal eye, for what I had diplomatically said was that I would be very surprised if His Grace wanted a privately owned fortress so close to his own great castle at Northampton. I admit that I knew how in the ten years of his reign, he had ordered over two thousand such strongholds razed to the ground. I have given kings unwelcome advice several times in my life since then, but even that first day, I knew better than to do so on my first audience.

"Clearly put. Whose man are you, Durwin?"

"Um . . ." In theory every man owed allegiance to someone. Even King Henry must do homage to King Louis for his lands in France. "Sire, I am not sure. I suppose my stepfather's, although

I have never met him. My father apprenticed me as servitor to Sage Guy Delany of Helmdon, but my father has since died, my mother is ailing, and I am the eldest. I need at least two more years at the academy to become a qualified sage. When I was certified as an adept this week, Guy told me I could not continue to work as a stable hand, so that relationship has ended." I was yet a few months short of my majority, but to mention that again would complicate matters even further.

The king's nod acknowledged a tactfully worded plea. "So you need a patron to complete your studies?" Sir Stephen would have told him this.

"Aye, Lord King."

"Were I to engage your services, Adept Durwin, would you always speak the truth to me as you know it?"

"Sire, I swear I would."

"So be it, then."

"I can imagine no greater honor than to serve Your Grace."

"Effective enchantment is almost as rare as honesty. In combination they are almost unprecedented. Sir Walter!"

One of the watching courtiers hurried over to attend the king. He was a ponderous man who carried a weight of years and had a worried, unhealthy look to him.

"This is Adept Durwin of . . ."

"Helmdon."

"Helmdon. Swear him in as . . . as a *familiaris*."

"Kneel, Adept," Sir Walter intoned. I knelt and laid down my cane so I could place my hands between the king's. Then I *repeat-after-me*'d the oath of allegiance and arose as a king's man. Missing my quarterstaff's support, I swayed, and it was the king who caught my elbow to steady me. A collective murmur of surprise sighed through the hall like wind in a forest.

"We grant him a pension of forty shillings for each of the next two years. In return, he is to complete his studies and then present himself to us, wherever we may be, no later than the Feast of Stephen two years from now. He can pay his own transportation."

"Your Grace is most generous!" I said, bowing. *Familiaris* can mean anything from slave to servant to friend. It undoubtedly had some specific meaning here, but I had no idea which. Forty shillings was a fair income for a priest or a senior clerk; I had found a sponsor beyond my brightest hopes.

"But we may call on you sooner if we find urgent need of your great skill."

I bowed again while assuring my king that I was always at his service. By the time I straightened up, he had left me and was returning to the group on the dais. Stephen caught my eye and grinned. It would do his own standing no harm to have sponsored such an appointment.

Court philosopher elect? I lurched down off the dais, half expecting to float. Two years of study uninterrupted by horses and wood chopping? It was beyond dreams. But then I did come down with a crash, figuratively, when I saw that I was being beckoned by a man wearing the green cape of a sage.

He was short and portly with a grizzled beard and mistrustful, heavy-lidded eyes. He stood within a group of other men, all of whom were narrowly watching me approach. Two of them wore green capes, and a younger pair in the background sported the white capes of adepts.

I bowed. "Adept Durwin of Helmdon."

The little man's smile was the most sinister I had seen in years. "Aubrey de Fours, enchanter general. We hear that you have been working miracles here at Barton, Adept."

He did not introduce his companions, some of whom were so grandly garbed that they could not possibly be his subordinates.

In my experience, you never get silver linings without clouds. Even then I knew enough of the world to understand that inner circles are always heavily fortified against newcomers, and royal favor always arouses jealousy. Here was an enemy—perhaps not the only one, but likely the most dangerous. When I went to court as a sage, I would be put under this man's orders.

"Then the stories you heard have been exaggerated, Your Wisdom. Ask the king. I told him the truth."

"It is unwise to do otherwise. We are told that you prevailed upon a bishop's ordained nephew to confess to three murders. You don't see that as a miracle?"

The onlookers—while always keeping a wary eye on the king—were enjoying the encounter. I, flush with triumph, was not inclined to toady to anyone. My future reputation, whatever it might be, must begin here.

"But you do, Your Wisdom? Which is the miracle—that he committed these crimes or that he admitted them?"

Grins widened in surprise and amusement: first point to the Saxon kid. De Fours was an expert and did not flinch.

"Oh, the latter, definitely. You could hardly have found a faster way to His Grace's heart just now than by exposing gross depravity among the clergy. What incantations did you apply?"

"My knowledge of herb lore told me the potions the killer used," I said, and a hint of a sneer told me that Enchanter General Aubrey put very little stock in herb lore. "Then I applied the *Ubi malum*, which located the child's body. That was the third murder discovered, but it predated the others by a week or so. Then the *Morðor wile ut* provided some very enlightening testimony." I couldn't be sure about de Fours, but most of the onlookers clearly did not know enough of the old tongue to translate that title. "And lastly, the *Malefice venite*."

"Impressive," the sage murmured. "How long have you been an adept?"

"Four days, sir."

Now the spectators were openly grinning at this battle of wits.

De Fours's eyelids drooped even lower. "Then you were excessively foolhardy! You ventured such incantations without supervision?"

"My only help was my squire. Fortunately he is a great tribute to Helmdon—fluent in Latin and scribing a very fair hand. He also sings well and enjoys all-in fisticuffs against men twice his size."

Now the sage sneered, detecting ridicule. "But you needed a third voice for the *Malefice venite*."

"I prefer the two-voice version. It's shorter and simpler."

"No one in two hundred years has managed to make that one work!"

I feigned surprise. I had no intention of revealing my secret editing. "It worked for me. I know of other texts corrupted by scriveners' errors. If you don't believe me, pray ask Sir Stephen de Mandeville. When the murderer obeyed our summons and came to confess, Sir Stephen was there as a witness."

And he had presented me to the king. Another hit for the Saxon.

"I should like to borrow your grimoire to see it, Adept."

"I can't lend you the book itself, Enchanter, for it belongs to Count Richard. At least I suppose it does, because it was the late Sage Archibald's. But I shall be happy to give you my copy of the text."

"Including a few scriveners' errors, no doubt," said one of the watchers, and they all laughed except the two in green capes.

Sage de Fours did not, and his eyes had narrowed to slits. "So to what office did His Grace swear you—adept general?"

That provoked some sniggers.

"*Familiaris*, Your Wisdom."

No one said a word, and I saw no change in Aubrey's expression, but out of the corner of my eye I noticed heads turning as looks were exchanged. Apparently my rank was to be somewhat higher than water bearer to the royal flowerpots.

At that moment our cordon of witnesses parted to admit a handsome, finely dressed page of around thirteen or so. It was to me that he bowed.

"Adept, Her Grace will receive you now."

chapter 32

i well remember the shiver of alarm I felt at that summons—the back of my neck prickled. I spun around and scanned the far end of the hall. It was not large, as I said earlier, but in my ordeal of meeting the king, I had completely overlooked the cluster of women at the far end. The queen? Ignorant as I was of etiquette, protocol, and politics, I knew enough history to know that there were always factions in courts, as dangerous as whirlpools. Heirs, queens, and royal mistresses could all have their own parties. I knew that Prince Henry was still a child, and Queen Eleanor was reputed to be both clever and beautiful, but that was the limit of my information.

I said something, and lurched off after the boy. I don't remember bowing to take my leave of the enchanter general as I certainly should have done. If I didn't, my apparent rudeness would not have warmed his feelings for me. Our rivalry would endure.

The count's chair still sat empty on the dais, but now I saw the countess's ahead of me, occupied by a lady. Six or eight women were gathered around her, some seated, some standing.

"By what name should I present you, Adept?"

"D-D-Durwin of Helmdon. How should I address Her Grace?"

The page glanced at me in surprise, and slowed his pace.

"'Lady Queen,' mostly. Sometimes 'Your Grace' or just 'my lady.'"

"Thank you."

"The prince just as 'my lord' or 'sir.'"

I looked again and this time noticed a boy standing beside the queen. The countess was seated at her other side. Everyone there was watching my approach. The page increased his pace again.

I repeated, "Thank you."

Then we arrived.

The page said, "Adept Durwin of Helmdon, Your Grace."

I knelt, hoping that the tremor in the hand holding my cane was not too obvious. I had *expected* to be summoned to the king, or at least had hoped for an audience, and so I had had time to think over what might be involved, but I had no idea what the queen could want with me. Since the countess was with her, she must know why the king had summoned me, and might even guess why he had accepted me into his service.

Aliénore d'Aquitaine had been renowned as the richest and most beautiful woman in Europe. After inheriting both the Dukedom of Aquitaine and County of Poitou in her own right, she had certainly been wealthier than most crowned monarchs. At fifteen she had married King Louis of France, and had later accompanied him to the Holy Land on crusade. She had borne him two daughters, but he had arranged for their marriage to be annulled in the hope that a second wife would give him sons.

Eleanor, aged thirty, had promptly married Henry, then count of Anjou, eleven years her junior. Henry had gone on to conquer Normandy and inherit England. That day, meeting her for the first time, I judged her to be in her mid-thirties. In fact she was forty-two and had already given Henry four sons—the first of whom had died in infancy—and two daughters.

Queens, of course, are well preserved and well dressed. I had never seen such a wonder as her scarlet gown, for it was of silk, embroidered with gold thread and pearls. A pearl-spangled French hood covered her hair and a wimple concealed her neck. Compared to such regal glory, the countess beside her looked like a rustic frump. Even Baroness Matilda, who was standing at the back of the group, was outshone by a woman twice her age, although clothing and ornamentation had something to do with that.

Eleanor must have seen my reaction, but she smiled graciously. "I am told that you used your magic powers to summon the triple-murderer and compel him to confess."

"My helper and I did summon him with an ancient chant, Lady Queen. I doubt very much that he would have confessed had Sir Stephen not been present."

"Modesty? You are refreshing, Adept. And you obviously impressed my husband. What office did he bestow on you?"

"*Familiaris*, my lady."

Enchanter General Aubrey de Fours had kept a straight face on hearing that news, but the queen raised her finely shaped eyebrows. "Did he, now? You are indeed special. You will be taking up attendance at court, then?"

"Not yet, my lady. His Grace is graciously sponsoring me to complete my studies." I wasn't going to show my ignorance by asking what a *familiaris* actually did.

She laughed. "He would have done better hiring you to teach that fraud, de Fours. He couldn't summon a sausage hawker at a joust."

"Can you prophesy, like Merlin?"

The question came from the prince. No one else would have
dared to interrupt Queen Eleanor. She did not reprimand him,
so I turned my attention to him.

"Anyone can prophesy, my lord." I was learning court equiv-
ocation already. "Would you like to hear a prophecy right now?"

Of course, he said, "Yes!"

I knew that Prince Henry, the king's heir and eldest surviving son, had been born a few months after his father's accession,
so he must be nine years old. He was tall for his age, with red hair
and the same piercing blue eyes as his father.

I raised a finger to Heaven and dramatically proclaimed, "It
will rain!" Then I held my breath. If this nine-year-old thought I
was mocking him, I would have made a lifelong enemy.

But his mother laughed, and he grinned.

"Only God knows what will really happen in this world,
my lord," I said. "Human prophecies must be considered very
carefully. Since I did not say *when* rain would fall or *where*, my
prophecy is undoubtedly true."

"What of Merlin's prophecies, though?" The boy was stubborn.

Here I knew I must be more cautious. There were dozens
of Merlin prophecies floating around England, and a prince
could easily have found one or more that he would like to think
applied to him.

"Sir, if the prophecy names names or gives a date for what is
foretold, then I will believe that Merlin himself made the prophecy, and I will believe it."

The blue eyes glinted angrily. "What about horoscopes, then?
Why does one horoscope say one thing and another say another?
Are the stars telling lies?"

Oh, so that was it, and he had trapped me nicely. "No, the
stars do not lie, my lord, but the men who interpret them can

make mistakes, just as hunting dogs can follow the wrong scent, or hawks strike the wrong bird."

"Or leave out the bad bits?"

I conceded with a nod. "And even add in a few good bits. Not everyone is honest."

"Can you make horoscopes?"

Trapped, hung, gutted, and skinned.

"Not here, sir. Back in the academy at Helmdon we have the charts and records required, and people more learned than I."

"I want you to cast mine!" Stubborn, stubborn, stubborn.

Before I could speak, the queen said, "A good horoscope is usually written in Latin. Is that not true, Adept Durwin?"

I thought I was saved. "The best ones certainly are, Your Grace."

"Learned, complicated Latin?"

"Precise, technical Latin, drawing subtle conclusions from obscure facts."

"You see, Richard?" she said. "If I ask Adept Durwin to draw up your horoscope, it will be a dangerous document to show to just anyone. Your enemies might get hold of it and use it against you. And you couldn't read it."

He saw the hook in the worm at once, and glared angrily at her. Then he nodded. "I will study harder, so I can read it for myself, as long as Durwin draws it."

Queen Eleanor, as she had shown many times already and was to demonstrate frequently in the future, was a fiendishly clever and dangerous woman. "Is that not fair, Adept? You, and my son means just you personally, will draw up Richard's horoscope for him, being completely honest, adding nothing and leaving out nothing. He is to study his Latin until he can read it. We shall of course reward your labors handsomely." She had just inspired her son to study harder and entangled me in her coils.

"I am honored beyond words, Lady Queen." Heaven was pouring blessings on me: *familiaris* to the king and astrologer to the queen? "And the date, time, and place of—" I suddenly realized that she had not been calling her son by the name I had assumed was his.

"Richard was born just after matins on the eighth of September in the year of our Lord, 1157, at Beaumont Palace, near Oxford."

So this was the second surviving son, just seven years old, but already his mother's favorite. His height had misled me. He grew up to be a giant, of course, eight or nine inches taller than me, and a mighty warrior, known as Lionheart.

At that moment King Henry decided it was time to go and kill deer, although everyone else was thinking longingly about dinner.

chapter 33

The king snapped out a few orders and ran, leaping from the dais to vanish down the spiral staircase. His men poured after him, almost rioting at the stair head.

Granted leave by the queen, I followed at my own pace, and was stopped by the clerks at the table, who proceeded to weigh out the first instalment of my royal pension in silver pennies. I signed for them, and we arranged how the balance would be paid to me by the sheriff of Northamptonshire. My tiny purse would not hold such a fortune, but they gave me a leather bag to carry it. Clutching more wealth than my father would have seen in his lifetime, I floated away in a rosy daze.

The usual guards on the door were missing. I hobbled down the long wooden stair, staying well to one side because men in ones and twos went tearing down past me. When I reached the bailey, the turmoil had moved out of sight, although I could hear much angry horse noise coming from the direction of the stables.

The only man in sight was the fool, slouched against a cottage wall, his single eye glittering inside his hood.

"One ear hears that one leg may climb much faster than most pairs do," he growled.

I decided to take that as a compliment. "On the first rung, 'tis sure. But if one leg slips it has no friend to keep it from falling."

"And sometimes one eye can see farther than two."

About to pass by, I detected a gleam of truth in that chaff and halted. "What do you see that I have missed, Sir Scur?"

"My bad eye sees no good, and my good eye sees much evil, but kings may see only what others show them." The monster would have been kept out of the royal view, no doubt.

"Aye, but was that what you meant before?"

"A man may sin alone, may he not?"

"He may," I said patiently.

"And two alone can sin together?"

"It has been known."

"And three is one too many." The old man twitched his hood so that his features disappeared altogether, and lurched into a shambling run, disappearing into the maze of cottages and sheds. Either he knew something he dared not put into words, or else his madness had flared up at news of my great success. But he had definitely been trying to tell me something, and this left me troubled.

In addition to the distant turmoil of king's followers madly trying to get their mounts saddled, all at the same time in a very confined space, I could hear loud male adolescent laughter. Tracking that, I came on a group of squires. Few of the Barton knights would be departing with the royal party, so their attendants could stay out of the way and avoid being ordered about. William was in the midst of the noisy pack, which included his former foes, Colbert, Delaney, and Kenric. They were all joking and mock wrestling, but the baiting was lighthearted now, since the despised squire had proved himself to be no milksop.

Someone spotted my approach and shouted a warning. They
all began bowing elaborately, uttering cries of "Make way for the
king's man!" Father Randolf had few supporters among these
hellions.

William certainly belonged in such company more than he
did in Helmdon. I had come from there with two companions; if
I had to go home alone how would I manage five horses?

William pulled loose and smartly saluted. "Congratulations,
Adept. I hear that your success has been justly rewarded."

"I could have done nothing without your skills and support,
Squire." His new friends were listening.

"Nor I without your example. Your commands, my lordly
master?"

"Just don't do any more fighting! I'm going back to the sanctum until dinner is ready."

"You heard!" a red-haired squire said, and punched him.
"You're not allowed to fight back."

William hooked a foot and pushed, spreading the attacker
flat on his back. "Now stand on him," Kenric suggested. "That
still won't be fighting." Other, lewder suggestions followed.

I left them to it. As well try to make a choir of cats sing in
tune.

Back at the sanctum, I hastened to hide my new wealth in the
secret closet. Then I sat down to let my heartbeat slow and my
mind absorb all that had just happened. I looked around almost
sadly. My job here was done. My duty to return the horses to
Helmdon required me to leave as soon as possible, and a brief
but epic chapter in my life would be over. I wished I had some
parchment so that I could copy out a few of the incantations
in Sage Archibald's grimoires. But the count would surely not

grudge me a few wooden panels. I settled down at the table to begin writing.

Before I could even open a book, I was interrupted by a thump on the door. Outside loomed Sir Kendryck, flaunting his inevitable big grin.

"My nose needs attention," he said. "So while you're not hobnobbing with royalty, I thought you might spare a humble wounded Saxon a few moments of your time."

"Happy to. You're much better company than most of them. Hold on a minute." I replaced all the grimoires in the cupboard, took up my satchel, plus—after a moment's indecision—my new cane. I was an adept now, and should not need a quarterstaff to assert authority. I set off with the knight to the infirmary.

Kendryck, as usual, was in a talkative mood. "That squire of yours, the one that mashed me . . . squires're calling him 'Wildcat.' . . . Wouldn't he be happier . . .? I mean, I don't want to offend, but . . ."

"You won't offend. Ask me."

There was a brief pause while we were passing the laundry and had to exchange innuendoes with the maids. Then Kendryck got back to business.

"Would you release him to me? He's a born fighter like I've never seen before, and I don't believe he's as happy as . . . I mean, I think he'd really like to get back into knights' training. Every squire in the castle is urging his master to swear him in. Kenric's giving me no peace. I expect some of them have asked you already?"

"Nary a one so far," I said. "I am certain William would be ecstatic to become your man, Sir Kendryck, but he isn't sworn to me. His father contracted with the academy to educate him as a sage. Dean Odo would love to be rid of him, because he's a rabid bear without a chain in Helmdon. But he's not twenty-one yet and has to do as his father tells him."

"I'll ask his sire, then," Kendryck said. "Anyone else asks, you'll tell them I'm first in line?"

"Not unless William wants me to, I won't. Knowing him, I'm sure he's already picked out the poor wretch he'd like to attach himself to. Here we are."

In the infirmary I laid out bandages and some fever-reducing herbs, while Kendryck continued to chatter. Told to lie down on a cot, he obeyed without stopping his monologue. He remarked how impressive the king was, and what an improvement he was over his late Uncle Stephen, how William ought to be whomped a few times for cracking his—Kendryck's—ribs and so keeping him out of the hunt, what a fantastic sage I would make if I stayed on at Barton as the count was sure to ask me to, but of course everyone knew that the king had claimed me.

"You a *familiaris* now?" he asked.

Here was the opportunity I needed! "What's that?"

"You'd better learn! The *familiares* are the king's friends, the confidants he sends out to do what needs to be done. His troubleshooters."

"All nobles."

"Not with this king, they say! Some commoners, too."

Small wonder my appointment had caused surprise. Of course the king could change it any time he fancied, if I did not measure up to his hopes.

Sir Kendryck was already off chasing another hare. "Loved the way you fixed that stuck-up priest! Yattering at us about our sins when he goes murdering children! What sin compares with that, huh? Bouncing a few buxom maidens doesn't—"

"A few?"

"A dozen or two, but hell's teeth, I'm twenty-two years old already. I'm not really lecherous like some I could name. And none of them were real maidens in the technical sense of the word, except maybe one. But where's the harm in that? Not one ever complained. Anyhow, I never liked the man. Old Father Christophe, now, he was an old dear, and his wife too. But Randolf? To listen to him, God made Heaven for Normans and us Saxon trash could expect nothing but the worst. Had to put up with him all the way to Northampton and back again until I wanted to punch his scrawny pompous nose."

"Hold still a moment," I said, "until I get this packing out."

"Ow!"

"Sorry. That's done. Hold this rag to it in case it bleeds some more."

"Poor Alwin's got the escort job this time, but he has it easy. The priest won't speak to him except if he confesses, and Alwin can always threaten to gag him and tie him to his horse, since he's a confessed murderer. What I think—"

"Hush!" I said. "I'm going to sing an enchantment that should make your nose heal straight. You don't want the girls to laugh at you for having a nose that bends to the left, do you?"

"Dunno. It might match the right bend on—"

"Shut *up*!" I said, which was no way to speak to a belted knight. The healing spell might work better a few days later in the healing process, but I wasn't going to be here then. Certain two-part enchantments might work even better.

I had barely finished before the much-delayed bell for dinner began to sound. The treatment was at once adjourned by mutual consent.

When knight and adept arrived at the scrum of diners waiting to wash their hands, Kendryck pushed me forward with a bellow of "Make way for the king's man!" and the crowd opened like the Red Sea for Moses. Squires and knights—lesser folk went elsewhere—stepped aside for the hero, touching forelocks and cheering me. I was a hero because I had unmasked the murderer, and I was the king's man. Surely any minute now I would wake up.

After that, when a belated dinner arrived, the king's friend was not at all surprised to find himself seated between the countess and the baroness again. The queen had departed, heading back to Northampton. William was down at the squires' table, between the two he had fought, Colbert and Delaney. Thanks to my ministrations, his black eyes and swollen face were in better shape than theirs. He was clearly just as popular among them as I was among the nobility. My promotion had been less painful, that was all.

As it was Friday, there was no meat other than fish, but the high table was served sturgeon, a gift from the king, a royal fish that tasted like fine beef.

Sir Bertrand du Blois, the steward, presided in the absence of count and marshal, but the countess pretty much ignored him, preferring to talk with me. The countess was much pleased with me. She had predicted who would turn out to be the killer, although for totally wrong reasons, and I had proved her right. Randolf might be a relation, but he wasn't from *her* side of the family.

"My husband will naturally reward you handsomely for your services, Adept," she purred. "How much did the king give you?"

"His Grace was most generous, my lady."

She shot me a withering look. "Well, don't expect a mere count to top the king."

I had already had a brilliant idea on this topic. "If I might be so bold, my lady . . . the sage's sanctum contains no less than five

283

grimoires, which is an astonishing collection for a single sage to have amassed. I suspect that most of them were there when you hired Sir Archibald, and so are technically yours. If I might beg a gift of one of them, that would be more than adequate recompense for what little I have achieved in your service."

She beamed. "That is easily granted. Take two, one from the count and one from me, with our thanks."

I felt more than a little guilty as I thanked her—not because the replacement sage would need those books, as he would probably arrive with his own grimoire, assembled during his training—but because selling off that little library might bring in enough money to run Barton Castle for a year, and she clearly did not know that.

"We may not even employ a house sage in future," she remarked. "Once this pile is razed, our need for staff will be much reduced."

"I am sorry. It must be a great blow to lose your ancestral home."

"It's not my ancestral home, boy. I am not at all sorry. I shall get to live in a proper house now, instead of this horrible old cage."

I had no reply to that. I wondered how many servants might find themselves homeless and jobless when the walls began to come down.

Baroness Matilda, on my other side, eventually acknowledged my existence, because she needed me to pass her the pickled eels. I congratulated her on her betrothal.

"Have you known him long, or was it love at first sight?"

She shrugged, as if my good wishes were of no account, and the upcoming marriage little more. "Love has nothing to do with it, Adept. Beds are warmer with two in them. I have been married before; he has had two previous wives. The only tricky point in the negotiations was how his estate will be divided if I give him more children."

"He has some of his own?"

"Four sons, three fully adult and one almost so. My son needs a father. When he is seven, I shall probably have to send him home to his uncle in Kilpeck. He is his late father's heir, if he can manage to live long enough to come into his own."

"*My lady!* You cannot mean—"

She tossed her head. "Of course I can mean it. Wicked uncles are as lethal as measles to young heirs, but my new husband is the king's chief forester, and the king's ear is strong protection."

"Chief forester is a very prestigious post."

"A very demanding one. Baron Weldon will be traveling a great deal, in attendance on the king when he is in England, inspecting the forests even when he is not." She smiled—at her own future, not at me. "But it does have its rewards."

"Fresh venison?"

She rolled her eyes: how naïve can a man get? "I am thinking of New Year gifts. Noble lords whose lands fall within the king's forest cannot hunt on them without permission from the king or his chief forester."

I raised my wine and toasted her future prosperity. She turned away to speak with Aveline, her other neighbor. I was trash and unworthy of the royal attention that I had been granted and she had not.

chapter 34

i sent William off to the infirmary to tidy up and bring back my satchel, while I returned to the sanctum to gloat over the five grimoires. Which to choose? I would return Guy's with thanks and innocently ask if he would now like to look over my two. Of course he would probably just have me copy them out in their entirety for his personal library.

I decided I could not choose between the five until I had listed all their contents, so I found a passably clean writing tablet and set to work. I had trouble concentrating. Being sworn in as a king's confidant was enough to justify a two-day drunk all by itself. On a darker side, I could foresee a massive headache in drawing up a horoscope for a juvenile prince with Caesarian ambitions, and my encounter with Scur had left me with a nagging feeling that I had overlooked something. So much had happened that day that I could hardly be blamed for failing to take in every word said or deed done, but I could not shake the notion that the one-eyed fool had seen something I had missed.

Then William threw open the door and bounced in, grinning from shoulder to shoulder.

"You look as if your day's been as good as mine," I said.

He dropped my satchel on the table. "Oh, better. You just had a king and a queen pestering you. I've got four knights begging me to swear to them!"

"Take all four. I gather that your injuries are no longer troubling you?"

"My gonads are still grumbling a bit, that's all."

"Lie down on the bench and I'll sing to them."

William had no sooner obeyed than there came a tap on the door. He jumped up and went to answer it, hastily adjusting his clothing on the way. My amusement turned to astonishment when he put on his flunky voice and announced the visitors.

"Baroness Matilda and the Widow Udela, master."

I bowed them in. "This is an unexpected honor, my lady."

"It should be." Matilda strolled across the room, looking around with disdain. "Now you have done all the damage you can, I assume you will be returning to your burrow at wherever it is very shortly?"

"Damage?"

"Disaster follows you like your Saxon stench. The king has ordered Barton Castle razed. Don't pretend that you had no part in shaping his decision. Our chaplain, my cousin, has been carted away in chains, having been bewitched by your evil arts. My father is distraught, my mother overwrought. You have cursed my family home like some bird of evil croaking on the roof."

My first impulse was to retort that the countess had seemed far from overwrought at dinner. My second was that if anyone was distraught, it must be Matilda herself. And my third was that her own betrothal should be included in that list of recent events.

"You will be leaving Barton before the demolition begins, though?" I asked.

"That depends on how long the king remains at Rockingham. He almost never spends two nights under the same roof, as you know, rushing all over England and half of France. His chief forester will rarely be apart from him at this time of year, but he has promised me that I will have a worthy home in either London or Winchester."

"Then the wedding will be soon?"

"Within the week. Baron Weldon has gone back to Rockingham to see that everything is in order for the royal hunt, but he has been given leave to return right after it to solemnize his marriage." She smiled demurely. "Before his, um, sudden departure, Father Randolf gave permission to waive the usual banns."

"A whirlwind romance!"

Indecent haste was what most people would call it, but I knew why the bride, at least, was in favor. I glanced at William to see what he thought, but William was concentrating on Udela.

Udela was concentrating on William.

Huh?

"I need a word with you," Matilda announced, heading for the ladder. "It will be more private up here. I will call for you when I am ready."

Udela examined the oak bench with disapproval. Then she sat on it and folded her hands demurely in her lap. William stepped in front of her, so I could not see either's face, but I suspected that they were exchanging smiles.

I was not so innocent that I didn't suspect what was about to happen; I just couldn't believe it, that was all. The grimoires and my satchel I removed and put away in the secret closet.

"I am ready, Saxon!"

William looked around in surprise, then up at the hatch. His eyes widened and turned in my direction. They asked, "What are you waiting for?"

"I will call you if I need your assistance," I told him. I did not expect to. I headed quickly for the ladder.

I was not totally naïve. Even then I was a sinner, and partly because nowhere in Helmdon had offered such privacy as my hayloft. In the previous three or four years more than one country lass had slipped into the academy's stable to visit with the young servitor. I was going to be very surprised now if a medical consultation was the only reason that I was being honored by the baroness's visit.

But why would a young beauty of the Norman nobility waste her charms on me? She was betrothed to be married within days and she could not be carrying a child, or even believing herself to be doing so, unless she already had a lover. If she wanted a last promiscuous fling before her marriage, why not a bittersweet farewell with him? Could she really be so wanton as to risk her future for a fleeting moment's pleasure with a transient Saxon servant?

Then my head rose above the trap and I almost fell off the ladder. She had closed the shutters for privacy, but they still let in enough light to show her leaning against a bedpost, toying with one of her long flaxen braids and watching my emergence with amusement. She was draped in one of the sheer scarlet webs from the closet, which hid absolutely nothing.

I laid my cane on the floor, closed the hatch, and then stood up to study her. "My lady, I have done nothing to deserve this honor."

"Then you will have to earn it with due diligence during the rest of the afternoon."

I limped closer. She was exposing her body to a man she barely knew, and yet she seemed entirely at ease. Her eyes were lustrous, her lashes had been darkened, her lips dyed with madder root. Her breasts were larger than I would have guessed, her waist more slender, and she showed no signs of having once given birth.

I was trembling. "This is not a necessary part of the procedure to abort a child." *Burbling idiot!*

"Of course not. Quite the reverse. But no matter what you eventually get around to doing, you can't put another one in me, so why don't you get started? Or are you going to stand there all day drooling, you uncouth Saxon lout?"

Ever since Eve, women have been temptresses, as the Church teaches us. What man could resist? I was twenty years old and didn't even try.

I took the neck band of her drapery with both hands and ripped it apart to her waist, then pushed the remains off her shoulders to let it fall around her ankles. She reacted with a twitch of surprise and perhaps even fear. Apparently being totally naked was different from being just totally exposed to view; and I, of course, was showing off my strength.

"I have dreamed of you like this for years," I said. Except that her name in my dreams had been Edla. "You are lovelier than the Romans' Venus, or Helen of Troy." Then I pulled her hard against me and kissed her, long and fierce.

"Oh!" she said when we parted. "Never mind the fancy talk. Take off your clothes." She sank back on top of the bed covers, not under them.

I stripped in a fumbling rush and joined her. Her lovemaking was quite unlike that of the hesitant girls of Helmdon, who had mostly exhausted their store of courage just by coming to visit me in the dark. Matilda demanded things and did things I had never even heard men brag of, until at last I could hold back no longer and insisted on my release. She cried out shamelessly a few times, but I suspected she was feigning.

As we lay there entwined, breathing hard and damp from our exertions, she murmured, "That was quite good, but far too short. Soon you will do it again, and take much longer, understood?"

"My pleasure, Your Ladyship, and I hope also yours." What a day! First the successful incantation, then the priest's arrival and confession, then the oath to the king and money to secure my future as a sage, and now a voluptuous Norman baroness in my bed. Any moment I would wake up and it would still be yesterday.

At that point we were both lying on our backs. She turned to me, squirming voluptuously against me. I rolled on my side to face her and clasp her breast.

That move saved my life, because my other arm was in the way, so I slid it up under the pillow. I found the knife there, just before her hand reached it. She clasped my wrist, but I was stronger than she was. She clawed at my eyes, and I grabbed that wrist and rolled my weight on top of her, keeping my crotch away from any attempt to knee me.

Two naked bodies with the man on top—it should have been sexual but it was a life and death contest.

We were nose to nose. She bared her teeth in fury.

I stared in horror at her eyes. The pearly gray irises had shrunk to tiny rims around gigantic black pupils. They had not been like that when she came to the sanctum, but she would have applied the *belladonne* just before setting out to visit me, because it blinds you in bright daylight and takes a little while to act.

"You meant to kill me!"

She smiled and squirmed like a cat. "Nonsense. I've got to marry a hateful old prune. I just came here for a good, hard fucking while I still have the chance. Do it again. Longer and harder this time."

"Fucking with an uncouth Saxon lout?"

"You're going away soon, where you can't gossip to the rest of the churls. Besides, you have a rank male smell that intrigues me."

"So why the dagger under the pillow?"

"I don't know. Do you always keep one there? Maybe it's Archibald's?"

"It wasn't there this morning. Where did you get the *bella-donne*?"

Again she smiled and squirmed sensually like a purring cat. "You like it? One of Sage Archibald's spells. He began by dipping a feather into a bottle and putting a drop of the liquid in each of my eyes. Then he put black stuff on my lashes with another feather, and finally he brought me up here and made me strip so he could dress me in that shameless red thing. By then I realized that he was not procuring a miscarriage, he was adding a baroness to his jousting score."

"And afterwards he gave you a bottle of that eye tincture?"

She kissed the end of my nose and squirmed again. "No. He did give me some of the inky stuff he had used on my lashes, but he said the pupil stuff was much too poisonous to let loose, it could kill people." She smiled—in anyone but a beautiful noblewoman that smile would have been called a smirk. "Do you think it improves my appearance?"

"No. I think you are as beautiful as humanly possible just the way the Lord made you. But you had to put up with Archibald's attentions more than once?"

"'Put up with' is a bit harsh. He was a lot more adept at fornication than you are, Adept Durwin, in spite of your title, although he was flabby where you are all-over solid, so you are more exciting. But when his enchantment produced no results, I realized that he had tricked me. I couldn't put up with that."

Now I knew why she had come calling. It wasn't lust that had brought her, although she might think so; it was *Malefice venite*. She had resisted longer than Father Randolf, that was all.

"So it was you who poisoned him?"

She shrugged. "Not personally. I came here for a second 'treatment' as soon as Wacian and his men had delivered the new wine. I warned Udela to make careful note of which bottle held the eye tincture, and while Archibald was busy bedding me up here, she drank a few swallows from his wine ration and topped it up with some of the tincture. When he finished his supposed enchantment, we dressed and went downstairs, and he insisted on some refreshment. Of course I declined to join him. I knew he would happily finish it himself."

"And you took the wine bottle away when you left?"

"Oh no! He was already suspicious of the taste. If the bottle had disappeared he would have guessed that we had tampered with it. Perhaps he drank more of it. An hour or so later he collapsed at dinner. Very dramatic of him, but I felt I had upheld my honor."

She had relaxed her hands, releasing her grip on my wrist, but continuing her seductive squirming, trying to lull me into releasing her. She was utterly crazy, a total lunatic. Was her story the truth, or a delusion, or just more of her perverted sex play?

"Then how did you get the tincture to make your eyes shine today?"

She laughed. "Udela again. After she'd doped the wine, she put the tincture bottle outside the door. She didn't have to go outside and risk the hex to come back in, just opened it a crack. When we left we took it away with us. There's still quite a lot left."

I shivered. If this madwoman was telling the truth she was a completely merciless and unrepentant killer in possession of enough poison to kill several more people. I could think of no way to get it away from her. This couldn't be true—it *mustn't* be true!

"Father Randolf told us that he committed that murder."

"He is a sweetie. He loves me madly, poor man."

But she didn't love him; she didn't love anyone.

"It was Father Randolf you thought had gotten you with child?" Why else would the priest have taken the blame, except to defend a lover?

"Of course. It was sweet of him to shield me, but he's always been crazy about me. I let him take my virginity when I was thirteen."

"How old was he?"

"Older, of course. It was just before he was to take his vows, and he begged me so nicely. Said it was his last chance! But when my husband died I came back here. . . . He was so handsome!"

Handsome was as handsome did. "So Randolf did kill Colby?"

She sighed. "Yes, that one was Randy's doing. Even as a child he always had a terrible temper, and that snotty little turd had been spying on us! He came to Randy asking for money, threatening to tell the count. Randy flew into a rage. He was very upset about it afterwards, I assure you; terribly upset."

"I am relieved to hear that." I pulled away and sat up, holding the dagger well away from her, and crossing my mismatched legs. "Sorry or not, killing a boy just to hide a secret love affair is too extreme for my taste. Surely the count would have just had the kid whipped and sent home?"

Matilda sniggered and tried to grab at my privates. I struck her hand away and jumped off the bed, moving back out of reach.

She sat up also. "Are you so shocked, boy? If I am so terribly depraved, you can copulate with me without feeling in the least guilty. It's all my fault. I lured you into it. Again, please?"

No doubt I should feel guilty, but mostly I felt soiled. "Which of you killed Sage Rolf?"

"That was Randy. He was furious at me for disposing of Archibald. He said the count would send for another sage, who would be able to track down the killer when he got here. And when he heard that Father had summoned Uncle Rolf, he was even more agitated. But he did absolve me, so I won't go to Hell."

Randolf had confessed to a murder he had not committed because he couldn't be punished any more for three than he would be for two. But I had lied to the count and my king. I had won royal favor under false pretenses. As I stood, still clutching Matilda's dagger and enduring her mocking stare, I realized that I couldn't admit to my mistake now. I had no evidence except her confession, which she would deny, and the fact that she had answered my *Malefice venite* summons—and we had promptly jumped into bed together. How would the sheriff interpret that testimony?

I stretched up as high as I could and slammed the dagger into a beam, so that it stuck there, out of her reach. "Get dressed!"

"Oh, I can't see with the potion in my eyes. You have to help me."

"Get Udela to help you." I began sorting out my own clothes.

Matilda stretched out her arms in supplication. "Lover, lover! Come back to me. I need you. Besides, if I know Udela, she's probably still busy with that squire of yours. At his age they can usually keep going for hours. Longer than you did, certainly."

I hobbled over to the hatch and opened it. I heard nothing and did not look down to see what was happening. Scowling, Matilda began fumbling with her clothes.

I let my attention wander for an instant; she leaped off the bed and jumped up to grab the dagger. Her weight pulled it free, but she stumbled as she came down, and that gave me time to snatch up my oaken cane.

"Drop it!" I said. "Or I'll break your arm."

For a moment we had a face-off. I took a step forward and she must have seen that I meant what I said, and then we might both face ruin. However much my account would be believed or disbelieved, her betrothal would end as suddenly as it had begun. She threw down the dagger and shouted a few curses at me. Her invective vocabulary was limited.

By the time I was dressed and had started to descend, Udela and William were sitting side by side on the bench. She looked more rumpled than he did, although his hair was a bramble bush. But they were respectably clothed.

No one said a word until the women had left.

chapter 35

illiam closed the door with a long sigh. "You were very quickly satisfied," he said regretfully. "I was hoping for a lot more."

I was flopped down on a stool with my face in my hands. My pride had blinded me, and I had mistakenly lied to my liege the king! I had taken royal money under false pretenses. To announce the true story now was unthinkable because no one would believe it. Matilda would deny it and even if she didn't, no one would take a woman's word over a priest's. I was a fraud and a perjurer. If I sought out a confessor, I might be told to put the king's money in the poor box. I knew I couldn't bear to do that, and it would still leave the murderess at large and unpunished.

"You were far too quick," William grumbled again.

Grunt.

"That Udela is no chicken, but she's still a really hot trollop. How was the baroness floozy?"

Another grunt. I could see no way to bring Matilda to justice.

After a moment I heard a peculiar noise, then another. I looked up. "What's wrong?"

"It hurts," he mumbled. He was rocking on the stool, hugging himself.

William complaining of pain? "What hurts?"

"My ribs, when I laugh." He made another spluttering, choking sound. "Did you put a piglet in the baronial sty, you suppose?"

"No chance. She's probably got one in there already." That was a breach of confidence, but in my present mood I didn't care.

"*She has?* Eeeey! Oh . . ." The squire hugged himself harder and made whimpering sounds, rocking in apparent agony.

"What is so accursed funny?"

"You are," William gasped. "You have just been sarding my future stepmother and by rights I should kill you for it. Now you tell me I'm to have a ready-made baby sister? God's blood! That's the funniest . . . thing I . . . oh, mercy, Lord, spare me!"

For a moment I could only sit there aghast. Kendryck had said that Matilda's betrothed was newly promoted to the barony of Weldon, a title William had never heard of before. Matilda had referred to her fiancé as William. Guy had named William's father as Sir William Legier, who had four sons. William himself had never withdrawn his threat to beat me to a pulp. Many men would say he now had cause to do so.

"Oh, William! I didn't know!"

He looked up with tears running down his swollen cheeks. "I didn't see him when he was here yesterday, remember? I just heard his name at dinner today. Now you say she's already baking the wedding . . . cake. . . . Ooooh, saints have pity, my ribs!"

William had surprised me many, many times, but never more than then. "You're not mad at me?"

"No, no! I'm delighted you put horns on the old lecher. I wish I could have done it myself. You think I'll get the chance if we stay here a couple of days?"

"I'm sure you won't. If she were spreading her favors widely, everyone would know it in a place this size. She had only one lover. She came here to knife me and avenge him."

"Oh, that was why you were shouting at her up there? Udela and I wondered what games you were playing."

"You'd better warn your father," I said, even as I realized how very unlikely it was that the old man would believe the story.

More painful efforts not to laugh. "Oh, I will. But not until he's safely married."

For a moment I wrestled with my conscience and my honor as a sage, and in the end friendship won.

"Jade isn't all she is, William."

He caught control of his mirth and nodded. "She was the one who saw Archibald off?"

"So she claims, but remember that the priest said he did."

"He couldn't have. He wasn't here. The wine was delivered that morning, but Randolf had gone to Northampton to visit his uncle the bishop on Sunday, and didn't get back until just before Monday dinner."

Oh, sweet Jesus! Of course that was true. Why had I not seen that? Kendryck hadn't mentioned a day, but he had complained about the priest's grumbling all the way to Northampton and back, and earlier he had said that he missed that meal. Of course the priest would have dismounted close to the keep, but the knights of his escort would have taken the horses to the stable, and would have stayed there to give them their rubdowns if the hands had already taken off to dinner. Horses were close to sacred to those who fought. Randolf had met Archibald and taken him in to the meal, but Kendryck had not made it in time.

"Who told you that?" I asked.

"Squire Kenric. He was annoyed that he missed seeing Archibald struck down at dinner. He was part of the priest's escort, attending his knight. He had to stay and tend to his horse, so he missed the meal. The rest I just worked out for myself. It was so obvious that I thought you had seen it and didn't care as long as you had Randolf's confession."

"You didn't think to warn me when I went upstairs with her?"

For once William hesitated. Then he admitted, "I thought you were collecting hush money. And I certainly wasn't about to stop you cuckolding my sire."

So Matilda had been telling the truth about the priest, or largely telling the truth. I had misled the king. And I should have seen that the priest was lying. He'd implied that both Archibald and Rolf had died from the same poison, which wasn't true. I'd missed that, too.

"Then everything's explained except the missing wine flask," I said. "Matilda says she left it here so that Archibald wouldn't get suspicious. So . . . so that evening, or the next day, whenever it was that she told Randolf, he realized that anyone entering the sanctum—the replacement sage, most likely—might suffer the same fate, and that would scream 'Poison!' to everyone. Or else, when he decided to poison the new sage himself and came here to get the nightshade . . . That doesn't make sense. Why did he not just take the flask that Udela had poisoned? Why take a new poison for Rolf?"

William shrugged. "Because it was already half empty?"

"No . . . probably because of that tomb-effigy bottler, Wacian. If his precious flask number seven had turned up beside Rolf's deathbed instead of here in the sanctum, he would have complained to the countess that the world must be coming to an end and they wouldn't have needed me to tell them what was going on. Randolf knew it was poisoned and didn't want the wine restored to the general supply, so he probably just dropped the bottle in the privy outside." Even a murderer could have some decency in him, perhaps.

William was happy again. "So my new brother or sister will be a priest's get?"

"Worse than that," I said. "A child of incest. Randolf and Matilda are first cousins. That was why she was so frightened of bearing his child and why he murdered the boy Colby. The Church will usually overlook a priest's fornication, but first cousins are within the fourth degree of consanguinity. His career would be ruined if their affair became known."

Someone hammered on the door. I sat down at the table as William went to answer, combing his hair with his fingers. He barked "Wait!" to stop the visitor just barging in, and turned to me. "William, Baron Weldon, Adept." His eyes were ablaze with mirth.

"Admit His Lordship, of course!" I stood up and bowed as the weather-beaten graybeard bounced in. "My abode is honored," I said. This was going to be a dramatic family reunion. I would happily watch, but I vowed not to get involved.

That decision was not contested, for the king's chief forester barely glanced at me before turning to address his son, who had closed the door.

"See where your contumacy has landed you—flunky for a Saxon clerk! Have you no honor, no shame, no sense of your ancestry?"

"It was your idea to—"

"Silence! I was utterly appalled when I was asked if I was any relation to William Legier, the adept's helper from Helmdon. Your brothers will probably kill you."

"They've all tried before now," William said with a smirk. "I'm ready whenever they are."

"Well, even though you have no honor, I still do. I have decided to give you one more chance. Since His Grace has conferred a barony on me, I shall need a larger train. I'll take you on as squire again, but strictly on probation, understand? One word of back talk and I'll disown you completely."

If this was the sort of treatment young William had been forced to put up with in the past from a tyrannical popinjay of a father, I could reconsider my past judgment of him. Any lad of spirit would fight back against that sort of humiliation, and his options had been very limited at Helmdon. I held my breath, waiting to hear him reveal the truth about Lady Matilda, his future stepmother; then the tables would be thoroughly turned. Evidently he wasn't quite ready yet:

"I thought you'd taken the king to Rockingham for some hunting?"

"His Grace changed his mind when he saw the flooding. He is returning to Winchester, and I shall join him there right after my marriage. You will accompany me." Baron Weldon glanced disapprovingly around the sanctum. "In fact you will come away with me immediately, this instant."

William strolled over to the corner, picked up the broom that stood there, and began to sweep the floor in front of the fireplace, where chips of bark and stray ash had collected. This was undoubtedly the humblest task he could find at the moment, the best way to infuriate his father even more.

"No," he said. "I won't. I'm going back to Helmdon with Adept Durwin to complete my training in philosophy, as you instructed me."

The elder William spat out some obscenities that I prefer not to remember. He almost screamed, "You will do as I say!"

Young William continued to sweep the floor, progressing until he was working around his father's feet. Now I knew how he had honed his ability to unhinge the sages at Helmdon.

The madder and louder the father became, the quieter the son did. William was obviously happy at the way the discussion was going. I still expected him to denounce Matilda at any minute, but still he didn't.

When at last the baron paused for breath, the squire said, "I am doing exactly what you said, Father. 'Go back there and finish what you started for once,' were the exact words you used."

"I am giving you fresh orders!"

"You can't. You signed a contract with the academy. As long as I do as I am told there, or accept punishment when I don't, they cannot evict me. And you can't withdraw me without breach of contract. That would be right, wouldn't it, Adept?"

"Absolutely," I said, although I had no idea what the contract's actual terms were. "Your son is the most promising recruit to come along in years, my lord, and the academy will resist to the full extent of the law any effort to remove him. As I told the king this morning—"

William Senior had no interest in my legal expertise. He went back to screaming at his son. "Ingrate! Serpent in my breast! The worst cur won't bite the hand that feeds it as you do. I disown you—"

"Then go to Hell," William said, raising the broom like a club and advancing on him.

The noise of Baron Weldon slamming the door was probably audible all the way to Northampton. The building shook with the violence of his departure. My squire and I looked at each other and then burst into laughter.

"You mean it?" I asked.

He grinned. "Absolutely. I shall obey my dear daddy's orders. I shall grovel on my knees to Dandelion Head and Sage Guy and swear to be a model pupil in the future."

"I am glad! You'll make an incredible sage. What changed your mind?"

He shrugged and went to replace the broom. "Watching you. I decided that if a lopsided, lowborn Saxon dung-shoveler can learn to work miracles, then I certainly can. Satan take me if I don't graduate sage before you do, Adept Durwin of Pipewell."

I doubted he could quite achieve that, but underestimating William Legier was never wise. I said, "You're on! I am delighted. And if your father refuses to pay your fees, then I will, out of the money the king gave me, because I couldn't have done all this without your help."

William snorted. "You really are soft in the head, but I'll take over your stable duties. How soon can we leave?"

Then my nightmare returned. I sat down.

After a moment William joined me at the table. "What's wrong?"

"You are. You didn't tell your father the truth about Matilda."

"Oh, I will. After the wedding." He grinned diabolically. Revenge must be very sweet after a lifetime of frustration.

"Have you forgotten the fifth commandment?"

He pouted. "I couldn't honor my mother because I never knew her, and my father has never honored me."

"The commandment only says that you must honor him, not that he must honor you. The implication is that you must earn his respect. William, you are going to let your father marry a killer who still owns enough poison to kill again, perhaps several times. Suppose he dies soon after the wedding? Your eldest brother will inherit the baronetcy, but I'm sure she's negotiated a big chunk of everything else to support her and raise her son. Will you be able to live with yourself after that? Will you be able to face your brothers or make confession?"

"Why would she do that? She's won herself a home in London. Her husband's a valued servant of the crown, with all the social status and corruption opportunities that brings. Why throw it all away by risking another murder?"

"That's the sane way to think," I retorted. "But she poisoned Archibald because he tricked her into bed. I don't like your father's chances of ever seeing her child born."

William glared at me, teeth bared. "And what do you suggest I do about it? Go and tell my father his bride murders people? Tell him she's a slut and half the knights in Barton have broken a lance with her? He will never believe me. The priest confessed to all the killings. You've already told the king so. How can you back away from that now?"

"I don't know," I said. "But I do know that I must try. If I can find a way, will you help me?"

He sat for a few minutes in rebellious silence, arms folded, teeth clenched. Then he said, "I suppose I must. The thought of Arnolph becoming a baron makes me puke. But I've got to see my sire's face when he finds out."

I handed him one of the grimoires and took another for myself. "Start looking, then. The answer's got to be in one of these."

chapter 36

It must have been an hour or longer, and we were both into a second spell book when William said, "Does *Oculos deceptus* mean what I think it does?" I saw that he was working his way through *The Wisdom of Abbot Tomas*, which contained a lot of very dark spells. They scared me and I would have forbidden him that grimoire had I thought of it in time.

"'Eyes deceived.' What are you thinking?"

"They won't believe you if you try to denounce the bawdy baroness now," he said. "And they certainly wouldn't believe me. Who would they believe?"

I knew enough by then to shiver when William Legier grinned that way.

We literally put our heads together so we could both read through *Oculos deceptus*.

"You are utterly out of your skull," I said.

"No. Think about it."

"Look at these glosses in the margin! Six, no seven, of them, and all disparaging. It doesn't work in sunlight, that's obvious. And most of them say the result isn't believable even by candlelight.

'Mountebank trickery, no more.' 'Good only to deceive children in a churchyard at midnight.' And here, 'The image ripples.'"

"That's what we want, isn't it?"

"Matilda's not going to fall on her knees and howl out a confession. She may be young but she's tough as chain mail, much tougher than Randolf."

"She's not the one we're trying to warn off. My sire is. He's gullible. If he sees a black cat, he runs home to bed and stays there for the rest of the day."

For the third or fourth time I said, "It'd never work!"

An hour later I was still saying that, but William had the bit between his teeth by then and there was no stopping him. He kept telling me to suggest something better and I couldn't. He also reminded me that I was the one who'd insisted we must warn his father. I protested that the count would hang us.

"He won't dare hang you, now you're one of the king's men. The priest lied to everyone, but we can't make people believe it. This will."

I could feel myself weakening. *Oculos deceptus* was a Release spell, meaning that it could be chanted in advance and then activated by speaking a single phrase, like pulling the trigger on a crossbow. So in theory we could spring it at any time, but the chances that we could make it work at all were very slim. I could see no trip wires in it, perhaps because the scribe had considered it too trivial to guard.

"We'd need help, because we don't know what Archibald looked like." I did know what he'd sounded like, though.

William admitted the point with a frown. "Um . . . who, though? Who could we possibly trust?"

We were saved from having to solve that problem just then by a hearty thump on the door. William opened it and invited the visitors to enter: the brothers from Stane, Kendryck and Kenric. The sanctum was suddenly crowded.

"We have come," Kendryck proclaimed in sepulchral tones, "to invite you to join a wake before all the ale gets drunk." The normally ebullient Saxon looked and sounded as if he had only hours to live. His squire was no more cheerful.

"Bad news?" I asked.

"Terrible. The king has ordered the castle razed. The stockade has to be torn down, the moat filled in, the keep demolished."

I felt no guilt. My counsel to the king had been lukewarm, but what I had said would have made no difference. He had known exactly how he was going to decide before he even left Northampton. He had probably been surprised to learn that any private castle, even a tiny one like Barton, had survived his purge. Who did Count Richard think he was? Why did he need a fortress manned by so many knights and men-at-arms in the very center of England when the kingdom was at peace?

"Did you ever think he would decide otherwise?" I asked.

Young Kenric nodded, but his brother shook his head sadly.

"Probably not. He's done it to thousands of others. But what are we to do, huh—Kenric and me? There isn't a decent war going on anywhere in Christendom just now. Turn our swords into plowshares and teach my destrier to pull a hay wain?"

"You're good at jousting," William said. "Kenric told me."

"Huh! That's a hard way to make a living—one loss and there went your horse and armor."

Jousting back then was not what it has become since. It was much less formal, usually a general melee, close to a real battle. Men could be mutilated or killed. The prizes might be good, but I suspected that Sir Kendryck would have trouble hanging on to his winnings for long. Brewers and trollops would empty his purse in very short order.

"The king of Jerusalem is always happy to swear in good knights to kill Saracens," I suggested.

The brothers looked at each other and mirrored each other's miraculous joy.

"*Hey!*" Kendryck roared. "What did I tell you? King Harry knows a good sage when he sees one." He thumped his squire's shoulder hard enough to make the lad stagger. "Let's go and drink to loads of dead heathens."

"We'll try and join you later," I said untruthfully. "Right now William and I have some serious work to do."

"Glad I never have to do that. Come on, then, killer, let's go and empty a keg or two." Knight and squire disappeared out the door.

William closed it. "Matilda's making a smart move—getting out of here before it's demolished, I mean. She may be crazy but she isn't stupid."

"She's cunning as a vixen. Let's leave the problem of an accomplice until later. Kendryck would be my last choice. Let's see if we think this incantation is worth the parchment it's written on."

"We have time enough, don't we?" William sounded wistful at being deprived of the chance to get roaring drunk with some like-minded thugs. "If the wedding isn't until next week, we have several days to plot our move."

I admit I was tempted. I had no desire to join in any mass carouse, and I doubted there was enough ale in the county for what Kendryck was planning, but a horn or two of the stuff would have gone down nicely about then. Count Richard and his men might have much to mourn; my day had been one long triumph. Before I could change my mind, we were interrupted by yet another knock on the door.

"Nice to be popular," William grumbled, going to answer. "Sir Bertrand! Enter, sir, and welcome."

The steward stepped over the threshold, but no closer, so the door remained open. His manner implied he was not planning to stay, and the way he glanced around at the crocodile and other gimcrackery suggested that they worried him. That might not mean much, because I had never seen him not look worried.

I had risen in respect for a man older than myself and a senior member of my host's household. "You honor us, sir. How may I help you?"

He glanced at the slate he was holding. "A couple of requests from Her Ladyship, Adept. Firstly, she wonders if you would be kind enough to sing a suitable ballad at her daughter's wedding tomorrow."

"*Tomorrow?*" William and I said in unison, and our emphasis made the steward jump.

"Oh, you haven't heard? There has been a change of plan. The king decided to head south instead of going to Rockingham as he had previously announced. So Count Richard and Baron Weldon—and the rest of their trains, all of them—have returned, and the wedding has been brought forward so that her husband can resume attendance on His Grace as expeditiously as possible. The baroness will follow as soon as can be arranged. Meanwhile, the bishop has agreed to officiate and the wedding will be celebrated in All Saints on Saturday, that is to say tomorrow. And the countess—"

"I shall be honored to sing at Baroness Matilda's wedding." Even as I spoke I knew that William had persuaded me to support his crazy plan, and the two of us were going to do our utmost to see that there would be no wedding. "And the second thing?"

"Oh, the family will have an informal celebration this evening in the parlor after supper: count and countess, baron and baroness, and so on. Her Ladyship asks if you would chant a blessing over the happy couple."

The bishop blessing their union in the church the next day would certainly refuse to let the proceedings include what he would see as blasphemous nonsense from a shyster magician. But it wasn't much more than two centuries since these Normans' ancestors had burned and slaughtered in the name of Odin and Thor; even yet some memories of the Old Ones lurked in the shadows at the back of their minds.

I was careful not to look at William. This unexpected invitation seemed like a God-given chance to carry out our treachery, and the only one we would get, but the timing was next to impossible. "I should be honored to do so. I may bring my cantor to assist?"

The steward consulted his notes doubtfully. "The parlor will be very crowded. . . . As long as he leaves right after?"

"Certainly," I said. "And I shall not presume to elevate myself to the status of a member of the baronial family. We shall both leave directly after we have completed our incantation." We might be on our way to the dungeon. Or everyone might leave, in a mad, people-trampling stampede.

"Thoughtful of you, Adept. I shall so inform Her Ladyship."

Sir Bertrand departed. Cantor and enchanter exchanged meaningful glances.

"We have about an hour to learn this thing and make it work," William said, looking at the sunlight.

"And if we can't, then we won't have a blessing ready to chant instead. Well, I know a solo I can use, if the words don't stick in my throat." Wish Matilda happiness and her husband long life? Him yes, her no!

"And we still need a helper!"

"Yes," I said, sitting down and reaching for a pen. "Scur. Go and find Sir Scur."

"That maniac? He's crazy."

"So are we, to be even thinking of this, but Scur already knows about the second murder. He as much as told me that the priest hadn't committed all three. And besides," I added triumphantly, "if he tries to tell anyone else what we're doing—or what we have done after we have done it—then no one will believe him. Find Scur. And be quick about it."

I set to work transcribing the incantation. I still wondered why I was going ahead with this crazy risk. Not to avenge the murdered Archibald de la Mare, for the man had been a thoroughgoing scoundrel. Not to clear Father Randolf's name, for he was a worse murderer than Matilda: he had killed a child and his own uncle. No, I reassured myself, it was to stop the demented baroness from poisoning anyone else. That, at least, was a worthy cause, and if I could only achieve a good end by very shady means, then I must be guided by Ovid, who taught us that the result justifies the deed.

Surprisingly soon the door flew open and in bounced William, fizzing with excitement.

"I saw him. He didn't see me this time, though."

"Who? Oh, your—"

"Yes. My father and the count and Marshal Hugh. They were just riding out the gate—going to inspect Matilda's dower lands, I shouldn't wonder. So we probably have a little more time than we thought. Scur's on his way." William sat down, grabbed the sandstone, and began scraping away at a writing tablet in a frenzy.

"I don't think we'll need that one," I said. "I'm copying out the responses for you. I think I can chant the versicles straight from the grimoire. It's more legible than most."

"Fox, Fox!" cried a discordant voice at the open door. "Have you gone to earth here, Fox?"

"Enter, Sir Scur," I shouted. "And be welcome."

"I jump in with both feet," the big old man said, filling the doorway as he came through. "Are you a sight for a sore eye, Adept?"

"I would hope so, except that I would not that your eye be sore. Now sit down and listen, for we need your help."

His solitary eye inspected me from the depths of his hood. "Ah, I am long past helping men with their troubles, excepting that I may ofttimes make them laugh at them."

Refusing to be distracted, I said, "You told me earlier that three is too many. Now I respond that beauty in fact may not be beauty in act."

He flinched and turned his head so that his face disappeared from view. "This is not to laugh at," he whispered.

I said, "William, will you sand some more tablets, please? And do it outside, so we are not distracted."

William glanced at the back of Scur's hood, took the hint, and departed with a couple of tablets and the sandstone, closing the door rather more loudly than necessary.

Now I had to find a way to handle the fool. I could not help but remember tales of Beauty and the Beast. How long had that hideously maimed old man worshipped his master's daughter from afar? Matilda would have been about seven or eight when Scur was mutilated.

"She must have been fair even as a child," I said.

"Fair of face, aye." As he emphatically was not.

"But never fair indeed?"

"'Never' is never fair." His voice was growing steadily quieter.

I wanted to say "Was Beauty beastly to the Beast?" but that would be too crude, too rough. If my guess was correct, I was tampering with the man's very soul. Had the child Matilda mocked the monster? Run from him screaming in terror? Did she mock the fool in the rabbit guise, as the others did?

"What of her soul, Sir Scur? Murder is mortal sin and she does not repent of it. Her lover has taken the blame and she hides behind that. She claims he gave her absolution, but absolution cannot be valid if she does not truly repent."

Silence. He did not move, but at least he was not heading for the door, as he had done on previous occasions when the talk veered too close to Matilda.

"With your help, I think we could make her repent," I said.

I waited patiently for a reply, and at last he whispered, "How?"

"I just need you to identify someone for me. I never met him, so I do not know what he looked like. She will not heed any other's warning, but there is one who might persuade her—her victim."

He turned his head until the single eye appeared, glittering at me.

"You would raise the dead, enchanter?"

"No, no! I lack such skill and hope I shall never feel the need. But I think I can charm my cantor so that he looks and sounds passably like Archibald de la Mare, at least for a few moments. If his shade can appear in a dim room and call her to repentance, surely by God's mercy she will yield and be saved from the eternal fires."

I had gone too far. The big man shuddered, then rose to his feet—slowly, almost reluctantly. If he reached the door I had failed.

"Wait!"

He stopped moving to listen, but did not turn to look at me.

"You see those goblets, Scur?" Neither William nor I had ever put them away, out of sight. It was almost as if we had left them there on the table, in full view, as a reminder of our mission to solve the mystery of the killings. "Matilda put poison in the wine and then only pretended to drink from her goblet. But

Sage Archibald did not know that, so he drank from his, and he died. She still has much poison left, Scur! How long will it be before she kills off that ugly old man she is about to marry? Will we, who could have stopped her, not share in the guilt of that murder?"

The old man groaned, then he lumbered back to his stool and whispered, "Tell me what you want me to do, Adept."

That was about the first coherent statement I had ever heard from him. There was still some trace of a human being inside the fool.

chapter 37

Scur departed with orders to return at sundown. William read out the remaining responses and I wrote them. Sunlight moved inexorably up the wall. We checked our work. By the time Scur returned, we had rehearsed the incantation backward twice and were ready to make our first attempt. William closed shutters and lit lamps.

This would be the second time we had performed before a witness, first the suave and confident Sir Stephen and now the hideous and embittered Sir Scur.

"These spells rarely work at the first attempt," I warned him. "If it does, then William here should change to look like Archibald de la Mare. If he looks like anyone else, we'll have failed. If he doesn't change, then we try again and again."

Scur dragged a stool over to the fireplace, turned his back on us, and did not answer. He did not wish to be involved in this deviltry.

Singing from the crabbed and faded grimoire text by candlelight was no easy matter, and I was not surprised when the first attempt produced no results. I reached for the ink bottle.

"Give me your first tablet," I told William. "There's a mistake in the fourth response."

Scur, hunched by the fire, peered around and said, "How can you know that?" I had not realized that he was paying so much attention.

"Inspired guesswork," was all I said. I was not going to reveal the secrets of my art to an outsider.

We began again, calling on spirits to give William the likeness of Archibald de la Mare. As we drew near the end I began to feel the glow of approaching acceptance. Then, suddenly, it was gone.

William was frowning. "I thought . . ."

"So did I. The second-to-last versicle? Ah, yes. Got it—a word missing. Start over."

The castle bell began to sound, signaling that supper was ready. My stomach rumbled. I ignored it.

Third time lucky. Even as I was chanting the final few versicles, I could heard William's voice changing as he sang the responses, and I think Scur must have heard the difference, too, because when I pronounced the concluding *Fac sicut dico!* he cried out in terror. The man across the table from me was no longer Squire William Legier. Scur jumped up and made a fast shuffle for the door. Archibald sprang after him and got to it first, pressing his back to it to keep the old man from leaving.

"It's all right, Sir Scur," he said in the London voice I recalled from the first time we had used the *Morðor wile ut* incantation. "I'm not dead. I'm still Squire William."

"He doesn't look quite real, does he?" I said, limping over to lay a hand on Scur's shoulder. "He sort of wavers. It's only an illusion."

Scur let me draw him back to the stool he had vacated, but he walked backward, never taking his eyes off the apparition. I could feel him trembling.

Archibald had been around thirty when he died. At first glance he did not look as I expected a notorious womanizer to look; his nose was too long, his ginger mustache too droopy, his beard too scanty, his eyes too sly. And yet . . . I decided he had a sort of smug confidence about him that might impress some people. He was studying me with arrogant amusement, even as his hands were exploring his own body.

The apparition's face was realistic, yet somehow unsubstantial, and his clothes were ill defined, somewhere between the belted blue tunic that William was wearing and a longer robe of indeterminate color, topped by a hint of a sage's green cape, but it was hard to concentrate on details. The general effect was one of a memory only poorly recalled. For people who had known him, he would suffice as an overall memory of Archibald and they probably wouldn't look at him more closely than they had to, especially since he was known to be dead and gone to Hell.

William finished patting himself. "I hope you can get me out of this, Adept. Pot belly, all my muscles gone to flab? Flat feet."

"I'm more worried that the illusion will fade before we have a chance to use it," I said. "I'll try the dismissal now. If it doesn't work, sunlight tomorrow will certainly free you. Stay away from the candelabras."

"The sun doesn't shine in dungeons."

Or in graves. I said, "Ready? *Dimitto!*"

William was back, instantly. Scur let out a burbling gasp of relief.

The glosses in the grimoire had been right, though. *Oculos deceptus* was a party trick, and a trick in very bad taste when used to impersonate the dead. Nevertheless, the shimmery, ambiguous image it produced was ideal for our purpose.

"Let's try the reprise," I said. "Ready? Here we go again, then: *Fac sicut dico!*"

Archibald leered across at me.

"*Dimitto!*"

William was back.

How many times the illusion could be recalled without repeating the whole incantation I did not know, and chanting the entire spell again might not work either. So we would have to go with what we had, and hope that it would serve. I took up my staff, feeling I needed the confidence that it gave me and the cane did not. William opened the door, but he and Scur let me lead the way.

I hated what I was doing and myself for doing it. Enchantment should be used to good ends—heal the sick, find the lost, frustrate evil. Never to deceive and entrap, which is what I was doing now. If we could trick Matilda into confessing, well and good, for she was a murderess and not deserving of pity. But we would necessarily have to fool the spectators as well, and might start a panic in which people would be crushed. William was no more talkative than I was.

Was I frightened? No, I was terrified. My day had been such a triumph and now it bid fair to end in utter disaster, with all my winnings lost.

Scur left us when we reached the keep. He ate in the kitchens, he told me gruffly, never in the hall, and we had no choice but to trust him. I was fairly confident that no one would believe the old wreck if he said he had just watched Adept Durwin raise the dead.

Stars were coming out as we plodded up the stairs to the door.

"I will try to signal to you by clapping you on the shoulder before I speak the command," I said. "We mustn't overdo it! Once the first shock wears off, people may start to analyze what they're seeing. There won't be any swords at a wedding party, but they might attack you with daggers. So call her to repentance, and I'll bring you back while everyone's eyes are on her, looking for her reaction."

William said nothing, and I realized how weak it all sounded. He was going to be more exposed than I was, although the count might have us both dragged out to the whipping post before the night was over. William probably wouldn't even care. He desperately wanted to watch his father writhe in horror and humiliation when he heard the truth about his future bride. Just how he was going to escape from the parlor without being unmasked seemed to bother him much less than it bothered me.

The previous night I had heard the party long before I got to it, but there was much less rejoicing now. The castle was to be torn down and many of the residents would see their livelihood vanish with it. The count would build himself a fine new home, no doubt, using the masonry salvaged from the keep. It would likely be a lot more spacious and comfortable than the two cramped rooms he and the countess lived in now, but the loss of his castle would make him feel degraded. He would not need nearly so many retainers.

The hall was even brighter than it had been last night, because there were fewer people there. I noticed that women outnumbered men. The knights and squires had all gone off to visit the village alewife, and I saw few stable hands either. Arth was fiddling his heart out, but the music seemed to dissolve unheeded in the pervasive gloom.

As before, food was laid out on a long communal table and eaten standing. The family had a separate supply up on the dais, and it was a reasonable guess that the people gathered around it were those who would retire to the parlor later: count and countess, knights Stephen, Hugh, and Bertrand. None of the knights had wives, so far as I had heard, although Stephen might have a family elsewhere. Aveline was there, but no priest yet, or my blessing would have to be canceled. Nor could I see Alwin, who would prefer to carouse with the boys. Two men I did not know wore green hunting dress. I decided they must be Baron Weldon retainers, brought along to even the odds a bit and support him in the wedding ceremonials. The bride and groom had not yet arrived.

Stephen was the one who worried me most. He lived in a more sophisticated society than Barton, probably accompanying the king back and forth to his lands in France. Others might flee or faint when the Archibald wraith appeared, but Stephen was far more likely to see through the masquerade and investigate what would happen if he stuck a sharp blade into the self-proclaimed ghost. Sir Hugh was another man of action, but the much younger Stephen was more dangerous.

Which way to turn, though? Should we gatecrash the gentry's party on the dais, or mingle with the commons at the other end of the hall until we were summoned? Discretion won: I headed for the servants' feast, with William at my heels.

I found that I had no appetite. I exchanged some small talk with Megan and other laundry maids, which pleased them greatly. I tried to comfort a couple of stable hands and a farrier. There was no shortage of horses in England, I said. I wished I was on one of them right then, heading anywhere at a full gallop. I even exchanged meaningless greetings with Lady Aveline, the first time we had spoken.

"Adept Durwin?" piped John the page at my shoulder. "Sir Bertrand says they are ready for you now."

I suppose I answered him civilly. I remember glancing at William and seeing his teeth bared in a grimace of sheer delight as he savored his forthcoming revenge for all those years of hectoring and abasement. I suspected he would look like that if he knew he would be beheaded right after. He never seemed worried by the prospect of future punishment. That is common in the young, but he carried it to extremes.

I desperately needed a privy, but William and I followed John along the hall to the dais, where Bertrand was waiting for us. He had the dais all laid out now: the food table at my extreme left, temporarily abandoned, then the count and countess standing in their finest finery, then two state chairs, back against the rear wall to receive the happy couple, and the parlor door, from which they would obviously emerge. Everyone else was clustered to the right of that, and behind them two heralds stood holding silver trumpets.

"The bride and groom are about to appear," Bertrand told me. "Her Ladyship decided that the parlor is too small for all the people who must attend, so you will chant your blessing out here. Wait over there if you please, until she signals for you to begin."

Oh, disaster! I had been counting on a small room, dark because there would be about as many people as candles, and so crowded that no one would see clearly what was happening or who was doing what. Instead we would have to perform our deception on stage, in clear view of a hundred eyes. I gave up hope. We could never pull it off.

"Forget it," I whispered to my accomplice as we moved in back of the guests. "We'll just have to sing a blessing."

"I don't know any flaming blessings," William said through clenched teeth, "and I'd sooner burn in Hell than bless either of those two."

He did have a point. Much as his son detested him, Baron Weldon was just a crabby, dictatorial old man to me, but how could I possibly call on the spirits to bless a woman as defiled and wicked as Matilda, Dowager Baroness Kilpeck? And what blessing? My mind was a blank page. I could remember nothing except the words of command. They raced around inside my head like brain mice: *Fac sicut dico! Fac sicut dico! Fac sicut . . .*

William and I hid behind the protective stockade of Hugh and Stephen. Troubadour Arth had given up his efforts to brighten the gloom-ridden feast with music. The chatter was dying down as people realized that something was about to happen. Bertrand glanced around, stepped up on the dais to join the rest of us, and signaled to the two heralds. The trumpets began to blare.

Everyone was facing the platform.

The fanfare ended, the door opened. Baron Weldon and Dowager Baroness Kilpeck emerged arm-in-arm and the congregation raised a cheer. The happy couple bowed to the count and countess, who returned the courtesy. Then they turned to acknowledge the commoner group that included us, hiding behind the two knights.

William rammed an elbow into my ribs so hard that I gasped. But my gasp came out carrying the fatal words: *Fac sicut dico!* I am sure I did not intend to say them, but say them I did.

Nothing happened. William looked down at his hands and then at me, dismay on his face. I shrugged and frantically tried to think of some blessing I could sing when given the signal. My brain was frozen.

A great wind sprang up from nowhere and whirled though the hall. Half the lights went out, and the rest dimmed. The temperature dropped to the depths of winter. The celebrants broke out in screams and howls of alarm—and I realized with horror that I had forgotten Sage Guy's warning. By speaking the words of the trigger, I had invoked *Oculus deceptus*, and thus performed magic during the forbidden hours of darkness.

chapter 38

The winds of Hell centered on Baron Weldon and his betrothed. They staggered, his cloak almost dragging him off his feet, Matilda clutching at her hood with one hand and her ballooning skirts with the other. Archibald's wraith appeared in front of her, leering at the audience. Then it spun around to point an accusing finger at Matilda.

"Murderess!" it shrilled in its London accent. "Repent, murderess! Repent, fornicator! Repent that incestuous bastard you carry in your womb, for it shall be accursed until the day it dies. Repent the poison your woman poured for me, for you have doomed her to eternal hellfire with yourself. Repent your debauchery with that priest who falsely confessed to your crimes and gave you false absolution for them. Repent your sins in my bed, with me and—"

"Dimitto!" I yelled, and the vision vanished. The wind stopped, the candle flames steadied, pushing back the darkness.

Matilda screamed. That is a gross understatement. I had never heard a human throat make such a noise, nor dreamed that any woman could. She would have drowned out the trumpets, had they tried to compete with her. Hysteria, as the learned

Galen taught us, is a disease of the womb, and no man could have shrieked so. There were words in there, just barely discernable: *Repent*, was certainly one, and *Penance* another. She had been raped. It had been self-defense. Forgiveness of sins. . . . She slumped to the floor in a faint. I thought I was about to do the same.

Our ploy had worked far more than I had intended. *Oculos deceptus* might not be true black magic, but it was close enough. I was extremely lucky not to have been blighted by it myself.

Count and countess dragged their daughter to her feet. She started screaming again. The countess swung a vicious slap at her. The impact seemed as loud as a crack of lightning and Matilda's clamor stopped instantly. Utter silence. Her mother dragged her away into the parlor. But then the whole congregation erupted, as if it had just realized that it had not been dreaming. The party was over. Terrified people began heading for the stairs.

The count went after his wife and daughter. After a moment's hesitation, Baron Weldon followed them, and we heard voices raised inside before he slammed the door. I saw, with relief, that the audience had been thinned out by the distance it had to cover to reach the various stairways and the need to discuss what they had seen, so it was leaving in a reasonably orderly fashion, not piling up. There might be some bruising and sprains, but no mass trampling.

I was grabbed and slammed back against the wall. Pinned there by a hand at my throat, I stared into the murderous fury of Sir Hugh Fiennes.

"You did that, you damned-to-Hell devil-worshiping necromancer!"

Beside him, white as a snowbank and teeth bared in a killer snarl, stood Sir Stephen de Mandeville. I had a vision of the pair of them tearing me apart between them, fighting for the privilege of killing me.

I made croaking noises; the pressure on my larynx eased a fraction. "She poisoned Archibald! She and Udela."

"You are lying! The priest confessed!" Hugh tightened his grip and I couldn't speak. I thought my last moment had come.

William was beside me, though. "Father Randolf was lying, Sir Hugh. They were lovers. He was protecting her!"

Hugh was the count's foster brother and knew the family relationships. "No! No!" But he did relax his grip enough for me to breathe.

"She carries his child," I gasped. "She came to me for an abortion and then changed her mind when—"

Stephen screamed and swung a fist at me, but Hugh struck the blow away with his spare hand. "Wait! Let's hear the rest of this filth."

"Randolf couldn't have poisoned Archibald," I babbled. "He said both men died of the same poison and they didn't. And he wasn't here that morning, when the wine was delivered. He'd gone to Northampton."

Stephen had been in the sanctum to hear that confession. He spun around and rushed to join whatever was happening in the parlor. The yelling inside seemed even louder, then the door shut it off again.

Hugh released me reluctantly, still seething. "Get out of here! You have done all the damage you can do. You are no longer wanted, understand?"

I nodded, swallowing painfully.

"Has Richard paid you?"

"Countess said I could take two spell books. There are five of—"

"Take the whole damnable lot and leave at dawn! We'll have no more Satan worship at Barton."

"Yes, Sir Hugh."

He stalked away, leaving me trembling after the narrowest escape of my life so far.

William gave me a sympathetic look and handed me the dropped staff. "That was close, Brother Durwin. Come and have a drink."

He held my arm as I stepped down from the dais, and then led me along the hall to the deserted food table. He filled a horn with beer for me, and I drained it.

"It went well, though," he said judiciously, smiling, but not gloating as much as I would have expected. "I think we can say that the wedding is postponed indefinitely."

"That would be the logical conclusion," I agreed. I took more beer. Then a meat sausage . . . a thick slice of cheese. I washed them down with more beer and began to feel better. After a few more minutes at the manger, we gave up and headed for the exit. I think we both knew we had better depart before Sir Hugh or the count discovered us still there.

We hadn't gone five paces before we stopped dead. Coming toward us was William Legier senior, Baron Weldon, with tears streaming down his weather-beaten old cheeks into his beard, and I could swear that beard looked grayer than it had fifteen minutes before.

He stopped. We stopped. For a moment there was silence.

"William?" he said.

"Father?"

"Oh, William!"

It was a cry for pity, and it was answered. Squire William stepped forward and embraced him.

Feeling very guilty and unwanted, I walked around them and went on my way. At the top of the stairs I glanced back. The baron seemed to be weeping on his son's shoulder and William was still hugging him tight, patting his back as one would comfort a child.

I began my story by telling you of three miracles. And so it ends with a fourth.

chapter 39

i left a candle burning in case my assistant returned in the night, but he didn't. I was wakened by the sound of the door closing. The candle had burned away, and a gray light showed through the shutter ports. I hoped I was hearing William arriving, not a lynch party of de Mandevilles.

After a moment William's head emerged through the trap. He regarded me with eyes like squashed strawberries.

"If you speak above a whisper, I will feed your guts to the hounds," he said.

"I know an incantation for hangovers," I said softly.

"Stuff it." He clambered up and looked around in the dimness. We had not been the tidiest of tenants, he and I. He went for his knapsack and began to collect his discarded clothes.

"How did it go?" I asked noncommittally. I was assuming that he had joined the hunting pack of squires in their mass booze-up.

He grunted. "I had no idea the old goat could drink like that." Then he chuckled softly. "But I won. I put him to bed. God's mercy, I do need that incantation."

I threw off my covers and began to dress. "You are coming back to Helmdon with me?"

William sighed. "No. Arnolph and the others have all gone. . . . He's all alone. His new job for the king terrifies him. The old fart needs me."

Which is what I'd been dreading to hear, selfishly. "I don't know how I'm going to manage five horses by myself." Not to mention my bag of silver and six massive grimoires, together worth a fortune.

"Oh, I arranged that yesterday," William said. "Goliath set it up with Alwin to have a troop of squires escort us. It'll just be you going now, of course. Good outing for them, and even as a king's man you don't rank knights."

"And Alwin agreed?"

"Of course he did. Alwin will do anything for Goliath."

I did not ask him to explain that remark.

Within the hour I bade farewell to my assistant. Our enmity had turned to friendship and mutual admiration, and we embraced. I said I fully expected him to become a king's man too before we met again. He called me Ironfoot, but now he said it with affection, not derision.

My six-squire escort was very subdued for the first few miles, but a persistent drizzle of rain and a cold wind soon sobered them up and returned them to their usual raucous selves. At Northampton we were advised that the bridge over the Nene was unsafe, so I retraced the route by which I had come, through the king's forest.

We reached Helmdon before nightfall, and received a warm welcome. The sages were almost as delighted to hear of William Legier's departure as they were amazed by the treasure of grimoires I had brought.

I had not intended to name my new sponsor, but my escorts were all blabbermouths, and the news boosted my status into the skies.

Younger members of the faculty were more interested in the load of fresh venison we had acquired. Kenric brazenly told them that it was a gift from the king, so we did not need to offer our prepared explanation of how we had stopped for some archery practice on the way and two fat bucks had run right into the arrows.

Stories have endings, but life goes on. Change came even to Helmdon. I progressed fast in my studies, becoming quite expert in reviving old incantations by picking out the trip wires in them. One by one the sages dropped their prejudices against tampering with the texts.

I spent much of the first month after my return working on Prince Richard's horoscope. As I had promised the queen, I drew it up myself, although I consulted a lot with Sage Alain, who kept our astrological records, and also with Guy, who checked my Latin prose for me.

"This is very convoluted," he complained more than once.

I assured him that it was meant to be so. Queen Eleanor's learning was legendary, so I was confident that she would be able to read it, but it would certainly challenge her son, if he were ever allowed to see it. Years later, when he was king, he was renowned for his fluency in Latin. He once remarked to me, his enchanter general, that my own style had improved a lot, which puzzled the listening courtiers.

Guy also warned me that I should be more tactful. "This prediction that the subject will be a great warrior? You must temper that!"

"Mars in Leo? What else can it mean?"

Guy conceded that point. "And you state categorically that he will be king of England. His older brother, Prince Henry, is heir apparent, so you mustn't say that."

"I don't say that. The stars do."

"Well then, you simply cannot tell a man that his beginnings will be greater than his endings!"

"I swore I would be strictly honest," I said. Of course time fulfilled the stars' prediction there. Richard as a crusader was to see Jerusalem from afar but fail to reach it; on the way home he got himself locked up in a castle on the Danube and had to be ransomed. He failed in a king's supreme duty to produce a legitimate heir, and died while besieging a minor castle.

Alas, somehow word leaked out that I had been commissioned by the queen. Soon half the gentry of the county were pestering me to draw up horoscopes.

A few years later, after I had left the academy to work for the king, I ran into Delaney of Carlton again, by then a belted knight, but still known as Goliath. He told me that the count had died of a broken heart while his castle was coming down; Stephen had inherited the title. Baroness Matilda had taken the veil, but Sir Delaney could not remember in which nunnery. Nobody knew what had happened to Father Randolf, although there were rumors that he had gone on pilgrimage to Jerusalem.

And Squire William? His eldest brother, Arnolph, died of a crossbow bolt in the throat, and the second of camp fever. The third son was by then an ordained priest, and ineligible to inherit, so when their father died, three years after the events related here, William became the second Baron Weldon. He married a rich heiress and fathered seven sons. I sang at his wedding.

afterword

The history is real. King Henry did hold a council in Northampton in October 1164, intended to bully Archbishop Becket into submission. Becket fled the country, but he was martyred six years later by four knights who claimed that they were acting on Henry's orders, which he denied.

All the places named still exist, except one. Of course the places themselves have changed very much in eight and a half centuries. Barton (which means "barley farm") is now called Earls Barton. If you Google it, you will find pictures of the wonderful old Saxon church tower that Durwin admired. The church is Norman, so that may be the one he knew.

The place that has disappeared is Pipewell, now just the name of some woodland on the outskirts of the city of Kettering. There is an "abbey church" there, but it is Victorian in age, and so much younger.

about the author

Dave Duncan is a prolific writer of fantasy and science fiction, best known for his fantasy series, especially The Seventh Sword, A Man of His Word, and The King's Blades. He is both a founding and an honorary lifetime member of SF Canada, and an inductee of the Canadian Science Fiction and Fantasy Hall of Fame. His books have been translated into fifteen languages.

Dave and his wife Janet, his in-house editor and partner for fifty-seven years (so far), live in Victoria, British Columbia. They have three children and four grandchildren.